Praise for Eller...

The Secret, Book & Scone Society

"Adams launches an intriguing new mystery series, headed by four spirited amateur sleuths and touched with a hint of magical realism, which celebrates the power of books and women's friendships. Adams's many fans, readers of Sarah Addison Allen, and anyone who loves novels that revolve around books will savor this tasty treat."
    —*Library Journal*, STARRED REVIEW, Pick of
    the Month

"Adams (*Peach Pies and Alibis*, 2013) kicks off a new series featuring strong women, a touch of romance and mysticism, and both the cunning present-day mystery and the slowly revealed secrets of the intriguing heroines' pasts."
    —*Kirkus Reviews*

"This affecting series launch from Adams provides all the best elements of a traditional mystery . . . Well-drawn characters complement a plot with an intriguing twist or two."
    —*Publishers Weekly*

"Adams's new series blends magical realism, smart women, and small-town quirks to create a cozy mystery that doubles as a love letter to books. Readers will fall in love with Nora's bookstore therapy and Hester's comfort scones. Not to mention Estella, June, hunky Jed the paramedic, and Nora's tiny house-slash-converted-train-caboose. . . . Overall this is a book that mystery fans—and avid readers—won't want to put down until they have savored every last crumb."
    —*RT Book Reviews*, 4 stars

The Book Retreat Mysteries

"[A] suspenseful and compelling read."
    —*Kings River Life Magazine*

"[A] delight . . . An idyllic mansion in a quaint village complete with secret passages and books, books, and more books—what could make for a more ideal setting for a cozy murder . . . ? Ellery Adams spins a fine tale full of jealousy, love, greed, aspirations, and poison . . . Highly recommended."
    —**Open Book Society**

"Adams . . . combines clever clues, a smart and courageous heroine and an interesting setting in a whodunit that will inspire readers to make further visits to Storyton Hall."
    —*Richmond Times-Dispatch*

"Adams makes Storyton Hall come to life . . . Readers will relish the way Ellery Adams weaves together books, mystery, and fantasy."
    —*Fresh Fiction*

"A mystery that takes place at a book-themed resort—it doesn't get any better. The author has woven in a bunch of suspects that will keep cozy mystery lovers guessing. The story is well paced and keeps you reading until you find out whodunit."
    —**MyShelf.com**

The Books by the Bay Mysteries

"Adams's plot is indeed killer, her writing would make her the star of any support group, and her characters . . . are a diverse, intelligent bunch."
    —*Richmond Times-Dispatch*

The Charmed Pie Shoppe Mysteries

"[A] savory blend of suspense, pies, and engaging characters. Foodie mystery fans will enjoy this."
—Booklist

"A sensory delight for those who like a little magic with their culinary cozies."
—Library Journal

"An original, intriguing story line that celebrates women, family, friendship, and loyalty within an enchanted world, with a hint of romance, an engaging cast of characters, and the promise of a continued saga of magical good confronting evil."
—Kirkus Reviews

"Adams permeates this unusual novel—and Ella [Mae's] pies—with a generous helping of appeal."
—Richmond Times-Dispatch

Books by Ellery Adams

The Secret, Book & Scone Society Mysteries
The Secret, Book & Scone Society
The Whispered Word

Book Retreat Mysteries
Murder in the Mystery Suite
Murder in the Paperback Parlor
Murder in the Secret Garden
Murder in the Locked Library

MURDER IN THE LOCKED LIBRARY

Ellery Adams

KENSINGTON BOOKS
KENSINGTON PUBLISHING CORP.
http://www.kensingtonbooks.com

KENSINGTON BOOKS are published by

Kensington Publishing Corp.
119 West 40th Street
New York, NY 10018

All Kensington titles, imprints, and distributed lines are available at special quantity discounts for bulk purchases for sales promotion, premiums, fund-raising, educational, or institutional use.

Special book excerpts or customized printings can also be created to fit specific needs. For details, write or phone the office of the Kensington Sales Manager: Attn.: Sales Department. Kensington Publishing Corp., 119 West 40th Street, New York, NY 10018. Phone: 1-800-221-2647.

Kensington and the K logo Reg. U.S. Pat. & TM Off.

First Printing: May 2018
ISBN-13: 978-1-4967-1563-0
ISBN-10: 1-4967-1563-2

eISBN-13: 978-1-4967-1564-7
eISBN-10: 1-4967-1564-0

10 9 8 7 6 5 4 3 2

Printed in the United States of America

*This is for the people who enter a bookstore and instantly
become giddy with happiness and anticipation. This is for
those of you who never tire of the feel, shape, and smell of
books. Those who are drawn to beautiful covers like a
moth to a bright light. Those of you who buy book-scented
candles and take photos of your book collection. Those of
you who can't wait to tell another person—or the whole
world—about the amazing book you just read. Those of
you who find respite from life's hardships by retreating
to your favorite reading spot with a good book.*

This is for you, lover of books, with gratitude.

"A little library, growing larger every year, is an honourable
part of a man's history. It is a man's duty to have books. A
library is not a luxury, but one of the necessaries of life."
—Henry Ward Beecher

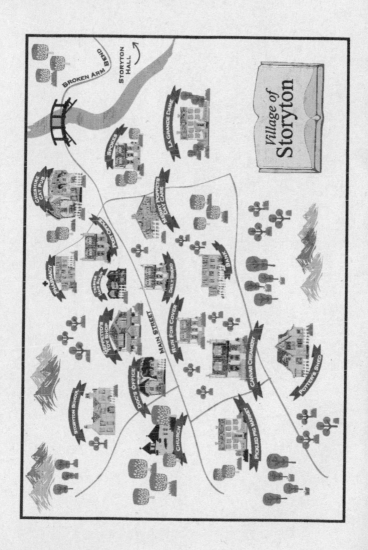

Welcome to Storyton Hall

Our Staff Is Here To Serve You

Resort Manager—Jane Steward
Butler—Mr. Butterworth
Head Librarian—Mr. Sinclair
Head Chauffeur—Mr. Sterling
Head of Recreation—Mr. Lachlan
Head of Housekeeping—Mrs. Pimpernel
Head Cook—Mrs. Hubbard

Select Merchants of Storyton Village:
Run for Cover Bookshop—Eloise Alcott
Daily Bread Café—Edwin Alcott
Cheshire Cat Pub—Bob and Betty Carmichael
The Canvas Creamery—Phoebe Doyle
La Grande Dame Clothing Boutique—Mabel Wimberly
Tresses Hair Salon—Violet Osborne
The Pickled Pig Market—the Hogg brothers
Geppetto's Toy Shop—Barnaby Nicholas
The Potter's Shed—Tom Green
Storyton Outfitters—Phil and Sandi Hughes

Robert Harley Rare Book Society Members:
Bartholomew (Bart) Baylor
Rosemary Pearce
Aaron Sullivan
Austin Sullivan
Levi Ross

Chapter One

"Don't touch that book!"

Thrusting his index finger out like a rapier, Sinclair, the head librarian of Storyton Hall, waved identical twins Hemingway and Fitzgerald Steward over to the far side of the reading table.

"Why not?" one of the brothers asked in surprise.

"You told us to be curious about what's between every cover in every library," the other brother added.

Sinclair pointed at their dirt-encrusted hands. "What else have I taught you about the proper treatment of books?"

"To make sure our hands are clean before touching a book," Hem said.

"I was going to say that." Fitz frowned, but quickly brightened again. "You also said never fold the corner of a page to mark our place. Civilized people use bookmarks."

Sinclair's stern expression morphed into a smile. "Correct on both counts. Scrub those hands until I can see pink skin and I'll tell you about this book. It holds a secret."

The twins cast matching glances of doubt at the modest leather volume before exiting the library at a speed their mother, Jane Steward, would have referred to as their "power-lurch" pace.

"At least they're not running," she said to Sinclair.

Jane had silently watched the exchange between the head librarian and her sons from the comfort of an oversized wing chair. She never interrupted Sinclair when he was instructing the twins. "It's a daily battle to keep them from knocking into little old ladies, especially when all three parties have their noses buried in books."

"I could think of far worse transgressions," was Sinclair's reply as he placed a wooden book cradle on the large reading table. He then laid two pair of white gloves, a selection of foam wedges, and a book weight next to the cradle.

At the sight of the gloves, Jane arched a brow and whispered, "I thought those were reserved for handling books in the secret library. And for initial contact only. Didn't you say that gloves can be more dangerous than bare fingers because one can't properly feel the pages and might accidentally rip them?"

"I did," Sinclair agreed amiably. "However, your sons and I have a markedly different definition of clean. I love those boys like they were my own flesh and blood, but their stained and jagged fingernails will *not* come into contact with this book."

Jane couldn't argue against this precaution. The twins had just started a new school year, and after three months of reading, swimming, archery, fishing, martial arts, falconry lessons, picnics, barbecues, and bike rides into the village, they were finding the adjustment difficult. Today, for example, was a Friday afternoon leading into a long Labor Day weekend, and the twins had been home for less than ten minutes. In that short amount of time, they acted like they'd just been released from prison.

Cleanliness had never been high on their priority list, and Jane was constantly reminding her sons to wash themselves and tidy their room. Now, with their earlier bedtimes, homework, and having to wear clothes that weren't riddled with holes or covered with stains, the twins were rebelling by blatantly ignoring their personal hygiene, and today was no exception. Even the handmade soap crafted by Tammie Kota, Jane's future spa manager, couldn't inspire the boys to do more than pass their grimy hands under running water before drying them on what was inevitably a freshly laundered white towel.

When Fitz and Hem returned to the library from the men's restroom in the lobby, Sinclair offered each of them a pair of gloves.

"Are we pretending to be Mickey Mouse?" Hem asked.

Fitz stared at his gloves. "Or *girls*?"

The twins exchanged horrified glances.

Sinclair deigned to reply. He gazed placidly at the boys until they donned their gloves.

"Now then, I told you that this book contains a secret. I'm going to teach you how to handle a very old book so that we can examine the secret together. When we're done, I'm going to package the book, along with the other eleven volumes in the series, for shipment. The set will be sold at auction. Your mother hopes that it'll fetch enough money to pay for part of the spa construction."

Fitz's eyes widened. He turned to Jane. "Didn't you say that it'll cost thousands and thousands of dollars?"

Jane nodded. "Remember when I showed you the plans? I explained that a spa like ours has to be fancy. We're going to have treatment rooms, a relaxation space, and a boutique selling all-natural botanical products. These rooms are expensive to build, especially when you include water features and custom—"

"And people are going to get wrapped in seaweed," Fitz interrupted.

"Like sushi!" Hem chimed in giddily.

Sinclair cleared his throat and all three Stewards snapped to attention. It didn't matter that Jane was the manager of

Storyton Hall Resort and technically, Sinclair's boss. Her position as manager carried little weight in the Henry James Library. The library was Sinclair's domain. In this cavernous room, with its reading tables, soft chairs, oil paintings, globes, mammoth fireplaces, and shelves upon shelves of books, only one person was in charge.

"The proper way to examine a rare book is to place it in a cradle like this," Sinclair explained to the twins. He gently transferred the book, which was about the length of his hand, to the cradle.

"What are those pieces of foam for?" Hem asked, reaching for one.

"I'm delighted you asked, Master Hemingway," Sinclair said. "Observe. When I open the cover, I meet with resistance when I get to . . . here. An angle of approximately one hundred and twenty degrees."

Closing the book, he looked at his pupils. "Would you like to try?"

Both boys did. Very carefully, they took turns opening the cover.

"I think I hear a little crack," Fitz said. "Like it's telling me to stop."

Looking pleased, Sinclair gestured at the foam blocks. "You have correctly interpreted the book's needs. Would you like the honor of placing this foam on the cradle and opening the cover again?"

His face shining, Fitz shot his brother a triumphant glance before doing as Sinclair directed.

Ignoring Fitz, Hem pointed at Sinclair's hand. "Why aren't you wearing gloves?"

"Excellent question. The answer is that it's best to turn the pages with clean hands. *Completely* clean hands. Now. Allow me to show you the first copperplate, which is opposite the title page."

The boys flanked Sinclair and bent over the book in anticipation. Sinclair revealed the illustration, which depicted a ship in wild seas, a wooden barrel being tossed by a rogue wave, and a formidable fish.

The boys released a stream of questions.

"Is there a storm?"

"What's in the barrel?"

"How can the fish be on *top* of the water?"

"Who's Jonathan Swift?"

Sinclair focused on the last question. "Among other things, Swift wrote *Gulliver's Travels*."

The twins were advanced readers for their tender age, which was no surprise considering they'd grown up surrounded by books and book enthusiasts. And while they'd yet to conquer *Gulliver's Travels*, they had seen an animated film adaption of Swift's famous tale.

"How old is this?" Fitz asked in a reverent tone.

Sinclair gingerly turned pages until he came to a copperplate of a map. "One of the reasons this book is so rare is that it's part of a series published between 1703 and 1740."

"Whoa, that's *old*!" Hem exclaimed, after a brief pause in which he seemed to be performing calculations in his head.

"Indeed," Sinclair said. "Most owners lost some of the books in their series. Or books were damaged. It is very unusual for the entire set to be together like this. And in such excellent shape. Look at the Moroccan calfskin binding of this volume. It's in sublime condition."

Fitz, who'd seen countless examples of leather-bound books, was indifferent as to its appearance. "What's the secret?"

"Ah, the secret is actually *part* of the book. It's literally been glued into the binding between the end paper and the back cover." Sinclair turned to the place in question and unfolded a sheaf of paper.

The twins stared at it in confusion.

"It's hard to read," Hem complained. "The writing is so curly. Is it cursive?"

"Wait. Is this about people getting married?" Fitz's voice was laced with indignation. The twins disliked any subject pertaining to romance. They were at "that phase" of their development, as Mrs. Pimpernel, the head housekeeper, tended to say. Mrs. Hubbard, the head cook, simply referred to it as a "three-year-long case of the cooties."

Sinclair chuckled. "I'm sorry to disappoint, but yes. This is a certificate of marriage between Jonathan Swift and Esther Johnson. See? Here's his signature. And hers. This third signature belongs to a man who witnessed what must have been a very small, very secret ceremony. His name is Alexander Pope. He's another famous author."

Because the boys were starting to fidget, Jane decided to add her two cents. "People have always wondered if Mr. Swift married Ms. Johnson. It's been one of history's mysteries." She grinned at her unintentional rhyme. "Mr. Swift definitely acted like he loved Ms. Johnson. He even made sure he was buried next to her. But until now, no one could prove that they were married."

Fitz was still unimpressed. "Last year, our teacher taught us about a man who went to jail for printing fake money. Can't people make fake letters too?"

"Absolutely," Jane said. "But this is the real deal. A close relative of Jonathan Swift gave these books to your great-grandfather after Mr. Swift's death. Mr. Swift's family didn't want anyone to know that he'd secretly married. For whatever reason, they believed Esther was the reason Jonathan wrote some . . . well, some strange things."

"I like strange things," Hem said.

Fitz looked at him. "Me too. People think wizards are strange. That's why wizards call nonmagical people Muggles."

It was obvious to Sinclair that the twins weren't exactly captivated by the book in the cradle, so after thanking them for their attention, he told them they were free to carry on with whatever they'd been doing before they'd wandered into the library.

"Where should we put these?" Fitz asked, pulling off his gloves.

Sinclair smiled. "Why don't you keep them? All great wizards own at least one pair of gloves, don't they? For handling toxic plants and such."

After mulling this over, Fitz said, "I guess so" and tucked the gloves in his pocket.

Jane threw him a stern look. He added a hasty "thank you," which was echoed by Hem.

The clock on Sinclair's desk chimed and the boys spun on their heels. They cried "teatime!" and bolted for the door.

Jane opened her mouth to chastise her sons for running indoors, but she wasn't fast enough. They were halfway to the kitchens before she could utter a syllable.

"I can't really blame them," she said to Sinclair as he began to wrap the Jonathan Swift book in tissue paper. "Even though the official Groundbreaking Ceremony for the Walt Whitman Spa isn't until tomorrow night, Mrs. Hubbard has been cooking as if she was serving royalty since Monday."

"Our guests have certainly been delighted by the tea offerings this week," Sinclair said. Having cocooned the book in tissue paper followed by an additional layer of white kraft paper, he was now securing the valuable volume in bubble wrap.

"Undoubtedly due to all the chocolate-themed treats,"

Jane said. "Apparently, the arrival of the earthmover and the mountain of dirt it created has inspired Mrs. Hubbard to bake platters of treats containing one or all of the following ingredients: chocolate cookie crumbs, chocolate shavings, chocolate chips, or nuts. I guess the nuts were meant to represent rocks."

Sinclair paused in his work. "Reminds me of a certain Halloween party from three years ago. The twins created a ghastly cake featuring chocolate pudding, crushed chocolate wafers, gummy worms, and red icing."

Jane laughed. "It didn't taste as bad as it looked."

Sinclair sniffed. "I wouldn't know. I don't eat food served in a litter box."

As if summoned by the mention of an object used by millions of his fellow felines, Muffet Cat plodded into the Henry James Library.

The rotund tuxedo made a beeline for a reading chair facing the window. A sunbeam lit the cushion, and though Jane couldn't blame the cat for wanting to doze in such a cozy spot, she had to prevent him from claiming it. Storyton Hall was currently hosting a very persnickety guest who'd blow her top should she encounter Muffet Cat a second time.

Mrs. Eleanor Whartle and Muffet Cat had first met in the lobby moments after Mrs. Whartle had disembarked from one of Storyton Hall's vintage Rolls Royce sedans. Upon entering the luxurious main lobby, the powdered and perfumed octogenarian had been greeted by Butterworth, the butler. As was his tradition, Butterworth offered Mrs. Whartle a glass of champagne. However, Mrs. Whartle had the distinction of being the only guest in Storyton Hall's history to help herself to two flutes of bubbly from Butterworth's silver tray.

"I just buried my husband of thirty-eight years," she'd

declared, as if she'd dug the grave herself. "After putting up with that odious man for as long as I did, I deserve his champagne too."

Butterworth had inclined his head and stoically replied, "Yes, madam."

Mrs. Whartle had drained the first glass and was raising the second glass to her mouth when Muffet Cat appeared from beneath a nearby sofa. Blinking groggily, he brushed Mrs. Whartle's calf with the length of his furry body.

This was atypical behavior for Muffet Cat. An aloof feline at best, he avoided mingling with guests unless they were dining alfresco. In that case, he made it clear that he'd like to sample choice tidbits from their plates. If a generous guest complied, the ungrateful feline would gulp down whatever morsels he'd been given and scamper off, surprising the guest with his agility, for Muffet Cat was approaching eighteen pounds.

Muffet Cat ignored most of the staff. He tolerated Jane and the boys. There was only one person he truly loved, and that person was Jane's great-aunt Octavia. Aunt Octavia was the equivalent of the dowager queen of Storyton Hall. In lieu of fur-trimmed robes, she wore voluminous housedresses in bold colors and wild designs and carried a bejeweled walking stick. Aunt Octavia's footwear was also unique. Following her diagnosis of type 2 diabetes, she'd taken to wearing orthopedic Mary Janes that produced a unique squeaking sound when the rubber soles met the lobby's polished marble floor tiles.

Mrs. Whartle's orthopedic shoes were identical to Aunt Octavia's, so it was no wonder that Muffet Cat mistook her for his favorite human. Not only that, but both women had a similar build. To Muffet Cat, Mrs. Whartle's calf looked just like Aunt Octavia's. Therefore, he assumed that if he rubbed said calf, he'd receive a treat.

Instead of pulling a piece of dried chicken or salmon from her pocket, Mrs. Whartle had screamed and hurled her champagne flute at Muffet Cat.

The coddled feline fled up the main staircase in a streak of black and white fur. When he reached the landing, he paused to cast a menacing glare down at the creature who'd splattered his coat with a foul-smelling liquid.

The broken champagne flute had been cleaned up within seconds, and Butterworth had apologized to Mrs. Whartle for the distress Muffet Cat's abrupt appearance had caused. However, it took several complimentary cocktails to finally appease her. Anyone within shouting distance of the Ian Fleming Lounge could hear Mrs. Whartle's tale of the wild animal in the lobby that had mercilessly attacked an old lady.

When Jane had phoned her room that evening in an attempt to repair the damage, Mrs. Whartle had made it very plain that she expected Muffet Cat to be banished from the house and grounds until the conclusion of her visit.

"I'll have *her* banished!" Great-Aunt Octavia had bellowed the following morning when Jane repeated the conversation she'd had with their flustered guest.

Great-Uncle Aloysius had pushed his fishing hat higher on his brow and murmured soothingly, "There, there, dear. Not everyone shares your affection for Muffet Cat."

"If that woman knew what a traumatic kittenhood that poor animal endured, she might not be so cold-hearted," Aunt Octavia had said. "I'm going to invite her to tea and tell her the moving tale of how Muffet Cat came to join our family."

Mrs. Whartle had thoroughly enjoyed the lavish tea, especially since it hadn't cost her a penny, but she'd yawned widely and often during Aunt Octavia's theatrical narrative of the stormy night when Muffet Cat had appeared on the doorstep, half drowned and no bigger than a man's fist. Mrs. Whartle didn't even crack a smile when Aunt Octavia explained that he'd been named Muffet Cat because everyone assumed that *he* was a *she* until the vet made his gender clear.

Now, Jane gazed at the portly feline and frowned. Muffet Cat was normally an excellent judge of character. If he growled or hissed at a guest—a very rare occurrence—it was because that person possessed an overtly negative character trait. Thankfully, most of Storyton Hall's guests were lovely people. Which was no surprise, seeing as they were all readers.

"Do you think Muffet Cat's radar is off?" Jane asked Sinclair. "Mrs. Whartle has already proven to be a rude, greedy, and impatient woman. And yet Muffet Cat gave her a calf rub."

"We all suffer lapses in judgment from time to time," Sinclair replied, and Jane wondered if the head librarian was referring to Storyton Hall's resident mouser or to the series of terrible events that had followed Jane's decision to allow the public to view an item from their secret library.

Placing a hand on the box containing the rest of the Jonathan Swift series, Jane said, "Many scholars believed Swift was secretly married. Having this fact brought to light won't hurt anyone. And in exchange, Storyton Hall can continue to compete in the luxury resort market. Without a world-class spa, we might lose potential clients."

Sinclair furrowed his brow and gestured around the library. "Isn't our main aspiration to provide a haven for readers? For those seeking an escape from the incessant buzz of a technology-saturated, overscheduled life?"

"Of course it is. Storyton Hall was meant to be a sanctuary for bibliophiles," Jane agreed. "But I don't have to tell you that it's so much more than that. Escape comes in many forms. People want to be close to nature. They want to stroll through colorful gardens, drink wine on a balcony while enjoying an incredible view, be offered a variety of activities, dine like kings and queens, have a multitude of different spaces to relax and read, be able to swim any day of the year, and give themselves over to pampering sessions."

Though Sinclair nodded, Jane had the sense her friend and mentor was unconvinced. "Sinclair, you know that I've wanted to start a tradition of giving away all-expense-paid weekends to couples or families who can't afford to stay at Storyton Hall. I've had to put that plan on hold for ages, but if we can increase our revenue, then I can mail our first Golden Bookmark by the end of the year."

"I like the Golden Bookmark. It's reminiscent of the golden ticket from *Charlie and the Chocolate Factory.*" Sinclair gazed at Jane affectionately. "I've seen the index cards on the Hopes and Dreams board in your office. I know what each one means to you."

Jane blushed. She sometimes felt that it was juvenile to hang a bulletin board pinned with pink, yellow, green, blue, and orange index cards in a place where the staff could see it.

"I know it's a bit silly," she said. "I'm like a girl hanging photos of her celebrity crushes. Still, I get such a rush of joy when I can move a card from the Hopes and Dreams board to the Current Project board. But ever since my Uncle Aloysius entrusted me with the management of Storyton Hall, it seems like all I do is write checks for repairs. Most of our projects have been necessary, but not very exciting. Or fun."

Sinclair gazed at the nearest set of shelves. After a moment's hesitation, he pulled down a slim volume and showed Jane the author's name.

"George Eliot," she read. "Aka Mary Ann Evans."

"She once said that 'adventure is not outside man; it is within.'" Sinclair pressed the book into Jane's hand.

Jane pulled a face. "Don't you think I've had enough adventure? For the last few years, I've done nothing but douse fires. Mysteries, murder, secret societies—a maelstrom of unexpected problems. All having to do with books." She shook her head. "And to think I once believed that the main purpose of books was to provide enlightenment and escape. I had no sense of their power until I came into possession of this."

Her fingers moved over the outline of the pendant she wore low on her décolletage. Because it was always tucked out of sight, no one realized that Jane's locket was more than a pretty piece of antique jewelry. Like so many things at Storyton Hall, it served a double purpose. If one were to apply pressure to the rectangular shape in its center, which resembled a closed book, while also pushing on the cluster of arrows on each side of the rectangle, the locket would spring open. Cushioned inside was a key to the Eighth Wonder of the World. Storyton's secret library. A treasure trove of rare, invaluable, controversial, and potentially dangerous books.

These books came in many forms and had been collected since man first began recording the human narrative. There were ancient scrolls, illustrated manuscripts, parchment documents, handmade books, and some of the first books printed using a machine.

And Jane Steward was Guardian to them all.

"What sort of adventure do you crave?" Sinclair asked, studying her with paternal concern.

Jane rubbed the pad of her thumb over the letters etched into the back of her locket. They were the same words engraved on every brass room key fob and emblazoned on the massive wrought iron front gates of Storyton Hall. The

Latin phrase roughly translated to "Their stories are our stories," and Jane had always interpreted the Steward family motto as meaning that people were united through stories— that words were the unbreakable threads connecting humans across time and space.

"Truthfully, you and George Eliot must have seen what I've been trying to hide," Jane said in a confessional tone. "I want an adventure of the heart, but I don't know if that's prudent. I'm a single mom. I'm a Guardian. My only living relatives rely on me to safeguard their legacy. Every day, I'm reminded that protecting the library is my purpose. Along with caring for the twins, of course."

"Of course," Sinclair echoed. Though Jane knew Sinclair must have dozens of tasks to see to before the next group of conference attendees swarmed Storyton Hall, he clasped his hands behind his back and patiently waited for her to continue.

Feeling a rush of tenderness for the man who'd helped raise her, Jane flashed him a crooked smile. "Maybe I just need a vacation."

"You decided to take a chance on Edwin Alcott." Sinclair was watching her closely. "Have you changed your mind about him?"

"No. Maybe. I don't know." Jane raised her hands and shook them in frustration. "He's away again—left the country on one of his enigmatic missions. How can our relationship be anything but fleeting if we're always keeping secrets from each other?"

Sinclair grinned. "Jane, my dear. All partners have their secrets. Earth-shattering or inconsequential as they might be, we all keep things to ourselves."

Jane frowned. "William and I didn't," she said, referring to her late husband. "We shared everything. His honesty was one of the things I loved best about him." She sighed.

"He would have been an amazing father if he'd lived to raise his sons."

"And Edwin?"

"It's hard for me to picture him in that role," Jane said. It was the first time she'd admitted this, even to herself, and it hurt. She wanted the man she loved to be father material. "Edwin's wonderful with the boys—when he's around," she went on. "He cooks for them and tells them amazing stories. And whenever he goes away, he comes back bearing gifts from exotic lands."

"Sounds like a doting uncle."

Jane made a noise of assent, but didn't elucidate further. The conversation was bringing her down, and it was too lovely a day to have the blues.

"Time will tell," she said with finality. At the mention of time, she glanced at the mantel clock and decided she could do with a cup of tea and a cookie. Or two cookies. "I'm going to join the boys. I bet they've found a shady spot on the garden wall—a perfect vantage point where they can see the earthmover carve out the space for our new spa. And I'm sure Mrs. Hubbard gave them an entire picnic basket worth of treats to snack on while they watch the construction workers perform their magic."

Suddenly, Butterworth appeared in the doorway. After clearing his throat, he took two steps into the room and abruptly halted. Seeing that no guests were present, he said, "I regret to inform you, Miss Jane, that the magic those gentlemen have performed may prove to be most distressing."

"Why can't anything go as planned?" Jane threw out her arms in exasperation. "Let me guess. The driver hit a water line or accidentally backed over one of our Gator carts."

Butterworth, whose expression was inscrutable in nearly

every circumstance, remained silent. However, there was a wary look in his eyes that immediately alarmed Jane.

"It's worse than that, isn't it? Butterworth, please. Please tell me that there hasn't been a terrible accident."

"An accident? On the cause of death, I couldn't say." Butterworth put a steadying hand on Jane's shoulder. "But we do have a Rip Van Winkle."

A Rip Van Winkle was code for a Storyton Hall guest who had expired on the premises.

"Not again!" Jane cried.

"This Van Winkle is unlike any other, however," Butterworth added. "He or she—the gender is unclear—is one for the record books."

Chapter Two

Jane stood very still.

"What do you mean?" she asked Butterworth in a near whisper, though there were no guests in the Henry James Library. "Exactly *why* is it one for the record books?"

"Our Rip Van Winkle is very old," was all Butterworth would say. Instead of elaborating, he gestured toward the hallway. "You'd better come with me."

Jane and Butterworth left the Henry James Library and entered one of the cool and dimly lit staff corridors that ran like rabbit warrens throughout Storyton Hall. Employees carrying fresh linens or pushing room service carts greeted Jane with cheerful smiles and hellos, but Jane was too focused on the Rip Van Winkle to do more than bob her head in return.

Even the pleasant cacophony in the kitchens—the thud of a cleaver striking wood, the hiss of steam, the rush of water, the scrape of metal against metal, and the endless dip and swell of voices as the staff chatted and bantered with each other—couldn't distract Jane. She burst through the rear doorway, hurried down the path next to the kitchen garden, and was met by a heavy silence. Behind the herb garden and inside the construction fence, the earthmover sat idle. A small crowd had formed a ring to one side of its shovel bucket, which hung open in the air like a giant claw waiting to seize unsuspecting prey.

Jane scanned the onlookers as she moved, and she quickened her pace when she spied two smaller figures among the construction workers.

"Why are Fitz and Hem here?" she asked, her voice tight with anger. "They hardly need to see a corpse at their age."

"There was no avoiding it, Miss Jane," Butterworth replied. "The twins raised the alarm in the first place."

Jane suppressed a groan. She hated to think of her sons having been exposed to a gruesome vision.

But when she reached Fitz and Hem, it was obvious that they weren't the least bit upset. On the contrary, they seemed quite jubilant.

"Mom! We're the ones who found him!" Fitz shouted, thrusting out his chest with pride. "Wait until Mr. Lachlan hears. He'll say we have falcon vision!"

"We were just sitting on the wall when we saw the head pop out!" Hem added. His face was shining.

Mortified by thoughts of a desiccated head, Jane glanced down into the fresh hole and met the empty stare of a skull.

She felt an immediate sense of relief. She hadn't known what to expect, but she'd anticipated a body—something that still resembled a human being. Not a skull and a scattering of bones. This sight, though unpleasant, wasn't grisly or gruesome in the slightest.

Jane turned to Butterworth. "Why would someone be buried here?"

"I don't know, Miss Jane."

Sinclair joined their ensemble several minutes after Jane as he'd had to lock the Swift books in his office. While the twins babbled excitedly to him, Jane's relief gave way to other feelings. The skull's vacuous stare inspired pity. And dread. It was as if another universe—a cold and lonely place—existed in the dark voids of its eye sockets.

I don't even know if you're male or female, Jane thought.

After a long moment, she looked at Sterling, the head chauffeur and another Fin. "Sterling, would you call the sheriff? He'll need to see this right away. We should probably contact Doc Lydgate too."

"I'm on it," Sterling said. Before he left, he put a hand on each of the twin's shoulders and squeezed. "Listen to your mother, gentlemen. Things are going to get a little crazy. You'll need to help her maintain order, okay? It's time to use your training."

Hem and Fitz responded by nodding and moving to Jane's side. "What can we do, Mom?" they asked in unison.

Jane wanted to enfold them both in a tight embrace, but she knew they'd prefer to be given a bona fide assignment. After all, they were being groomed as future Guardians, and she didn't want to undermine the importance of that role. "We must keep the guests away from the bones," she said. "We have no idea what we're dealing with and we can't have them trampling the area. I know we already have the construction fence, but once the word gets out that a body's been discovered, people will move mountains to see it."

"We should put up a tent," Fitz suggested. "That's what they do on TV."

Jane wasn't sure how Fitz had gained this television crime drama knowledge, but she suspected that he and Hem had watched such programs at one of their summer sleepovers with Uncle Aloysius and Aunt Octavia. The octogenarians were prone to falling asleep in front of the TV well before eight o'clock, and Jane could easily picture the twins enjoying shows with more mature ratings than Jane permitted while their older relatives dozed away in blissful oblivion.

"That's a good idea, Fitz," Jane said.

Butterworth inclined his head in agreement and reached for his cell phone. "Billy and I will see that a covering is erected immediately."

"I guess I should send the workers home," Jane muttered. "I can't afford to have them standing around with nothing to do, especially when there's no telling how long it'll be before construction can continue."

"All will depend on what the sheriff finds when he climbs into that hole," Sinclair said. "At least this happened late on a Friday afternoon leading into a long weekend. It gives Sheriff Evans several days to investigate and make a ruling. The construction would have been paused until Tuesday in any case."

Though Jane was also aware of this, it didn't make her feel any better. Neither did standing around, idly waiting. Tugging on Hem's sleeve, she said, "See if Mr. Lachlan is at the Recreation Desk. If he is, ask him to bring us several pairs of binoculars. If he's not there, just borrow the binoculars."

"Why don't you call him?" Hem wanted to know.

Tamping down her impatience, Jane said, "Because he might be training a falcon. You know how sensitive they are. Fitz, go with your brother."

"I'll speak with the foreman," Sinclair said once the boys were gone.

As Jane stepped closer to the edge of the hole, she heard Sinclair say the words, "sheriff" and "temporarily cease work" before she stopped listening. The skull, what appeared to be a femur, and several small bones that Jane couldn't identify, had completely captured her attention.

Who are you? she silently wondered.

Jane didn't know how long she stood there, but when she eventually looked around, the construction team was gone and the twins were ducking under a section of the orange netting with Landon Lachlan in tow.

Lachlan, head of Recreation and Storyton Hall's Falconry Program, approached the hole wearing a guarded expression.

A former army ranger, Lachlan had seen terrible atrocities during his two tours in Afghanistan. Though he'd retired from active duty, he hadn't managed to escape violence, for it was as a civilian that he'd witnessed his brother's murder.

Jane believed that Lachlan suffered from PTSD, and though the other Fins—all former military men—shared their methods of coping with stress and anxiety with Lachlan, there were moments when he withdrew deep inside himself. Jane noticed that it could be difficult for him to resurface.

Watching him, Jane wondered if the skull in the freshly torn ground would trigger one of Lachlan's traumatic memories, but it was evident that his concern was more for the twins than for himself.

"Miss Jane," he said, hurrying to her side. "The boys told me it was okay for them to be here. But . . ."

Lachlan was too polite to say that he thought Fitz and Hem might be stretching the truth.

"It's okay," Jane assured him. "They spotted the bones first, so there's no keeping them out now." She gestured at the backpack slung over Lachlan's shoulder. "You have the binoculars?"

In reply, Lachlan reached into the pack and handed her a pair.

Most people would have bombarded her with questions, but that wasn't Lachlan's style. He used words sparingly—a trait that Eloise Alcott of Run for Cover Books, his girlfriend and Jane's best friend, often found exasperating.

"What are we looking for?" Lachlan asked as Jane adjusted the focus on her binoculars.

"Anything that could tell us more about this poor soul," Jane said. "If all that's left of this person is bones, then he or she might forever remain a mystery."

Fitz jiggled Jane's arm to get her attention. She frowned because the movement prevented her from training her binoculars on the area near the skull. "What is it?" she snapped, without bothering to see which boy she was addressing.

"Mom," Fitz whispered. "We think we saw the driver pick something up."

"Yeah," Hem added, echoing his brother's secretive tone. "When we yelled at him to stop digging, he turned off the engine and got out of the truck. He was really mad that we were on this side of the fence. His face was as red as a candy apple."

Fitz nodded vigorously. "I don't think he could hear what we were saying—about the skull—because he was wearing headphones. But when we pointed—"

"At the bones, he finally got it," Hem finished his brother's sentence. "He walked to the front of his truck and saw the bones. We thought he'd call someone, but he didn't. He just jumped into the hole."

"And then he bent down and moved some dirt," Fitz said, rounding out the narrative. "That's when we saw him put something in his pocket." He paused before tacking on, "Well . . . maybe."

Jane fixed her sons with her most intense stare. "This could be very serious, so you need to be sure."

Lachlan raised his index finger, signaling that he had an idea.

"Why don't you show us?" he suggested to the twins. "Repeat exactly what you saw the man do."

Hem gestured at the hole. "You want us to go in there?"

"No," Lachlan said. "Just copy the man's actions. Like you were playing a game of Simon Says in slow motion."

The twins nodded in understanding. Turning their backs on Lachlan and their mother, they squatted on their heels and brushed the top of the grass with their right hands. Their movements were like a synchronized dance, and there was no mistaking the furtive behavior they were replicating as they pretended to pinch something between their fingers before hurriedly standing and slipping the same hand into their pocket.

"That's what we saw," Fitz said when he and Hem were done.

Lachlan glanced into the hole. "If he took something, the object must have been small. Did you see it at all?"

"No," they said, clearly wishing that they had.

"All right," Jane said. "Thank you, boys."

Having listened to her sons, Jane didn't feel comfortable confronting the driver. Though they believed they might have seen him pocket something, they simply weren't positive, and Jane could hardly accuse the man based on a possibility. At the moment, her main goal was to examine the ground before the sheriff arrived. She had plenty of experience with Rip Van Winkles—as well as less peaceful deaths—at Storyton Hall, and she knew that once the authorities showed up, there'd be few opportunities for quiet observation and reflection. Or stealthy searches.

Jane and Lachlan began their sweep of the ground surrounding the visible bones. The twins followed suit, but as soon as Sinclair returned from speaking with the foreman, Fitz passed him the binoculars he'd been using and shared with his brother instead.

"I can see a few more bones," Jane said.

Lachlan mumbled in agreement. "There's something else too. Just behind the skull and to the right. It looks like the edge of a piece of metal."

"Rusted." Sinclair lowered his binoculars and faced

the twins. "Gentlemen. You have the sharpest eyes. After Mr. Lachlan, that is. Can you spy anything else?"

To their great disappointment, the boys couldn't.

"It doesn't matter," Jane said. "If there's anything near the surface, the sheriff and Doc Lydgate will find it. Here they are now."

Two brown sedans emblazoned with the county seal pulled up next to the maintenance shed. Sheriff Evans and Doc Lydgate alighted from one car while Deputy Phelps got out of the second. Butterworth and Billy stopped to greet the lawmen and, Jane assumed, to explain why they were taking one of the white folding tents traditionally used for outdoor weddings into the construction zone.

As Butterworth escorted the officials toward what Jane now thought of as the grave site, she was struck by the differences between the five men.

Deputy Phelps, who was quick and lean, trod over clumps of dirt and rocks with the easy confidence of a man in his prime. Doc Lydgate stepped with more care. He kept a firm grip on his kit with one hand and held the tip of his white beard with the other as he picked his way to the edge of the hole. Sheriff Evans and Butterworth were both in their late fifties. But while the sheriff was fair haired, stocky, and had a slight paunch, Butterworth was tall, fit, and commandeering. He'd chosen an apt partner in Billy the bellhop, who was compact, strong, and had an unending supply of energy.

"Just leave the tent here, Billy," Butterworth told his fellow staff member. "Mr. Lachlan can assist me when the sheriff is done with his initial investigation. Would you keep an eye on the new arrivals in my place?"

"Yes, sir!" Billy cast a wide-eyed glance at the skull before hurrying back toward the kitchen entrance.

Sheriff Evans made a beeline for Jane. Tipping his hat, he said, "I see you've been gardening, Ms. Steward."

"Bumping into you in the village every so often isn't enough, so I had to come up with a reason for you to visit." Jane smiled at the sheriff and then extended her hand to Doc Lydgate.

Setting his kit on the grass, the village doctor took her hand in his. "Jane, my dear. How are you?" Releasing her hand, he turned to beam at the twins, who'd been his patients since birth. "Boys! I see you've made a new friend."

The twins giggled, and Jane guessed that Doc Lydgate had made his silly remark to ascertain whether her sons were upset by the discovery of the skeleton. Satisfied that they weren't the least bit distressed, he looked at the sheriff and said, "I'll wait here until you call me."

The sheriff and his deputy spent fifteen minutes photographing the site from every angle before pulling on gloves and scrambling down into the hole. When Evans was within reach of the skull, he motioned for Phelps to hang back and for Doc Lydgate to come closer.

Using two hands, Evans carefully picked up the skull and carried it to the edge of the hole where he passed it up to Doc Lydgate. Next, he and Phelps began collecting and bagging the other bones. Jane, the twins, and Lachlan gathered around Doc Lydgate while Butterworth and Sinclair took up sentinel positions just inside the construction fence.

"He doesn't have very nice teeth," Hem said, studying the skull with fascination.

Doc Lydgate made a noise of assent. "No, he doesn't. This poor fellow is missing a few choppers—because of time or decay I couldn't say—but he has cavities in three teeth. Look here."

Very gingerly, the physician cradled the skull in his palm and pointed at the deep craters present in two molars and one incisor.

"Is it a man?" Fitz asked.

Doc Lydgate shook his head. "I don't know. I certainly

couldn't tell you by looking at the skull. If the sheriff or Deputy Phelps finds an intact femur or pelvis, then I might be able to say if you've unearthed a John Doe or a, er . . ."

Jane put a hand on the doc's shoulder. "If she's female, we'll find something else to call her." The skull rested in the doc's hand like a Halloween prop, and Jane had to look away because it suddenly seemed so small. So fragile. When her gaze landed on the sheriff, she saw that he was brushing dirt from around the metal edge Lachlan had spied through his binoculars.

Looking through her own pair again, she watched Evans carefully shift dirt until he was able to wriggle the rusty metal object free from the ground's firm grasp. The object, which was rectangular in shape, turned out to be a pad-locked box.

"Sinclair—" Jane began, but the head librarian was already in motion.

"Sheriff?" Sinclair called from the edge. "Perhaps we could open the box in the garage? We have the necessary tools, as well as a sink, should you require one."

The sheriff passed the box to Deputy Phelps. "Fine by me. I'll give everyone a pair of our fashionable regulation gloves. I've bagged all the bones I found near the surface." He made a sweeping gesture at the area where the skull had once sat. "Doc Lydgate can examine the findings in the shed while Phelps digs around with a trowel. In case I missed something."

"Mr. Lachlan can lend Deputy Phelps a hand," Jane said, and the sheriff readily accepted her offer.

Instantly, two arms shot in the air. "Can we help too?" Fitz and Hem pleaded.

Evans was clearly torn. After a moment's hesitation, he said, "Tell you what. Why don't I give you some of our special gloves and put you both in charge of bagging any evidence found by Deputy Phelps or Mr. Lachlan? You won't be in the hole, but it's a very important job. Can I trust you with something this important?"

"Yes, sir!" the boys said in unison.

For the next thirty minutes, Phelps and Lachlan used garden trowels and rakes to shift through the soil. Both men managed to retrieve additional bones and bone fragments from the ground. The twins swelled with pride each time they were allowed to seal an evidence bag and place it with the others grouped inside the body bag the sheriff had brought along. Jane avoided looking at the body bag. She'd seen more than one guest wheeled away from Storyton Hall on a gurney and knew that they'd all ended up in identical cocoons of plastic at the morgue.

"That's not a bone!" Hem exclaimed, breaking Jane out of her macabre reverie.

Fitz peered at the bag in his brother's hand. "Maybe it's money. Like a coin?"

"It'll have to be cleaned," Jane said, reaching for the evidence bag. She gave the disc inside a jiggle, and though some loose dirt came off, the object was too encrusted with dirt to be identified. "We'll bring it to Mr. Sterling. He'll know what to do. Unless you'd prefer to clean it at the station, Sheriff?"

Sheriff Evans paused in his digging. "No, I'd rather ask Mr. Sterling to take care of it now. If it is a coin and we can read its date, we might get a clue as to our skeleton's age. Mr. Lachlan, let's stop and join the others."

With the boys proudly toting the evidence bags, the hot and perspiring party gratefully entered the cool garage.

Someone had brought a pitcher of ice water and glasses down from the kitchens, and after Jane washed her hands and splashed her face with cold water from the sink, she poured water for Lachlan and the sheriff and gestured for the boys to hand over the evidence bags and hydrate.

In the short time Jane and her group had been outside,

the skull and the other bones exposed by the earthmover had been spread out on a folding table covered by plastic sheeting. Doc Lydgate was turning what looked like a femur over and over in his hands. His bushy brows were nearly touching and multiple furrows creased his forehead. His concentration was so intense that he didn't respond when Jane asked if he'd like a glass of water.

"Er, what?" he said only after she touched his arm. "Sorry, Jane. It's just that there's something unusual about this bone. See the dramatic curvature? If I didn't know better, I'd say this person—an adult, judging by the size of this femur—suffered from rickets."

"Crickets?" asked Hem from the other end of the table.

Doc Lydgate chuckled. "No, young sir. Rickets with an *R*. It's a bone disease resulting from a lack of vitamin D. Do either of you boys know where you get your daily dose of vitamin D?"

Fitz raised his hand. "From our Flintstones."

It took the doctor a second to comprehend the reference. "Ah, your chewable vitamins. Yes, that's correct. But you also get vitamin D from playing outside in the sunshine and eating foods like eggs, tuna fish, salmon, and Swiss cheese."

"I hate Swiss cheese," Hem said.

Doc Lydgate pointed to the end of the bone, which was missing part of its hip joint, and invited his audience to lean in. "The round hip joint, or femoral head, is incomplete on our mystery skeleton. This allows us a clear look at the quality of this fellow's bone. And the quality isn't good, my friends. Whoever was buried in the yard had soft, weak bones. My guess would be that the skeleton's other bones will have the same spongy appearance. A result of rickets."

Jane glanced from the femur to the doctor's animated face. "That disease was eradicated, so that means this skeleton was buried a long time ago, right? As in the nineteenth century."

Sinclair answered before the doctor could. "To the contrary, rickets hasn't been eradicated. A number of Victorian era diseases have begun reemerging in first-world nations. Hospitals have reported cases of scurvy, gout, tuberculosis, and rickets. Some of these diseases are making a comeback."

Doc Lydgate stroked his beard. "Sadly, Mr. Sinclair is correct. In most of the cases cited in my medical journals, the patients were subsisting on very imbalanced diets. Luckily, the parents of most of my patients know what to feed their children. There are a few, and they shall remain nameless, who insist that soda is an acceptable substitution for milk or water at mealtimes, but you can't convince folks of facts they don't want to believe."

Sheriff Evans, sensing that Doc Lydgate might go off on a tangent, cleared his throat. "We might determine the skeleton's age by cleaning the muck off this coin. Mr. Sterling? Any suggestions?"

"We'll probably need something stronger than water. I'll grab some supplies," Sterling said. "Be right back."

Sterling vanished through a doorway marked STAFF ONLY, and Jane guessed that he'd entered his private chemistry lab to collect some exotic solution to use on the coin. She was surprised when he returned with a bottle of vinegar and a box of table salt.

Upon seeing these household items, Butterworth grunted in disapproval. "I would ask, Mr. Sterling, that you only use these agents out of desperation."

The sheriff cocked his head at Butterworth. "Is something wrong?"

"Most numismatists would advise against cleaning a coin with anything but water," Butterworth said. "The agents Mr. Sterling has selected could damage the coin on a chemical level and should be avoided. Unless such cleaning is required for identification purposes, of course."

"I'll do my best with the water first," Sterling assured the head butler, who was a passionate coin collector. "Unless you'd like the honors, Sheriff."

"You go ahead. I'll watch," the sheriff said, shooting Butterworth a nervous glance before moving to stand next to Sterling.

There wasn't enough room around the sink for everyone to observe the cleaning process, so the rest of the group had to wait while Sterling passed the coin under the water multiple times while rubbing at layers of grime with the pad of his thumb.

Jane found it difficult to be patient, but Butterworth and Sinclair were using the lull as a teaching opportunity. Both men had selected an evidence bag and were pointing at bone fragments and holding a quiet exchange with the twins. Doc Lydgate had returned to examining the femur and Deputy Phelps was scrolling through text messages on his cell phone.

Involuntarily, Jane met the skull's gaze. She experienced a fresh pang of pity for this nameless soul—this individual who hadn't eaten a balanced diet. What sort of life had this person led? And why had he or she come to Storyton Hall in the first place?

"I can't see the last two numbers, but the coin was minted in the eighteen hundreds," Sterling suddenly announced over the sound of the running water.

All other conversation ceased.

Sterling squinted down at the coin and then looked across the room and grinned. "I believe this individual is a countryman of yours, Mr. Butterworth. The profile on this coin isn't one of our presidents."

Butterworth marched over to the sink and, keeping his hands clasped firmly behind his back, leaned forward.

"That is most definitely *not* an American president. It is Her Royal Highness, Queen Victoria. You hold a farthing, Mr. Sterling. A coin minted of copper until 1860. At that point, the coins were made of bronze. This coin is of the copper variety."

"How can you tell?" Sheriff Evans asked, joining the men at the sink.

"The queen gives it away," Butterworth said, straightening to his full height again. "When the coins were produced of bronze, Her Majesty's bust was also changed to include a laureate and a draped robe over her shoulders. In later years, there were other alterations. However, this is not the time for a history lesson on British coinage."

Everyone in the room now turned to face the skull.

"Whoever this person is, he or she has probably been in the ground for well over a century," Jane said. "But why were they buried at Storyton Hall? It wasn't a hotel then. It was Walter Steward's home."

Sheriff Evans sighed. "I know you don't want to hear this, Ms. Steward, what with your construction project and all, but this case is out of my league. I'll have to call the state and request the assistance of a forensic anthropologist. It'll be up to them to decide what happens next."

Fitz and Hem started a bout of animated whispering. Jane thought she caught the name "Indiana Jones," and tried not to be annoyed with her sons. After all, it wasn't their fault that a skeleton had surfaced and threatened to ruin her dream of building a world-class spa.

"How long do you think the anthropologist will take to conduct an investigation?" Jane asked, already fearful of the answer.

"I hate to say this, Ms. Steward, but the real question is how long will it take to *get* an anthropologist," the sheriff replied glumly. "The state isn't exactly teeming with them, and the ones we have are already overworked."

Jane felt despondent. As she watched Sterling hand the evidence bag containing the farthing to Sheriff Evans, she considered mentioning what the twins had told her about the driver of the earthmover and their belief that he'd taken something from the grave site. Seeing as her sons weren't reliable witnesses, she decided that it could wait. Unfortunately, if she were to take what the sheriff had said to heart, the wait could be quite long.

"What about the box?" she asked instead. "I know you need to call in certain people, but is there harm in seeing what's inside?"

The sheriff shrugged. "I suppose not. Besides, I'd be lying if I said that I didn't want to open it."

As if he'd been expecting the request, Sterling produced a pair of bolt cutters and held them out to Sheriff Evans.

The sheriff easily snapped off the old lock and placed it inside an evidence bag. He then popped open the box latch and attempted to lift the lid. After several seconds, it became obvious that the lid was stuck fast. "Phelps? Can you get the other side?"

Together, the two men worked their gloved fingers under the lid and pulled upward. Without warning, there was a sigh of escaping air and the lid sprang open.

Jane stood right behind the sheriff's shoulder as he removed bits of cloth so tattered and stained that it was impossible to determine their original color. Under the cloth was a rectangular object. An object made of paper and bound in leather.

Releasing the breath she hadn't known she'd been holding, Jane whispered, "Oh my. It's a book."

Chapter Three

Sinclair was at Jane's side in a flash. "The remains of a book, at least."

"If you say so," the sheriff said, tilting his head. He stared down at the time-ravaged object, which was barely recognizable as a book, and peered intently at its cover of threadbare forest-green cloth. He then glanced at Jane, clearly confounded by all the excitement. "Isn't it ruined?"

"Most likely," Sinclair said. "Unfortunately, the box wasn't air tight. The damp crept in and ate away at the paper, spine, boards, and cloth. Grain cloth, to be specific."

Sheriff Evans looked from Sinclair to Jane. "I see that you two would like to investigate this part of the mystery, but I'd better close this up and hand the book over to the forensic anthropologist in an undisturbed state. I cut the padlock and opened the box and will take full responsibility for those actions, but I don't want to compromise the anthropologist's work any more than we already have."

"Quite so," Doc Lydgate agreed. "When you speak with the fellow, please let him know that I'd be glad to help reassemble the skeletal remains. I have a great deal of experience repairing bones."

"Because of Broken Arm Bend?" Hem asked.

The doc chuckled. "Mostly. People have accidents in other parts of the village, but that piece of road has brought me quite a few patients over the years."

Jane, who'd been gazing fixedly at the book cover, saw that the sheriff was on the verge of closing the box lid. Instinctively, her hand shot out to stop him.

"Could I take a photo of the cover?" she asked. "I'd like to research this book while we wait on the anthropologist. Like Doc Lydgate's experience with bones, our expertise with old books might produce quicker results."

The sheriff had no objection, so Jane used her cell phone to capture images of an embossed shape that might have once been covered by gold. Though it had lost its shiny decoration, Jane hoped to identify the mystery book by this design.

Sinclair understood why Jane was zooming in on one section of the cover and shone a flashlight on the area. The sheriff gave them a solid five minutes before he announced that it was time for Phelps to return to the station with the box and collection of evidence bags.

"Ms. Steward, I'll call this in from your office, if that's all right," Sheriff Evans went on to say. "I'd like to know how the anthropologist wants us to handle these bones. The skull seems pretty fragile." He turned to Sterling. "Can we cover this table with another piece of sheeting and move it to a safe place until I get an answer?"

"Of course." Sterling moved off to gather the necessary supplies.

The sheriff was making it clear that their involvement in the case was now at an end. Taking the hint, Lachlan ushered the twins toward one of the John Deere utility vehicles. Jane heard Lachlan say something about feeding the birds and flashed him a grateful smile, for the boys could spend hours at the mews. Next to the kitchens, it was their favorite place on earth.

Phelps slid the metal box into a plastic bag and carried it back to his car, taking care not to jostle its contents. Butterworth escorted the sheriff to the main building while Jane and Sinclair followed at a distance.

"The book shouldn't deteriorate any farther," Sinclair said in an attempt to console her.

"I really wanted to examine it," Jane said. "I know you did as well. My disappointment isn't just about the book either. After all, the box was buried with a dead Englishman from another century—I'm going to refer to the body as 'him' until we learn otherwise—who literally went to his grave with that book. Why? Was it so valuable that the man couldn't part with it, even in death?"

Sinclair scrunched his lips. "Valuable? Or dangerous? He could have been protecting others by hiding it where no one would find it. His grave."

"In the old rose garden?" Jane asked wryly. "That site was never a cemetery, not even for family plots, and that man wasn't given a proper burial. There's no coffin. Unless it was made of wood and completely decomposed, which seems unlikely."

"At least you had the foresight to photograph the cover. Somehow, we'll identify the book," Sinclair said, unfazed by Jane's tone.

Jane looped her arm through Sinclair's. "I'm sorry. I'm just crushed by the idea that the spa could be delayed for weeks. Or, heaven forbid, for months! I'm also a bit unnerved over the thought of someone being buried on Storyton's grounds while Walter Steward lived in the manor house. There are countless rumors about his mental state."

"Which began circulating only after he dismantled Storyton Hall and had it shipped, brick by brick, from his seat in the English countryside to a remote valley in western Virginia," Sinclair said in Walter's defense. "Prior to that, he was known for his learnedness and charity. My personal opinion is that his British countrymen were affronted by his decision to immigrate to America and chose to blacken his name because of that decision."

Though this made sense, Jane still wasn't at ease. As she and Sinclair headed for the herb garden, a thick knot of clouds blanketed the sun. The bright marigolds Mrs. Hubbard had planted around the garden's perimeter looked wilted and dull, as if they'd suddenly aged.

Jane felt like something was lurking just beyond her field of vision—that something from the past had been woken the moment the earthmover had raised those bones from the ground. She knew she was being fanciful, but that didn't stop her from glancing back at the orange construction fence.

"What if someone followed Walter from England?" she asked quietly. "A person with bad intentions. Maybe Walter's Fins had to take this person out, and this man, this threat to Walter and to the secret library, had to be buried swiftly and covertly before anyone learned that he'd been here."

Sinclair tightened his hold on Jane's arm. "Beware of creating fiction, Miss Jane. We may enjoy reading it, but we're not writers. I'm a Fin and you're a Guardian. We must work with facts or risk being led astray."

At the door to the kitchens, Jane froze. "I know one fact. Mrs. Hubbard will be bereft when I tell her that I'm canceling the Groundbreaking Ceremony. She already started baking for the event. What will we do with all the extra goodies?"

"We'll have to serve them to the rare book convention attendees," Sinclair said. "After all, if we can't identify the mystery book from your photos, then a member of the Robert Harley Rare Book Society might recognize it."

"That's true." Jane brightened at the thought. However, when she entered the kitchens to find Mrs. Hubbard assembling a tiered cake, her bubble of optimism popped.

Mrs. Hubbard lowered the top tier onto a set of plastic supports and released a grunt of satisfaction. As she wiped her hands on her apron, she spied Jane. "This cake will be one for the scrapbook, my dear. I'm planning on fondant lotion bottles, a robe made fuzzy with finishing sugar, candied cucumber slices, and edible flowers. It'll be so colorful. So inviting. Just like the future spa!"

There was no avoiding telling Mrs. Hubbard that the official Groundbreaking Ceremony had to be canceled. However, sharing details about the discovery of old bones was tantamount to taking out an advertisement in the local paper. Mrs. Hubbard was one of the most famed gossips in all of Storyton. The other was Ms. Eugenia Pratt, Jane's friend and a member of the Cover Girls Book Club. Between Mrs. Hubbard and Mrs. Pratt, the news of the mysterious skeleton would be known by everyone in the village before Sheriff Evans hung his hat that evening.

"Can you freeze that cake?" Jane hurriedly said. "And could you use the fondant to create colorful books instead of towels or lotion bottles?"

Mrs. Hubbard twisted a corner of her apron—something she did when she was unnerved. "Why? What's happened?"

Jane told her.

"A skeleton?" Mrs. Hubbard's round, apple-cheeked face glowed with interest. She would dine on this tale for days, and Jane knew that her head cook would mete out the details of the discovery like a commissary officer distributing wartime rations.

"That's all I can share with you for now," Jane said.

"Until Sheriff Evans can find a forensic anthropologist to continue the investigation, the spa construction is at a standstill and the skeleton will have to wait a little longer to introduce himself to us."

Mrs. Hubbard gave Jane's hand a pat. "What you need is comfort food. You've had a shock and a major disappointment at the same time, you poor dear. I know you were worried about my feelings, but I can change my cake design like that." She snapped her fingers. "It's not quite so easy for you. You have bank loans and deadlines and such. I should be fretting about you."

Jane squared her shoulders. "I'm sure everything will work out."

"Always putting on a brave face. That's our Miss Jane."

Jane suddenly found herself enfolded in Mrs. Hubbard's warm embrace. Mrs. Hubbard's hair smelled like oranges and cinnamon and Jane closed her eyes and breathed in the cook's familiar scent of fresh-baked dough and love.

"I know I'm not Edwin," Mrs. Hubbard murmured. "No one can comfort you the way your man can. And he really should be here to hold you. He should cook you dinner and rub your sore feet. Where is that good-looking devil, anyway?"

Jane gently disengaged. "Abroad" was all she could say because she honestly didn't know. Her last communication with Edwin had been two weeks ago. He'd called from "the road," and hadn't explained where he was heading, or which rare scroll, document, incunabula, or other priceless artifact he was pursuing or what he'd do with it once it was acquired.

My life is a revolving door of secrets, Jane thought as she left the kitchens for her small office.

She'd barely nudged her computer out of sleep mode

when one of the front desk clerks called on the intercom to inform her that Sheriff Evans was holding on line two.

"Ms. Steward, I have good news," the sheriff said cheerfully when Jane picked up the phone. "We won't have to wait for an anthropologist."

Out of habit, Jane grabbed a pen and held it over her desk calendar. "We won't?"

"We got really lucky," Evans continued. "It just so happens that a forensic anthropologist is serving as a visiting professor at the University of Virginia. When the state office contacted her, she offered to drive down to Storyton straightaway. Not only that, but she's also bringing along a small team of grad school students to help out. They'll be arriving around eight. Can you put them up for a couple of nights if need be?"

"Of course. What's the anthropologist's name?"

Jane heard the rustling of paper. "Hold on a moment. I wrote it on the case file." There was a pause and more rustling. "Ah, here we go. Doctor Celia Wallace. But she insists on being called Celia. Nice lady. Anyway, I'll be over first thing in the morning with the box and the evidence bags."

"What about the bones in the garage?" Jane asked. "Did Doctor Wallace, er, Celia, tell you what to do about them?"

"She asked that we leave them as they are. That's not a problem, right?"

Jane shook her head, even though the sheriff couldn't see her. "No, no."

"You don't have to be nervous about Celia's arrival, Ms. Steward. I believe she'll fit in well with everyone at Storyton Hall. She was positively giddy about visiting a place filled with books."

She sounds promising, but initial impressions can be deceiving, Jane thought.

The moment she ended the call with Sheriff Evans, she phoned Sinclair and told him to run a background check on Celia Wallace.

"I have my book club meeting tonight," she told her head librarian. "So I'm going to let you and Butterworth play the hosts to Doctor Wallace and her students. However, if she raises any red flags . . ."

"Rest assured, I'll inform you at once," promised Sinclair. "In the meantime, try to enjoy yourself. Remember what another Wallace wrote. In this case, I'm referring to Wallace Stegner."

Jane smiled. She loved when Sinclair quoted obscure lines from novels she'd read once, and often, over a decade ago. For some reason, he expected her to remember every word of every book. Jane wished she could. What she did recall was the feeling each book inspired. Sinclair, on the other hand, had what was nearly a photographic memory when it came to works of literature. He could accurately quote thousands of lines.

"Which was?" she asked him.

Sinclair cleared his throat and intoned, "'Another fall, another turned page: there was something of jubilee in that annual autumnal beginning, as if last year's mistakes and failures had been wiped clean by summer.'"

"That's lovely."

Sinclair made a noise of assent. "So get together with your friends, pour a glass of wine, and find something of jubilee."

The Cover Girls appeared to be of the same mind as Sinclair.

Jane had just finished feeding the twins and had sent them upstairs to get ready for bed when the doorbell rang and Eloise Alcott let herself into the house. Two other Cover Girls, Violet Osborne and Phoebe Doyle, were close on Eloise's heels. Like Eloise, both women were Storyton Village merchants. Violet owned Tresses Hair Salon and Phoebe owned the Canvas Creamery, which was not only a frozen yogurt and coffee bar, but also an art gallery.

"Is it true?" Eloise demanded breathlessly. "Was a body dug up today? And if it's true, then why didn't you call me?"

Jane waited until her friends were completely in the kitchen before saying, "Because I knew you'd hear about the skeleton within hours after my telling Mrs. Hubbard. Also, I knew we'd be seeing each other tonight. It's much better to share this story in person."

"I wish you'd had time to drop in at Run for Cover, but I'm sure you had to call the sheriff and . . ." Eloise trailed off, her lovely face clouding over. "What *is* the protocol when a skeleton suddenly surfaces on your property?"

Violet nudged Eloise, who was blocking the doorway, aside. "Can we put the lasagna in the oven before we bombard Jane with questions?"

"More to the point, can we pour the wine?" said Anna, setting two bottles on the counter. Anna worked at Storyton Pharmacy. She and Violet were the youngest members of the Cover Girls.

The doorbell rang again and the rest of the Cover Girls burst into Jane's house with Mrs. Pratt leading the charge. She hurried into the kitchen, clutching two loaves of bread in one hand and her copy of their club's most recent read, *The Storied Life of A. J. Fikry*, in the other.

"Jane Steward, whenever I entertain thoughts of buying a beach condo—just a tiny place where I can warm myself when we have a winter with too much freezing rain—I think of what I might miss if I ever left Storyton!" She drew in a breath before continuing in the theatrical manner she was known for. "What would I do for *excitement*? Having a friend and neighbor like you is better than paying for premium cable channels."

"I'm glad my troubles have entertainment value," Jane muttered grumpily.

Mabel Wimberly, the proprietor of La Grande Dame Clothing Boutique, placed a wooden salad bowl on the kitchen island and put her arm around Jane's waist. "You most certainly have value! You're the sun of our solar system! We gravitate to your house week after week to eat delectable food, drink delicious drinks, and talk about anything and everything that matters. Sometimes, we even get around to discussing the book we read."

This elicited a laugh from Betty Carmichael. She and her husband, Bob, ran the Cheshire Cat Pub. "Oh, come on. We always start with the book. We just get sidetracked by other subjects. I think that's okay. We're women, which means we can multitask. We always return to the key themes before we call it a night. We never part without arguing about who'd be the best book boyfriend, sharing beautifully written lines from the novel, and spilling something on Jane's rug."

Mrs. Pratt glanced around at her fellow club members with an incredulous look. "How can you all act like this is any other night? Isn't anyone else *dying* to hear what happened today? With the *body*?"

"Of course we are," Eloise said soothingly. "And Jane promised to tell us. But first, wine!"

As Eloise and Anna opened wine bottles and filled glasses, Betty and Mabel put the finishing touches on the salad. Violet grated fresh Parmesan cheese for the lasagna while Jane added napkins and flatware to the table.

"I like that we've basically made the same meal served by one character to another," Phoebe said, pointing to her own copy of *The Storied Life of A. J. Fikry.* "Because the setting mostly takes place in Nantucket, I was afraid we'd be having a fish course, and you know I'm not a big seafood fan."

"But you *are* a big lemon fan, and I baked lemon shortbread bars for dessert," Betty said. "Jane? You have the strawberries and cream to put on top, right?"

Jane gave Betty a thumbs-up before accepting a wineglass from Eloise. The two best friends clinked rims and Jane took a grateful sip.

After granting herself a second sip, Jane gave her friends a recap of her day, omitting the part where the twins had purportedly witnessed the driver pocketing an object from the grave site. By the time she was done, her wineglass was empty.

"A forensic anthropologist?" Anna cried. "And she's coming to Storyton Hall tonight?"

"She should be here any minute now," Jane said.

Mrs. Pratt sighed. "I'd prefer a male, à la Sean Connery from *Indiana Jones and the Last Crusade*."

"You're just saying that because Mr. Connery is a Scot and you like your men in kilts," Mabel teased.

The women laughed and raised their glasses to Mrs. Pratt. It was a known fact that Eugenia Pratt, a devoted fan of romance novels, had read nearly every Scottish-themed romance both in and out of print.

Always delighted to be the center of attention, Mrs. Pratt smiled. "It sounds like your mystery skeleton was an Englishman. Could he have been a relative? Was there a family burial plot in that location?"

Jane shook her head. "According to the original drawings, it was once a rose garden. There were multiple gardens. Kitchen gardens. Herb gardens. Topiary gardens. Hedge mazes. And so on. Milton's Gardens is the only one we've managed to restore to match the original plan. The folly and the orchard are on my Hopes and Dreams board, but I wanted to build the spa first."

"Why bury a person in the garden? Like he was a pet?" Phoebe asked.

"Or something you wanted to hide," Betty added.

Mabel made a time-out gesture. "Hold on, ladies. Do we know that this man is a man at all?"

"No," Jane said. "But by the end of tomorrow, I'm sure the anthropologist will have identified the skeleton's gender. Which means you'll know."

"*If* you tell us." Eloise pretended to pout.

Suddenly, the oven timer chimed.

Jane cupped her hand over one ear. "The oven's playing my song. Cover Girls? Shall we feast?"

The women spread out the food buffet style in Jane's bright, cheerful kitchen, served themselves, and then sat around her table to eat and discuss Gabrielle Zevin's novel.

"I just want to say, Jane, that this is my favorite of all our reading themes to date," Violet said. "Books about books. I had fun when we chose titles starting with certain letters too, but I really love this theme."

"Me too," Betty agreed. "I was surprised by how much I liked the nonfiction-book-themed books. I learned so much about bibliophiles and bibliomania from *How Reading Changed My Life, A Pound of Paper: Confessions of a Book Addict, The Man Who Loved Books Too Much,* and *Rare Books Uncovered.* I thought *we* were book crazy, but we're not as crazy as some of the people we met in those books."

Mabel used a slice of garlic bread to point at Betty. "I don't know about that. Have you seen Eugenia's living room? The place is wall-to-wall books."

"It's beautiful," Jane said. "You clearly know what's important, my friend."

"Thank you." Mrs. Pratt preened. "I guess I'll have

plenty to talk about with the dashing men attending the rare book conference."

Anna giggled. "Do you think they collect romance novels featuring hunky Highlanders?"

Mrs. Pratt shrugged. "If the books are hardbacks, in the original dust jacket, and signed by the author, it's possible. They can't *all* collect religious texts bound with vellum or parchment pages filled with diplomatic treatises. If so, this will be a seriously tedious convention."

The Cover Girls shared another laugh.

As was their tradition, the friends discussed a host of topics about *The Storied Life of A. J. Fikry.* At one point, Jane popped upstairs to give the twins a good-night kiss and to check under their blankets for stashed paperbacks, comic books, and flashlights. Satisfied that her sons were worn out from the day's excitement, she returned to the kitchen and prepared individual servings of lemon shortbread bars topped with sliced strawberries and whipped cream.

Over dessert, each of the Cover Girls took turns reciting a quote from the novel that had resonated with them.

"Mine should be pretty obvious." Eloise smiled broadly. Tossing a lock of honey-blond hair off her shoulder, she placed her hand over her heart and said, "'A place is not really a place without a bookstore.'"

There were numerous murmurs of agreement and Mrs. Pratt suddenly grabbed Eloise by the hand. "It's so true. I can't imagine life in Storyton without you or Run for Cover. It would be colorless and dull."

The two women exchanged affectionate, teary-eyed glances.

"You'd better say yours before things get too emotional," Betty whispered to Mabel.

Mabel nodded and pulled a piece of scrap paper from her copy of the novel. Multicolored sticky notes protruded from three of four sides of the book, indicating lines or passages she'd found memorable. "Here's the quote. Actually, it was more of a question that kept me up until all hours of the night. I'm not kidding, either. I couldn't fall asleep because I wasn't able to answer this question. Just when I thought I had the answer and I'd start to drift off, another answer would pop in my head and I'd be awake again."

Violet was on the verge of biting into a strawberry topped with cream, but she was so intrigued by Mabel's dilemma that she lowered her fork to her plate. "What's the quote?"

"'You know everything you need to know about a person from the answer to the question, What is your favorite book?'" Mabel threw out her hands, nearly knocking over her wineglass. "See what I mean? Can you name just one favorite? Because I can't. After hours of tossing and turning, I whittled it down to three. *Charlotte's Web*, *The Secret Life of Bees*, and *The Bluest Eye*."

Phoebe rolled her eyes. "I can't limit it to three. I might be able to do five. Let's see." She gazed into the middle distance and said, "*Anne of Green Gables, Gone with the Wind, Naked in Death, The Pillars of the Earth,* and *Girl with a Pearl Earring*."

The rest of the Cover Girls had lapsed into silence, a list of beloved book titles scrolling through their brains.

Jane watched her friends. She wasn't even going to take a stab at the exercise. She knew she needed a minimum of ten titles if she were to create an all-time favorite list, and while she could write down a few fairly quickly, such as *A Wrinkle in Time, The Hobbit, The Once and Future King, To Kill A Mockingbird,* and *The Secret Garden,* the second half of the list would require several minutes of quiet and solitary rumination.

"If my life depended on it," Mrs. Pratt began with a dramatic air, "I could force myself to a mere two titles. *Outlander* and *Pride and Prejudice*."

Eloise grinned at her. "You are such a hopeless romantic. May you never change."

Mrs. Pratt responded with a hapless shrug. "I don't think Gavin would agree with you," she said, referring to Storyton Hall's former head of Recreation. "He wanted me to change. He wanted me to move to another state. All along, I thought I'd been waiting for just such a proposal. A good-looking, intelligent, Scottish gentleman who occasionally wears a kilt comes along and would have probably asked for my hand if I'd agreed to the move. But I hadn't. Why? Because it turned out that I didn't want the fantasy from my romance novels. I realized, after half a dozen dates with Gavin, that I'd have to compromise for our relationship to work. I would've gladly done that if we stayed in Storyton, but to leave this place would mean losing the life I'd built here. It would mean losing too much of myself. And it would mean losing you, my dear friends. In the end, a man in a kilt who wanted to whisk me away *wasn't* what I truly wanted."

Anna folded her arms over her chest. "Sometimes, I read for the sole purpose of driving Randall's monotone out of my head. All day long, he stands on his elevated platform in the pharmacy like he's the pope, delivering sermons on head lice, good and bad bacteria, flu shots, and seasonal allergies. It's no surprise that my favorite books are escapist reads. Tamora Pierce, Jonathan Kellerman, and Mary Stewart. I also reread my Nancy Drew collection every few years."

Eloise looked at Jane. "You've been awfully quiet. Is it too hard for you to hone down your list?"

"I was focusing on titles for a bit," Jane said. "But then I started thinking about the nonfiction books we read for our book-related theme. There were so many anecdotes about the lengths bibliomaniacs will go to possess certain works. They'll lie, cheat, and steal. They'll take incredible risks. Foolish risks."

"Why do I have the feeling we're no longer talking about our current novel?" Violet whispered softly.

"Because I think we're talking about a skeleton and a box containing an old, decrepit book," Phoebe whispered back.

Jane went on as if neither of her friends had spoken. "What would a book collector do to protect his most valuable prize?"

"Anything," Eloise blurted. "He might even—" She stopped, put her hand to her mouth, and then slowly lowered it. "Take it to his grave."

Chapter Four

Eloise's words stayed with Jane long after the Cover Girls went home.

The next morning, Jane woke early. There was a tangible difference to the air, and when she pushed back the covers and felt a breath of coolness in the room, she knew that summer had finally given way to autumn.

The change was subtle. There was a slackening of humidity, as if the morning had less weight to it. The twins must have noticed the shift too. Even though they couldn't verbalize it, they were more raucous at the breakfast table than usual.

"Is the bone lady here?" Hem asked as he poured a river of syrup over his pancakes.

Jane watched him out of the corner of her eye. Over the summer, she'd been trying her hand at pancake art. She didn't attempt the complicated creations she'd seen online—celebrity portraits or three-dimensional architectural structures—but stuck to basics like hearts, stars, cats, dogs, birds, or other easily recognizable animals. Today, however, she believed she'd topped all of her previous creations by forming batter letters. She'd then sprinkled each letter with mini chocolate chips prior to flipping it.

When she presented her sons with their names spelled out in polka-dot pancake form, she expected a better reaction than the one she got. The twins murmured a hurried thanks, but that was all. They were too focused on wolfing down their breakfasts as quickly as possible so that they might catch a glimpse of "the bone lady."

"I was told that Doctor Wallace and her students arrived last night," Jane said to her sons. "However, I have no idea if you'll be allowed near her work site. We'll have to ask for permission."

"But *we* found the bones!" Fitz protested.

Jane gave him a stern look. "I realize that, Fitzgerald. You and your brother are observant and you have excellent eyesight. You also stopped the earthmover driver just in time. But neither of you are trained scientists. Therefore, you will *not* go near that area unless you are specifically asked. Do you understand?"

The boys murmured "yes, ma'am" into their plates while Jane tried not to roll her eyes. Women on her staff were constantly telling her to be grateful for sons because girls were far more dramatic. But these women hadn't been around to witness Fitz and Hem when they embarked on one of their lengthy sulks, and Jane could see that they were heading in that direction.

"Tell you what," Jane said in a softer tone. "Let me finish my coffee and throw on a pair of jeans, and we'll walk over to the garage together. If the bone lady and her team are up and about, that's where we'll find them."

The boys responded by devouring their pancakes, loading their plates into the dishwasher, and offering to fix Jane a travel mug of coffee.

In lieu of accepting, she gestured at the mixing bowl, whisk, measuring cup, spatula, and pan and suggested that they get a firsthand experience of how many tools pancake art required.

Fifteen minutes later, with the kitchen relatively clean, Jane trailed after her sons on the very brief trip from their house, which was originally the back half of the hunting lodge on Walter Steward's estate in England, to the garage. This larger front half contained the fleet of Rolls Royce sedans used to collect Storyton Hall guests from the train station as well as Sterling's living quarters and lab. There was also a spacious basement where the Fins did much of their physical training and Jane and the twins honed their martial arts skills.

This morning, a small crowd of people dressed in jeans and T-shirts occupied the garage. They stood in a loose circle around the table where the bones had been laid out the day before. Because their heads were bent and they were so quiet, they looked like a group at prayer.

Drawing closer, Jane noticed that the plastic sheeting covering the skull and larger bones had already been removed and that several powerful lights had been positioned around the area. A woman with round glasses and dark hair laced with filaments of silver was speaking in a hushed, but animated tone. Not only were the graduate students giving who was undoubtedly the forensic anthropologist their full attention, but so was Sinclair.

Unlike the students, Sinclair was a Fin. As soon as he sensed Jane's approach, he signaled to Celia Wallace that he needed to interrupt her.

"Doctor Wallace? This is Jane Steward, the manager of Storyton Hall." Sinclair introduced Fitz and Hem next. "These gentlemen are her sons. They're responsible for finding our Englishman."

"Please call me Celia. We living are all friends among the dead." The anthropologist came forward to pump Jane's hand while the boys received enthusiastic high-fives and a string of compliments for their discovery.

"Is he a man, ma'am?" Hem asked.

"He is," Celia said. "One of my students"—she pointed at a pretty young woman with an auburn ponytail—"has already given him a nickname. We're calling him Oliver."

"Like *Oliver Twist*?" Fitz peeked out at the grad student from under his long lashes and she rewarded him with a friendly smile. Flustered, he instantly dropped to a catcher's pose and pretended to tie his shoe.

Celia was noticeably impressed. "Wow," she said to Jane. "I didn't expect them to get the reference. Not many kids their age would. Then again, not many kids are lucky enough to grow up in this paradise. After we're done with the site, I'm not sure I'll want to leave."

It was impossible not to warm to Celia. "You're fond of books, then?"

"Fond?" Celia laughed, and the sound was so replete with unchecked merriment that everyone in the room laughed with her. "I'm an addict. A junkie. A hoarder. I openly admit to having a serious problem when it comes to books. Ask my students. They had to fight for seat space with the books I keep in my truck. I ride around with books to read at cafés, or during boring movies, dull lectures, or at *really* long red lights. People are constantly honking at me."

She began chortling again, but tapered off when she noticed Hem studying her with a wary eye.

"I love books, but my real passion is old bones. And the stories they tell. Ah, the lessons we can learn from the silent past," she added in a far more sedate, almost melancholy tone. She then took off her glasses, rubbed at a smudge on the left lens, and addressed the twins. "Would you like to learn how we knew this person was an Oliver and not an Olive?"

The boys said that they would, and while Celia showed them Oliver's femur as well as the partial pelvic bone, Sinclair motioned for Jane to join him away from the others.

"Sheriff Evans is on the way with the rest of the collected

evidence. Doctor Wallace—I cannot bring myself to use her Christian name—has informed me that she intends to grid the area where the remains were found. It's her hope that she and her team will take what's already bagged as well as what they find back to the university two days from today."

Jane was both astonished and delighted. "Two days? That's all?"

"Apparently, once she gets her hands in the dirt, she doesn't stop digging." Sinclair shot Celia Wallace an appreciative glance.

"It sounds like she shares your work ethic," Jane said.

Sinclair's lips formed the ghost of a smile. "We seem to have several common interests. Doctor Wallace also enjoys reading everything she can get her hands on, from autobiographies to historical fiction to romantic poetry."

Jane gave Sinclair a gentle bump with her shoulder. "Maybe I shouldn't want such an interesting woman to leave us so quickly."

For the briefest moment, Sinclair looked like he might agree. "On the contrary," he said instead. "We must do all we can to assist her. Keeping the construction project on schedule is of paramount importance."

"Mom!" Hem and Fitz suddenly materialized in front of Jane.

"The bone lady said that we could help!" Fitz exclaimed. He opened his mouth to continue, but Hem didn't give him a chance.

"If we follow her directions, and you say that it's okay, we can shake dirt through special screens!"

Jane smiled. "It's okay with me. I see it as an educational opportunity."

This earned her a hug from her sons.

"You'd better wear boots!" she cried as they dashed off. "You'll be spending the day in the dirt."

When Jane turned to look at Celia, she saw that the

anthropologist was grinning at her. "They seem pretty amped about playing in the dirt."

"It's their favorite medium," Jane said with a laugh. Growing serious again, she asked, "Did Sheriff Evans tell you about the other artifacts found with the bones?"

Celia nodded. "One of my students is proficient in coin cleaning. He'll get going on that as soon as it arrives. As far as the book fragment, I'd planned to ask you and Mr. Sinclair—he insists on being so formal—to lend us your expertise. This is the first time I've encountered a book buried with human remains."

One of Celia's male students, who wore a faded Cheerwine T-shirt, waved to get his mentor's attention. "PoPo's here."

When Jane saw that Deputy Amelia Emory was with Sheriff Evans, she smiled. She liked the young deputy. Emory was an art aficionado and a chronic reader, and Jane suspected that she'd volunteered to come with the sheriff today.

After dispensing with introductions, Jane gave Sheriff Evans the floor.

"I'm going to sign the evidence over to you, Doctor, er, Celia," the sheriff said. "But if you need manpower from our department, just say the word. We're a bit short, seeing as it's a holiday weekend, but I can always find a few deputies willing to work extra shifts."

Celia's eyes were already moving over the evidence bags, and she seemed pleased by what she saw inside. "Thank you, Sheriff. I appreciate all that you've done already. We'll be sure to let you know what we find. Won't we, team?"

The grad students murmured in agreement, but the disarticulated remains had transfixed them as well. Though no words were spoken to the effect, it was plain that Celia and her team were eager for the sheriff and his deputy to depart so they could be alone with the bones and the British coin.

Sheriff Evans was an intuitive man. Tipping his hat, he wished everyone a pleasant day. As he headed toward his car, Jane heard him say, "Don't worry, Emory. If they need help, you'll be the one I send over. But for now, we have the glamorous job of responding to Mrs. Hogg's complaint."

"Not the rooster again," Emory muttered before the pair moved out of earshot.

With the arrival of the evidence bags, Celia's demeanor changed. She clapped her hands and began assigning tasks with the loud, rapid-fire speech of a general launching a full-scale assault.

Jane realized that if she didn't interrupt, she might spend the rest of the morning waiting for an opening, and she had plenty of things to do before the conference attendees checked in that afternoon.

"Celia." Jane touched the anthropologist lightly on the arm. "I'm leaving you to your work, but before I go, could we discuss the book found with the body? My guess is that it's too humid out here for something in such delicate condition, so I'd like to take it inside Storyton Hall for safe-keeping and further study. With your permission, of course."

"The book!" Celia shook her head. "Forgive me, but when I'm near a pile of bones, I completely lose myself. They're the most fascinating puzzle. And it's much more than the reassembly of the broken pieces. The bones ask so many questions. Am I male or female? Am I young or old? Rich or poor? Healthy or Unhealthy? Did I die of natural causes? What was my diet? Did I take care of my teeth?"

Jane glanced at the skull. "When I look at that, *I'm* full of questions, not the other way around."

Celia nodded encouragingly. "Such as?"

"Why were you buried without a coffin or headstone? Why did you come to America? Why did you take that book to your grave?"

"Excellent questions," Celia said approvingly. She scanned the room until her gaze landed on Sinclair.

Storyton Hall's head librarian had just left the twins in the care of the pretty grad student who'd smiled at Fitz earlier. Celia had asked the girl, whose name was Petra, to take the boys under her wing for the day, and she'd happily agreed.

"Are we talking books or bones?" Sinclair asked, joining Jane and Celia next to the table bearing the skull, femur, pelvis, and other large bones.

"Both," Celia said. "However, I'd like to entrust the book to you and Jane. After an initial examination, including photographs, I'll send the book inside and out of harm's way."

Sinclair was satisfied with this outcome, so Jane left the occupants of the garage to their tasks and headed into the kitchens to get a cup of coffee before proceeding to her office.

She bumped into Mrs. Hubbard refilling her personal mug from the staff coffeepot.

"It's nice and strong this morning," she said, settling on a stool. "I heard that our special guests are already hard at work."

She must pay her spies with baked goods, Jane thought.

Instead of supplying Mrs. Hubbard with details, she ordered a tray of sandwiches to be prepared for the anthropology team by lunchtime, poured herself a mammoth cup of coffee, and continued to her office. She spent the next two hours answering e-mails and meeting with various staff members to ensure that all was ready for the kickoff of the rare book conference.

At noon, Jane helped two waiters from the Kipling Café carry platters of sandwiches, fruit kebabs, homemade potato chips, and drinks to the garage.

The grave site was now completely covered by a white

event tent, and when Jane ducked under one of the flaps, she was stunned by the transformation she saw within. Hours ago, there'd been a jagged hole in the ground. Now, the shape of the hole was a perfect rectangle and a grid of strings covered the entire opening. A grad student armed with trowel, sieve, brush, and a pair of buckets occupied each grid square. Celia remained in the garage. Spotting Jane, she announced that Oliver's bones had been cleaned and were now drying in shallow pans.

"Your sons made another discovery," she told Jane, sounding like a doting aunt. "A halfpenny! Both the halfpenny and the farthing are in great shape. I wish I could say the same of Oliver's clavicle bones."

Hem and Fitz couldn't wait to show Jane their find. After she admired the coin, which was about the size of a contemporary quarter, she convinced the boys to leave the treasure and eat.

"The halfpenny lady is called Britannia," Hem told her as he selected a smoked ham and mozzarella sandwich from the platter.

"She's holding a thing that looks like a pitchfork," Fitz added. "Poseidon had one too."

Jane looked on with amusement as Fitz grabbed a roast beef with herbed goat cheese and far too many potato chips. To make up for his excessiveness, she skipped the chips, putting a spoonful of fruit salad on her plate next to her prosciutto and fig sandwich.

"A trident?" she guessed.

"That's it!" Fitz exclaimed. "Ms. Celia is going to put our names in her article. She said it's important to give credit where credit is due. I don't know what that means, but we're having our names in a magazine. Isn't *that* awesome?"

Jane smiled at her son. "Yes, it is. And what Doctor Wallace means is that you should be recognized for what you found. For your hard work as well. No matter what your age."

"I like her," Hem said as Jane led her sons to a bench in Milton's Gardens.

"Me too," Jane said.

Fitz, whose mouth was stuffed with potato chips, began to speak, but Jane pointed at his cheek and shook her head.

He hurriedly swallowed and began to tell Jane how he and Hem had helped sift the dirt of Petra's grid through a screen. While they'd worked, Petra shared stories of the other digs she'd been on.

Hem said, "She's done two others, but she said that this one's her favorite."

"Not because of us," Fitz added. "It's Oliver. They have lots of his bones. And Ms. Celia is excited because he had a disease just like Doc Lydgate said."

Hem examined a brown spot on his potato chip. "They all think diseases are cool, but we saw pictures of germs in our science book and I think they're gross."

"Plus, Aunt Octavia has a disease and it makes her unhappy," Fitz added.

Jane put down her sandwich. "Some adults are interested in how diseases mark human bones because it helps them know what kind of life that person lived. It helps them understand that person's story. It would be like if, one day, they found your Aunt Octavia's diary and they read about how sad she was when she learned that she couldn't sample all of the teatime treats everyday."

"Because too much sugar isn't good for her," Hem said.

Fitz had stopped eating and was frowning in thought. "Oliver must have eaten a ton of candy. He had holes in his teeth. Remember how Doc Lydgate showed us three cavities?"

"Probably not from candy," Jane said. "But who knows? Tooth decay is another kind of disease. See? These are the things Celia and her team will study when they take Oliver back to their lab."

"I want to study bones when I grow up," Fitz announced.

Hem stared at him in astonishment. "I thought we were going to be explorers. We made a *pact*."

Imagining pinpricks on pinkie fingers and the swearing of a blood oath, Jane spoke up before her sons could begin one of their endless arguments. "You could do both. Anthropologists travel quite a bit. So do archaeologists."

"But I don't *want* to study bones," Hem complained. "I don't want to be stuck in a building. I don't want to wear a tie and be quiet all the time. I'd *die!*"

Many of Storyton Hall's guests felt as Hem did. Their professions required that they spend countless hours in cramped spaces—walled cubicles, labs, operating rooms, offices—and when they dreamed of a vacation place, they dreamed of a setting with tall trees, rolling hills, and a wide swath of bright blue sky. They longed for the tranquility of muted phones and e-mails set to out-of-office reply. Only with this combination could they hope to finally unwind, take a deep breath for the first time in a very long time, and pursue their love of reading. Which is exactly what Storyton Hall offered.

And a dead body from time to time, Jane thought ruefully.

After lunch, the twins wanted to continue working with Petra.

"They've really been helpful," Celia assured Jane. "And we're making wonderful progress. If tomorrow goes as well as today, I expect to be Charlottesville-bound before suppertime."

"That's incredible." Jane wanted to hug the anthropologist. "When the sheriff first mentioned this process, I was under the impression you'd be here for weeks."

Celia laughed. "We have no structure to excavate. The

metal detectors aren't signaling large buried objects, so what I expect to find at this juncture would be more coins, a belt buckle, buttons—that sort of thing. We've probably found all the bones we're going to find. The rest have likely been destroyed, but we'll continue searching."

"In the meantime, we can study the book here?" Jane asked.

"Mr. Sinclair told me that an entire army of rare book experts is descending on Storyton Hall. If the book remains a mystery to you two, why not show it to these folks? I'm not one of those scientists who secrets her discoveries in a lab cabinet where they never see the light of day. I believe, that by pooling knowledge and sharing information, all disciplines benefit. The human race benefits."

Jane thought of how she'd previously tried to convince Uncle Aloysius to display items from their secret library and of how the words she'd said to him had sounded similar to Celia's.

"I agree," she said. "And I can't imagine there'd be anything a bibliophile would love more than to help solve a book-related mystery."

All of Storyton Hall's rooms were booked by conference attendees. Jane had no idea what she and the staff would have done had Celia and her grad students needed to stay another night, so she was infinitely relieved when Sinclair informed her that the anthropologist and her team would complete their work on the site by that evening. Most of them would be returning to Charlottesville to examine the findings in the university lab.

"The process isn't finished, however," Sinclair said. "And Doctor Wallace has a request. She'd like the dirt previously removed from the site by the earthmover to be kept off-limits. She's leaving two grad students behind to sift through it and would welcome any help our groundskeepers can offer. We're not to worry about accommodations for her students, as one of them has family living about fifteen minutes away who'll not only put them up, but will also loan them a car for the duration."

"Sounds good." Jane gestured toward the narrow door leading to Sinclair's office. "Can you show me the book fragment now? I thought I'd get over here earlier, but you should have seen the twins' bathroom. The things I have to do to make their tiles white again."

Sinclair grinned. "I expect they slept very soundly."

"I didn't hear a peep."

"I admit to burning the midnight oil to no avail. I've had no luck identifying Oliver's book." Sinclair raised his hands in supplication. "While I may find the nickname a trifle flippant, it's preferable to referring to our unknown guest as the skeleton or the Rip Van Winkle. Oliver sounds more innocuous."

Once Jane was inside Sinclair's office, he closed and locked the door behind them. Sinclair was in charge of vetting guests, which meant he performed background checks on everyone who booked a room at Storyton Hall. The Fins had learned from experience to step up security measures during conferences. As a result, index cards covered every inch of wall space above Sinclair's desk. Each card contained the name and a color photograph of the conference attendees.

Jane's eyes roved over the cards. "There are more men than women," she observed.

"The numbers seem slightly skewed by the addition of the Robert Harley Society, which has traditionally been all male." Sinclair arched a brow. "And before you become offended on behalf of your gender, women are permitted to join. In fact, there is one female member, but it's a very small society as a rule."

"I wonder why," Jane mused aloud. However, her interest in the subject vanished as soon as Sinclair showed her the metal box buried with Oliver.

Sinclair handed her a pair of latex exam gloves and donned his own.

"The box itself houses no clues," he said. "It's empty, unmarked, and corroded by rust. I've placed it in a rubber bin and will give it to Doctor Wallace before she leaves this evening."

As for the book, its sad remains sat in one of Mrs. Hubbard's roasting pans in the center of a small table on the far side of Sinclair's office.

"Did you ask to borrow this?" Jane asked.

Sinclair shook his head. "If word gets out, Mrs. Hubbard will have my head." He gestured for Jane to take a seat and switched on a powerful desk lamp. Two pieces of foam, a magnifying glass, a jeweler's loop, a razor blade, and a pair of tweezers were lined up alongside the roasting pan.

"I'm afraid the typeface has literally vanished from what's left of the pages," Sinclair said morosely. "But your eyes are younger than mine. Perhaps you'll spot something I missed. Go ahead. You know how to handle fragile materials and it won't be harmed much more than it already has. It's barely recognizable as a book now."

It clearly galled Sinclair that he might never know what treasures had been between the book's covers due to how thoughtlessly it had been buried, but he moved away to give Jane room to work. She placed a foam block in the pan and opened the cover onto it for support. Both the inside cover and endpaper were stained a dark russet. There were also black speckles and pockmarks throughout, as if the book were diseased. Every page looked like it had been gnawed by starving rats, and despite Jane's deliberate inspection, she couldn't find a single word or illustration.

And then, just when she believed the book had no secrets to reveal, she realized that two of the pages were stuck together.

Using the razor blade and a great deal of patience, she parted the pages at the top corner. She continued sliding the blade down the fore-edge and was horrified when minute flakes of loose paper floated down into the pan. She nearly stopped, but the pages were almost separated, so she took a steadying breath and finished the job.

Jane slowly peeled the pages apart and immediately spied the ghost-pale shapes of letters. Readjusting the angle of the desk lamp, she picked up the magnifying glass and stared at the faded print.

"Have you found something?" Sinclair asked from his desk.

Jane turned to face him. "Three words. They make no sense. And I'm not sure I want to understand their meaning."

Sinclair was at her side in an instant.

Accepting the magnifying glass Jane held out, he bent over and read the words aloud: "'Skin the tongue.'"

He then straightened and looked at Jane. "A bit graphic for Oliver's time, wouldn't you agree?"

Before Jane could reply, her cell phone vibrated. She glanced at the screen and said, "We'll have to continue this later. The conference attendees are starting to arrive." After a moment's hesitation, she added, "Having seen those three words, I'm relieved that by the time we found Oliver, there was nothing left of him but bones."

Chapter Five

Mrs. Hubbard's book-themed tea service looked like a scene from a fantasy novel.

The conference attendees lined up in the hallway outside the Agatha Christie Tearoom, and when the waitstaff opened the doors, the guests standing close enough to glimpse the magical spread gasped with delight.

Mrs. Hubbard and the sous chefs had been playful in the past when shaping finger sandwiches. Jane had seen them use cookie cutters to form flowers, leaves, and Christmas trees. However, this was the first time the staff had made platters of sandwiches shaped like open books.

"Using marbled rye helped create the illusion of text," Mrs. Hubbard had explained to Jane as the tea buffet was being arranged. "The grill lines on the sourdough and white toast created a similar look. That was Juan's idea," she said, smiling at her fry chef. "And because we also made open-faced sandwiches, we were able to use condiments as text."

Jane examined a tiered glass platter. The bottom tier featured smoked salmon sandwiches topped with herbed cream cheese squiggles while the top tier held roast beef and arugula rolls garnished with delicate scribbles of roasted red pepper sauce.

"These are wonderful, but the desserts are beyond magnificent. I can't imagine how much time you put in making that cake."

The cake, which stood proudly on the end of the buffet line next to orange Jell-O books topped with whipped cream pages and a platter of book-shaped cookies filled with homemade strawberry jam, had a black-and-white theme.

"Make sure you're here when it's cut or you'll miss all the fun," Mrs. Hubbard had said.

As the guests began entering the tearoom, Jane saw the space through their eyes. She took in the snowy tablecloths, the placemats resembling old book pages, and the centerpieces of chrysanthemums, feathers, and fresh greens. Each linen napkin had been tightly rolled and tied with a satin ribbon. Nestled inside every napkin was a quote by a famous scribe, bookmaker, or modern publishing mogul. The speaker's identity was intentionally left blank, for Jane hoped the quotes would serve as conversation starters.

Jane could see that these wouldn't be necessary, as the guests were already talking to each other about Mrs. Hubbard's cake.

The entire confection was black and white. The bottom and top tier were white and the middle tier was black. The tiers were lined with black-and-white fondant book spines in different sizes and shapes, complete with real book titles penned in edible icing. There was also a fondant topper fashioned into an open book. On its white pages, Mrs. Hubbard had written "welcome" in a curly script.

The end result was a bit of a surprise to Jane, considering how excited Mrs. Hubbard had been to make a colorful cake for the Groundbreaking Ceremony.

"Would you like a piece, sir?" the waitress charged with cutting the cake asked the first person in line.

The man, who was tall, slender, and heavily freckled,

leaned over to read a few of the icing book titles. "I never say no to cake. If the cake is uncut, that is. If I get the first piece, I know the knife has touched only my food. It's one of my quirks, and it's not always well received at other people's birthday or anniversary parties."

He didn't smile to indicate that he was joking, and the waitress clearly didn't know how to respond, but Jane did. She realized that the man must be Bartholomew Baylor, president of the Robert Harley Rare Book Society. He'd explained, in a detailed e-mail to her, that he suffered from obsessive-compulsive disorder, and that his visit to Storyton Hall would be made more comfortable if Jane would fulfill certain requests.

These requests weren't difficult or demanding. Mr. Baylor asked for an even-numbered guest room on the second floor. He wanted an even number of towels and pillows. If a single candy or mint was to be left on the bed during the evening turndown service, he'd asked for an extra candy or mint or none at all. Finally, he requested nightlights—the kind he could plug into wall outlets. An even number of nightlights.

Jane had replied that her head housekeeper, Mrs. Pimpernel, would personally prepare his room.

"I'll do whatever it takes to make him feel at home," Mrs. Pimpernel had said after reading the e-mail. "I have a cousin with this condition. He turns the lights on and off sixteen times before leaving the house, and he washes his hands for exactly five minutes. No more, no less."

Determined to put Mr. Baylor at ease, Mrs. Pimpernel went into room 222 and started counting. She removed the single neck roll pillow. She added extra toiletries and arranged the bottles by matching pairs. Mrs. Pimpernel also relocated the Storyton Hall stationery and pen sets. Normally, one set resided on a nightstand with the second on the desk, but she decided that Mr. Baylor would prefer them side by side.

"I also brought in an extra reading chair and floor lamp," she'd told Jane when the room was ready. "I believe the symmetry will appeal to Mr. Baylor."

Now, as he stood waiting for his piece of cake, Bartholomew Baylor sensed that he'd said something unusual. Smiling awkwardly at the waitress, he said, "I hope someone photographed this cake. It's magnificent, despite its three tiers. Four would have been better."

Jane stepped forward. "I'll pass your compliment on to our head cook. She keeps a scrapbook of all her masterpieces. I'm Jane Steward. We've exchanged e-mails."

"Bartholomew Baylor." The awkwardness vanished and he smiled at Jane with genuine warmth. "Please call me Bart. You've been most accommodating, Ms. Steward. My room is very comfortable. As for the rest of the resort?" He released a rapturous sigh. "I've heard of Storyton Hall. I know people who've stayed here and lauded its wonders, but I didn't understand why they were so enamored until I entered a reading room."

"Which one did you visit?"

"I wandered into the Isak Dinesen Safari Room," Bart said dreamily.

Jane was about to ask Bart if he'd had the chance to explore other parts of Storyton Hall when someone cried, "Look at that!"

The woman behind Bart stared at Mrs. Hubbard's book cake, her mouth forming a perfect O. When she recovered, she said, "How brilliant. This cake reminds us not to judge a book by its cover—that the magic of books is the journey the reader embarks on because he or she dared to open the cover."

Jane couldn't glance away from the slice on Bart's plate, which revealed a kaleidoscope of colors. Swirls of red, yellow, orange, green, blue, and purple cake existed beneath the layers of black and white buttercream and fondant.

Exclamations of amazement and anticipation reverberated down the buffet line.

Bart turned to the woman behind him. "It's good to see you, Rosemary. Let's sit together."

He didn't shake hands or hug Rosemary, but the lack of physical connection didn't faze her. She was obviously sensitive to Bart's needs, because she immediately gave him her napkin and then asked a waiter for a replacement for herself.

Two middle-aged men who looked like they'd just stepped from the pages of *Country Life* magazine soon joined Bart and Rosemary. The men wore expensive but casual clothing and radiated good health. After vigorously shaking hands with Bart and Rosemary, the men, whose features were so similar that Jane guessed they were brothers, tucked into their food. When the siblings weren't eating, they smiled and laughed easily, as if they'd never known a moment of strife in their entire lives.

An older man with round spectacles and strands of gray woven through a coarse, dark beard approached their table and performed a little bow. Instantly, one of the brothers jumped up and shouted, "Levi!"

The smaller man was enfolded in a bear hug.

As soon as Levi was released, the second brother clapped him on the back. Levi's smile was reserved but friendly, and he accepted a seat next to Rosemary with evident delight. He took her hand in both of his, raised it to his lips without making contact, and waved at Bart. Jane found this odd, considering Bart had shaken the brothers' hands, until she recalled that there were two of them. Even numbers put Bart at ease.

The five companions quickly fell into easy conversation. They seemed to have much to share with each other and there was a great deal of amiable interrupting.

Their behavior reminded Jane of her meetings with the Cover Girls, and she felt content as she meandered through the room, greeting her newest guests. She always tried to make everyone feel welcome from the moment they entered Storyton Hall.

She was on the verge of leaving the room when an elderly woman grabbed her hand.

"I hear my alma mater has lent you one of our visiting professors." The woman's eyes sparkled with interest. "Is the find of historical importance?"

"Doctor Wallace hasn't been able to draw any firm conclusions yet," Jane said. "However, she's returning to the university this evening. Perhaps you could call her department and make inquires."

The old woman's face fell and Jane saw that she'd disappointed her guest. She couldn't blame the woman for being curious. Most people, upon learning that human remains had been found at one's resort, would ask questions about such a fascinating subject.

"I *did* overhear a theory presented by the village doctor, however," Jane whispered conspiratorially. "He believes that the person buried in our grounds was afflicted with rickets. Not only that, but he explained that several Victorian-era diseases are making a comeback. Gout, for instance."

"Oh, yes!" the woman exclaimed, and proceeded to launch into a dramatic narrative featuring her next-door neighbor and his struggles with gout the previous winter. When she turned to focus on her tablemates, Jane slipped out of the tearoom.

In the garage, she found Celia and her team packing their skeletal remains.

"Any luck with the mystery book?" she asked Jane.

"Not yet," Jane said. She saw a pair of Celia's students exchange a flirtatious glance and wished Edwin wasn't thousands of miles away. Not only could he possibly help identify the book, but she also missed him. She missed so much about him. His voice, the feel of his hands moving over her body, the sound of him banging around in her kitchen, the bedtime stories he told the boys, the way she'd catch him staring at her from across a room. She missed all of it.

Celia paused in the act of snapping the locks on a case. "Don't look so forlorn! This is how these things go. It's a big puzzle where all the pieces are broken, damaged, or scattered to the four winds. And sometimes, no matter how hard we work, the mysteries remain unsolved."

"I know. It's just that I like to have the whole story—not just the excerpts." Jane gestured at the manor house behind her. "Do I have your permission to show the book to some of the rare book experts? A group called the Robert Harley Rare Book Society might have access to specific resources or experts."

"Absolutely!" Celia called to one of her students to give Jane a box of examination gloves. "You may not need these, but it'll make me feel better to leave them with you. I'll be in touch with any findings on my end." She stopped packing and looked at Jane. "I realize that this is your home, Ms. Steward. Your ancestral land. Somehow or other, this man—the puzzle—that we're taking away, is a part of your history. I understand your interest in discovering how his threads are woven into your family's tapestry, and we'll do all we can to provide you with answers."

Celia's sincerity touched Jane. She gave her a grateful smile and asked her to communicate directly with Sinclair. "Because I'll have my hands full with the conference."

This wasn't exactly true, but Jane had a sneaking suspicion that Sinclair would enjoy receiving phone calls from the forensic anthropologist.

"Of course," Celia said.

Before turning away, Jane caught an unmistakable glint of pleasure in the other woman's eyes.

* * *

The first official event of the rare book conference was unlike any other group meeting held at Storyton Hall. Sponsored by the Robert Harley Society, the conference kicked off with a cocktail party in the main lobby. The drinks invented by the Ian Fleming Lounge staff the previous week had names like Antiquarian Aperitif, First Edition Fizz, Whiskey and Watermark, Octavo on the Rocks, and Virgin Vellum. For the wine fans in attendance, the bartenders had gone the extra mile and applied handmade labels to the wine bottles. Jane grinned every time she heard a guest order Copperplate Chardonnay, Mint Condition Merlot, or Signed Copy Cabernet.

The attendees sipped their cocktails, nibbled hors d'oeuvres, and mingled until book dealers, auctioneers, librarians, archivists, and collectors took turns at the raised podium Butterworth had erected in the middle of the lobby. From this spot, the rare book enthusiasts regaled the crowd with anecdotes of the worst behavior they'd witnessed over the past year.

"All in the name of collecting," the first speaker added by way of introduction.

A book dealer from London spoke of how a J. K. Rowling doppelgänger had tried to sell signed copies of the Harry Potter novels from the back of her van for hundreds of pounds each.

"You'd think the van would be a dead giveaway," the woman said. "It probably rolled off the factory line the same year the Beatles released *Abbey Road*. Still, people believe what they want to believe. The imposter J. K. sold several cases—all hardbacks too—before someone reported her."

The other stories were equally entertaining. A representative from a New York auction house spoke of how a desperate collector had hired the distant relative of a

well-known socialite to spread rumors about a folio of
Audubon's *Birds of America* during the preview party.

"The guy had half the bidders convinced the folio was a
fake," the auction rep said, dabbing his forehead with a
cocktail napkin. It was clear that the memory still haunted
him. "I'm in charge of rare books acquisitions and my job
was on the line, so I had to stop this guy's tongue from
wagging. Luckily, my good friend is a detective. One of
NYPD's finest. A call to him and I find out that the guy
strutting around the gallery, gulping down champagne and
Wagyu beef on toast, doesn't own six car dealerships in
Connecticut, but is an out-of-work actor. Even after security
had him removed from the building, some of our prospec-
tive bidders still questioned the Audubon. To this day, I
swear we could have gotten a better price for that folio if not
for that scam artist."

A murmur swept through the crowd, and Jane could see
that most of the attendees sympathized with the auction representative.

However, she soon learned that there were just as many
guests who weren't shy about expressing their admiration
for bibliokleptomaniacs.

When a rare book dealer from Miami reached for the
microphone, a hush fell over the crowd. "Last week, a boy
was arrested in Paris. I do not exaggerate when I use the
term 'boy,' for this kid was no more than thirteen. He was
spotted jumping from the roof of a private collector's house
onto a neighbor's roof. He was as lithe and sure-footed as
a cat. When he was caught, he told the authorities that
nothing would stop him from becoming the next Stephen
Blumberg."

This caused a rush of animated twittering from the crowd,
and Jane understood why. Known as the Book Bandit,
Stephen Blumberg had stolen thousands of books from

museums and universities in forty-five states. The net worth of these books was over five million dollars, and that was back in the 1990s. Blumberg never had the slightest intention of profiting from his crimes, which earned him plenty of fans. He had his fair share of critics as well. Either way, most people in the book business knew of him.

The Miami book dealer finished his tale and passed the microphone to Bart Baylor, who introduced himself as the president of the Robert Harley Rare Book Society. Keeping his eyes fixed on a matching pair of striped wing chairs, he added, "If this is your first time attending, you might not have heard of my other name. I'm also known as the Book Doctor. If you have a rare book in need of restoration or conservation, I can help. My areas of expertise are in water and age-related damage and in customized archival housing."

"The Book Doc's the best!" a voice called, and Jane guessed that it belonged to one of the two brothers who'd had tea with Bart that afternoon.

The outburst distracted Bart and he tapped on his lips with his index fingers several times in an agitated manner.

"Thank you, Aaron," he said, once he'd mastered his thoughts again. "Each year, we gather to celebrate our dedication to the preservation, protection, and collection of rare books. I'm bundling other types of rarities in that term to keep this speech brief. I'd never ignore the significance of your maps, Charles, or the beauty of your etchings, Edith."

Bart continued to name several dealers and collectors and Jane could sense a feeling of unity swelling among the conference-goers. There had to be a measure of competition among the dealers and collectors, but in this moment, they were all people who'd congregated to celebrate a shared passion.

"There are those who mock collectors of rare books," Bart

went on. His voice had grown louder and more confident as his speech progressed. "They reference Sebastian Brant's medieval German allegory, *The Ship of Fools*, in which one of the fools headed for the Fool's Paradise was a book collector. The man who hoarded books without ever cracking a cover to gain the wisdom from the contents."

Bart removed two index cards from the pocket of his dinner jacket and, using a censorious tone, recited the following lines,

"For I rely upon my books,
Of which I have a great supply,
But of their contents know no word,
And hold them yet in such respect,
That I will keep them from the flies."

Someone gently bumped Jane's elbow and she pivoted to find Eloise offering her a First Edition Fizz.

Jane accepted the cocktail and mouthed her thanks.

"Future generations will thank us for keeping rare books from the flies," Bart intoned. "Private collectors are accustomed to being called fools. But you'll find that the shelves of libraries and museums are filled with the donated collections of *foolish* men and women—the visionaries who hunted for, cherished, and saved priceless treasures for future generations. Let's raise our glasses to them, and to all of us, who continue to honor Brant's Fool of Useless Books." Bart held up his glass of water. "To useless books!"

"To useless books!" shouted the attendees, the staff of Storyton Hall, the Cover Girls, and the villagers.

When Jane turned to speak to Eloise, she saw tears in her friend's eyes.

"It's silly, I know," Eloise said, sniffing. "I don't sell rare books in Run for Cover, but that speech was very moving."

"It wasn't just the speech," Jane said, understanding exactly what Eloise meant. "We're among our kind. We're with book people. People who love *everything* about books. The history of books. The illustrations. The typography. The paper, covers, edges. The significance of an original manuscript or a signed copy. These people also understand the power of books. They understand how books can impact the world, one reader at a time. They respect the book, as we do."

Eloise nodded. "This is going to be an amazing five days. I'm going to learn things I never knew."

Jane thought of the black-eyed stare of the skull and the book fragment waiting in Sinclair's office. Under her breath, she whispered, "I hope these discoveries don't bring us harm."

Later that evening, after the attendees had dined in either the Madame Bovary Dining Room or opted for a casual meal in the Rudyard Kipling Café, Butterworth rounded up the members of the Robert Harley Society and escorted them to the Henry James Library.

"Thank you for coming," Jane said when they were all seated. "The library is officially closed, so it's the perfect place to ask if you'd be willing to look at a book that we found buried in our back garden." She paused. "I should add that the book was buried with human remains and is in very poor condition."

The Robert Harley members exchanged quick, excited glances.

"You may have already heard about the body and that we had a forensic anthropologist on our grounds today," Jane continued. "Our staff was instructed to be completely transparent on this topic. And while Mr. Sinclair and I had hoped to identify the book on our own, we've been unsuccessful. Therefore, we'd be grateful if you five would take a look at it. Mr. Sinclair is very knowledgeable about books—"

"But my knowledge pales in comparison to yours." Sinclair smiled humbly at their guests.

"We'd love to!" one of the brothers exclaimed. "I'm Austin Sullivan, by the way. This is my older brother, Aaron. We work in public relations, but we're not that devoted to work. We're devoted to collecting all things related to American history. That's where all our time and money goes."

"The Sullivan brothers come off like socialite playboys, but that's not who they are," Rosemary said. "They're constantly raising money for the humanities—whether it's a new library wing or an after school arts program—these two will be chairing the committee and beating the bushes until the funds are raised."

Aaron and Austin pretended to scowl at Rosemary.

"Ro, we have a rep to maintain," Aaron whispered. "Don't sell us out."

"I don't travel in their circle much," Rosemary continued. "I'm shackled to a desk in my little corner of the Library of Congress. I'm an archivist."

"An archivist with famous politician parents," Austin said. "Daughter of an ambassador and a senator. Not that she lets that define her. Ro kicks ass on her own."

"I've had the pleasure of meeting Ms. Pearce's parents in Israel," said Levi. "I'm Levi Ross, purveyor of rare books and manuscripts. Levi Ross Rare Books has locations in London, Chicago, New York, and Tel Aviv."

It was now Bart's turn. And though he and Jane had already met, he and Sinclair hadn't been introduced, so he said his name, occupation, and then added, "The Sullivan brothers and I attended the same college. We sort of came into manhood and book collecting together. And now, here we are."

Again, Jane felt an aura of genuine warmth fill the space around her. She felt completely at ease among this group.

"Is everyone comfortable with my locking the main doors?" Sinclair asked. "I'd prefer we weren't disturbed."

Bart tapped his lips and muttered a string of numbers under his breath.

"Bart?" Rosemary whispered. "Are you all right?"

"Gloves," Bart said. "I need my gloves."

Sinclair shot Jane a worried glance. The plan was for the Robert Harley members to look at the book, not touch it.

"Doctor Wallace, the forensic anthropologist assigned to this case, entrusted the book to me," Sinclair said. "For now, I'd rather no one else handle it. I hope you understand."

Bart nodded multiple times, but this revelation seemed to allay his anxiety. "I have a latex allergy, so if gloves were necessary, I'd need to get mine from my room."

"Of course," Sinclair said in a soft, soothing voice. "Shall we proceed?"

Bart indicated that he was ready and Sinclair motioned for Jane to lock the door while he retrieved the book from his office. Their footfalls echoed in the silence, and when Sinclair placed the sealed rubber box in front of the five book aficionados, not one of them moved.

Sinclair pried off the box lid and lifted out the wood cradle holding the remains of the book.

Rosemary sucked in a breath at the sight of the ruined cover, but Levi immediately put a jeweler's loop to his eye and leaned closer to the cradle.

Austin also bent closer. Unlike Levi, he closed his eyes altogether and inhaled deeply. His brother glanced at Sinclair. "Are the pages just as bad?"

"There's nothing left to see. Except . . ." He glanced at Jane for permission and she nodded. "A single legible phrase that said, 'skin the tongue.'"

Levi removed his loop and frowned down at the book.

Bart tapped his lips. His expression matched Levi's.

Suddenly, the two friends looked at each other. "Do you think—?" they began in unison.

Jane suppressed a grin. They reminded her of Fitz and Hem.

"Go ahead," Levi said graciously.

Bart kept his eyes on the book. "It's likely a cookery. A book of receipts. Rosemary? Aaron and Austin? What do you make of the age?"

"Mid-eighteen-hundreds," Aaron said, his focus still on the cover. "Not American."

"Maybe a smidgen earlier. Based on that shade of green," Rosemary added. "A London publisher, Austin?"

Austin nodded. "I think so. I'd need to view the typeface before I could say for certain. Could we see the page with that line of text?"

The room was plunged back into expectant silence as Sinclair shifted the fragile pages to the place where Jane had found what she'd originally believed to be a gruesome phrase.

The Robert Harley Society members concurred that the mystery book was most likely a cookbook, and that "skin the tongue" was a line of instruction from a recipe.

"Levi and Rosemary can search their databases for records of other nineteenth-century cookeries with an embossed wheat bundle on a green cover," Bart said after Sinclair returned the book to its rubber bin. "It shouldn't take them long to come up with a title."

Jane and Sinclair thanked their guests for their time and expertise.

In return, their guests thanked Jane and Sinclair for allowing them to see the mysterious artifact buried with human bones.

"But why?" Jane said to Sinclair after the five friends had left the library. "Why go to your grave with a cookbook?"

Sinclair gazed down at the damaged cover. "Perhaps the pages weren't filled with traditional recipes. Perhaps they contained receipts written by an unusual woman—an herbalist, for example."

"Those herbalists were known by less favorable names," Jane said after a long hesitation. "Sometimes, they were called witches."

Chapter Six

Though the twins did their best to convince their mother that they should spend Sunday morning helping the grad students instead of attending church services, their efforts were in vain.

"You're going, so put on your church clothes and be quick about it," Jane said. At this rate, they'd be even later than usual meeting Uncle Aloysius and Aunt Octavia.

To say that Aunt Octavia disliked tardiness was an understatement, and Jane's brow was damp from more than the heat by the time she and the boys arrived in the lobby.

Aunt Octavia wasn't standing next to the grandfather clock as was her custom, pursing her lips in disapproval and tapping her walking stick against the carpet as if counting every second she was being kept waiting.

In fact, Jane's great-aunt wasn't standing at all. She was comfortably ensconced on a lobby sofa with Muffet Cat curled up against her left thigh.

The sight of Storyton Hall's resident feline reminded Jane that Mrs. Whartle had checked out yesterday. Muffet Cat, who'd been unhappily sequestered with Aunt Octavia and Uncle Aloysius since the "champagne incident," had happily regained his freedom.

"Mom," Hem whispered. "Why is Aunt Octavia reading?"

"Yeah. Aren't we late?" Fitz asked. "Doesn't she *hate* being late?"

Jane had no answer for her sons, for her great-aunt did have a book splayed on her lap. To her right sat a man who bore a close resemblance to a badger. He also had a book open on his lap and was gesturing between the two books.

"There you are!" Aunt Octavia called upon noticing Jane and the boys. "Come see! Mr. Rolf is letting me travel back in time. It's not often that someone as old as I am can be a child again. You've given me quite a treat, sir, thank you."

"It's a pleasure to share the delights of these books with such a receptive audience." Mr. Rolf beckoned to Jane and the twins. "Don't worry, I don't bite."

He smiled a crooked-toothed smile and the twins hesitated. Jane looked beyond his teeth and the white and gray-streaked tumbleweed that was his hair to the book on his lap and was immediately drawn to it.

"Is that a pop-up book?" she asked.

"*The Pop-Up Mother Goose*," said Aunt Octavia. "From 1933. *I* had this book, and I remember it well. There were only three pop-up pages—such things weren't common at that time—and I thought they were magical. I moved the pages again and again." Suddenly, she looked bereft. "Once, I wasn't careful and I tore off Humpty-Dumpty's legs. It was awful. I felt like I'd killed the poor thing!"

Fitz rushed to lay his hand over Aunt Octavia's. His brother was a heartbeat behind him.

"It's okay, Aunt Octavia," they consoled her in unison.

"My angels!" she cried, her eyes growing damp with tears.

Mr. Rolf, clearly worried that his rare book was on the verge of getting wet, scooped it off Aunt Octavia's lap and passed it to Jane.

Jane was amazed by the pristine condition of the old

book. She cradled it in her right hand while carefully turning its pages. Her sons watched as each of the three pop-up illustrations unfolded and took shape and then fell flat again as she turned the next page.

"Would you like to trade?" Mr. Rolf asked, offering Jane the book from his lap. "This one's from 1880." He held up a finger. "No pop-ups this time. This is a panorama picture book."

"Show the boys, Jane. After that, we should be off." Aunt Octavia pointed at the grandfather clock. "I'm sorry to rush off, Mr. Rolf, but I hate to walk in after the first organ notes have been struck. The best seats are already gone by then."

Knowing she was being given a subtle hint, Jane opened *Wild Animal Stories* and gingerly turned the pages. The twins were instantly enraptured.

"These panoramas are called chromolithographs," said Mr. Rolf. "My favorite is the leopard with the monkeys. The leopard is so serious, but the monkeys look like they're about to laugh, don't they?" He smiled at the twins and this time, the twins smiled back.

"I like the polar bears," Aunt Octavia said.

"I like the elephants," said Uncle Aloysius from behind Jane.

Because she hadn't heard her great-uncle's approach, Jane flinched in surprise. She gently returned the book to Mr. Rolf, thanked him for sharing his treasures with her family, and was on the verge of scolding her great-uncle when he wagged his finger.

"As a gentleman, I wouldn't dream of rushing you ladies—especially my beautiful bride—but Sterling has a full schedule this morning and he's anxious to get underway. I told him that he needn't wait, but he insists on seeing us off." Uncle Aloysius walked around to the front of the sofa and offered Aunt Octavia his elbow. "My love? Shall we?"

"Madam. Sir." Mr. Rolf leapt to his feet. "I'll have many

more wonders on display during the conference. Most of which are for sale."

At this news, Aunt Octavia clapped her hands. "Splendid! We'll look for you."

The Stewards piled into the Rolls Royce, and as Jane sped up the long driveway toward the massive iron gates that separated Storyton Hall's grounds from the public easement, Aunt Octavia gushed about the current guests.

"Jane, my girl! We've had some quality people stay at Storyton Hall, but this group will be my favorite. I just know it."

"Because they like old books?" Hem asked.

Aunt Octavia laughed. "That's part of it. You can't understand because you're too young, but when you're as old as I am, you appreciate people who preserve the precious things from your childhood. How can I explain this?" She snapped her fingers. "What's your favorite possession right now? The thing you'd most hate to lose."

Jane glanced in the rearview mirror and saw both boys concentrating hard.

"The puzzle box Mr. Alcott brought back from his last trip," Hem said after a moment.

Fitz took longer to answer. "The paperweight Mom gave me," he finally said. "The one with the glow-in-the-dark jellyfish inside."

"All right. Now imagine you're both grown men with grandchildren." Aunt Octavia's voice took on a nostalgic quality. "You've worked, traveled, and had many experiences. It's been over fifty years since you even thought about your childhood toys. Then, one day, you go to a museum. In a display case, you see your puzzle box, Hem."

Jane stole a quick peek in the mirror and grinned at the quizzical expression on Hem's face. "Why's my box in a museum?"

"Because there aren't many of them left in the world.

Your puzzle box is *that* old. And *that* rare. The same thing goes for your paperweight, Fitz. Wouldn't you be happy to see your box or your paperweight again?"

Hem was the first to reply. "I guess. But it would make me feel sad too. I'd be sorry I didn't keep it." He glared at Jane. "Mom. Why do you make us give stuff to the church thrift shop if we're just going to miss it when we get old?"

"Yeah!" Fitz cried in righteous indignation, while Uncle Aloysius began to chuckle.

"Very funny," Jane muttered to her great-uncle as she pulled into a parking space.

Fitz opened the back door and was about to dash off, with his brother a heartbeat behind him. Jane shouted their full names in a don't-mess-with-me-tone that brought both boys to an abrupt halt. "The question you just asked me, Hem?" Jane said calmly, once she had her sons' attention. "I want you to ask that same question to your Sunday School teacher, and I expect you to share her answer with us on the ride home."

"Yes, ma'am," the twins said, and slunk into the church.

Uncle Aloysius, on the other hard, wasn't able to enter the sanctuary because he was laughing too hard.

"Stop it, Aloysius," Aunt Octavia chided. "Imagine you just caught the biggest fish of your entire life. You're about to pull it into the boat when *snap*, your line breaks. There goes your fish."

Uncle Aloysius, who loved fishing more than anything other than his family and Storyton Hall, instantly sobered.

Aunt Octavia marched up the short flight of stairs leading into the church and grabbed the door handle. Turning to Jane, she said, "I'm going to pray that those people from the rare book society find the title of your mystery book. Won't it be wonderful to learn which piece of history we've been walking over for years?"

Despite the fact that the members of the Robert Harley Society believed the dead man had been buried with a cookbook, Jane found the thought of both man and book slowly rotting away so close by more than a little disturbing.

Entering the church, Jane and her family were met by the sound of the opening hymn. And though Jane sat at the end of the pew where she was bathed in a rainbow of light streaming in through the stained-glass window, she was unable to dispel a deep sense of disquiet.

That afternoon, the conference-goers could attend one of three lectures: The History of Paper, Attracting the Collector-Donor, and A Study of Bindings. Following the lectures and tea service, the guests would have a few hours to rest and relax before gathering on the great lawn for a buffet supper and party game involving costumes and word puns.

Bart had told Jane about the Word Search game in one of his e-mails. He'd explained that the game was a tradition at their annual conference. During this event, attendees wore cocktail attire with costume-type embellishments that transformed their regular clothes into literary puns. Participants then competed to see who could correctly identify every pun.

Jane now had the answer sheet in hand and she couldn't wait to watch the Word Search take place. The game was restricted to conference attendees, but the public had been invited to purchase buffet tickets. Proceeds from the meal would be donated to the World Literacy Foundation and dozens of locals were already lining up to fill their plates. It was clear that the costumed conference-goers would be mingling with all the book lovers of Storyton Village.

Mrs. Hubbard had enlisted the most artistic staff members to help her create a beautifully bookish buffet. Dozens of blocks of wood had been painted to resemble antique books. These were stacked at intervals along the length of the table. In between the food platters, Mrs. Hubbard had scattered quill pens, tea lights, and what appeared to be rolled pieces of parchment sealed with wax. The center-piece was a potted tree covered with fairy lights. The leaves, made from book pages taken from a pile of damaged library books that a Storyton staff member had found in a recycling bin, had been dipped in tea to lend an aged appearance. Each one featured a different typeface.

"Look there, Monica," Jane heard a woman say to an-other. "It's my favorite. Old Style."

"Modern is superior, and you know it," her friend said. "You just don't like it because it was invented by a French-man, and you're British."

"That is simply *not* true."

A man put his arm around both the women. "There's nothing to fight about, ladies. The Germans reign supreme with Futura."

A good-natured debate broke out in front of the center-piece. The delay gave Jane and the Cover Girls, who were seated at a table on the terrace above, an excellent opportu-nity to study some of the word play costumes.

"No spoilers, okay? The rest of us don't want to see the answer sheet," Eloise told Jane.

Jane held up a folded piece of paper. "I haven't looked at it. Cross my heart. Sue printed it at the registration desk and handed it to me just like this."

"I wouldn't be able to resist." Mrs. Pratt surveyed the guests, her eyes shining. "I like knowing what's going on far too much."

"Oh, we know!" Anna said with feeling.

She and Violet giggled into their hands.

Up to this point, Mabel had been too interested in her scallop kebabs to decipher any of the word play costumes, but when she put down her empty bamboo skewer and dabbed her mouth with her napkin, Jane knew her friend was ready to start guessing.

"I'm stuffed," Betty said, miming Mabel's movements. "I know we can't compete for the prize, but can we play this game for the fun of it?"

The other Cover Girls were quick to echo Betty's request.

"Of course," Jane said to her friends. "Eloise? Would you distribute the answer sheets? We'll have to drum up some clipboards and pencils, but I think Butterworth left a basket of extra supplies on the back terrace. Here's how to play: There are forty-eight blank spaces on your sheet. That's how many rare book conference-goers are participating in the Word Search game. Each guest is wearing a name tag with his or her number. If you guess their pun, write it next to their corresponding number. Got it?"

Phoebe raised her hand. "Are we allowed to ask the guests questions?"

Jane shook her head. "Hints are not permitted. And the rules for the costumes are quite strict too. Each person is allowed to add five items to their cocktail attire. Any more than five and the participant will be disqualified. Also, if their costume requires another person, they cannot separate from that person until the game is over. Not even to use the restroom."

"Whoa," Violet murmured. "This is serious."

"Seriously serious," Anna agreed. "Why? Is there a big cash prize or something?"

Jane gave Anna a long look. "If you had to guess what it is . . ."

"A rare book!" Eloise shouted. "Jane? Do you have it?"

"Thankfully, no," Jane said. "Storyton Hall isn't responsible for any of the valuables belonging to the conference attendees. Our room safes are too small to accommodate most of their needs—especially those of the book dealers—

so their items were delivered by special freight services. Along with safes."

Mabel whistled. "Sounds expensive."

"As is the value of the prize," Jane said. "I can't wait to see it, either."

Betty threw out her hands in exasperation. "You're pulling a Mrs. Eugenia Pratt right now. Stop holding us in suspense."

Jane and Mrs. Pratt exchanged a conspiratorial grin. "I need to give you a little background first," Jane said. "In this case, the prize reflects the theme of the dinner dance—the conference's final event. And you all know that the theme for this event is the Pre-Raphaelites."

"I can't wait to see everyone in their dresses!" Phoebe exclaimed. "Mabel, you worked wonders with mine. I actually look slim! Must be the empire waist."

Eloise waved at Jane to continue.

"The prize is a first edition of *Poems by the Way,* by William Morris. *The* William Morris. Founder of Kelmscott Press, writer of poetry and novels, and designer of beautiful textiles." She turned to Betty. "Your dining room curtains are his Strawberry Thief pattern, right?"

Betty nodded. "I've always been a fan of his designs. But back to the book. How much is it worth?"

"Being one of only three hundred copies, the book is valued at six thousand dollars," Jane said.

"That's more than I make in . . ." Violet began, but didn't finish her sentence.

The other Cover Girls expressed their astonishment over the cost.

Eloise was especially peeved. "Imagine what a difference that kind of money would make if it was donated to a literacy fund."

"I agree. It seems over the top to spend six grand on a

prize for a party game," Jane said in an effort to placate her friends. "However, the prize was donated by Aaron and Austin Sullivan, and I've read up on the Sullivan brothers since their arrival. They're the Sullivans of Only Natural Foods. They're worth millions. Despite their financial status, they both work regular jobs. And when they're not working, they're busy raising money for various humanities organizations. They've saved libraries, museums, and independent bookstores from extinction and have helped fund after-school art, music, and reading programs."

"Millionaire book nerds with big hearts?" Anna nudged Violet. "If they're single, there's one for each of us."

Betty picked up her answer sheet. "What happens in the event of a tie?"

"I was told to anticipate that scenario," Jane said. "I'm going to put all the correct sheets in the box the twins used for their school Valentines last year. One of you will draw the winning name."

Phoebe reared back. "Count me out. I can't handle the pressure."

"Who's up for it?" Jane arched her brows in question. "I can introduce a local merchant and brag about her business."

"I'll volunteer," Mabel said. "One of your guests might need a last-minute accessory for the Pre-Raphaelite dinner dance. I have some lovely shawls and a few extra hairpieces. I put the best aside for my friends, of course."

With this important matter settled and their meals finished, the Cover Girls left the table, collected clipboards and pencils, and headed off to participate in their own form of the Word Search game.

Naturally, Jane and Eloise paired off. The first participant they came across was a man with a fake beard carrying a clay pot and a garden trowel. The best friends exchanged a quick smile before filling in the name on their answer sheets.

"Harry Potter" Jane wrote next to number 37.

Next, they encountered a couple. Like the Harry Potter entry, this man also wore a false beard, but his was very long and white. His other accessories included a white wig, Coke-bottle glasses, and a cane. Finally, he'd drawn wrinkles all over his face using black eyeliner. He leaned heavily on his cane, while the woman holding his free arm paused to smell the flowers. One by one, she took in the fragrance of the Russian sage, monkshood, asters, anemone, hyssop, witch hazel, and goldenrod plants blooming along the garden path.

She bent over so frequently that Jane had a difficult time figuring out her costume. The woman wore a lovely cocktail dress in an ocean-blue hue, but no obvious accessories. She didn't even carry a purse. Jane glanced at Eloise to find her friend looking equally baffled. Suddenly, Eloise's face brightened and she wrote something on her answer sheet.

Jane turned back to the woman. She saw a sparkly letter *C* attached to the sash of her dress.

"Old man and the sea" was the answer Jane filled in for numbers 14 and 15.

"I love this game," Eloise said after they encountered a man wearing a cape trimmed in faux fur, a feathered cap, and tights. He also had the Olympic rings stitched on his medieval-style tunic, indicating that he was "Lord of the Rings."

Not all the costumes were based on book characters. Near the Anne of Green Gables Gazebo, Jane and Eloise ran into a woman wearing a black dress and a man's suit coat. The duster end of several feather dusters had been attached to the coat, which looked like it had spent a decade hanging in someone's attic.

Jane wrote "dust jacket" next to number 9.

She and Eloise continued to meander through Milton's Gardens. The best friends were having a ball.

Jane's answer sheet was nearly complete when she paused to say hello to Tobias Hogg of the Pickled Pig Market. Tobias was dating popular romance novelist Barbara Jewel, and when he wasn't lavishing affection on her, he was busy spoiling his pet, a miniature potbellied pig named Pig Newton.

"Another marvelous evening, Miss Jane," Tobias said. "Barbara's off talking to a book dealer. She's had a ball checking out the costumes. As for me? I focus on the food. My compliments to Mrs. Hubbard."

Suddenly, Eloise cleared her throat and jerked her head to the left, so Jane thanked Tobias, told him to say hello to Barbara, and fell into step with her friend.

"Sorry," Eloise said. "But someone wearing a costume we haven't seen yet is headed toward the koi pond."

They rounded a bend in the garden path and came upon a group of guests milling around the pond. Randall, from Storyton Pharmacy, and Phil and Sandi Hughes, from Storyton Outfitters, were also among the assemblage.

"In my professional opinion, ragweed is the likely culprit, though goldenrod is mistakenly blamed for causing hay fever symptoms on a regular basis," Randall was saying to Bart Baylor in the dull monotone that drove Anna crazy. "Seventy-five percent of people who are allergic to pollen-producing plants are also allergic to ragweed. Therefore, it's logical to conclude that you are allergic to ragweed."

Randall droned on, but Jane was distracted by the sight of a woman in a bronze-colored dress wearing some kind of animal tail. She was speaking with the Sullivan brothers, neither of whom was in costume. Jane also noticed the peace symbol attached to the end of the woman's tail, but she decided that it was more important to rescue Bart from Randall than figuring out the woman's word pun.

"I don't get it," Eloise said, staring at the woman in bronze.

"I can't worry about puns right now," Jane whispered. "If Bart drowns himself in the koi pond in an attempt to escape Randall's lecture, I'll never forgive myself."

Jane called Bart's name. He turned his head to locate her and, without saying a word of farewell to Randall, jogged over to where Jane and Eloise stood. When he reached them, he didn't relax, but shifted restlessly on his feet.

"Ms. Steward, I've been searching for you for over an hour! Could we return to the Henry James Library for a few minutes? There's something I want to show you. In private."

Eloise murmured a low "oh my."

"Forgive me, Mr. Baylor, but my book club is trying to solve the Word Search game," Jane said. "Just for fun. Eloise and I are currently stuck on this lovely lady in bronze and—"

Bart darted a glance at the woman. "She's a tailpiece. Piece with an *IE* not an *EA*. A tailpiece is the decorative typography or ornament found in the blank space toward the bottom of the page at the end of a chapter or poem. All right?" He raised his brows in question. "Can we go to the library now? What I have to show you concerns your, er, special book."

Jane realized that Bart didn't want to reveal any information about the mysterious cookbook in front of Eloise. After all, he didn't know that Eloise was Jane's best friend.

"Of course." She smiled at him. To Eloise, she said, "I won't be long. After all, that incredible prize still has to be awarded."

"Thanks for the clue on tailpiece," Eloise told Bart. "I never heard that term before. It's nice to learn new things about books. Especially since they're my life."

"Ray Bradbury once declared that the women in his life were all librarians, English teachers, or booksellers. The man had excellent taste," Bart said before turning away with Jane.

As they walked, Jane sent a text to Sinclair. She had no intention of meeting with Bart alone, and when she noticed that Bart was pulling something out of the inside breast pocket of his suit coat, she abruptly stopped. "What do you have there?"

Taken aback, Bart held out a pair of purple exam gloves. "I didn't mean to presume. I brought them to demonstrate—" He shook his head, exasperated. "It's too difficult to explain here. Can it wait until we're inside the library?"

Relaxing a little, Jane said that it could.

She relaxed even more when she saw not only Sinclair standing by the Henry James Library doors, but Butterworth as well.

"Good evening, Mr. Baylor," the head butler formally greeted their guest.

Bart managed a brief smile, though it was obvious that he was too impatient to share what he'd learned to bother with pleasantries.

Sinclair unlocked the doors and everyone entered the library except for Butterworth, who signaled to Jane that he'd take up a sentry position outside.

Bart pointed at the doors in appeal. "Please lock them again. What I have to say is quite serious."

Sinclair complied, and only after Bart heard the click of the lock turning did he act less agitated. "I can explain everything without your cookbook present, but it will be easier to show you if it's sitting in the middle of us. Will you trust me?"

Sinclair looked to Jane for direction. She studied Bart for a long, drawn-out moment before she finally responded. "Yes, Mr. Baylor. We will."

The rubber bin was brought out from Sinclair's office

and placed on a reading table. Bart took out his cell phone from his jacket pocket.

"When I first saw the embossed wheat sheaf, I thought it looked familiar," he began. "That's no surprise. I've seen thousands of book covers over the course of my career and have repaired a dozen books with a variation of a wheat decoration on the cover or spine. Still, I felt like I'd seen this sheaf before. Not on a cover I'd handled, but mentioned in the text of a book I'd repaired. It wasn't a recent repair. This was a long time ago, back when I was first learning the trade. I had to sit in my room and go to a quiet place in my mind so I could remember, but right before I came down to dinner, I was able to recall the instance."

Bart took out a pair of his purple gloves from his coat pocket and pulled them on. He then put his cell phone on the table and asked Sinclair to remove the box lid.

Bart gave Jane and Sinclair a minute to compare the image of the book cover on his phone screen with the tattered remains in the rubber bin.

"*Mrs. Tanner's Everyday Receipts.*" Jane read the title aloud.

The book looked unremarkable. Other than matching sheaves of wheat, the green cover was embossed with gold decorated dishes. There was a platter with a roasted chicken or duck, what looked like a plate of cookies or rolls, a fancy jellied dessert, and some sort of rolled food Jane couldn't identify.

"I did a few calculations and, based on this photograph, the middle stalk of wheat should be exactly four centimeters from the top edge." Bart produced a ruler from his breast pocket. "May I?"

"Go ahead," Jane said, feeling more than a little anxious.

Bart performed the measurement. "Exactly four centimeters. A good number. Four."

He put the ruler on the table and, staring down at it, frowned at it in distaste.

Jane moved to Sinclair's desk, plucked the ruler from his top drawer, and laid it next to Bart's ruler. He nodded in gratitude and released what sounded like a pent-up breath.

"Ms. Steward. What you have before you is an extremely rare book. I do not think it is missing any words. I believe they're all still there. On every page. They've been hidden, but can be revealed by means of a simple chemical process."

"Why were they hidden?" Sinclair asked. "Didn't you identify our artifact as a Victorian cookbook?"

Bart kept his gaze on Jane. "Yes, but it was known by another title."

Involuntarily, Jane's eyes strayed to the book in the bin. She sensed that she'd been right to feel repulsed when she'd first read its only legible line. "What was it called?"

"It was originally published as *Mrs. Tanner's Everyday Receipts*," Bart said. With an unsettling lack of emotion, he continued, "But later, it was known as *The Devil's Receipts*."

Chapter Seven

Sinclair made a noise.

It was almost inaudible. It wasn't even a grunt—just a hitch of breath—but Bart looked at Storyton Hall's head librarian and said, "You know the title."

As this was clearly a statement, not a question, Sinclair nodded. "I've heard of a cookbook called *The Devil's Receipts*. If the tales are true, the book was printed, but never distributed. The warehouse where the cookbooks were stored was deliberately set ablaze, leaving no surviving copies. I don't know why."

Bart smiled with delight. "Very few people could have said that much. Bravo, sir. However, there's even more to the book's colorful history. Rumors, mostly. All of what I'm about to tell you is hearsay." Glancing down at his hands, he began peeling off his gloves. "Purportedly, half a dozen copies of *The Devil's Receipts* survived the warehouse because they were given away as gifts days before the fire was set. The author received six copies. Five of these were recovered and also destroyed. Somehow, a single copy made it out of London and was never tracked down."

Jane waved a hand. "Excuse me. Before you go any

farther, I'd like to know the meaning behind the title? *Why* were those books burned?"

Sinclair, seeing that Bart was unsure what to do with his gloves, grabbed a trash can from under the reading table and held it out to him. After depositing his gloves in the can, Bart returned his attention to Jane.

"The recipes were supposedly hazardous to the public's health," he said. "Some of the ingredients were actually toxic and if ingested in large enough quantities, could be poisonous to the very young, very old, or infirm."

"That's horrible," Jane said. "Why was such a reprehensible book published in the first place? And under such a benign title?"

Sinclair moved next to the rubber bin. He replaced the lid and covered it with his hand in what looked, to Jane, like a protective gesture. "I believe the book was given its nefarious title long after the fire," he said to Jane. "I must defer to Mr. Baylor's expertise on this matter."

Bart's gaze grew distant and he absently tapped his index finger against his lip. This was a physical tic Jane had witnessed on multiple occasions since Bart's arrival at Storyton Hall, but it was the first time he looked like he'd kissed something covered in baby powder.

Though Jane wasn't about to interrupt Bart to tell him that the cornstarch from his gloves had been transferred to his mouth, she didn't want to stare at the white smudge, so she glanced out the window instead. For a brief moment, she wondered if the Word Search participants were still working on their answer sheets or if they were milling about, impatiently waiting to find out who'd won the game.

"There was a scientist. A chemist," Bart said, breaking the silence. Jane turned to look at him and saw that the powder on his lips was gone. "He wasn't British—I'm not sure where he was originally from—but he moved to

London to work and to study." Bart paused and a funny expression came over his features. "He began writing a series of articles for the *London Times* called . . ."

Suddenly, Bart spread his fingers and turned his palms to the ceiling. His eyes bulged and Jane saw terror reflected in the enlarged orbs.

"Are you all right?" she asked, instantly concerned.

"The *gloves*!" Bart's shout was shrill with fear. "I don't think they're latex free! I don't feel right! I can't . . . I can't breathe."

At first, his words burst out like water pouring from a broken pipe, but his final phrase sounded choked.

Jane tried to control her own feelings of panic.

"You're going to be okay," she assured her guest. "Do you have an EpiPen?"

Bart fixed his bug-eyed gaze on her. "Ye-es," he gasped. "My. Room."

Uttering those words used more oxygen than Bart could afford to give. He seemed to deflate. His shoulders sagged and he grabbed his throat in panic.

"The EpiPen's coming," Sinclair told Jane. His phone was pressed to his ear.

Jane was grateful that her friend and mentor didn't fetch the EpiPen himself. She needed him with her. He kept her calm.

"Bart, help is seconds away," Jane murmured soothingly.

She pulled out a chair. Bart dropped into it with a moan, followed by a noticeable increase in breaths. Jane didn't know if he was having a panic attack or if his body was already going into shock because of the latex exposure.

Why didn't this reaction happen right away? Jane thought as someone banged on the library door.

Sinclair unlocked the door and Sterling rushed into the room, clutching the EpiPen in his fist. He removed the safety cap as he ran, dropped to his knees next to Bart, and pressed the EpiPen into his thigh. There was an audible click, signaling the release of the medicine.

"You heard the click, Bart." Knowing that he didn't like to be touched, Jane tried to comfort Bart with her voice instead. "The medicine is pumping through your body right now. Mr. Sterling will hold the EpiPen in place for a count of ten. Ten's an even number. Let's count together by twos."

Jane began with "two," but Bart's breathing continued to accelerate until he sounded like a panting dog.

"Try to calm down," Jane pleaded.

Behind her, she could hear Sinclair speaking into his phone. He was calling for an ambulance. In between Bart's frantic breaths, she heard Sinclair say "rapid pulse" and "beet-red skin." Jane suddenly realized that Bart's face looked sunburned. This was scary, seeing as he'd been his pale and freckled self a few minutes ago.

And then, without warning, he keeled over in his chair.

Jane stretched out her arms, but it was Sterling who caught Bart before he could hit the floor.

Sterling was still holding Bart when his body began to twitch and twist as if he were being electrocuted.

"He's seizing!" Sterling shouted.

Sinclair hastened to move the chair Bart had been sitting in away from his flailing limbs.

The seizure seemed to end as abruptly as it had started. And just as quietly.

That was what terrified Jane now. The silence. The lack of Bart's panicked breathing. The complete lack of sound.

Sterling, who'd managed to keep Bart's head on his lap despite the violence of the seizure, used his index and middle finger to check for Bart's carotid pulse.

He held this position for a long minute before looking up

and meeting Jane's stare. Withdrawing his fingers from Bart's neck, he shook his head.

"He's gone?" Jane whispered in disbelief.

"Miss Jane—" Sinclair began. But Storyton Hall's head librarian was clearly at a loss for words. For the first time since Jane had known him, Sinclair's composure was shaken. He was completely unnerved by Bart's death.

Jane could see why. After all, this was Sinclair's sanctuary. His haven. And a fellow book lover had just expired on the floor at his feet.

"He always used his own gloves," Jane murmured, glancing between Sinclair and Sterling. "He said as much, remember? He carries them wherever he goes because of the severity of his latex allergy. So why would he have accidentally worn the wrong pair? He wouldn't. He wouldn't make such a thoughtless mistake. He was far too careful." As she listened to her own speech, she realized what alternative remained. "No, no, no. Not again."

Sterling grabbed a pillow from a reading chair and placed it under Bart's head. The gesture was tender and reminded Jane of a parent tucking a child in for the night.

"Mr. Baylor's gloves must be tested." Sinclair spoke to Sterling in a hushed voice. He then retrieved the gloves from the garbage bin using the tip of his pen and dropped them on the reading table.

Because of the white powder on Bart's lips, Jane thought. *That's what we need to test.*

The exam gloves Sterling used in his lab were powder free, and the only gloves Sinclair owned were made of white cotton. He'd never allow cornstarch within a mile of his beloved books.

"Why didn't we realize something was wrong?" she asked the men in the room. Her voice held both anger and accusation.

When they didn't reply, she moved closer to Bart and

took his hand in hers. It was too late to comfort him, but the touch wouldn't unsettle him now either. And in a strange, illogical way, holding Bart's hand gave Jane comfort. Very little, but it was better than nothing.

"I should have known that you wouldn't wear powdered gloves. No book person would." Jane's eyes filled with tears and she glanced up at Sinclair. "I didn't want to embarrass him by mentioning the white smudge on his lips. And I was so caught up in the story of this stupid book. Yes, I said *stupid book*! Because we were distracted by bits of paper and cloth, a man was poisoned right in front of us."

Jane squeezed Bart's hand as if begging forgiveness. His long, elegant fingers were cold. Any life that had allowed those digits to repair wounded books from the past had gone. Five fingers. Bart wouldn't like that she was only holding five, but she couldn't touch his other hand. Those fingers had met his lips. Those fingers had delivered his death. Jane was sure of this fact without knowing exactly how or why.

In the distance, she heard the whine of an ambulance. The noise reminded her that there were more important things to consider than her emotions. The safety of her family, her guests, and the secret library was paramount, so Jane placed her forehead against the back of Bart's hand in a final, apologetic gesture and got to her feet.

She accepted the tissue Sinclair proffered. Once her eyes and cheeks were dry, she said, "Sterling, we need a sample of whatever's inside those gloves, but we should also test a tiny piece of the actual gloves. Those things tear all the time, so hopefully, the medical examiner won't make anything of a missing sliver."

"Mr. Butterworth has spoken with the sheriff," Sinclair said as he studied his cell phone screen. "He'll meet Evans and the ambulance crew at the loading dock."

Jane wondered how many guests would gather to see

which of their fellow conference-goers the ambulance had come to collect. She'd learned long ago that it was human nature to be curious about such things. However, when she realized that most of the guests were still in Milton's Gardens, she also remembered *why* they were outside.

"The Word Search game!" Jane cried, pulling the answer sheet from her clutch. "Sterling, can you get this to Eloise? Ask her to use the Cover Girls to help identify the winning entries as quickly as possible. Once that's done, Mabel should draw a name from the box on the back terrace. The Sullivan brothers have the prize."

Sterling hurried off, passing Lachlan on his way out.

Before surveying the rest of the scene, Lachlan scanned Jane from head to toe to ascertain whether she'd sustained any injuries. He then knelt next to Bart's body. He didn't touch the Book Doctor, but stared intently at his flaccid face. Jane saw pain in Lachlan's eyes. And sadness.

"Was it murder?" Lachlan asked quietly.

It was the first time anyone had spoken the word out loud, and Jane wished Lachlan hadn't uttered it here. Not so close to Bart. Or in this library. This was a place where Jane and the twins had spent countless hours reading, working on projects, looking up exotic cities on one of the spinning globes, and snuggling on chairs close to a blazing fire.

Stow your emotions until later, Jane reminded herself.

"Bart has a severe latex allergy, but Sterling used an EpiPen, so he should have been okay," Jane said, not realizing that she'd referred to Bart in the present tense. "Something else must have killed him."

Lachlan pointed at Bart's thigh. "Here? And you heard a click?"

"Yes." Jane's reply was curt. She didn't want to be interrogated right now. There'd be enough questions when

Sheriff Evans arrived. "Unless the device was tampered with, the medicine should have been delivered."

"There was white powder on his lips, which was most likely transferred from the inside of Mr. Baylor's gloves," Sinclair said. "We could be looking at cyanide poisoning."

Lachlan turned back at Jane. "Did it happen fast?" When she nodded, he said, "That must have been horrible to watch. Are you okay?"

"No," she said, hating how weak and thin her voice sounded. "But we have a duty to find out what happened to Bartholomew Baylor and to protect Storyton Hall and the people and treasures housed within its walls. Speaking of which—"

"I'll check on your family," Lachlan said, and darted through the open doorway.

Immediately following his departure, the Henry James Library erupted in noise and activity. First, Butterworth escorted three EMTs into the room. The paramedic in charge had barely started his assessment when Sheriff Evans and Deputy Phelps arrived.

The sheriff usually tipped his hat to show his respect for Jane, but when he saw Bart's immobile body and his slack but ruddy face, he removed his hat and pressed it against his chest. Phelps followed suit, and the two men paused for a moment to recognize that a fellow human being had passed from this world to the next before they both donned their hats again and approached the emergency medical crew.

Evans exchanged words with the paramedic kneeling by Bart's right shoulder, and from her position near the door, all Jane caught was, "We'll take him whenever you're ready."

Sheriff Evans then turned to Jane. "Mr. Butterworth told me about Mr. Baylor's EpiPen. Where is that device?"

Moving deeper into the room, Jane showed the sheriff the EpiPen, which had rolled under the reading table. Sheriff Evans signaled for his deputy to bag the item.

"Could you walk me through what happened?" the sheriff asked, taking a notebook and pencil from the pocket of his uniform shirt.

"Yes, but before I do, could you also bag those?" Jane gestured at the purple gloves. "I can't say for sure, but they might be important."

Once Phelps completed this task, Jane reviewed the evening's events. She started with the moment Bart requested a private meeting in the Henry James Library and ended with her helplessly watching his body jerk and thrash on the floor.

"And just like that, he was gone," she concluded while blinking away the tears moistening her eyes.

Sheriff Evans tapped his pencil against his notebook and frowned.

"Any thoughts on the white powder?" he asked the paramedic. "Sounds like something was transferred from inside the gloves to Mr. Baylor's lips. What are those gloves normally lined with?"

"Cornstarch," the paramedic said. He opened Bart's mouth and pointed his penlight inside. "Though you won't find powder-lined gloves anymore. FDA banned them in 2016. Either this guy has old gloves or they're lined with something else." He looked at Jane. "Was his face flushed earlier in the day?"

"Like he had a sunburn? No," Jane said. "He's normally pale skinned. Look at his arms."

The paramedic turned his back to Jane and murmured to Sheriff Evans, but not quietly enough. She heard him say, "I'd put my money on cyanide. Between the bright red skin and the traces of black vomit in the victim's mouth, it's the likely culprit. The ME will tell you for certain."

The sheriff thanked him and swung around to face Jane again.

"Has anyone threatened Mr. Baylor since his arrival here? Or expressed any ill-will toward him whatsoever?"

"No. Quite the opposite, in fact," Jane said. "Everyone seemed to either like him or, at the very least, admire his work. Mr. Baylor was known as the Book Doctor because he repaired rare books."

The sheriff glanced at the inert form on the floor. "All right. It's time to give us the room now, Ms. Steward. At some point, we'll need to speak with everyone who interacted with Mr. Baylor tonight. I realize that's a tall order, but you and your staff have been invaluable to our department in the past and we could use your cooperation again. However, we can't proceed without learning what was inside those gloves. That's our top priority, so Deputy Phelps will accompany Mr. Baylor over the mountain. After I'm done here, I'd like to see Mr. Baylor's room."

"Over the mountain" was the local's way of referring to any town outside Storyton. Storyton was a sleepy village surrounded by hills. It had no strip malls, no car dealerships, and no hospitals. This meant that people had to go "over the mountain" for many of life's modern conveniences.

"Of course. Just call me on the house phone if you need anything," Jane said, and waited for Sinclair to follow her out of the Henry James Library.

Sinclair didn't follow right away. "Sheriff Evans. When you're finished documenting the scene, may I return the excavated book to its secure location? Doctor Wallace entrusted it to me, and I'd like to assure her that it has met with no harm."

"Yes. For now, we'll keep the book at Storyton Hall," the sheriff said. "And for now, Ms. Steward and Mr. Sinclair, we'll refer to Mr. Baylor's passing as an accidental death. There's no sense in raising an alarm."

"I agree," Jane said before slipping out of the library.

Never before had she wanted to escape a library. Libraries had always been places she'd wanted to escape *to*, not *from*. This realization almost brought fresh tears to her eyes, but she blinked them back. Her cell phone vibrated and, seeing the caller's name, she immediately answered the call.

"Lachlan?"

"Your family is fine. The twins are asleep. Ned's reading on the sofa," he said, referring to the young Storyton Hall employee who watched Jane's boys whenever she had to work late. "I just came from upstairs, where your great-uncle is also reading and your great-aunt is watching a rerun of *Downton Abbey*. She thought you'd sent me to count the number of scoops in her ice cream sundae."

Normally, this would have made Jane smile. Now, because she'd gotten to know a man named Bart Baylor, she wondered if Aunt Octavia's bowl had contained an odd or even number of scoops.

"Tell the other Fins to meet me in Sterling's office," she said into the phone. "I want to make a list of everyone Bart spoke with in Milton's Gardens. Someone must have swiped his room key. If we're lucky, one of the cameras captured the footage."

Jane pocketed the phone and headed for the staff corridor when Sinclair grabbed her hand and said, "I have an alternative plan."

Without releasing his hold, Sinclair led Jane into the Ian Fleming Lounge. "Two coffees with whiskey," he told the barkeep. To Jane, he said, "You need this. We both do."

Jane knew that her old friend and mentor was right. She needed the steadying influence of the hot coffee and the calming effects of the whiskey. The way her hands trembled as she picked up her coffee cup proved that her body was still processing her shock.

"Tell me about Bart," she said to Sinclair, several sips later. "Do you remember anything unusual about his background report?"

"Only that he's very wealthy," Sinclair said. "After we finish our coffee, we'll go to Sterling's office. I'll access my files and print out copies of the report. We can review it together."

Jane reached out and straightened Sinclair's bow tie. The head librarian was always impeccably dressed and wouldn't want to be seen with a crooked tie. For some inexplicable reason, Jane thought of how challenging it would be for Sinclair and Celia to share a closet. For the most part, Sinclair's wardrobe consisted of his tailored suits, bow ties, and pocket squares. Celia's was most likely comprised of jeans and whatever tops the weather called for.

It was ridiculous, Jane knew, to be thinking of such a thing at this moment. But Bart Baylor had died alone in a locked library in the company of two relative strangers. She didn't want Sinclair to have only his duty to Storyton Hall and a room full of books when his time came. Jane wanted him to be with someone as wonderful as he, and she had a strange feeling that Celia Wallace might be that someone.

Jane swallowed the last of her coffee. It heated her body and helped create a sense of normalcy in a world that had once again been turned upside-down.

She and Sinclair put down their cups, thanked the barkeep, and took the staff corridor to Sterling's office.

Lachlan and Butterworth were already inside and had started reviewing the feed from the security cameras covering Milton's Gardens. Of course, the coverage was limited, so if Bart had spent part of his evening in a secluded nook or conversing next to topiary where one of the gravel paths came to a dead end, they'd be out of luck. Years ago, when their surveillance system was installed, Jane had insisted that the cameras be hidden. She didn't want guests to feel like they were being spied on. Not only that, but too many cameras could also send a message to outsiders that there was something inside Storyton Hall worth protecting. Which, of course, there was.

"Mr. Sterling will join us shortly," Butterworth told Jane. "He's testing the piece taken from Mr. Baylor's gloves. I removed a pair from the box in Mr. Baylor's guest room to use them for the purpose of comparison. There was also a box of white cotton gloves and I took a pair of these as well. I thought it was prudent to examine the room before Sheriff Evans conducted his search."

"And?" Jane tried to read Butterworth's face. As usual, it was an inscrutable mask.

"Though I didn't have the time to search as thoroughly as I would have liked, I do not believe that Mr. Baylor felt threatened. In short, I believe his death was as much a surprise to him as it was to you and Mr. Sinclair," Butterworth said somberly.

Jane was puzzled. "What led you to that conclusion?"

"Mr. Baylor's laptop was left open on his desk. I was able to log on because the password was disabled. I checked the activity log to determine whether this was a recent occurrence, but it wasn't," Butterworth continued. "Mr. Baylor didn't feel the need to protect his device. Therefore, I must conclude that he wasn't concerned about having his privacy invaded."

"Maybe he didn't keep sensitive material on his computer," Jane suggested.

Butterworth nodded. "That's quite plausible. I glanced briefly through his files and saw no personal or financial information. Everything was book related. As were his most recent Internet searches. The last thing Mr. Baylor did on his computer was visit a website showing an artist's rendering of the cover of an early nineteenth-century cookbook called *The Devil's Receipts.*"

"Which was officially published as *Mrs. Tanner's Everyday Receipts,*" Sinclair said.

Butterworth's brows twitched.

"I don't get it," Lachlan said, swiveling in his seat. "How does the devil figure in? Did Mrs. Tanner recommend that every woman should stir poison into their husband's tea or something?"

Sinclair shook his head. "We don't know the exact meaning behind the title yet. Mr. Baylor died before he had the chance to fully explain the book's history. However, he was able to tell us two significant facts. The first is that a reversible chemical process may have concealed the typeface on the pages. Secondly, the book was considered a public health hazard at the time of its publication. That's why it was intentionally destroyed."

"A health hazard?" Butterworth asked.

"Some of the ingredients listed in the cookbook could make people very sick," Jane said.

Butterworth inclined his head toward his seated colleague. "It sounds like Mr. Lachlan wasn't far off the mark."

Someone knocked on the door three times in quick succession and, a second later, Sterling entered the room. In the original manor house, this space had been a butler's pantry. Now, Sterling's office doubled as the center of hotel security and the home of the copier machine. With all the bodies added to the mix, it felt rather cramped.

"The powder in Mr. Baylor's gloves is cyanide," Sterling said without preamble. "I ran the test twice. Iron sulfate combined with the sample of the suspected cyanide. Next, I added mineral acid. Both times, I ended up with Prussian blue. A positive result for cyanide."

"Prussian blue? As in the pigment Van Gogh used in his *Starry Night* painting?" Jane asked.

Sterling nodded. "It's a chemical—one with many uses. As for the glove, it matches the others from the box in Mr. Baylor's room."

This news baffled Jane. "Wait. The gloves *were* latex free?"

"Yes."

Jane let this sink in. "If Bart wasn't reacting to the latex, then the sole source of his physical distress was the cyanide." She stared in the middle distance and replayed the horrible scene from the Henry James Library in her mind. "After he took off his gloves, he tapped his lips. I saw a white smudge on his mouth and assumed it was cornstarch from the gloves. Oh, Sterling." Jane struggled to control the quaver in her voice. "Could I have saved Bart's life simply by handing him a tissue?"

"I don't think so. And if anyone in this room is responsible for his death, that person is me," Sterling said. "I believe the killer correctly guessed that we'd react to Mr. Baylor's symptoms by utilizing his EpiPen. By injecting him with adrenaline, we increased his heart rate."

"His heart would have already been operating at an accelerated rate following the absorption of the cyanide powder," Butterworth said, understanding at once.

Sterling shook his head in dismay. "We were manipulated like marionettes on strings."

"Show me the video feed," Jane said, her shock and grief giving way to anger. "It's time to hunt for our puppet master."

Chapter Eight

Jane sat down to watch the video feed.

"Unfortunately, we don't have a clear shot of the buffet," Lachlan said.

Because Sterling had been busy in his garage lab, Lachlan had already begun reviewing the footage from the security cameras and now gave the group a rundown of what he'd seen so far.

"Unfortunately, I was only able to start tracking Mr. Baylor after his meal."

"I saw him on the buffet line," Jane said. "He stood out because he wasn't first, and he preferred to be the first person in line because he liked to know that no one else had handled the serving utensils. I guess he was late because he was up in his room, researching our infamous cookbook. Bart didn't see me because I was up on the terrace. Otherwise, he probably would have skipped his meal altogether in his haste to tell me what he knew."

"Did he speak with anyone on the buffet line?" Butterworth asked.

Jane thought back on the charming scene, of Mrs. Hubbard's amazing book-themed decorations and the wonder and delight on the faces of her guests. How could it have been one of Bart Baylor's last meals? Why would anyone want him dead? He seemed utterly harmless.

No one is harmless, she reminded herself. *Everyone is capable of hurting others.*

"The people I can identify that I saw Mr. Baylor interact with tonight include the members of the Robert Harley Society, Eloise, Barbara Jewel, Sandi and Captain Phil, and Randall Teague of Storyton Pharmacy. I doubt I interrupted a conversation between Bart and Randall. It would be more accurate to say that Randall was delivering a monologue on ragweed while Bart was looking for a means of escape."

"Do you recognize this man?" Lachlan asked, pointing at the frozen image of a man with a cloud of white hair streaked with gray, bushy eyebrows, and a rotund belly.

Jane peered at the video screen. "I do. He's a book dealer named Mr. Rolf."

"He also had an exchange with Mr. Baylor," Lachlan said. "And though we can't hear it and I'm not very good at reading lips, it's pretty obvious that it wasn't friendly."

Jane and the rest of the Fins watched in silence as Lachlan played the footage.

A camera mounted to the roof of the Anne of Green Gables Gazebo showed Bart's approach along the gravel path. His body was stiff, and though he smiled at his fellow conference-goers, the smile was brief.

"Mr. Baylor's expression, lack of eye contact, and posture send a message that he doesn't wish to engage in conversation." Butterworth, who was adept in reading body language, peered intently at the screen. "He appears to be focused on finding someone. I suppose that someone was you, Miss Jane."

Before Jane could voice her agreement, Mr. Rolf scurried out from inside the gazebo. He was just a blur at first, and his sudden appearance startled Jane. He'd apparently startled Bart too, because he reared backward in surprise.

Mr. Rolf immediately made a series of apologetic gestures, and Bart quickly recovered and seemed eager to continue on his way. However, the book dealer stood directly in the center of the path. Mr. Rolf's lips moved rapidly as he reached into his jacket pocket and produced an object wrapped in tissue paper.

"A book, I assume," Sinclair said.

Mr. Rolf barely had the book unwrapped when a group of Word Search participants meandered down the path. He shot them a nervous glance and beckoned for Bart to follow him into the gazebo.

Bart shook his head and remained where he was.

His refusal clearly angered the book dealer. His furry eyebrows drew together and he took a menacing step toward Bart.

Watching the feed, Jane could almost sense Bart's acute agitation and she found that her own fists were clenched. Was Mr. Rolf on the verge of touching Bart?

Stop! she shouted internally. Aloud, she said to Sinclair, "We'll need to hear two background reports before we leave this room. Mr. Baylor's and Mr. Rolf's."

Onscreen, the arrival of the other conference-goers gave Bart the opportunity to skirt around Mr. Rolf. As soon as he made it past the book dealer, Bart continued deeper into Milton's Gardens. His pace was brisk and he kept his head down.

After she uncurled her fists in relief, Jane realized that the gazebo camera had recorded something that could have escaped their notice had they not been watching very closely. It had captured Mr. Rolf's chameleonlike nature.

One moment, he was furious with Bart. It was easy to imagine a cartoonist's black cloud hovering over his head.

In a flash, his expression cleared and he was smiling and exchanging pleasantries with the partygoers. Once they'd moved along and he was alone on the path again, his smile vanished and his shoulders drooped. He looked tired and defeated. When he turned and slunk off toward the main hall, he reminded Jane of an injured animal retreating to its den.

Lachlan paused the feed on Mr. Rolf and tried to locate Bart again. With no cameras near the koi pond, there was no record of the people Bart had spoken with between the time he was ambushed by Mr. Rolf and the time Jane rescued him from Randall's lecture.

"I'll continue to review the footage while we talk," Sterling assured Jane, and took the controls over from Lachlan.

"Good. I'd like to examine the background information. I need a more complete picture of Bartholomew Baylor, because right now, I don't understand why anyone would want him dead. In my view, he was a smart, interesting, and unusual man whom we failed to protect."

Sinclair bowed his head. When he looked up again, his eyes met Jane's. "We will not fail to bring him justice."

They had to wait a short interval while Sinclair made copies of the reports, and Butterworth, who somehow always managed to act as both Fin and butler, ordered a coffee tray from the kitchen.

"Please ask the staff to put some nibbles on our tray too," he said before replacing the receiver.

Lachlan tried not to grin, but failed. "Nibbles?"

This was one of Aunt Octavia's code words for sweets, and Jane was touched that Butterworth had used it, knowing the silly term might make her feel better.

"As you can see from your printouts, Bartholomew Baylor was very wealthy," Sinclair said after distributing sets of papers. "Mr. Baylor was the only child of Leo and Penelope Baylor of Lilyfield Farms, Inc."

Sterling reacted to the name immediately. "Isn't Lilyfield one of the largest food manufacturers in the United States?"

"Yes," Sinclair said. "They're on par with Nestle or Kraft."

Lachlan let out a soft whistle.

Jane wasn't interested in Bart's fortune. She was interested in his story. "His parents are gone?"

"Yes. They died in a boating accident off the coast of Long Island when Mr. Baylor was a boy. His paternal grandfather raised him for a decade. Upon the grandfather's death, he was cared for by a series of servants and tutors until he received the first of his trust fund payments."

"If he had a fortune, he had enemies," Lachlan said.

Butterworth grunted. "I would agree. According to Mr. Sinclair's research, Mr. Baylor was worth millions."

"Though one wouldn't know it." Sinclair took off his glasses and wiped the lenses with his pocket square. "Mr. Baylor was an unusual man in many ways. His life was seemingly uncomplicated. His interests were limited to rare books, classical music, architecture, and touring museums. The luxury items many of the megarich possess held no appeal for Mr. Baylor. He didn't care for sports cars, multiple residences, private jets, or the like. He lived in a modest home in upstate New York where he spent his time plying his trade. The house overlooks the Hudson River and must be very peaceful."

Jane, who'd been staring at the photocopied image of Bart's driver's license, said, "There has to be a dark secret in Bart's past. Something that followed him to Storyton Hall. Something that prompted the killer to lace those gloves with cyanide, knowing that Bart would use them tonight."

Sterling turned away from the bank of television screens to look at Jane. "What you just said is important. How *did* the killer know that Mr. Baylor would be using gloves tonight? That person could only have that knowledge if Mr. Baylor shared what he'd learned about the cookbook *before* he shared it with you."

Jane dismissed this theory with a flick of her wrist. "He might have used those gloves at any time. We have no idea *when* the poison was inserted."

Butterworth cleared his throat. "I must concur with my colleague, Miss Jane. During my search of Mr. Baylor's guest room, I came to the conclusion that Mr. Baylor arrived at Storyton Hall with an unopened box of disposable gloves. That box remained unopened until today. When Mr. Baylor removed his first pair of gloves, he most likely did so after teatime."

"How on earth could you know that?" Jane asked.

Butterworth's shoulders moved in the ghost of a shrug. "The trash bins are emptied at the same time each day, give or take a few minutes. The housekeeping staff cleans Mr. Baylor's guest room between eleven and eleven-thirty every morning. According to Mrs. Pimpernel, Mr. Baylor prefers not to be in his room when the housekeepers are present, so he would have exited before eleven. Considering he had lunch plans, followed by a lecture and teatime with his friends from the Robert Harley Society, I don't think he would have had the chance to open the box until four at the earliest."

"Impressive," Sinclair said, inclining his chin at the head butler.

Though Jane was listening to Butterworth, a line in Sinclair's report had diverted her attention. "Bart contributed huge amounts of money to a charitable organization called the Literacy Ark. Is it legit? And who operates it?"

"Give me a minute and I'll have your answer." Sinclair's fingers flew over his laptop keyboard. "The goal of the Literacy Ark is 'to combat illiteracy across the globe by training teachers, providing instructional materials, and building or improving public school and library facilities at no cost to those who benefit from its use.'"

"A wonderful cause," Jane said. "I'm not surprised that someone who devoted his life to the preservation of books and knowledge would support such an organization."

Lachlan, who'd been reading over Sinclair's shoulder, pointed at the computer screen. "I'm sure Mr. Baylor's buddies, the Sullivan brothers, were pretty influential when it came time for him to write a big check. Aren't they famous for their ability to raise impressive amounts of money for humanities-related fund-raisers? And since they founded this charity, I bet they put even more effort into the Literacy Ark."

Jane sighed. "I hate to say it, but we'll have to dig deeper into this charity. The Sullivan brothers might not be the altruistic philanthropists everyone believes them to be. Maybe they're motivated by the huge donations because they're skimming off the top." She shook her head. "Lord, when did I become so cynical? Can't anyone be what they seem? Can't Bart have been a decent person who lived a quiet life? Can't the Sullivans truly want to make the world a better place through books, music, and art?"

Butterworth was about to speak when there was a knock on the door. "That should be someone from the kitchen staff."

The aroma of fresh-brewed coffee filled the room as Butterworth placed a tray in the center of the table. In addition to coffee, there was a basket of croissants, corn bread muffins, Mrs. Hubbard's famous dill rolls, and crispy cheddar breadsticks—kept warm beneath a cotton napkin.

"I ordered a bold decaf. Eventually, you will need to sleep." Butterworth served coffee to Jane first before offering it to his fellow Fins.

Jane helped herself to a croissant, but decided to forgo the butter. The pastry was so light and flaky that it was perfect as it was.

"What of Mr. Rolf?" she asked Sinclair. "After his behavior by the gazebo this evening, I'd like to take a closer look at his profile."

"Mr. Felix Rolf is a rare book dealer hailing from New Orleans," Sinclair began. He scanned his notes and then nodded as if silently confirming a fact. "His antiquarian bookshop is best known for its selection of rare and unusual children's books."

"I saw two such books this morning. They were magical." Jane proceeded to describe the pop-up book and the panorama picture book that Felix Rolf had shared with Aunt Octavia.

"As we've already seen, the rare book world is a small one," Sinclair continued. "One's reputation is everything. Mr. Rolf enjoyed a spotless reputation until he was linked to a forgery two years ago."

Jane put down her unfinished croissant. "A forged book?"

"Not a book. An etching by a famous nineteenth-century children's book author and illustrator," Sinclair said. "Mr. Rolf sold the etching to a private collector. Within a year of making the purchase, the collector passed away and the etching was bequeathed to a museum. The museum curator questioned the drawing's provenance. You see, the author's etchings were based on tracings of her watercolor paintings, but the animals in the etching Mr. Rolf sold were slightly smaller than those in her painting. This raised a red flag in the curator's mind. He thought the animals should be the same size. He also found the paper suspect and declared the piece a forgery. An investigation into its origin commenced."

"Were arrests made?" Butterworth wanted to know.

Sinclair shook his head. "None. Mr. Rolf cooperated

with the authorities, but since he'd purchased the etching online and the seller was long gone, there was no hope of finding the culprit. Those in the business claim that, after so many years of experience, Mr. Rolf shouldn't have made the purchase from an unknown source. Some believe that his story is a complete fabrication while others believe he was a hapless victim. Those who continue to patronize his shop admit that even the shrewdest rare book dealers can be duped. That's all I was able to glean about his reputation based on newspaper articles."

Sterling, who was still focused on the television monitors, suddenly swung his chair around to face the rest of the group. "I don't know the man, but I can tell when a person won't take no for an answer. Watch this." He pointed at the center screen. "When we left Mr. Rolf, he looked like he was heading back to the main building, having been turned down by Mr. Baylor."

Onscreen, Felix Rolf had nearly reached the back terrace when he ran into Rosemary Pearce and the Sullivan brothers.

Rosemary seemed happy to see Felix. She signaled for Aaron and Austin Sullivan to keep walking and flashed a warm smile at the rare book dealer.

As for Felix, he beamed at Rosemary. Once again, he started talking rapidly and with great animation. At one point, he gestured in the direction from which he'd come. He was clearly complaining, and Jane guessed that his complaints centered on Bart.

Rosemary appeared to listen patiently until Felix's tirade was finished. She then gave him a friendly pat on the shoulder and opened her purse. She pulled out a plastic bag and handed it to Felix before continuing on her way.

"Ms. Pearce rejoins the Sullivan brothers and the trio engage in a lengthy conversation with a man wearing a feathered cap and Olympic rings on his chest," Sterling explained to the room at large.

Jane recalled the costume well. "He was dressed as Lord of the Rings."

Sterling nodded. "I like it. However, you might not like this, Miss Jane. Do you see Mr. Rolf? He's going to do an about-face and head back toward the gazebo."

"And Mr. Baylor?" Lachlan asked.

"I assume he was Mr. Rolf's target," Sterling said. "However, there's no way of knowing if Mr. Rolf and Mr. Baylor have a second exchange because we don't have coverage around the koi pond. What we *can* see is Mr. Rolf's return to the main building twenty minutes from this point. How would you describe his appearance?"

Jane stared at a still frame of Felix in the elevator cab.

"He looks weary," she said. "Like he can't wait to crawl into bed."

Sinclair nodded. "I agree. The man is nearly gray with fatigue."

"Even so, we need to speak with him," Butterworth said. "We must know what he discussed with Mr. Baylor."

"Before we call Mr. Rolf, I'd like to ask Rosemary Pearce a quick question," Jane said. "I want to find out what was inside that bag. I want to know what Felix Rolf did with whatever Rosemary gave him."

Sterling rewound the footage of Felix walking from Milton's Gardens to the manor house, but it was impossible to determine what was in his pockets. After all, he'd pulled a tissue-wrapped book from the right one. There was no telling what he had in the left.

Jane reached for the phone and dialed the front desk. After asking to be connected to Rosemary's room, Jane remembered how Rosemary had given Bart her flatware in the Agatha Christie Tearoom so that he'd have an even number of utensils. Rosemary obviously cared for Bart. She was his friend.

Jane felt a twinge of guilt. Instead of telling Rosemary that Bart was gone and offering her comfort, Jane was planning to question her.

I have no choice. I am the Guardian of Storyton Hall, Jane thought.

It had not been an easy role to embrace, and Jane often wrestled with what the title required of her. Especially at moments like this one.

Rosemary's phone rang and rang, so Jane put down the receiver and said, "It's late, but the Ian Fleming Lounge is still open. Most of the guests were outside when the ambulance arrived, but some of them will have noticed the presence of the sheriff and the paramedics. Maybe Rosemary already guessed who was taken away in the back of that ambulance."

Sterling switched to the camera feed in the Ian Fleming Lounge and there was Rosemary, ensconced in a leather club chair with a glass tumbler in one hand and a book in the other.

"She doesn't look distraught," Sinclair observed.

Jane rose to her feet. "No, she doesn't. In fact, she seems to be genuinely focused on her reading. Lachlan, you're my wingman for this mission. I'm hoping your good looks and quiet presence will throw her off guard. Also, I believe you'll be able to tell if she's trying to hide feelings of guilt. Butterworth might be our body language expert, but women of a certain age have a tendency to let their guard down when you're around."

Lachlan, who was unaware of his effect on the opposite sex, reddened in embarrassment.

Butterworth, on the other hand, seemed to relish Lachlan's discomfort. After informing Jane that he would make himself available should Sheriff Evans require assistance, the butler clapped Lachlan on the shoulder and said, "Into the trenches, Mr. Lachlan."

The mood in the Ian Fleming Lounge was tranquil. Not many guests remained at this late hour, and most sat at the bar. Rosemary and another man were reading in club chairs, but as they were sitting on opposite sides of the room, Jane wasn't worried about the man overhearing their conversation.

"It must be a good book," was how Jane interrupted Rosemary's reading.

Rosemary showed Jane the cover so that she could see the title.

"*Library: An Unquiet History*, by Matthew Battles. Sounds interesting."

"It's kind of like a library world tour," Rosemary said. "I'm enjoying it immensely."

Jane pretended to hesitate. "I hate to come between a reader and her book, but could I talk to you for a moment?"

"Sure thing." Rosemary immediately closed her book and set it aside.

"This is Mr. Lachlan, our head of recreation."

Lachlan and Rosemary shook hands and Rosemary seemed too captivated by Lachlan's green eyes and rugged good looks to wonder why he was joining them.

"This might sound strange, but would you mind sharing what you know about Felix Rolf?"

Rosemary was clearly surprised by the question, but she answered all the same. "Felix? Well, he can be an odd duck at times, but so can I. People who devote their lives to the study, preservation, or sale of books are bound to be a little odd. I mean, we spend most of our lives indoors, hunched over books, manuscripts, and maps. Felix is just as devoted and passionate as the rest of us. He's amazing at finding really unusual children's books. His store is truly a magical place."

"I'd love to see it one day," Jane said. Thinking of the books Felix had shown Aunt Octavia before church service, she realized she really would like to visit such a shop. "Does every member of the Robert Harley Society know him well?" she asked Rosemary.

"The Sullivan brothers don't collect juvenile-themed Americana, so they've never dealt with Felix. I'm sure they know him by sight. Most people do." She finished the last sip of her drink and studied the empty glass, her eyes shining with humor. "I've always been surprised that Aaron and Austin didn't go in for children's books. Even though they have almost a decade on me, they're so boyish and carefree. A side-effect of having truckloads of money, maybe."

She delivered this line without the slightest trace of spite or jealousy, and Jane believed that Rosemary was perfectly content with her lot in life. Jane rarely met anyone who found complete fulfillment following their passion. However, it was possible that both Bart and Rosemary were such people.

Lachlan interrupted her musings by pointing at Rosemary's glass. "May I get you another drink?"

She smiled shyly. "No, thank you. I never have more than two." And before Jane could slip in another question, Rosemary began asking Lachlan about the Falconry Program.

"I'd be glad to give the Robert Harley Society a tour of the mews," Lachlan said. "Would your friends enjoy holding birds of prey?"

Rosemary considered this. "We'd be wearing gloves, right?"

"Yes, but . . ." Trailing off, Lachlan looked to Jane for help.

Picking up on her cue, Jane said, "The gloves aren't sterilized between uses."

"Oh." Rosemary pulled a face. "That might be a problem for Bart. Unless he could wear his own gloves underneath."

"Does he carry an extra pair of latex-free gloves wherever he goes?" Jane inquired in what she hoped was an innocent tone.

Rosemary shrugged. "Sometimes he goes for the latex-free. Other times, he wears white cotton. It depends on the occasion. I started keeping an extra pair of cotton gloves in my bag in case of emergency. For Bart. Not for myself. I decided to do this following an incident at our conference two years ago. You see, Bart didn't participate in this great activity because he didn't want to touch something that everyone else was handling."

Jane felt her pulse quicken. "That's really thoughtful of you. Has he needed your emergency gloves since he's been here?"

"Yes, tonight! Well, maybe." Rosemary laughed. "Let me explain. I ran into Felix on my way out to the gardens and Felix asked for advice on how to convince Bart to examine a book he desperately needed repaired. I gave Felix the gloves and explained that Bart had issues with germs. The gloves were in a plastic bag, of course."

"But they were cotton? They weren't purple, latex-free gloves?"

Though Jane had to clarify this point, she could instantly see that she'd gone too far. Rosemary knew something was amiss.

Jane reached out and touched the other woman's arm, silently imploring her not to speak. Turning to Lachlan, she said, "Please get Ms. Pearce that refill and meet us in the Daphne du Maurier Morning Room."

After Lachlan moved away, Jane leaned closer to Rosemary. "Ms. Pearce. I need to tell you something confidential, and it would be best if I could do so in private. Would you please follow me?"

Rosemary nodded nervously and collected her book.

Jane wanted to walk slowly through the hallways of Storyton Hall. She wanted to delay breaking such difficult news to this lovely young woman. She wanted to avoid the pain she was on the verge of inflicting. She could only pray that Rosemary would take a small measure of solace from knowing that the very last thing Bart had seen before his death had been books. Rows and rows of beautiful, timeless, dependable books.

Chapter Nine

Jane invited Rosemary to make herself comfortable in one of the yellow damask chairs facing the back terrace. Lachlan set Rosemary's whiskey on the table near her elbow and withdrew to a chair in the far corner of the room.

Though the September sky was dark, it was drenched with stars. A large moon hung low on the horizon and illuminated the hills surrounding Storyton Hall with an ethereal light. Jane believed the view might lend Rosemary more comfort than the empty hearth or shelves of paperback novels elsewhere in the room.

"I won't increase your anxiety by delaying what is bound to be hard news," Jane said. "I had to ask those questions about the gloves because I'm trying to understand what happened to Mr. Baylor. I'm so sorry to tell you this, but he passed away earlier this evening. It was very sudden. Though we tried to save him, I'm afraid we failed."

Jane fell silent. She knew she needed to give Rosemary time to process the terrible tidings. Studying her guest, she saw a range of emotions flit across Rosemary's face. There was disbelief, confusion, and sorrow. And then, as expected, the burning need for clarification.

"How?" Rosemary demanded, an angry glint in her eyes. "I saw Bart in the gardens during tonight's party. He was fine. A little overexcited, maybe, but fine! *How* could he just *suddenly* die? You must have the wrong man. You *must*!"

She jumped up, plunged her hands through her hair, and sank back into her chair again.

Jane wanted to take the other woman's hand. After all, Rosemary's reaction was normal in the face of such incomprehensible news. She was trying to make sense of senseless.

"Only the medical examiner can determine the cause of death, but Sinclair and I believe that Mr. Baylor may have had a reaction to the gloves he put on to show us something he'd discovered about our excavated book." Jane took a breath and hurriedly continued. "I don't think Mr. Baylor planned on touching the book, which is why he wore purple latex-free gloves instead of white cotton gloves. I'm sure he was more concerned over coming into contact with the bin or another object in the Henry James Library that many guests had previously handled, such as a reading chair or magnifying glass."

Rosemary shook her head. Her body still refused to accept what her mind had already begun to process. "If Bart wore his latex-free gloves, then why would he have a reaction? And please call him Bart. He wouldn't want you calling him Mr. Baylor. He liked you, Ms. Steward."

"Thank you," Jane said. Though touched by this remark, she had to get answers out of Rosemary. She couldn't afford to be sentimental. "The gloves raise questions for us too. Bart wore them for several minutes before he showed any sign of distress. When his symptoms came on, they came on very swiftly. When Bart struggled for breath, we called another staff member to fetch his EpiPen. Mr. Sterling administered the medicine, but it didn't help. Either that, or we just didn't get him what he needed fast enough."

Rosemary looked out the window. Tears rolled, unchecked, down her cheeks. "It's just so hard to accept that he's gone." She turned back to Jane. "Bart and I usually saw each other twice a year. We also e-mailed about this and that, but I've had a soft spot for the guy from the first." She shrugged. "Maybe it's because I'm an only child and I enjoyed fussing over Bart. He was so grateful to anyone who could see beyond his quirks. Or maybe it's because I could always be myself around him, just as he could always be himself around me. Isn't that the best kind of person to be around?"

"It is," Jane said with feeling. "And it's rare to meet someone like that, as we all wear so many faces. It's almost a necessity in this complicated world."

Jane reminded her guest that she had two fingers' worth of whiskey at the ready should she need a dose of warm fortitude, but Rosemary politely demurred.

"I want to *feel* the loss of Bartholomew Baylor," she said. "He's worth the pain."

To Jane, this was a strange, but beautiful sentiment. "Ms. Pearce, I need to know as much as possible about Bart's movements this evening. Even in cases involving an accidental death, the sheriff's department will conduct an investigation. My staff and I also want to know what happened. After all, Bart was a guest under my roof."

Rosemary dug a tissue out of her handbag and wiped off her damp cheeks. "I'll tell you what I can, but I wasn't with Bart the whole time."

"Could you make a list of the people you saw Bart with during tonight's event?"

Rosemary nodded. "It'll be a short one. He had dinner with the Robert Harley members. After that, I barely saw him. He was very distracted. What he'd discovered about your cookbook made him more fidgety than usual and he was anxious to share what he'd learned with you. However, when he saw you, you were having dinner with a group of women. You were all laughing and seemed very merry. He didn't want to interrupt your time together. He said that moments of true merriment are few and far between and should be protected." Rosemary smiled sadly. "He was very sensitive of other people's feelings. Sweet Bart."

"Did he tell you what he'd found?"

"About the cookbook? Of course." Rosemary seemed surprised by the question. "It was way too fascinating to keep to himself. Bart's life revolves around books. As does ours. It was only natural for him to share such an interesting story with his closest friends and fellow bookaholics."

Jane gave Rosemary a plaintive look. "I don't think Bart had the chance to tell me the whole story. Would you repeat what he told your group?"

Rosemary did. The details were the same until she said, "The cookbook was akin to a modern vanity press project. The bigwigs behind three of Britain's most successful food and beverage companies created the recipes. The Mrs. Tanner of the title was probably some random woman who served tea to one of these men and agreed to lend the book her name for a few pounds. Either that, or she was told to pretend she'd written the book or she'd be out on the street."

"So who started the fire?" Jane wanted to know.

"No one claimed responsibility. According to the *Times*, it was a clear case of arson. The businessmen were furious and tried to blame the publisher, but dozens of witnesses put him at the opera house while the warehouse burned."

Jane mulled this over. "What about the scientist who wrote the articles decrying the adulteration of the food?"

Rosemary reached for her whiskey glass and took a sip. She'd been so caught up by the tale of how *Mrs. Tanner's Everyday Receipts* had come to be and of how it had almost disappeared into obscurity, that she momentarily forgot her grief. Jane was also freshly hypnotized by the story of a cookbook that later became known as *The Devil's Receipts*.

"By the time of the fire, Doctor Otto Frank had already fled the country." Rosemary stared into her glass tumbler as if she were an auger who could see into the past. "Apparently, he received multiple death threats after his articles were printed. Bricks through the window with messages attached—that sort of thing. Frank named specific products made by specific manufacturers. He took a serious risk writing what he did. In my mind, he was a hero."

"Because the good doctor's findings threatened the bottom line of those food manufacturers," Jane said. "If people believed him and heeded his warnings. Did they?"

"Bart believed that *Mrs. Tanner's Everyday Receipts* was created to divert attention from Frank's articles." Rosemary's glance strayed to the bookshelves. "The point of that cookbook was to charm the public with its illustrations, approachable language, and the vast variety of recipes. It was also priced lower than competing cookbooks. Everything seemed geared to encourage the masses to purchase the book."

Jane wondered if she should ask about the concealed typeface, but decided against it. If Bart hadn't mentioned that detail to his peers, there may have been a reason he kept it to himself. Perhaps he hadn't trusted all of the Robert Harley Society members. And because the companions had sat together at dinner, it was impossible to know which he'd trusted and which he hadn't.

"Did he say anything else about the cookbook?" Jane prompted.

"Just that yours was most likely the last copy in the known world." Rosemary frowned in confusion. "He was incredibly excited by this possibility, which baffled me. What was dug up in your garden looks like a desiccated shoebox." She pointed at the bookcases across the room.

"As obsessed as we rare book nerds can get about bindings, printings, paper, signatures, engravings, et cetera—what value is a book without words? I'm not including illustrated works, like children's books, in this rhetorical question. I'm talking about the idea of capturing the story of humankind on parchment or paper and binding those pages together between two unyielding, protective covers."

Rosemary took another healthy swallow of her whiskey. "Bart was probably just thrilled by the thought of one of the cookbooks escaping the fire. To him, no book was detrimental. Only their authors. All it took to truly upset Bart was the mention of a book burning. He could never stomach *Fahrenheit 451*. It was too painful."

"I can see why he'd feel that way," Jane said.

Then again, Bartholomew Baylor's existence wouldn't have been threatened by the publication of a book, she thought. *He was an educated man with a trust fund. He wasn't a woman in early twentieth-century Europe who could have been forcefully sterilized by a publication touting eugenics. Neither was he an African-American who would have been institutionalized because of a phrenology book. Both of those books were brought to Storyton Hall before they could be mass produced, and the words found between their covers deserved to remain in the dark for a period of time.*

Jane shook her head, returning her thoughts to the moment at hand.

"Do you know how Bart came to love books with such fervency?" she asked in a reverent tone. "It's something I wonder about all my guests, but don't always get to ask them. Sometimes, they'll tell me about a family member, teacher, or librarian—that special person who started the fire in their soon-to-be reader's heart."

"My mom kindled my fire," Rosemary said. "We had mother-daughter library dates. These days, when we can find the time, we have bookstore dates. Bart's story is much sadder." She paused to gather herself. "His parents and older brother were killed in a boating accident. I'm no psychologist, but I think that's why Bart hated odd numbers. One is an odd number. Four is even. He was once part of a family of four. See? He was supposed to go out on the boat too, but he'd just broken his foot and was still laid up in bed. Before his family left for their outing that fateful morning, they gave Bart a picnic basket filled with boredom busters. One of these was an old book. A beautifully illustrated copy of *The Goblin Market,* by Christina Rossetti."

Jane smiled. "I remember that poem from my college days. It was about two sisters. Because one sister ate the goblin's food, she became gravely ill. The other risked her life to save her sister from death. Wasn't Dante Gabriel Rossetti the illustrator?"

"As well as Arthur Rackham. At least, he illustrated Bart's 1933 edition. I'd bet my collection of hand-colored maps that Bart's copy is in his guest room right now. He never went anywhere without it. That book is . . . was . . . his talisman."

Rosemary set her empty glass down and Jane reached for one of her hands and held it. "I want you to know that Bart wasn't alone at the end. His gaze searched for, and found, a wall lined with books. They were the last things he saw."

"I hope that eased his fear," Rosemary whispered.

Unable to assure her on that point, Jane decided to leave her guest to her grief.

Lachlan offered to escort Rosemary to her room. Once they were gone, Jane's next move was to summon Felix Rolf. Unfortunately, Sheriff Evans foiled her plans by calling her to the Henry James Library.

When she arrived, she found him pacing around Sinclair's desk while murmuring into his cell phone, which gave her the necessary time to adjust to her surroundings. The signs of an ongoing investigation gave the library an alien appearance. Glancing at the yellow evidence markers on the floor, Jane guessed that they'd been placed to mark where the EpiPen had rolled, Bart's gloves had been discarded, and where Bart had fallen.

"Ah, Ms. Steward." The sheriff pocketed his phone. "That was the ME. The blood work won't be ready until tomorrow morning, so we'll have to wait a little longer for the official cause of death. Mr. Butterworth and I have searched Mr. Baylor's room and nothing seemed amiss. I'll take Mr. Baylor's laptop with me and give it to a deputy to examine. If we can access Mr. Baylor's files, perhaps we'll discover the motive for what happened here tonight."

"Is the investigation on hold until tomorrow?"

The sheriff nodded. "Until then, I'd like this room to remain locked. No one should enter without me. I also realize that you'll need to make an announcement to your guests in the morning. Without more information from the medical examiner, we'll stick to the accidental death ruling. But should anyone attempt to check out—"

"That would certainly raise a red flag, seeing as all the guests are attending the same conference and it doesn't end for several days," Jane interrupted.

"Good to know," Evans said. "I'd like a copy of the conference schedule as well as a list of attendees when I come back. And if there's a particular guest or guests you think I should interview first, let me know."

An image of Felix Rolf's badger-like features immediately appeared in Jane's mind, but she kept her response limited to, "I will."

Butterworth showed the sheriff out and stood by the front door. When the taillights of the cruiser were faint red blurs in the distance, the butler turned to Jane. "Shall I disturb Mr. Rolf's slumber?"

"Yes." Jane continued to gaze out into the darkness. "And I don't want to make him as comfortable as we made Rosemary Pearce. Please escort him to the William Faulkner conference room."

Jane turned on the lights in the conference room and tried to decide where to sit. Though she didn't want to take the chair at the head of the table and risk looking like a dictator, she wanted to make it clear to Felix Rolf that he had one chance to be honest. If he lied to her this night, she would make him pay for his deceit.

She sat down at the head of the table and waited.

When Butterworth ushered Felix into the room, the book dealer was obviously anxious. Jane couldn't leap to the conclusion that his darting eyes or fidgeting revealed a guilty conscience, however, because anyone would be nervous in his position.

"I apologize for disturbing you at such a late hour. I would never do so without an urgent reason," Jane said. "And because I don't want to keep you a moment longer than necessity requires, I'll get right to it. Would you tell me about the conversation you had with Mr. Baylor by the gazebo earlier this evening?"

Felix stared at her. "Ex-excuse me?"

Jane didn't respond. She simply returned his stare. Only his was wide eyed and fearful, while hers was as flat and cold as a snake's.

"It was nothing, r-really," Felix stammered. "Just a brief exchange about a book. Why? Did Mr. Baylor lodge a complaint against me?"

"I'll explain why I need to know in due time," Jane said, infusing her tone with a steely edge. "Please repeat the conversation in as much detail as possible."

Felix glanced from Jane to Butterworth. The butler stood discreetly off to the side. His posture was as stiff as a wooden soldier's. Finding no reassurance in Butterworth's bland expression, Felix looked at Jane again.

"I don't know why Mr. Baylor has turned against me," he said despondently. "I've always been able to trust him with the finest pieces in my inventory. I've been fortunate enough to hire him to work wonders on a damaged book many times, but quite suddenly, he changed. He refused to do a repair for me. When I e-mailed him per usual with a written description and images of the requested repair, Mr. Baylor immediately responded by saying that he wouldn't accept the project. That's the word he used. 'Wouldn't.' Not couldn't. Wouldn't. I have no idea why."

The subject was transforming Felix. His anxiety had morphed into indignation. As he spoke, spots of color bloomed on his jowly cheeks.

"You can't think of any reason why Mr. Baylor refused your request?" Jane asked skeptically. "None at all?"

Felix's pique was instantly replaced by embarrassment. Without meeting Jane's searching gaze, he said, "My name was mixed up with a forgery case. I didn't realize that the item in question wasn't genuine. I swear it on my honor as a southerner and a gentleman. Certain people refused to deal with me following this unfortunate incident. But Mr. Baylor was *not* one of them. In fact, he repaired a signed, first edition of *Little House on the Prairie* for me two weeks after that wretched case was publicized."

"Then what happened by the gazebo? We heard of tension between the two of you."

Seeing that it was futile to protest, Felix shot another furtive glance at Butterworth and swallowed. He then spoke so quickly that his words were almost unintelligible. "It's been a difficult year for my shop. Sales have been weak. I'm not sure if people's interest in rare children's books are waning or if my customer base is aging and passing on, but I need every sale I can get." He paused for breath before launching into another hurried speech. "I have a customer with a fondness for adventure tales, especially those involving survival against great odds. This customer is both wealthy and discerning, so when I came across an 1814 first English edition of *Swiss Family Robinson*, bound in tan calf with gilt titles and marbled endpapers at a reasonable price, I knew I could make a profit if Mr. Baylor would help me improve the book's very good condition into fine condition. This was the very book he rejected via e-mail. I brought it here, you see. I thought if I showed it to him, he might be persuaded. . . ."

Jane had listened closely to Felix's tale. Now that it had reached its end, she was baffled by it. Why did Bart suddenly develop such an aversion to Felix? Or was it the book itself that he disliked with such intensity?

"Mr. Rolf, you've been very accommodating. May I beg one more favor? If you don't mind, I'd like to see this book."

Without giving Felix a chance to speak, Butterworth waved at the door. "I'll accompany you, sir."

"Yes, yes. Of course." Felix jumped out of his chair and scurried from the room.

Jane followed them out, but she headed for the lobby restroom to scour her hands with hot water and soap.

When Felix and Butterworth returned, Felix placed the book on the table in front of Jane.

"May I touch it?" Jane asked. "I just washed my hands."

Felix gave his assent and Jane made a cradle of her left palm before opening the cover and gently turning pages. She made it as far as the frontispiece when she suddenly understood why Bart hadn't wanted anything to do with this book.

"Mr. Rolf. How familiar are you with Mr. Baylor's personal life?"

He shook his head. "All I know is that he's *very* well off because his family owns Lilyfield Farms. Or most of its stock. Or something of that nature."

"Were you aware that Bart was the only surviving member of the Baylor family?"

Felix looked stricken. "No. How *terrible*. Was their passing recent? Perhaps that explains his odd behavior." He bit the end of his thumbnail. "How selfish of me—to think I was being rejected when he—"

"You weren't being rejected, Mr. Rolf," Jane interrupted. "Mr. Baylor was rejecting this book. In particular, this plate." She moved to the chair next to Felix so he could see more clearly. "It depicts a frightening image of a family on the deck of a ship. It's storming. The family members are clearly terrified. They're huddled together, staring up at that bank of ominous clouds with their big, dark eyes. To you and me, this is merely a black and white engraving from two hundred years ago, but to Mr. Baylor, this scene was probably very painful to view. Mr. Baylor's family—his father, mother, and older brother—died in a boating accident."

"Ooooooh!" Felix cried. He clamped a hand over his mouth as if pushing any additional noise back inside. When he'd mastered his emotions, he said, "That image must have been torturous for Mr. Baylor to look at, and I kept pushing it on him, even after he politely refused me." The book dealer shook his head in self-loathing. "My actions were beyond insensitive. Please, Ms. Steward. I would dearly like to make amends. Mr. Baylor is a good man, a champion of book preservation, and the finest book doctor in all of America. I apologize to *you* for causing any distress and I must apologize to Mr. Baylor as soon as possible."

Jane would have liked nothing more than to arrange a meeting between the two men the following morning. Instead, she touched Felix's arm and said, "Your mistake was unintentional. Don't be so hard on yourself. And you don't owe me an apology. I'm honored to have you as my guest. And though you may have temporarily lost a sale in your *Swiss Family Robinson* customer, I have a feeling you'll gain quite a few more in Octavia Steward."

Felix smiled. "That's very kind of you."

"Again, I'm sorry to have disturbed your rest." Jane got to her feet, signaling the end of the interview.

Butterworth turned to Felix. "Sir, may I offer you a nightcap? Or a cup of herbal tea to assist in your slumber? We stock a smooth chamomile blend flavored with a hint of orange blossom that should do the trick."

"I'd like that, thank you," Felix said.

When the two men were gone, Jane headed to the kitchens. Butterworth's suggestion had resonated with her as well. Though she was physically and emotionally exhausted, she knew sleep wouldn't come easily. She could use whatever help she could get to keep her mind from replaying the final moments of Bart Baylor's life. And if she managed to do that, she'd also have to put a stop to the endless doubt that there was something she could have done to save him.

She was just reaching for the kettle when Butterworth's hand gently closed over hers. "Allow me, Miss Jane. It's best to leave the preparation of tea to the British."

With a grateful nod, Jane plopped onto a kitchen stool and watched Butterworth's graceful and efficient movements.

"What was your assessment of Mr. Rolf?" Butterworth asked once he had the kettle on the stovetop.

"I believed him," Jane said. "I also believed Rosemary. Which means we have no leads."

Butterworth frowned. "Indeed."

They fell silent, each lost in their own thoughts, until the whistle of the teakettle shattered the stillness.

After filling a small teapot with boiling water and wrapping the pot with a napkin to keep it warm, Butterworth added a teacup, small cream pitcher, lemon slices, a selection of sweeteners, utensils, and two pieces of shortbread to a doily-lined tray. He then filled a second teapot for Jane.

"I could deliver yours as well," he offered, but she

squeezed his arm, told him she'd manage, and wished him a good night.

As she crossed the lawn, her phone alert indicated the receipt of a new e-mail. Normally, Jane would ignore incoming correspondence at such a late hour. However, nothing about this evening had been normal, so she let herself into her house, where she was met by the sounds of Ned snoring on the living room sofa, and poured herself a cup of tea. She resolved to have a single sip and glance at the e-mail before waking Ned and telling him that his long night of babysitting was finally over.

The message on her phone was from Celia Wallace. It read:

I know it's late, but I wanted to tell you about today's discovery. My team finished reconstructing Oliver's bones. Your friend Doctor Lydgate was right. Oliver suffered from rickets. His spine is also riddled with holes, indicating he was also inflicted with tuberculosis. Fascinating as these diseases are, they aren't the reason I'm contacting you. I wanted you to know that Oliver has a fractured wrist and forearm. These breaks never healed and are indicative of self-defense wounds. And here's the doozy. After examining the X-ray film, we noticed an object buried in his shoulder blade. That object was an arrowhead. Between the defensive wounds and the arrowhead, I believe that Oliver may have been murdered. I can't say why this act of violence occurred, but Oliver probably had two assailants. The first struck him head-on, creating the fractures. The second attacker was a coward, seeing as he shot Oliver with an arrow in the back. That's all I have for now. Will check in with you again soon. Let me know how the dirt mound progress goes.
—Celia

Jane picked up her teacup, but the liquid was already tepid, so she set it back down. Tiptoeing into the living room, she gently shook Ned's shoulder and whispered her thanks to him.

After Ned was gone, she climbed the stairs and peeked into the twins' room, drawing comfort from the rhythmic sounds of her boys' soft exhalations.

In her room, she sat on the edge of her bed and reread Celia's e-mail. She paused when she came to the lines referring to Oliver's assailants.

The first struck him head-on, creating the fractures. The second attacker was a coward.

"He wasn't a coward," Jane murmured wearily into the darkness. "He was a Fin."

Chapter Ten

The next morning, Jane saw the twins off to school before meeting Sheriff Evans in her office.

When she entered, she found him standing in front of her Hopes and Dreams board. His posture was stiff. His expression, grave.

"I'd like to gather the guests and tell them of Mr. Baylor's passing," the sheriff said. "Unless you can point us toward other individuals, we'll start by interviewing the members of the Robert Harley Society."

Jane thought back on last night's interactions with Rosemary Pearce and Felix Rolf. The sheriff had seen Storyton Hall's video surveillance room and would understand why Jane had conducted her own inquiries, so she recounted both conversations to him.

"Doesn't sound like either of them wished Mr. Baylor harm," the sheriff said when Jane was done. "Maybe the killer wasn't close to Mr. Baylor. He may have been well liked, but he was also very wealthy. In my experience, the very wealthy accumulate enemies. Just goes with the territory."

"Because of envy?" Jane asked.

The sheriff nodded. "That's usually the case. It's what I'll be looking for this morning. A sign that someone wanted what Mr. Baylor had."

"You wouldn't know he was rich by his dress or demeanor," Jane said. "He was humble. Understated."

"Maybe the killer asked Mr. Baylor for money and was turned down. With that kind of money in his bank account, he must have been constantly solicited," said Evans. "At this juncture, money is the obvious motive. Unless you think Mr. Baylor was murdered over something to do with that buried book?"

Jane's heart skipped a beat. Involuntarily, her hand moved to the pocket where her cell phone was nestled. Last night, after reading Celia Wallace's text, she'd been unable to sleep. Her body was beyond fatigued, but tumultuous thoughts kept her mind from shutting down.

You have two murders on your hands, spoke an unquiet voice in her head. *Two murders. One old. One new. Are they related?*

Jane didn't want Sheriff Evans focusing on the cookbook. She and the Fins needed to determine how the words on its pages had been rendered invisible and reverse the process. Only then could she determine if the book was connected to Bart's murder.

"I can't imagine who'd want to stop Mr. Baylor from sharing what he learned about a deteriorated book," Jane said in what she hoped was a light tone.

But Sheriff Evans wouldn't be put off that easily. He rubbed his bristly chin with slow, contemplative movements and said, "Mr. Baylor was the majority shareholder of one of the largest food manufacturing companies in the United States. The cookbook discovered in your back garden was controversial because it could have harmed the uninformed public of nineteenth-century England. Those two facts make me want to have a closer look at certain food manufacturers. Especially those who would have benefited from the cookbook's distribution."

Jane saw where Evans was heading. "Is there a link between Lilyfield Farms and the food company that published *Mrs. Tanner's Everyday Receipts*?"

"None that I can find," the sheriff said. "But I know next to nothing about this cookbook of yours."

Does he think I'm withholding information? Jane wondered.

Ignoring the anxious feeling in the pit of her stomach, she spread her hands in a gesture of transparency. "If Sinclair and I discover any new information, we'll tell you straightaway. We plan to research the book more thoroughly today. Up to this point, most of what we know came from Bart. This is no surprise, seeing as there's nothing left but a partial cover and pages that have been so ravaged by time and weather that the ink has literally seeped away."

"Luckily, we have an entire resort filled with rare book experts at our disposal," the sheriff said. He collected his hat from where it was perched on the corner of Jane's desk. "After I inform the guests of the sad news about their colleague and my desire to speak with certain individuals, I may ask for their help. I want to learn more about this book and everything I can about Mr. Baylor's life. Someone wanted him to put on those gloves and transfer the cyanide to his lips. According to your statement, this lip tapping was a prevalent behavior of Mr. Baylor's. The killer used this knowledge to his or her advantage."

"Which means that person is here, in Storyton Hall," Jane said unhappily.

Sheriff Evans donned his hat. "More often than not, a murder is deeply personal. The killer felt compelled to end Mr. Baylor's life using a quick, but painful method. This murderer is observant, clever, and capable of blending in with your current group of guests. This person won't be easy to ferret out, and because we have no idea what precipitated their actions, we have no idea if their goal has been achieved."

Jane didn't like the sound of that at all.

First, Bart was killed. Hours later, she learned that the two-hundred-year-old man buried on the grounds of her ancestral home was also a murder victim. Now, Sheriff Evans was suggesting the possibility of more violence.

I won't allow it, she silently vowed.

Squaring her shoulders, Jane promised to assemble the guests in the Shakespeare Theater without delay. This was an easy task, seeing as the day's first event was being held there. What was heart-wrenchingly difficult was witnessing the reactions of the conference-goers when Sheriff Evans broke the news of Bart's death.

Gasps rose throughout the room and people turned to each other, eyes wide with shock and sadness. Jane saw heads shaking in disbelief and hands reaching for tissues.

The hardest hit were Levi Ross and Aaron and Austin Sullivan. Rosemary had been told the previous night, of course, though this didn't prevent a fresh round of tears from wetting her cheeks. The men in her group fussed over her, but they were equally shaken. Not one of them managed to hold back tears.

Jane caught Sterling's eye. Like the rest of the Fins, he'd been carefully studying the faces in the crowd, hoping to spot a tell—the slightest indication that something was off about a person.

He shook his head. He hadn't seen a thing.

Jane made eye contact with the rest of the Fins. One by one, they responded as Sterling had. None of the guests had reacted suspiciously.

Though Jane hadn't expected to identify the killer following the sheriff's announcement, she still wanted to let that person know that they were being watched. If the killer became nervous, perhaps he or she would make a mistake.

I just pray that mistake doesn't involve more violence, Jane thought.

The sheriff finished his statement and said that he was willing to answer questions if there were any.

Hands shot up around the room.

Signaling for Sterling and Sinclair to exit the theater, Jane led them away from the doors. "We need to find out what's written inside that cursed cookbook." Her voice was an urgent whisper. "Sterling, there must be an early nineteenth-century formula for creating invisible ink and another for revealing it."

Sterling surprised her by saying, "There are several. For example, rice water becomes invisible when dry. When rubbed with iodine, it turns blue. This ink was used during the Indian Rebellion of 1857, which probably occurred after the publication of our cookbook. However, I've been focusing more on inks made with foodstuffs. Specifically, the juice from onions or turnips. Seems more fitting, considering it's a cookbook."

"I agree," Jane said. "What chemical process would reveal onion or turnip juice?"

"We don't need one," Sterling said. "We just need to apply heat."

Sinclair, who'd yet to speak, arched a brow. "As in, the heat from an iron?"

"Exactly," replied Sterling.

Jane looked at Sinclair. "Would you assist Sterling? If Sheriff Evans takes the book as evidence, we might not get another crack at it."

He hesitated. "I will. But before I go, I must ask if you heard from Doctor Wallace last night? I received an e-mail from her."

"Unfortunately, yes. What are your thoughts on her message?"

Sinclair raised two fingers. "First, we must complete her request regarding the dirt mound. Her students are already working, but we should lend them an extra pair of hands. Or two. If another piece of evidence is hidden in that mound, it must be brought to light as swiftly as possible."

Jane pointed at his second finger. "I know what that finger represents. The earthmover driver. He's a question mark in our minds. Did he pick up an object from the ground and drop it in his pocket? We set this issue aside because the boys weren't sure of what they'd seen, but we can't let it go any longer. The man must be questioned, and he has to be questioned in such a way that he doesn't dare lie or refuse to answer."

"Which means we need to intimidate him." Sterling's eyes gleamed. "As soon as we finish with the cookbook, Sinclair and I will get his name from the contractor—"

"I'll do that. And when I have it, I'll give it to Mrs. Pratt," Jane interrupted. "If this guy's a local, she'll have a mental dossier on him." She sighed. "We have so much to do. I wish there were more of us. I wish . . ." She trailed off, unwilling to give voice to her deepest desire.

Sinclair touched her shoulder. "Edwin would come home? Have you heard from him?"

"Not a whisper," Jane said. "I haven't received cryptic postcards, surprise packages, or hurried phone calls with bad reception. Nothing." She shook her head. "Edwin would have been helpful, but he isn't here. I have my Fins and I have my friends. Along with the twins, Uncle Aloysius and Aunt Octavia, you're my family. That has, and always will be, more than enough."

When Jane stepped back into the theater, it was clear to her that Sheriff Evans was no longer taking questions. According to Butterworth, who hastily filled her in, the guests had been told to try to enjoy the remainder of their conference. Evans then asked the members of the Robert Harley Society to meet him in the Madame Bovary Dining Room.

"Why there?" Jane murmured under her breath. She had no time to reflect on the question because the sheriff was headed straight for her.

"I'd like to form a better picture of Mr. Baylor. Would you please see to it that we're not disturbed?" Evans gestured at the distraught and ashen-faced group following him at a leaden pace. Levi came first. His eyes were downcast and his hands were buried deep in his pockets. Aaron Sullivan had an arm around Rosemary's waist and Austin walked on her other side, looking lost.

Jane realized that she'd never seen the Sullivan brothers with somber expressions. Their faces had always been lit by smiles. Watching them now, Jane saw the heaviness of their limbs and the dullness in their eyes and felt responsible for the loss of their joie de vivre.

She was so fixed on the pall clinging to the group that she didn't notice Deputy Emory until the younger woman stood directly in front of her.

"Are you okay, Ms. Steward?"

Jane summoned a smile. "I didn't sleep well last night. Thanks for asking."

Deputy Emory's eyes, which reminded Jane of cornflowers, filled with sympathy. "I can understand why you'd have a restless night. What I don't understand is why people seem so bent on doing bad things in Storyton. I'm referring to our whole area. I just don't get it. It's one of the most peaceful places I've ever seen. That sense of peace is why I moved here after graduate school." She shook her head in dismay. "I could have gone to another place. There were so many other careers I could have chosen. But I had to be in this *place*. It chose me."

"Even our oasis is vulnerable to the outside world," Jane said. "As long as there are people, there will be violence."

"I know," Emory said. "I just thought it would be a rare occurrence in these parts. And I expected to face less serious crimes. The worst I thought I'd see would be domestic disputes or barroom brawls. Instead, I've assisted with multiple homicide investigations and I've been with the sheriff's department for only two years."

Sheriff Evans and the Robert Harley Society members left the theater, but Emory lingered behind.

"Do you regret your choice?" Jane asked.

"No," the deputy immediately answered. "If I stood on those famous roads from Robert Frost's poem—where they diverged in the woods, I'd take the untraveled one again. No matter what happens, I belong in Storyton." Smiling sheepishly, she tucked a lock of auburn hair behind her ear. With her rosebud lips and smooth skin, the lovely deputy looked like one of Dante Gabriel Rossetti's models. "I stopped to check on you and instead, you made *me* feel better. Let me know if I can do anything."

Jane gazed at Emory intently. "You can. You can catch Bart Baylor's killer. He didn't deserve that death, Deputy Emory. I didn't know him well, but the impression I had was of someone who liked to fix books, preserve the past, and help people when he could. He was my guest, and I failed him. I'm asking you to be his champion now."

Deputy Emory responded with a solemn nod and hurried from the room.

As for Jane, she would have loved to watch Sterling conduct his experiment on *The Devil's Receipts*, but she turned in the opposite direction of the garage. Enclosed in her office, she began to scour the Internet for references on Levi Ross.

There wasn't much, and most of what Jane found centered on Levi's bookstores. Levi didn't post personal information on social media accounts and seemed to live a quiet life. At least, according to cyberspace.

The opposite was true for Aaron and Austin Sullivan.

There were hundreds of links, photos, and references to the gregarious duo, and the more Jane scanned through articles of their charitable endeavors, the more she liked the siblings. Her search came to an abrupt halt, however, when she came across a *Wall Street Journal* piece entitled ONLY NATURAL FOODS DEALS WITH BACKLASH OVER UNNATURAL INGREDIENTS.

"That doesn't sound good," Jane murmured.

Embedded in the text of the article was a photograph of Aaron Sullivan at what looked like a press conference. The caption read, "Aaron Sullivan, public relations director of Only Natural Foods, blames supplier for presence of chemical in olive oil."

According to the article, this was the second Only Natural Foods recall in the past six months. The company was currently under fire for their olive oil, a product labeled as 100 percent extra-virgin olive oil. After being tested, the oil was found to be 70 percent olive oil and 30 percent sunflower and soybean oils. Worse than this, copper sulfate was detected in the oil.

"Not a great ingredient for a company called Only Natural," Jane said, examining the image of the olive oil bottle near the bottom of the article.

The piece went on to describe how Only Natural had been in hot water with the Department of Agriculture's Food Safety and Inspection division that spring after a test revealed that their organic, sun-ripened tomato basil soup contained yellow dye number 5. That incident caused a major dip in the company's stock value. The dip turned into a sharp decline following the olive oil incident. By the time she was finished reading, Jane realized that Only Natural Foods was trading at its lowest value since the company opened its doors in 1914.

Jane leaned back in her chair. She thought of how wealthy Bart had been and how his killer was likely motivated by money. That's what Sheriff Evans believed, at least. As for

Jane, she still felt there might be a connection between Bart's death and *The Devil's Receipts*. Someone knew he'd discovered the book's secret identity and wanted to silence him. But if so, why? How could an old book threaten anyone?

"That damn book," she muttered, a phrase she never thought she'd speak.

After printing the *Wall Street Journal* article to share with the Fins, Jane called the contractor in charge of the Walt Whitman Spa project and pretended that Doctor Wallace needed the contact information of the earthmover's driver.

"When can we start work again, Ms. Steward?" the contractor asked after fulfilling Jane's request. "The weather's supposed to be great this week. Clear skies and smooth sailing."

Jane glanced at her Hopes and Dreams board and suppressed a mournful sigh. She wasn't going to let anything stop the spa from being built. "I'll check in with the anthropologist and the sheriff and let you know the moment we're given the green light. No one wants to see you and your crew back here more than I do."

Next on Jane's list was a call to Mrs. Pratt.

"Kyle Stuyvesant?" Mrs. Pratt repeated the driver's name. "No, he doesn't live in the village." She paused long enough for Jane to feel weighed down by disappointment. Then, she added, "He might not live in Storyton, but he drinks here."

Jane sat a little taller in her chair. "Drinks? At the Cheshire Cat?"

"If he could, he'd probably carve his name in his favorite bar stool," Mrs. Pratt said with disapproval. "I'm all for a cocktail or two, but this man approaches drinking like it's an Olympic event. And at the end of the night, he begs people to drive him home because he lives too far away to walk. It's very irresponsible. And he's mean to the cats to boot. He tries to kick them, but he's always too unsteady to land a blow. He needs help, but he won't admit to having a problem." A derisive snort echoed down the line. "Ask Betty. She'll gladly tell you about Bar-stool Kyle."

However, Betty wasn't glad. She was quite reticent, in fact.

"I don't know, Jane," she said. "Bob and I believe in the Tenders' Code. It's an unspoken agreement between barkeeps and their customers that most things spoken while under the influence of alcohol are best forgotten. I don't work the bar as often as Bob, but when I do, I hear hard things. Things I'd never repeat. I feel like I'm part therapist, part legal counsel, and part doting aunt when I man the taps. I can't betray the trust of my patrons by divulging what they've said during moments of weakness."

Jane surprised Betty by laughing. "This is exactly what I love about you, Betty. You and the rest of the Cover Girls are such rare people. People of integrity. I wouldn't dream of asking you to break your Tenders' Code without an excellent reason. It has to do with the buried book and with a possible theft of an archaeological artifact." Jane went on to repeat what the twins thought they'd seen.

"Kyle wasn't on a Cheshire Cat bar stool when he took that object. He was lucid and sober," Jane added. "*If* he took it, that is. I don't want an innocent man to be accused without justification. However, if it's true . . ."

"Then he has to turn it in because it might help identify the man buried in your garden," Betty finished miserably. "As if you don't have enough stress. I heard what happened to Mr. Baylor. Word has it that you were in the room with him when he collapsed. You poor thing. How are you holding up?"

Mrs. Hubbard was busy this morning, Jane thought, picturing the round-cheeked, round-bodied cook buzzing through the kitchen, sampling sauces, frying bacon, and pulling biscuits from the oven—all while keeping a phone pressed to one ear.

"I'm okay," she told Betty. "I'll see you at the workshop. I have to run because the sheriff's here now. If you can help out with Kyle the next time he comes in—"

"Which will be five o'clock today," Betty said with confidence. "With the spa job on hold, he'll be on his favorite stool, reciting his favorite quote. It's by Oscar Wilde and we hear it whenever he enters the Cheshire Cat. 'Work is the curse of the drinking classes,'" she recited in a deep voice. "Anyway, Bob should have what you need by eight at the latest."

Jane thanked her friend and hung up. For the next twenty minutes, she delved deeper into the history and financial structure of Only Natural Foods, where Aaron Sullivan worked as the head of public relations and Austin ran the advertising department. Jane realized that the Sullivan brothers had a similar background to Bart Baylor. All three men had parents who were majority stockholders in one of the nation's leading food manufacturing firms. Not only that, but Bart and the Sullivan brothers had also attended the same university.

It was at this point that Jane found a tiny blurb—a bit of financial hearsay that representatives from Lilyfield Farms firmly denied—that there were talks of a merger between Only Natural and Lilyfield Farms.

Jane's phone buzzed and she read the text Sterling had sent.

We've exposed the words. Come see.

Needing no further incentive, Jane grabbed the printouts and hurried through the staff corridors, out the loading dock door, and down the driveway to the garages.

Sterling was watching for her approach. He ushered her into his lab and locked the door behind her.

"The book is more unique than we originally thought,"

Sinclair said. He sat on a backless stool, gazing fixedly at the cookbook through an LED magnifying lamp. Jane could see brown squiggly shapes on the pages. But what she saw made no sense. Typeface wasn't squiggly. It was neat and uniform.

"Is that handwriting?" she asked.

Sinclair finally looked at her. "Yes. Apparently, this is a bound version of the original draft. It's quite rough in places. Lines are crossed out here and ingredients added there. The editor must have had a hell of a time making sense of it all. Mr. Sterling and I have made two important discoveries. Mr. Sterling? Would you care to explain? You figured out that the writing had been done in turnip juice."

"A lucky guess." Sterling gestured at the book. "The recipes are all brand specific. They repeatedly recommend the use of ingredients produced by three food manufacturers. Mr. Sinclair and I have made a list of the manufacturers as well as the ingredients we believe could have been harmful if ingested in large quantities. I'll have to do more fact-checking on those, however."

Jane moved closer to the magnifying lamp and Sinclair immediately vacated his stool to give her a clear view of the exposed writing.

SAUCE FOR A BOILED CHICKEN. PUT THE FOLLOWING INGREDIENTS INTO A MORTAR: ANISEED, DRIED MINT, AND A SMALL QUANTITY OF MUSTARD SEEDS. COVER WITH RACKLEY'S VINEGAR . . .

"I assume the Rackley's Vinegar is the adulterated product." Jane stepped away from the lamp. She hadn't liked the book from the moment she'd heard its negative moniker. Now, the thought that it could have been used to poison children, the chronically ill, and the elderly made her dislike it even more.

Sinclair, who'd always been adept at reading Jane's expressions, edged closer to her. Perhaps he sensed that she needed comfort, but guessed that she also didn't want to appear weak. "Though we haven't delved into Rackley Manufacturers yet, Mr. Sterling believes that copper was added to many of their products. Their pickled vegetables, for example. The copper would have made them a brighter, more robust green."

Jane turned her back on the book to face Sterling. "What effect does ingesting copper have on people?"

"In mild cases, it can cause stomachaches, nausea, vomiting, headaches, and fever. In more severe cases, anemia, liver or kidney failure. And death."

Jane wanted to rip the book to shreds. It was an utterly foreign sensation, and though it quickly passed, she felt ashamed. The book wasn't at fault. The men behind its creation were. "I could understand why someone would take this book to their grave. It is literally filled with poison. I find myself wondering if that chemist, Otto Frank, the doctor who exposed the companies behind the food adulteration, didn't end up at Storyton Hall in an effort to hide that book. But if that *was* the case, then why would he have an arrowhead embedded in his scapula?"

Neither Sterling nor Sinclair could supply an answer.

"Sterling, I'd like you to research the companies behind the creation of this cookbook," Jane said, cutting her eyes at the book in question. "They might be long gone, but the practice of adulterating food is very much alive. In fact, we're currently hosting two guests whose family has been in the food business since 1914."

Sinclair cocked his head. "You're referring to the Sullivans, I take it?"

"I am." Jane handed Sinclair the *Wall Street Journal* article and patiently waited for him to read it. When he was done, he frowned and passed it to Sterling. Though Sinclair conducted background checks on every guest, there was simply too much information and too many guests coming and going to know every nuance of their lives.

"The sheriff should see this article," Sterling said. "Maybe those playboy philanthropists pressured Mr. Baylor to do what was necessary for the merger of their companies to take place. When he refused their proposition, they decided to eliminate the competition. The Sullivan brothers had motive and opportunity. If we could link them to the cyanide, we'd give the sheriff the necessary evidence to tie up this case by day's end."

Though this sounded too good to be true, Jane was willing to indulge in fantasy for a moment. The trouble was, she wouldn't feel relieved to see Aaron or Austin hauled off in the back of the sheriff's cruiser. Their demise wouldn't raise Bart from the dead or restore the atmosphere of happy camaraderie that had been fractured by an act of premeditated violence.

"I have a feeling that things will shift before our eyes multiple times as this day progresses," Jane said. "By the end of it all, I might be at the Cheshire Cat, sitting next to Bar-stool Kyle."

"To investigate or to drown your sorrows?" Sterling quipped.

There was no humor in Jane's voice when she said, "Maybe both."

Chapter Eleven

Jane had less than an hour before she was supposed to join the Cover Girls for one of the most anticipated events of the conference: a letterpress workshop.

Jane had been looking forward to the workshop since she'd first heard of it. Though she very rarely participated in the same activities as her guests, this was a learning experience she couldn't resist. However, she wouldn't feel right spending the afternoon enjoying herself if there was a fresh lead to follow, so when she saw Deputy Phelps standing guard outside the William Faulkner Conference Room, she asked for an update.

"The sheriff's still with the victim's friends," Phelps said. "It took a while before they were able to calm down and talk. They were pretty upset and the sheriff realized that we needed to relocate. When that dining room is empty, there's an echo."

"And the sounds of grief carried," Jane guessed. "I understand that you can't fill me in on what's being discussed in the conference room, but what about Mr. Baylor's laptop? The sheriff mentioned the possibility of having it examined last night."

Phelps issued a hapless shrug. "There's nothing on that machine that I wouldn't show my granny. Most people have *something* worth hiding on their computers. Whether it's a secret bank account, an ex-girlfriend's phone number, or a browsing history that reveals, er, certain interests, I've never scanned a computer as—well, there's no other way to say it—as nerdy as Mr. Baylor's."

This didn't offend Jane. It made her smile. "In other words, he used his computer to focus on his passion for books?"

"He also watched tons of travel videos and listened to music," Phelps said. "He searched for photos on architecture and nature too. And he had a bunch of art images. Mostly pieces that were famous for their symmetry. He also read up on his OCD. All the latest research. Like he was always looking for new treatments and coping strategies."

Jane's smile faded. "It takes a strong man to acknowledge his problems and to do his best to manage them." When Phelps didn't reply, she returned to the subject of the investigation. "What about Lilyfield Farms? Bart wasn't directly involved in the business, but were there any indications that he kept track of the company?"

"He checked the stock prices, but not often. It wasn't a part of his daily routine," Phelps explained. "He did receive e-mails from Lilyfield Farms. Most were about charity events."

Jane mulled this over. "The Sullivans are involved with several charities. I did some research last night and discovered that their family owns the majority shares of a large food manufacturing firm—just like the Baylor family. Did you notice any correspondence between Bart and Only Natural Foods?"

"None," Phelps said.

Bart could have deleted it, Jane thought. *I could see him permanently erasing anything that increased his anxiety.*

"What about Aaron or Austin Sullivan?" she pressed.

"Did they contact Bart about topics other than the Robert Harley Society?"

Phelps stiffened and Jane realized that she'd pushed too hard.

"Never mind." She held up her hands in a show of apology. "I shouldn't be asking so many questions. It's hard to sit and wait for things to progress. I wish I could be of more help."

Relaxing, Phelps told Jane that he'd let her know when the sheriff needed her.

Knowing she'd been politely dismissed, Jane toyed with the idea of sneaking into the broom cupboard in the hall. The cupboard had a false back that led into a narrow passageway dividing the two conference rooms. This secret space had been designed as both a hidey-hole and a way of eavesdropping on those gathered in either room. Jane had previously used it to listen in on the sheriff's interviews, but she didn't dare try to sneak into the broom cupboard with Phelps standing so near. He might see her go in, and Jane doubted that proclaiming herself a diehard enthusiast of *The Chronicles of Narnia* would serve as a sufficient explanation as to why she'd suddenly ducked into a cupboard.

Heading to the staff corridor, Jane's hand closed over her locket. This was a habitual gesture and she always felt a thrill of pleasure when she thought of the treasures stored high above her head. Her current guests would go weak in the knees at the sight of just one or two selections from the secret library. The door at the back of Great-Aunt Octavia's closet that granted access to the library's spiral staircase was truly a Narnian gateway, for every time Jane stepped into that windowless room, it was as if she'd entered another world. A world of words, preserved for all time in a fireproof, climate-controlled space. Unpublished Shakespeare folios. Famous literary masterpieces with alternate endings. Maps, poems, drawings.

Bart would have loved them all, Jane thought. *Even the books meant to incite conflict or cause harm.*

This thought led to thoughts of food adulteration. Jane suddenly picked up her pace, bound for the spa construction area.

She'd been so preoccupied by Bart's abrupt and violent death that she'd neglected to check on Celia Wallace's grad students. Their sifting through a mound of dirt seemed less significant in comparison to her goal of identifying Bart's killer and bringing him or her to justice. And yet Jane couldn't shake the feeling that there was a connection between the diseased murder victim buried in Walter Steward's garden nearly two hundred years ago and Bart Baylor.

Ducking under the flap in the construction fence, Jane recalled how concerned she'd been that the discovery of skeletal remains would delay the next phase of construction on the Walt Whitman Spa.

"If that was all I had to worry about today, I'd be grateful," she muttered.

Her mood lifted the moment she came upon the grad students—both of whom were young women—exchanging lighthearted banter with two of Storyton Hall's oldest groundskeepers. All four looked hot, sweaty, and dirty. They also looked delighted to be scooping shovelfuls of dirt from one pile to another.

"Hello, Miss Jane!" One of the groundskeepers paused in his work to greet her.

"Wow. You've made incredible progress so quickly," Jane said, pointing at the diminished dirt mound. "Have you found any treasure?"

The grad student with the blond pigtail braids said, "So far, just a coin."

"Another halfpenny?"

The second grad student, a slim Hispanic woman with caramel-colored eyes, shook her head. "This one's German. We haven't cleaned it, so I can't read the year or denomination. We'll bring it back to the university just as we found it because Celia prefers artifacts to be delivered untouched if possible."

"Makes sense," Jane said, and glanced up at the sun. "I'll send out pitchers of ice water and Mrs. Hubbard's homemade limeade. You're all working so hard, but you need to stay hydrated."

This was met with a chorus of "thank yous," and Jane felt a trifle guilty for having an ulterior motive in sending Butterworth to deliver the cold drinks. When he appeared in her office twenty minutes later, however, the guilt quickly vanished.

"It is decidedly German," Butterworth said, his eyes glinting with excitement. "An early piece, predating the formation of the German Empire in 1871."

At Jane's blank stare, Butterworth elaborated. "Prior to this event, Germany was comprised of separate states and the various regions issued their own coinage. There were guldens, marks, hellers, groschens. I'm no expert in German numismatology, but I believe the coin discovered today is silver and was minted in Hamburg."

Jane was impressed. "How do you know? Is Hamburg stamped on the coin?"

"An image of its fortress is. With its three-tower castle, the structure is clearly recognizable."

"Recognizable for those with your breadth of knowledge." Jane's phone buzzed and she glanced at the screen. "The sheriff has finished interviewing the Robert Harley Society members. They're signed up for the letterpress workshop, as am I. Not only will the event give me a chance to observe the Sullivan brothers, but I could also use some time to reflect on these two murders. Quietly setting type might give me that time."

Butterworth looked dubious. "Forgive me, Miss Jane, but quiet contemplation is unlikely seeing as you'll be in the company of your friends."

"They can't all make it, which is a shame. The Cover Girls have as much passion and respect for books as any of our current guests," Jane said. "And while they lack the combat training of the Fins, they often help me tackle complicated problems. I don't tell them every detail, but sharing the broad brushstrokes often gets me to that allusive a-ha moment."

"I hope your a-ha moment occurs," Butterworth said, his mouth twitching slightly at the corners.

Jane made to leave when she was struck by a thought. "Speaking of friends, have Sinclair tell Celia Wallace about the coin's provenance as well as my wild theory that the man buried in our garden is Otto Frank."

Holding the door for Jane, Butterworth said, "Mr. Sinclair thinks your theory is a valid one."

"He does?" Jane asked.

"Mr. Sinclair found an article mentioning Doctor Frank's state of health. It was written shortly before he fled London and was never seen again."

Jane knew exactly what Butterworth would say next. "He had tuberculosis, didn't he?"

Butterworth nodded. "His condition was no secret among those in his circle. He was not expected to reach old age."

"It's difficult to age with an arrow in your back," Jane said. "Have Sinclair ask Celia for an image of that arrowhead, please. I don't know why, but I'd like to see it."

The head butler left and Jane ordered lunch trays for herself, Sheriff Evans, and his deputies and requested that they be delivered to the William Faulkner Conference Room. Over walnut chicken salad sandwiches and roasted sweet potato and ginger soup, Jane shared what she'd found regarding Only Natural's financial difficulties.

"During their interview, the Sullivans said that they've known Mr. Baylor for a long time," Emory said. "It would be a shame if they turned on their friend because he didn't support the merger of their companies."

Having finished her soup, Jane put down her spoon. "When did they first become friends with Bart?"

"All three gentlemen attended the same boarding school and college," the sheriff answered. "Mr. and Mrs. Sullivan were also godparents to Mr. Baylor."

"I had no idea they had such close ties," Jane said. "Did their families live in the same town too?"

Sheriff Evans had just taken a bite of his sandwich, so Deputy Phelps replied in his stead. "Different states. But both families summered in Newport. According to Aaron Sullivan, that's how they first met."

Deputy Emory looked aggrieved. "The brothers were so upset when they heard about Mr. Baylor, that they're either skilled actors or their grief is genuine."

"It's possible to commit a crime and still express remorse," the sheriff said. "A murderer isn't without feelings. Sometimes, when finally confronted, a killer can be completely overwhelmed by emotion."

Jane suddenly found it difficult to swallow her mouthful of sandwich. She saw that Deputy Emory was no longer eating and sat quietly with her hands in her lap. Deputy Phelps had already devoured everything on his tray. Perched on the edge of his chair, he was clearly eager to get back to work.

"We need to delve deeper into Only Natural Foods and the roles Aaron and Austin Sullivan play in the company." The sheriff placed his napkin on the table. "Ms. Steward, thank you for lunch. Keep your eyes and ears open during the afternoon workshop, if you would."

The sheriff obviously had things to discuss with his deputies, so Jane left them in the conference room and made her way to the Great Gatsby Ballroom, which was where the letterpress workshop was being held.

As the session was already underway, Jane silently maneuvered around the other tables, bound for the one marked with a sign reading, RESERVED FOR COVER GIRLS.

"Is everything okay?" Eloise whispered once Jane was seated. "I know it's not, but are *you* okay? When you weren't here at the start, we got worried."

The other Cover Girls in attendance—Mabel, Betty, and Mrs. Pratt—nodded in agreement.

"I'm better now that I'm with you," Jane said, and meant it.

She turned her attention to their workshop leader, a retired professor named Michael Piech. The professor was describing the various works created by letterpresses.

"In my opinion, this press was made to produce poetry," he said, directing his audience to the screen at the front of the room. "Just look at this broadside of a Rumi poem."

"What's a broadside?" Mabel whispered.

Jane grew rigid, unable to reply.

Don't be that *Rumi poem*, she silently prayed. *I don't want to think about Edwin right now.*

"It's a sheet of paper printed on one side. Like a poster or an advertisement," Eloise whispered to Mabel.

Professor Piech raised his pointer. "Printed on Crane's Lettra Pearl White using a Vandercook cylinder press. The typeface is Open Sans. Black. The mountain design, done in red ink, is from a hand-carved woodblock."

Staring up at the screen, the professor read the lines of

poetry aloud. And though Jane knew a much older man was speaking, she heard Edwin's voice fill the air around her.

> *"A mountain keeps an echo deep inside itself.*
> *That's how I hold your voice.*
>
> *I am scrap wood thrown in your fire,*
> *and quickly reduced to smoke."*

"How beautiful," Eloise murmured.

Mrs. Pratt put her hand over her heart. "That poet must have made millions of women swoon."

Mabel also chimed in with a comment, but Jane was lost in a memory and didn't hear it.

In the memory, she and Edwin were sitting on the low wall surrounding the herb garden behind Storyton Hall's kitchen. It was twilight. Shadows were stretching out along the gravel paths and stars were beginning to spangle the periwinkle sky.

On that garden wall, Edwin had given Jane a gift. It was an original Rumi poem. Because it had been written in Persian in the sixteenth century, Edwin had translated the words, saying that the gift was his way of pledging himself to her. He told Jane that he loved her and that the echo of her voice had carried him through his most difficult time. He was forever hers. If she'd have him.

Jane had responded by saying that she wanted him, despite the complexities of such a relationship, because she'd fallen in love with him.

Afterward, they'd walked, hand in hand, across the great lawn and through a cloud of fireflies, to Jane's house.

It had been an enchanted evening.

"Psst!" Eloise waved a hand in front of Jane's face, snapping her back to the present. "You haven't blinked in over a minute. Is there something we should know?"

"I'll tell you later," Jane murmured.

The professor clicked his remote and the image on the screen changed. "Though we're focusing on Pre-Raphaelite-style broadsides today, I still wanted to show you a few examples from contemporary printers. Many small presses use fresh, bold interpretations of classic works. Take this version of Shakespeare's Sonnet Thirty-Five, for instance. The Optima typeface and the clever eclipse design, which progresses from black to yellow to red and is a nod to the eclipse referenced in the poem, are arguably more effective than multiple colors and ornate typeface. This design allows the sonnet's themes to shine."

A woman near the front said, "It's unique, but I believe William Morris and Kelmscott Press were the perfect match for Shakespeare's works."

"Fair enough," the professor said amicably, and signaled for the house lights to be turned up. He then asked the participants to select a poetry sample from the center of their table.

"This is what you'll be printing today," he explained. "At the end of the workshop, you'll have a beautiful piece of art to take home. I'm sure some of you are wondering why you aren't being given the chance to print an entire poem."

The audience murmured their agreement and the professor laughed. "It's okay, it happens every time. You'll be surprised to find that setting movable type is neither quick nor easy. You must set the type in reverse, and even the most detail-oriented individuals will make mistakes along the way. Typically, these mistakes go unnoticed until the plates meet the press. When the ink is on the rollers, things tend to become clear."

To Jane, the professor might have been describing a murder investigation. She felt like she'd been given an assortment of random bits of information and was somehow expected to fit them together until they formed a complete picture. But the information she and the Fins had gathered thus far might as well be backward and upside-down letters from a nineteenth-century poem. At this point, their sleuthing was all theory and no concrete evidence.

"Which poem did you get?" Mabel asked Mrs. Pratt.

"'The Honeysuckle,'" Mrs. Pratt answered. "The poet is Dante Rossetti. You?"

"I have the other Rossetti. Christina," Mrs. Pratt said. "It's a rather gloomy verse from 'A Daughter of Eve,' but I don't mind. The Victorians were obsessed with death, so I don't expect a poem filled with sunshine and daisy imagery."

Eloise was grinning over her selection. "Mine is 'Violets,' by George Meredith. It's very sweet. I'll have it framed and we can give it to Violet on her birthday. She was so disappointed that she couldn't come, but she couldn't reschedule her clients. Who wrote your poem, Jane?"

"William Morris. I've never heard of this one. It's called 'Our Hands Have Met.'"

Mrs. Pratt craned her neck to see Jane's paper. "Oh, it's romantic! 'Our hands have met—our lips have met'"—she paused to wriggle her brows before continuing—"'our souls—who knows when the wind blows?'"

"Quite an abrupt change in tone at the end," Eloise said. "Sounds like someone who can't quite commit."

Though Jane briefly wondered if Eloise was referring to Edwin, Lachlan, or both men, she didn't want to be bogged down by thoughts of her complicated love life, so she scanned the room in search of the Robert Harley Society members.

All four of them were concentrating on their poems. Their faces were taut, as if the strain of holding back their sadness and shock was stretching their skin.

I won't learn a thing by watching them, Jane thought.

I need to set my type quickly and visit their table when I'm done.

There were wooden boxes filled with metal type tiles on every table. Each wooden box was divided into compartments by letter. The box the Cover Girls had been given was labeled "Goudy Modern 12 pt."

Professor Piech walked everyone through the steps of setting their first line of type, and Jane became completely absorbed in the task of selecting tiles and positioning them in her composing stick. It was delicate work that required deep concentration, and though the room was at capacity, hardly anyone spoke. This was understandable, seeing as a single mistake in one line, such as omitting punctuation or forgetting to insert a text tile in reverse, often meant redoing the entire line.

Jane found the exercise very therapeutic. It helped to have long, thin, and deft fingers, which she did. It also helped that she loved the feel of the tiles and how each line of poetry grew as she worked.

"I feel like a modern day Gutenberg," she whispered to Eloise, after finishing her third out of five lines.

"You're much better looking," Eloise quipped.

To her right, Mabel cursed softly. "I can't believe it. I inserted a comma when I was supposed to use a semicolon. Lord, how am I ever going to fix that mess? It's in the middle of the second line and I'm on the fourth."

"I could see why people resisted child labor laws," Mrs. Pratt grumbled half-heartedly. "Their little fingers are better suited to this kind of work. Mine were made to turn pages and lift pieces of chocolate to my mouth."

"Can you picture Fitz and Hem doing this?" Jane asked with a grin. "I *could* see them switching the *p*s and *q*s in every box, however."

Their laughter was raucous enough to draw attention from neighboring tables. Still smiling, Jane got back to work. She was thoroughly enjoying this workshop. Not only was she learning new information about books, but she was also clearing her mind. She knew this would be beneficial when it came time to think about the murder investigation again.

The workshop participants finished setting their type at different times, and a dozen people had already stepped away from the letterpress carrying beautiful poems printed on thick, oversized paper. These were put on racks to dry, and the guests returned to their seats to chat with their friends.

Once Jane's broadside was on a drying rack, she made a beeline for the Robert Harley members and quietly asked to join them. She knew that the empty chair at their table had been meant for Bart. Even after the group invited her to sit, she hesitated to take Bart's seat, but Levi got to his feet and pulled out the chair for her.

"Please," he said. "We could use the company."

Jane asked after their poems. All four members read their poems to her, which lightened the mood. It also led to a discussion about the Pre-Raphaelite dinner.

"I know it won't be the same without Bart," Jane said, addressing the group as a whole. "But he'd want you to savor every moment of this conference, wouldn't he?"

"He would," agreed Rosemary. "He enjoyed seeing others enjoying themselves. Must have been why he loved you buffoons so much."

This remark was directed at the Sullivan brothers, who responded with bittersweet smiles.

"We balanced each other out. Like weights on a scale," Aaron said. "Bart was serious, studious, and careful. Austin and I were the opposite. Bart taught us to care about our education—something our parents and teachers never managed to do. We could never repay him for that gift."

"And we like to think we helped him realize that he had

the power to control his life," Austin said. "A terrible thing happened to him, but he didn't have to keep letting it happen to him. He held the key to his happiness. We believed in him long before he was the Book Doctor."

Aaron nodded. "We believed in each other. The three of us. That's what I mean by balancing each other out. We were good for each other."

"To our parents and their peers, Aaron and I were spoiled brats who'd never amount to anything. We proved them wrong. And Bart?" Austin smiled though his eyes were growing moist. "Almost everyone predicted that he'd end up in a psych ward—that he'd never be able to find his own way. But he did. He found his passion and he followed it. Not only that, but he shared it with us along the way. Lucky for us."

Seeing that his brother was becoming emotional, Aaron squeezed his arm.

"You three were like the Pre-Raphaelite brotherhood," Rosemary said. "Instead of pursuing a new style of paint- ing, you sought to celebrate and preserve rare books. And then, you found Levi. He became the fourth brother."

"And you became the fifth," Austin said with a wink. "Because it's hard for me to think of you as a sister. You're more of a library goddess."

The men beamed at Rosemary. She colored prettily and rose from her chair. "I'm off to have my poem printed. Levi? Are you ready too?"

Levi said that he was and followed Rosemary to the front of the room.

"Ms. Steward, Austin and I were hoping for the chance to speak with you alone," Aaron said. Seeming even more troubled than before, he kept clasping and unclasping his hands. "Earlier today, the four of us met with the sheriff. He seems very capable, but something isn't right about the way Bart . . . went. He's always been healthy. If he had an illness—anything other than his latex allergy—he would have told us."

Austin looked at Jane. "It's true. We're closer to him than anyone. We've known him since we were kids."

"And were things always friendly between you three?" Jane asked. "Forgive me, but I can't imagine you two as teenagers, hanging out with the quirky boy who had to be first in line and who hated odd numbers."

The Sullivans stared at the table in unconcealed shame.

"We weren't nice to him at first," Austin admitted sheepishly. "We teased him. We wanted to fit in so badly that we were probably meaner to him than the other kids."

Aaron passed his hands over his face. "I still feel terrible about those days. We were such jerks. But we changed." He glanced at his brother. "I guess it's more accurate to say that Bart changed us. We were going to fail out of school, so we offered to pay him to tutor us."

"Except he didn't want money. He wanted us to be nice. That was the payment he asked for," Austin said. "We agreed, and within a few months, we actually became invested in our schoolwork. More than that, we respected Bart's cleverness, toughness, and integrity. From that time on, we had his back. If anyone messed with Bart Baylor, they'd have to answer to the Sullivan brothers."

"I wish we'd had his back last night," Aaron said, and turned his head to hide his expression of agony.

However, Jane saw his face. She saw the pain written across it.

As she left the ballroom, she felt very conflicted.

Bart was like a brother to them, she thought. *Could they betray their brother for money?*

Unfortunately, she knew the answer to that question. She also knew that the grief the brothers were exhibiting could be something other than grief.

It could very well be guilt.

Chapter Twelve

While Jane was setting type, Sheriff Evans had been busy investigating. According to Butterworth, he'd searched all of the Robert Harley Society member's guest rooms. Having gained permission from the guests that morning, he, Phelps, and Emory inspected every nook and cranny, but found nothing of interest other than a note on Levi's writing desk. The note cited an estimate of the current market value of the exhumed cookbook.

Jane listened to Butterworth's summary with reluctance. She'd just come from afternoon tea with her family. It had been such a lovely diversion to listen to Hem and Fitz talk about fishing with Uncle Aloysius and to watch Aunt Octavia serve Muffet Cat a saucer of whipped cream, that Jane had wanted to linger at the table for hours.

Normally, she restricted her teatime treats to a single pastry or two cookies. She'd overindulged today, succumbing to the temptations of Mrs. Hubbard's two-bite apple scones, pear tart, and butter cookie sandwiches layered with raspberry jam. Having downed two cups of tea along with these heavenly pastries, Jane was feeling somewhat torpid.

Despite her desire to evade her duties, Jane touched her

locket and thought of the generations of Guardians who'd come before her. Her lethargy vanished.

"Would you pay five figures for a deteriorated book?" she asked Butterworth. "I don't care if it's the last copy on earth, it can't be worth that much in its current state. Or, in its previous state, I should say. Now that the writing is legible, it might be worth a small fortune."

"Precisely," Butterworth said. "But Mr. Ross wasn't aware that ours was a bound copy of the manuscript with hidden ink. Or was he?"

Jane considered this disturbing possibility. "Is Mr. Ross facing financial hardship?"

"None that Mr. Sinclair can find. Mr. Ross's business earns a handsome profit each year and he's judicious with his personal funds." Butterworth contemplated for a moment before adding, "I don't think he's motivated by money. Prestige is another matter. Each time Mr. Ross acquires an extremely rare book to sell in one of his shops, he gains prestige. Judging by his interview with the sheriff, that's what matters to Levi Ross."

"Even if that's true, Bart's death doesn't grant Mr. Ross possession of our cookbook. He can't sell it. Bart's passing simply removes someone with knowledge about *Mrs. Tanner's Everyday Receipts* from the picture."

Butterworth's shoulders rose and fell in the ghost of a shrug. "Knowledge is power. Not many people were aware of the book's secret."

"One of Bart's friends might be a book thief," Jane whispered. "They'll have to be watched around the clock. The Sullivan brothers. Levi. Even Rosemary."

"Not only did they know of the cookbook's secret, they were also familiar with Mr. Baylor's habits," Butterworth said. "Who else would be able to swap his gloves for gloves that were identical in every way except that the imposter gloves were lined with cyanide powder?"

Jane raised a finger. "What about the accessibility of the murder weapon? It can't be easy to obtain cyanide."

"Surprisingly, it is not difficult to acquire." Butterworth pulled a sheet of paper from the breast pocket of his uniform jacket. "There are several websites offering cyanide powder for sale. The quantities are small. However, they are large enough to suit the murderer's purpose. Obtaining a fake credit card is a simple task as well. Gone are the days of risky, back alley transactions. These have been replaced by marketplaces on the Dark Web. One can purchase almost anything using untraceable currency called bitcoins. The accessibility of illegal drugs and documents leaves us with no lead on the murder weapon."

"Even so, we should share this information with Sheriff Evans." Suddenly, an expression of dismay crossed Jane's face. "How will we explain the sudden appearance of words in the cookbook? The sheriff saw the book in its previous, blank-page state. I didn't mention Bart's hidden ink theory to him nor ask his permission to experiment on what's sure to become a key piece of evidence in his murder investigation."

Butterworth mulled over this conundrum. "You could say that you accidentally spilled tea on the book and the tea revealed writing. This happy accident led you to research invisible inks from the nineteenth century and to proceed with Mr. Sterling's experiment. It's probably best to confess now and emphasize that you were only trying to help. As I recall, Sheriff Evans asked for assistance researching this book."

Jane did as Butterworth suggested. Though Sheriff Evans looked dubious when Jane spun her ridiculous story about an accidental spill, he was too fascinated by the ruddy handwriting to question her.

"Food manufacturing and books. Seems to be the running theme," he said while examining the cookbook in the privacy of the Henry James Library.

"Sinclair is looking into the three companies behind the book's publication," Jane said. "What we *do* know is that it's very rare. Because this book is one of, if not *the* only surviving copy, it's probably quite valuable. Especially now that its words have been brought to light." Jane shot a brief glance at the spidery letters. "The killer may have known about the hidden ink all along. And of the book's worth. If he intends to steal it, he might have deemed it necessary to eliminate anyone possessing similar knowledge. That unfortunate person was Bart."

The sheriff creased his brows in thought. "There's a way to put your theory to the test."

"Yes," Jane said without the slightest hesitation. "We can set a trap with *The Devil's Receipts* serving as bait."

Evans stared at the cookbook. "If we can use the devil to catch a demon, we will."

After Jane and the sheriff outlined a plan, Jane went home to make supper for the boys.

When presented with his bowl of chicken noodle casserole, Hem blurted, "I wish Mr. Edwin would cook for us!"

Fitz eyed his bowl with unconcealed dislike. "Me too. I bet he never makes casseroles."

Jane scowled at her sons. "Maybe not, but you have home-cooked meals every night. For that, you should be grateful. You *should* simply thank the person who cooked for you and keep your negative comments to yourselves."

Hem was instantly contrite. "Sorry, Mom. You're a good cook. It's just that Mr. Edwin just makes everything fun. Remember how he showed us how to sear steaks?"

"Or flip omelets?" Fitz added. "Plus, he tells stories when he cooks."

Jane realized that she'd been so preoccupied with murder that she'd barely spoken to the twins since she got home.

She normally bonded with her boys in the evenings. They'd talk over supper, watch television together, and wrap up the night by listening to an audio book while they worked a jigsaw puzzle. On colder nights, all three of them would change into their pajamas, snuggle on Jane's bed, and read until it was time for the twins to go to sleep.

"I can tell you a story about invisible ink," Jane said. "I'll use vanilla ice cream and chocolate sauce to illustrate my point. When I'm done, you can eat the ice cream. How does that sound?"

The boys cheered and attacked their casseroles with gusto.

Jane told them how the book that had been found along with Oliver, the skeleton, appeared to be filled with blank pages. As she described Sterling's discovery and the spidery handwriting done in reddish-brown ink, the twins hung on her every word.

"What did the writing say?" Fitz asked breathlessly. "Is it a spell book?"

"Or directions to a buried treasure?" Hem wanted to know.

Laughing, Jane put the lid back on the ice cream carton. "It's a book of recipes."

The boys exchanged disappointed glances. "Why would someone hide recipes? That's dumb."

"Actually, some of them were dangerous," Jane said, lowering her voice to a whisper. "They included poisonous ingredients. They're *still* dangerous; so don't tell anyone what I've told you. Pinkie swears?"

The boys performed their most solemn of oaths before devouring their ice cream. After putting their bowls in the dishwasher, they launched into a debate over which jigsaw puzzle to begin next.

"Let's do rock, paper, scissors," Hem said. "Two out of three wins."

Jane finished cleaning the kitchen and joined the boys at the table. Fitz, who'd won the right to choose the puzzle, had selected one of his favorites. The puzzle featured the covers of R. L. Stine's Goosebumps books. Jane's gaze was drawn to a particular cover that showed a mansion in purple with a blood-red door. It was titled, *Welcome to Dead House*.

Pretty soon, that's what people will call Storyton Hall, she thought glumly.

Fitz put his small hand over hers. "Are you okay, Mom? You look sad."

She pulled him in for a hug. "Sad? No way. This is my favorite time of the day. Being with my boys is like having a giant sundae with sprinkles and a cherry on top." She smiled at her sons. "Fitz, why don't you fire up the audiobook? I'm ready for a tale of adventure."

The twins were barely settled in their beds when Jane's cell phone rang. Betty was calling from the Cheshire Cat.

"Kyle just left," Betty said. Her voice was quivering with excitement.

Jane glanced at the clock on her nightstand. "Is he calling it an early night?"

Betty snorted. "Hardly. He started drinking at five. Three hours later, he paid his tab and wobbled out of the pub."

"Was Bob able to get anything out of him?"

"Bob's a wonderful listener, but he's not a great talker. Bless his heart," she added loyally. "So I took over. I told Kyle how fascinated I was by the archaeological investigation— which is no lie—and asked what happened when the boys first signaled for him to stop his machine. The question made him squirm on his bar stool."

Jane sensed that Betty was drawing out the scene. She couldn't blame her. It made for dramatic storytelling, but she was in no mood for drama. "And? Were you able to confirm that he picked something out of the dirt?"

"Not exactly," Betty said, sounding deflated. "He clearly didn't want to discuss that day and shut down the conversation by grumbling about the project being on hold. Luckily, when he was on his fourth or fifth round, a bunch of locals showed up. It's our monthly trivia contest night, so the pub was pretty full, and several villagers grilled Kyle about the Storyton Hall skeleton."

Jane could picture the locals gathering around Kyle in hopes of learning juicy tidbits to mete out the next day in their shops. "Who were some of these villagers?"

"Sam from Hilltop Stables, all three Hogg brothers, Magnus and the cook from Daily Bread, Captain Phil, and Wes from Spokes. Randall was there too. He wasn't able to deliver any lectures because everyone was focused on Kyle. In exchange for a beer, he offered to describe the skeleton. After another, he exaggerated his role in discovering the bones. I was mighty upset that Kyle failed to mention the twins, but I let it slide."

Jane smiled into the phone. "It was nice of you to think of the boys."

"Well, they're such darlings!" Betty exclaimed fondly. "But back to Kyle. He droned on until eventually, he ran out of things to say. The rest of the men settled down at tables to wait for the trivia contest to start."

Jane sighed. "Why do I feel like your tale is almost over?"

"It is, and it isn't," Betty said cagily. "You see, over the course of the evening, I noticed Kyle touching the front pocket of his shirt. He wore a button-down in khaki canvas. The kind of shirt with pockets that have flaps. Oh, I wish I had Mabel's description for fashion."

"It's okay, I know what you mean," Jane assured her friend.

Betty released a small breath. "Here's the crux of it, Jane.

I could see that something was in his left breast pocket. I have no idea what it was. All I know is that Kyle would repeatedly brush his fingers over the bottom of that pocket like he needed to make sure whatever he had in there hadn't gone missing."

"Did he seem to make that motion when the subject of the skeletal remains was raised?"

"Yes," Betty said. "There's one more thing. When he asked for his bill, I might have made an error in judgment by pretending to have heard a rumor about an artifact disappearing from the site. I even went on to say that I hoped the culprit wasn't a Storyton Hall staff member, seeing as I'm fond of the ones I know, and I didn't want anyone to face jail time due to a spur-of-the-moment mistake."

Jane was confused. "That sounds like a clever ruse. Why are you questioning your judgment?"

"Kyle's face went a bit green after my speech," Betty said. "I don't know if it was the beer, a guilty conscience, or both. He didn't beg for a ride home as usual. He simply walked out of the pub, past all the yowling cats gathered around the Cheshire Cat statue, and turned left."

"Left?" Jane asked, wanting to be sure she'd heard correctly.

"Left," Betty repeated. "Toward Storyton Hall."

The Fins were summoned to Jane's house. After a flurried exchange of whispers in her kitchen, it was decided that Butterworth and Sinclair would remain with the sleeping twins while Jane, Lachlan, and Sterling set off to find Kyle Stuyvesant.

"How will we convince him to show us what's in his pocket?" Jane asked Sterling once they were underway.

Without taking his eyes off the road, Sterling said,

"We'll offer him a ride. If he refuses, Mr. Lachlan and I will encourage him to accept. And by encourage, I mean force. Then, we'll take him to the dig site and insist that he hand over what he stole."

Having no better ideas, Jane nodded. Because she was sitting between the two Fins on the bench seat of a pickup truck used by Storyton Hall's groundskeepers, she had to put her palm against the dashboard to keep from ramming against one of them with every curve in the road.

The night seemed darker than previous nights. A cool wind had sprung up and it carried the scent of impending rain.

Lachlan glanced out his window. "There's no moon. It'll be easy to pass our guy if he sticks to the shadows. If he ducks behind a tree, we might never spot him."

"He should be beyond Broken Arm Bend by now. And you'll spot him. You have raptor vision." Sterling used the truck's high beams to illuminate the road ahead. The light bounced off a pair of large, yellow eyes peering out at them from the gloom.

Jane pointed at the shoulder. "Watch for the deer."

Sterling eased up on the gas.

Suddenly, there was a disturbance in the underbrush bordering the road and a massive buck leapt in front of the truck. Sterling hit the brakes and the truck came to a rough stop.

The buck, unperturbed, turned to stare at them. At that moment, the moon emerged from behind the clouds and the magnificent animal was bathed in a radiant white light.

Jane's breath caught in her throat. To her, the deer had transformed into the mystical stag as described in the Harry Potter novels, *The Chronicles of Narnia*, or *The Hobbit*. It stood completely still, its proud head held high, as if its massive antlers were made of air.

And then, it bounded across the road and sailed over the split-rail fence, vanishing as abruptly as it had appeared.

"That's the biggest buck I've ever seen," Lachlan murmured in awe.

Sterling hadn't tracked the deer's departure. His gaze remained fixed on the place where it had burst from the cover of the underbrush and surrounding trees.

Jane now saw what Sterling saw. There was a shadow that seemed darker than the others near the roadside. It was as if the night had congealed into a man-sized lump.

Man-sized, Jane thought with a start. She was on the verge of telling Sterling to turn off the ignition when he pulled the truck to the side of the road.

"Stay here," he told Jane. He then asked Lachlan, "You good?"

"I'm good," Lachlan said, peering straight ahead.

The two men jumped from the truck with the quiet grace of big cats. They crept forward, their shoulders nearly touching. The moment they reached the dark shape, their postures changed and they visibly relaxed. Seeing this, Jane knew that there was no immediate danger. She grabbed a flashlight from the glove box and walked toward the men.

Sterling immediately turned and called out, "Wait there, Miss Jane. You might not want to see this."

Jane's feet continued to carry her forward. As she closed the distance between herself and the Fins, the lump on the ground became more defined. She recognized a booted foot. Next, she identified a hand with the fingers partially curled.

"A body," she whispered. "Is it . . . ?" Her voice seemed out of place among the insect sawing and other night noises. Somewhere in the distance, an owl hooted. It was a lonely, plaintive sound.

"It's Mr. Stuyvesant," Sterling said in a hushed tone.

Jane glanced to where Lachlan knelt on the ground next to Kyle's body. "He's dead, isn't he?"

"Imagine what one of those deer would have looked like had I hit it with the truck," Sterling said. "It appears that Mr. Stuyvesant met such a fate."

Jane took another step forward. "A hit and run? That's so cruel. What if he was alive after it happened? Alive and suffering. What if it wasn't accidental?" After a long moment of silence, she asked, "Did you search his pockets?"

"Mr. Lachlan?" Sterling turned to his colleague.

"If he left the bar with anything in his pocket, it's gone now," Lachlan said. "All he had on him was his wallet and cell phone. I'm checking out his phone now. The screen is cracked, but it's still operational."

Jane touched Sterling's arm to reclaim his attention. "If this man is dead because of what he took from the construction site, then his death is tied to Storyton Hall. And to me. I'm not going to shy away from his body because it could upset me. He might have taken something that didn't belong to him, but he shouldn't have been mowed down and left on the side of the road like an animal. For all we know, he was headed our way to return what he'd taken."

"I suppose we can give Mr. Stuyvesant the benefit of the doubt," Sterling said. "If you insist on seeing him, let's get it over with."

Jane gripped her flashlight tightly and moved with a confidence she didn't feel.

She trained her gaze on Lachlan's face. He was preoccupied with Kyle's phone and the illuminated screen cast an eerie glow over his features. Despite his spectral appearance, Jane stared at him until she was ready to look down at the dead man.

Sterling was right. In the seconds it took for Jane's mind to comprehend that the bloodied, twisted, and misshapen thing on the ground had once been a man, her body was already reacting.

Pushing past Lachlan, Jane ran toward the forest and tried to draw in deep breaths. It was no use. Bending over, she was violently sick to her stomach.

When her retching finally ceased, Sterling offered her a tissue.

Jane leaned against a tree until the nausea receded. "We can't leave him like this," she whispered. Her throat was raw and there was a foul taste in her mouth. She wanted nothing more than to get home, clean up, and crawl into bed. None of these options were acceptable, however, so Sterling fetched her a water bottle from the truck.

"How will we explain our presence if you call the sheriff?" he asked, handing her the water. "I'm assuming that's what you intend to do."

"I'll stick as close to the truth as I can, but I couldn't live with myself if we drove away and left him here like a piece of trash." Jane pulled out her phone. "There's also a driver on the loose who committed vehicular manslaughter tonight. Sheriff Evans needs to be made aware of that."

Sterling put his hand over Jane's, preventing her from dialing. "There's vehicular manslaughter, which could be accidental, and there's murder. Seeing as Mr. Stuyvesant's pockets are empty, I'd say the latter is true."

"I think I know what he had in his pocket." Lachlan held up Kyle Stuyvesant's damaged phone. "Let me show you."

Still feeling unbalanced, Jane suggested they move away from Kyle's body.

Back at the truck, Lachlan cradled the phone in his gloved hands. At first glance, it was difficult to make sense of the image because the cracks in the screen created distortions, but Jane soon realized that it was a photograph of a ring.

"It's a signet ring," she said. "Gold, maybe? With a coat

of arms. I'll take a picture and we can research it later. I don't know if it means anything, but it looks old." Using her phone, Jane captured an image of the ring and then called the emergency operator to report Kyle Stuyvesant's death.

Sheriff Evans arrived with Doc Lydgate and a middle-aged deputy whom Jane had never met. The lawmen focused on Jane, Sterling, and Lachlan while Doc Lydgate examined the body.

"Did you see any other vehicles on the road?" Evans asked.

"No," Jane said. She'd already explained how she and her two staff members had found Kyle, and she expected the question about other cars to be the sheriff's last. It wasn't.

The sheriff closed his notebook and frowned. "Why didn't you mention what your sons saw at the construction site earlier?"

The censure in his tone wasn't lost on Jane. "If they'd been sure, I would have. But they weren't, and I didn't want to falsely accuse this man of stealing from what became an archaeological site. Mr. Stuyvesant could have been picking up a penny, for all the twins knew."

"I don't think he was hit by a car over a penny," the sheriff said tersely. He turned away from Jane. "Doc? What have we got?"

"Death by blunt force injury," was the reply. "Multiple broken bones. Both legs. Pelvis. The skull is also fractured. A brain hemorrhage is likely the cause of death. There's a great deal of blood loss from the head wound. Some from the deep lacerations on his lower legs as well." His eyes met Jane's. "Did you know this man?"

Jane shook her head. "Not personally. He was involved in the spa construction project. He operated the earth-mover."

Doc Lydgate got to his feet and addressed the sheriff. "It won't be much comfort to his family or friends, but the end came quickly. He may not have been aware of what happened at all. With the severity of his head injury, it was lights out the moment he struck the ground. He didn't suffer. That's my belief. The ME will tell you more."

Sheriff Evans offered his thanks and then fell silent, watching a pair of headlights approaching along the dark road.

"It's the ambulance," said the deputy, and waved at the oncoming vehicle.

The driver pulled over at a safe distance from Kyle's body. Though he turned the engine off, he left the head-lamps on, and the dual beams illuminated the woods on the opposite side of the road.

Jane thought of the magnificent deer. If only Kyle had possessed a wild animal's sense of danger or the ability to leap into the tree cover when threatened by the approach of a speeding car.

As she searched the woods for signs of life, it began to rain.

"Damn it all," the sheriff grumbled. "Just what I need when I'm trying to find and photograph tire tracks."

"There are no skid marks," Lachlan said. "I checked. I wanted to know if the driver attempted to slow down. There's no indication that someone applied the brakes. If anything, the driver swerved across the lane and struck Mr. Stuyvesant full force. The car must have sustained notice-able damage. Mr. Stuyvesant wasn't a small man."

Sheriff Evans eyed Lachlan warily. "How do you know these things?"

"From my time in the army, sir." Lachlan met the sher-iff's gaze without flinching.

For a moment, it seemed like Evans would ask more questions. However, the rain began falling harder and faster and he muttered more expletives before waving at Jane, Sterling, and Lachlan. "You can go now. I'll see you in the morning." To his deputy, he said, "We'll do what we can to capture the scene. After this, we're off to the Cheshire Cat."

The deputy, who wasn't one of the department's sharper minds, asked, "For a drink, sir?"

"That would be nice, but no," the sheriff said, and signaled to the ambulance crew to unload their gurney.

Jane, Sterling, and Lachlan climbed into the pickup truck. They didn't speak on the return trip to Storyton Hall. The sound of the raindrops battering the roof and windshield lulled them into a gloomy silence.

Jane kept her gaze on the passing farmland. She'd love to see the herd of deer once more—to watch the buck racing through the field of tall grass. She knew the sight of such beauty would help restore her flagging spirit. However, the field was empty of deer or any other sign of life.

There was only the rain, sliding sideways down the truck windows like a flow of tears.

Chapter Thirteen

The next morning, the conference goers attended either a presentation on state-of-the-art archival storage methods or a lecture called The Evolution of Ink. After lunch, they had the afternoon to themselves. Many had booked archery lessons, tours of Storyton Mews, fishing excursions with Storyton Outfitters, or had rented bicycles through Spokes. The rest, Jane suspected, would seek a comfortable chair in one of the reading rooms and while away several blissful hours lost in a good book.

Jane was on her second cup of coffee when Sinclair asked to see her in his office. To say that she hadn't slept well the previous night was an understatement. When she'd first seen her face in her bathroom mirror, she decided she looked like one of George R. R. Martin's White Walkers.

She'd tried to brighten her washed-out appearance with makeup, but it was difficult to conceal a glassy-eyed gaze, and Sinclair noticed it at once.

"Jane, my dear." He ushered her into his office and pulled out his chair for her. "Can I get you anything?"

"It's a bit early for whiskey, so how about a murder suspect?"

Adopting a hangdog expression, Sinclair asked, "Will

information on the image from Mr. Stuyvesant's phone do for now?"

Jane said that it would and Sinclair took a seat next to her. He directed her attention to his computer screen where he called up an enlarged image of the ring.

"As you inferred, this is a signet ring. When compared to rings of similar style, shape, and ornamentation, my guess is that it belongs to the neoclassical era. This era occurred between 1760 and 1830 and featured classical motifs borrowed from architecture. Greek columns, for example."

"The design looks very medieval to me," Jane said. She wasn't trying to be argumentative, but she recalled no references to a coat of arms in her Greek or Roman history classes.

"Be that as it may, this type of ring, called an intaglio armorial seal ring, was not purely ornamental. It was pressed into warm wax to create a signature. The seal on this ring bears the owner's family crest."

Jane glanced at Sinclair with interest. "It's definitely a man's ring?"

"Yes. A woman's ring could certainly have been made of carnelian, but based on my research, a ladies ring from this period would more likely feature a cameo or an ivory miniature than a crest."

Jane scooted her chair a little closer and peered intently at the screen. "Even with the cracks disrupting the image, I can see a helmeted knight at the top of the shield. What are those things on either side of the shield? Plumes coming out of the helmet?"

Sinclair nodded. "That's my assumption. In the center, we have an armored hand pointing to a column. The hand represents leadership and the column symbolizes fortitude and constancy."

"Sinclair, I don't mean to be rude, but all I care about is

whom this ring belonged to," Jane said impatiently. "Were you able to find that answer?"

"*I* wasn't, but a friend of mine is a heraldry expert and he recognized the family represented by the crest. The family is of Nordic origin and has British *and* Germanic crests. The armorial seal ring on Mr. Stuyvesant's phone bears the German crest of the Frank family."

Jane slowly exhaled. "Otto Frank. He was born in Germany. It was only later in life that he went to London to work and study. That explains the mixed coinage found with his remains. I bet he kept the German coin for sentimental reasons. Or for luck. It was a tie to his homeland—something he could touch or look at when he felt lonely."

A hush fell on the office as Jane and Sinclair became lost in thoughts of a man they'd never known. A man whose body had likely been buried in secret in what had once been Storyton Hall's rose garden.

"The ring was probably given to him by his father," Sinclair said, finally breaking the silence. "If any of Doctor Frank's personal correspondence or the articles written for the *Times* remain, we have a chance of matching his seal to those documents."

"But how to prove the ring came from the same grave as the bones? That is *if* we can successfully retrieve it from the person who used a car as a murder weapon."

"Celia will find soil remnants in the crevices; I have no doubt of that." Sinclair's gaze turned cold. "However, it's up to us to hunt down the assailant."

Feeling a renewed sense of frustration, Jane excused herself and walked into the Henry James Library. She ran her fingertips along the book spines. The feel of the supple leather brought her immediate comfort.

Jane moved past row upon row of books until she reached a section on the library's eastern wall. Suddenly, she was standing at eye level with another Frank. Not Otto, but Anne. She didn't have Sinclair's memory for quotes, but as she looked at the poppy-red spine of *Anne Frank: The Diary of a Young Girl*, Jane could hear the words of one of history's most courageous heroines flow from her lips, "'People are just people, and all people have faults and shortcomings, but all of us are born with a basic goodness.'"

Sensing Sinclair behind her, Jane turned to him. "Maybe Kyle took a photo of that ring because he planned to sell it. He may have posted it online and the killer saw the photo and contacted Kyle to request more details." Jane gazed across the room, addressing the faceless, nameless murderer. "But why? Why do you need Otto Frank to remain unidentified?"

"There is another, more disturbing possibility to consider," Sinclair said.

Jane absently laid her hand over a group of books before asking, "Which is?"

"That we're dealing with two killers and two separate crimes." With a frown, Sinclair went on, "The discovery of a decrepit book shouldn't have precipitated a murder. If the crime was committed in the name of possessing the book, we'll catch the killer tonight by using it as bait. If one subscribes to Miss Frank's belief that all people are born with a basic goodness and are led astray by their faults and shortcomings, then Mr. Baylor's killer has been led astray by greed or pride."

Jane reflected for a moment. "What you're saying is that it doesn't make sense for Bart's killer to target Kyle. Who cares about the identity of those old bones? Unless—!" Jane grabbed Sinclair's hand. "Unless this crime isn't about greed or pride at all. Sheriff Evans said it himself. The repeating theme is food adulteration. I know we're talking about different centuries, but a big corporation is a big corporation. Money and power can corrupt. That hasn't changed over time."

Sinclair pointed at a biography of Charles Dickens by G. K. Chesterton. "Indeed."

"We're obviously missing key pieces of evidence," Jane said. Her lack of sleep and fear over being outsmarted by Bart's killer were filling her with a tension that no book could ease.

"If there's a clue on Mr. Stuyvesant's phone, the sheriff will have it by morning's end." Sinclair squeezed Jane's hand.

Knowing he was trying to instill her with hope, she rewarded him with a smile and left the library.

Despite Bart's death and the discovery of a body in the garden, Storyton Hall was still a working resort, which meant Jane had to attend to her duties. After pouring her third cup of coffee from the urn in the lobby, she greeted the front desk clerks and was about to head to her office when one of the clerks cleared her throat.

"Ms. Steward," said Sue, one of Storyton's most amiable clerks. "The postmistress is here. She made it clear that this is a quick visit, but that she had to see you in person." Sue shrugged. "That's all I could get out of her. She wouldn't even accept coffee or tea."

Jane jerked a thumb toward her office. "She's waiting for me in there?"

Sue nodded and Jane continued walking, her lips pursed in puzzlement. Nandi, the local postmistress, loved a good, long chat. She loved to tell newcomers how she was part Zulu and part British and that she was named after Shaka Zulu's warrior mother. This usually led to a history lesson on Shaka Zulu's establishment of an all-female fighting force. Nandi also knew a vast array of African folktales and never failed to entertain the children waiting in line with stories of Anansi the spider, leopards and tortoises, elephants and juju trees, or kings and their magic drums.

It was completely out of character for Nandi to say that she didn't have time to linger, and Jane was worried that more bad news was about to land on her lap.

"Good morning, Nandi," she said, infusing her voice with a cheerfulness she didn't feel. "What a lovely surprise."

Nandi didn't smile or return the compliment, which made Jane even more anxious. "I'm not replacing Monroe as your mailman," Nandi said. "I've come because I made a promise to Mr. Alcott."

Jane grew very still.

Nandi reached into her uniform jacket and withdrew a postcard. "You know I like to spin a good yarn, but I can keep my mouth shut when it matters. I promised to put anything Mr. Alcott mailed to the post office directly into your hand. So I'm doing it. Please hold out your hand."

Jane complied and Nandi got to her feet and reverently laid the postcard on Jane's palm. She then smiled and it occurred to Jane that the postmistress was relieved to have completed her task. She was now free to be her lighthearted self. After wishing Jane a wonderful day, she showed herself out, closing the door behind her.

Alone in her office, her cup of coffee totally forgotten, Jane held the postcard with quivering fingers.

"Edwin," she said.

Her eyes filled with unbidden tears.

It had been too long since she and the man she loved had connected. So much had happened since Edwin had left Storyton—since he and Jane had shared a meal, a laugh, or a touch—that the receipt of this simple card made her ache for him.

She gave in to her feelings of longing and loneliness. For a few moments, in the privacy of her office, she wasn't the

Guardian of Storyton Hall. She was just a woman missing her man.

After a time, she grew calmer. She dried her eyes and looked at the image on the postcard.

"Where are you, Edwin?" she asked, though she knew the picture could be misleading. Her lover could be miles away—another continent even—from the place the card had been posted.

A lifelong fan of Egyptology, Jane recognized the image as a scene from *The Book of the Dead*. It was a scene of judgment, but the soul being judged had been a good man during his lifetime and would continue his journey to paradise.

"Not the most romantic choice," Jane murmured, flipping the card over to discover that it had been mailed from Alexandria.

Her eyes hungrily took in Edwin's elegant script:

*A strange passion is moving in my head. My heart has become a **bird**, which searches in the sky. Every part of me goes in different directions. Is it really so that the one I love is Everywhere?*

Jane read the lines again and again. They were beautiful, but she didn't think they were Edwin's. Turning to her computer, she entered the first line into Google's search box and got an instant hit.

"Rumi." She grinned. "I should have known."

The words, unlike the picture on the postcard, were definitely romantic. But Edwin hadn't written anything personal. Not a single thing. This concerned her on two levels. Did he need to be secretive because he was in danger? Or was he incapable of expressing how he felt about the woman he supposedly loved?

That's not it. She immediately pushed her doubt aside. *He's expressed his love openly and honestly dozens of times. Something else is going on.*

Examining the lines of poetry more closely, Jane noticed that the word "bird" was slightly darker than the rest of the words. It was as if Edwin had gone over it twice with his fountain pen.

Jane's instincts told her that this was no accident. Edwin was sending her a message about a bird. But what bird?

Flipping the postcard over again, Jane scanned the bird-headed gods in the tomb scene as well as the much smaller bird hieroglyphs. Her eyes moved from left to right, very slowly, until she thought she saw something odd.

She pulled out a magnifying glass from the top drawer of her desk and held it over Thoth's foot. Thoth, the god with the head of an ibis and the body of a human, didn't usually have a symmetrical heart symbol hovering above his big toe. In fact, this symbol wasn't Egyptian at all. Following the heart symbol was a vulture glyph.

Turning back to her computer, Jane searched for an online hieroglyphs translator. She'd used these in the past and knew they weren't completely accurate, but they'd point her in the right direction. According to the translator, the vulture glyph represented the letter *E*.

Heart plus E meant *Love, Edwin.* Jane was sure of it. But what about the other symbols he'd inserted above those two?

With careful scrutiny, Jane realized that Edwin had added the entire column to Thoth's left. She plugged each symbol into the translator and then waited for the result. When it appeared on her screen, the initial thrill over having discovered Edwin's hidden message quickly morphed into cold dread.

BEWARE OF FALSE FIN

What did Edwin mean? What false Fin? Surely, he wasn't referring to Butterworth, Sinclair, or Sterling. Those men had been a part of Jane's life since her girlhood. Could he be warning her against Landon Lachlan? He was the newest Fin, having come aboard following Gavin's retirement. But Gavin had handpicked Lachlan. The men were blood relatives, for crying out loud.

Jane trusted her Fins with her life. More significantly, she trusted them with the lives of her family. Not one of them would betray her. Of that, she was certain. If any man had the potential to let her down, that man was Edwin.

Yanking open her desk drawer, she swept the magnifying glass and the postcard on top of a messy collection of pens, pencils, paper clips, sticky notepads, and lip gloss. Slamming the drawer shut, she gripped her computer mouse, determined to focus on her daily tasks.

At first, it was impossible to concentrate. Inventory documents and budget spreadsheets blurred as she kept gazing off into the distance. But eventually, she came to the realization that neither the Rudyard Kipling Café nor the Madame Bovary Dining Room would be updating their autumnal menus if she didn't place produce orders from local farmers today. All it took was an image of Mrs. Hubbard's face when one of the braver members of the kitchen staff informed her that there'd be no Granny Smith apples for her famed Apple Brown Betty or pumpkins for her curried pumpkin soup, to shake Jane from her stupor.

By lunchtime, she'd checked several items off her to-do list and had almost forgotten about Edwin's postcard.

Almost.

In an effort to turn her thoughts toward the investigation,

Jane asked Sinclair to meet her in her great-aunt and -uncle's apartments.

"This is a treat!" Uncle Aloysius met her at the door. He gave Jane's shoulder an affectionate squeeze and led her into the living room to say hello to Aunt Octavia.

Aunt Octavia tapped her cheek and Jane obediently planted a kiss on the powdered skin. She loved that her great-aunt smelled of magnolia blossoms and old books. Today, however, there was an additional scent. A very strong and rather unpleasant fish odor.

"Have you eaten, dear?" Aunt Octavia asked. "We just finished our lunch, but we could call down for another tray."

"No, thanks. I've had so much coffee that I'm not hungry yet. What did you two eat?"

Aunt Octavia laughed. "Don't play coy—I know you can smell that tuna from a mile off! It's all Muffet Cat's fault. He was a *very* naughty boy and jumped up on my lap just as I was about to take a bite of my favorite sandwich: an open-faced tuna melt with tomatoes and arugula. Simply *divine*!" She made a kissing noise. "Apparently, Muffet Cat concurs. Only I didn't know he was with us. The little devil snuck into our apartment on the delivery cart. Our feline acrobat was balanced on the frame, completely concealed by the tablecloth, and didn't make his move until I was on the verge of my first bite. He frightened me near to *death* and I dropped the whole half sandwich!"

"It bounced once." Uncle Aloysius touched his own chest to demonstrate. "And then, it landed upright on the carpet. Muffet Cat pounced like a wild panther and began gulping it down. He growled too, making it quite clear that he was staking his claim over my wife's lunch."

Jane glanced around. "Where is his Portly Highness now?"

Aunt Octavia gave an amused snort. "He's on the bed, in a tuna-induced coma."

There was a knock on the door and Aloysius let Sinclair into the apartment.

"Oh, so this *isn't* a familial visit?" Aunt Octavia asked Jane, looking hurt.

Taking her aunt's hand, Jane said, "I'd love to spend an afternoon with you. We could drink tea, discuss books, go over the details of the Pre-Raphaelite dinner and dance, and feed Muffet Cat feline breath mints. I really miss our summer afternoons, when the twins were preoccupied with fishing, canoeing, archery, falconry, and their other activities, because it gave me a chance to share a precious hour or so with you and Uncle Aloysius. You're both so important to me. But ever since this rare book conference began and someone was killed, all those lovely stolen moments have become impossible to reclaim."

"Nothing is impossible. Especially not for you, my sweet girl," said Uncle Aloysius.

"I assume you and Sinclair are heading upstairs." Aunt Octavia pointed overhead, her eyes bright with curiosity.

Jane removed her locket. "We are. I want to see if our collection contains any books, published articles, or personal correspondence written by the man buried in our back garden."

"You've identified the skeleton?" Aunt Octavia clapped her hands with glee.

Hating to spoil her aunt's mood, Jane looked to Sinclair for help.

"I wish it were cause for celebration," he said solemnly, and went on to describe the arrow found in Otto Frank's back. Next, he explained how Kyle Stuyvesant had been the victim of a hit-and-run and that the ring taken from his corpse had undoubtedly been buried with Doctor Frank.

"Fins only commit violence if the Guardian or the secret library is threatened," Uncle Aloysius said when Sinclair was finished. "What if those bones belong to someone else altogether? A man who stole the cookbook and Doctor Frank's ring, perhaps. A man who also suffered from rickets and tuberculosis. Those afflictions weren't uncommon during the nineteenth century."

This theory didn't ring true to Jane. "I admit that it's possible, but why would an imposter be buried in the garden? If Frank wasn't murdered, then where did he go? And why bury the cookbook with the body? Why didn't Walter Steward add it to our secret collection?" As she spoke, Jane pressed the book-shaped engraving on her pendant. It sprang open to reveal a key nestled in a bed of velvet.

"That is indeed a mystery," her uncle said. He sounded disappointed.

Aunt Octavia looked deflated. Even the electric orange hue of her batik print housedress seemed duller.

Wanting to restore confidence, Jane said, "That's why we're going up. To search for clues. To find answers. To do the impossible." She smiled first at her uncle and then at her aunt. "You raised me to handle situations like this. It isn't easy, but I can do it. Because I have you, and I have the Fins, I can do it."

She waited until Aunt Octavia returned her smile before making her way into the bedroom and to the back of her aunt's walk-in closet. She was glad to be alone and hoped there'd been nothing telling in her voice or facial expression when she'd mentioned the Fins. For when she had, she'd flashed on an image of Edwin's postcard and of its disturbing hidden message.

She pushed the shoe rack away from the air vent and removed the four screws holding the vent cover in place to reveal a small aperture. And just like that, her mind emptied of all thoughts.

Jane slid her key into the tiny keyhole and turned it clockwise at the same time she turned the metal lever to its right counterclockwise. She heard the sound of something large and heavy moving along the sitting room wall.

After replacing the vent cover and shoe rack, Jane met Sinclair in the sitting room. The bookcase housing Aunt Octavia's prize collection of Meissen porcelain, which was firmly held in place by pieces of wax, had swung away from the wall. It was into this slim, dark opening that Jane slipped, followed by Sinclair.

Jane never tired of the thrill she experienced when she pulled a lever on the wall and the bookcase slid back into place. The lever also activated the emergency lighting. The lights were dim, but they allowed Jane and Sinclair to make their way up the narrow stone staircase into the secret library.

The library was a climate-controlled, waterproof, fireproof room outfitted with metal storage drawers. These looked like those found at a bank, but were designed more like the archival boxes found in the deepest recesses of the Library of Congress.

"I bet Rosemary has seen repositories like this," Jane said to Sinclair.

"And wondrous materials as well," Sinclair said. "In addition to reams of works from presidents, statesmen, and other prominent Americans, the Library of Congress Rare Book and Special Collections Reading Room has a perfect Gutenberg Bible printed on vellum, seventeenth-century publications on cryptography, dime novels, the African-American Pamphlet Collection, and the personal library of Harry Houdini to name a few." He paused and then added, "There's also the Third Reich Collection."

Jane, who'd opened a drawer marked "ephemera" and was frowning over an ad for a "fasting diet" for chubby babies, looked up sharply. "How is that categorized?"

"As one of their collections with unusual provenance."

Gesturing at the wall of drawers in front of her, Jane said, "We have those too. Written records of man at his worst. The Library of Congress is right to preserve and display these things. It's only by studying our history that we can learn from it. If things are hidden or destroyed, aren't history's mistakes more likely to be repeated?" She sighed. "At least, that's what I once thought. Now, I don't know. It seems like whatever decision I make about these materials is wrong. If I sell one item in an effort to share our human story and to improve Storyton Hall, I bring danger our way. On the other hand, if I keep every item locked up here until I pass the mantle to the twins, I risk nothing."

"Faulkner said that 'you cannot swim for new horizons until you have courage to lose sight of the shore.'" Sinclair opened a drawer near the back wall and peered inside. "Ah. This begins the record of Walter Edgerton Steward as Guardian. His son, Cyril, became Guardian after Walter's death. So if you can find the drawer marked with Cyril's signature, the section we'll need to search will be made clear."

Jane moved to the middle of the wall and opened a random drawer. The signature on the bottom of a piece of paper listed the acquisition date and the description of the treasure housed within: an inscribed copy of Christopher Marlowe's *The Massacre at Paris*. The signature belonged to her great-uncle.

Closing the drawer, Jane walked over to Sinclair. "Since we know when Otto Frank fled London, we can concentrate on that time period. We don't have to sift through everything Walter amassed."

"Excellent point," said Sinclair. "And one I should have come up with myself. I'm afraid I've been distracted by thoughts of another doctor."

Jane was stunned by this admission, but hid her surprise because she didn't want to dissuade Sinclair from saying more. "I assume you're referring to Celia. Did you call her about the ring?"

"Yes and yes." Sinclair kept his gaze fixed on the contents of another drawer. "She's en route to Storyton Hall as we speak. I tried to dissuade her, but she wouldn't be deterred. At least, she had the good sense to leave her students behind. Also, the two grad students she left here have completed their work and returned to Charlottesville."

"Then why is she coming?" Jane asked.

Sinclair's fingers, which had been rifling through sheaves of paper like rustling bird wings, fell still. "She read about Mr. Baylor's passing in her local paper. Having heard about Mr. Stuyvesant, she can't stay in her lab when she feels that these events are somehow tied to the discovery of Otto's bones. That's what she said." The look he turned on Jane was one of concern. "When I tried to warn her off, to hint at the danger awaiting anyone who might interfere with the person who stole the ring from Mr. Stuyvesant's pocket, she laughed. She laughed and claimed that she'd been through worse."

Jane didn't know how to respond, and there was nothing to be done in any case. Celia wouldn't be put off. Perhaps, she'd prove to be helpful.

Unless she's in collusion with the killer, came a sudden, unpleasant thought.

"I believe I have it!" Sinclair said. He removed a small, leather-bound book from a drawer. "This, dear Jane, is Doctor Otto Frank's diary."

Jane's relief was so immense that she felt like she was being bathed in sunshine. "Oh, Sinclair! How wonderful!" She gave him a hug. "Let's take it back down to the sitting room, order some food, and start reading."

However, as Sinclair studied the paper that rested on top of the book, his jubilant grin turned into a frown.

"What is it?" Jane asked.

"The diary was written in German. I know several languages, but German isn't one of them." Jane opened her mouth to speak when Sinclair suddenly brightened again. "However, guess who happens to be fluent in German?"

Jane thought she knew the answer, but decided to humor Sinclair. "Who?"

"Doctor Celia Wallace." He spoke her name as if every syllable were a musical note.

Chapter Fourteen

Jane didn't wait for Celia to arrive. She decided to leave Sinclair and the forensic anthropologist alone to have a more intimate meeting.

With the conference attendees dispersed throughout Storyton's manor house, grounds, and village, Jane decided to take advantage of the calm by getting a little fresh air and exercise. She also decided to check in with the sheriff at the station instead of waiting for him to contact her.

After telling Butterworth she was heading into town, Jane filled her thermos with cold water, placed it in the straw basket attached to her handlebars, and began pedaling her bicycle up Storyton Hall's long driveway.

It felt wonderful to be out on a sun-dappled September afternoon. So wonderful that Jane had to shove down feelings of guilt. One of her guests was dead. A second man, who'd been hired to work on the Walt Whitman Spa, was also dead. What right did she have to revel in the beauty of the day? And yet she did. The fields lining the road were painted gold and green and masses of honeysuckle vines still clung to the fence rails. As Jane zipped by an enormous clump, the sweet, cloying scent burst into the air like a spritz from a perfume bottle.

She rode past the brown-and-white pinto who had a fondness for apples and called out promises to bring him several, as well as a few carrots, when she next rode out with the twins. After the pony pasture, Jane inadvertently slowed her pace. She was coming up to the spot where they'd discovered Kyle Stuyvesant—where he'd been left in a heap on the side of the road like discarded trash or a wounded animal. An inconsequential creature left to perish alone. In the dark. Without hope or comfort.

Jane swallowed hard and pedaled faster. Becoming morose would serve no purpose. Kyle was gone and his killer hadn't been apprehended, but she and the Fins weren't the only ones investigating the crime.

Maybe, just maybe, the sheriff has caught a break, Jane told herself.

Holding on to this optimistic thought, she rounded the sharp curve of Broken Arm Bend, making a mental note to ask the twins to share the latest version of the song commemorating the infamous curve.

At the start of school, the boys had been singing,

> *Broken Arm Bend,*
> *where rides come to an end,*
> *in Farmer Mackey's*
> *field of corn.*
>
> *Yellow as the bus,*
> *try not to cuss,*
> *and next time,*
> *use your horn!*

Involuntarily, Jane began humming the tune. She was full on singing the ridiculous ditty by the time she parked her bike in front of Run for Cover. The song vanished, however, as she concentrated on which word stepping stones to choose en route to the bookshop door.

"*Persevere, Fortitude, Strength.*" She paused and then took a detour toward the garden bench to hit the stones marked *Wisdom* and *Courage*.

Pivoting where she stood, Jane drank in the sight of Eloise's garden. The yellow coreopsis, salmon-colored yarrow, and purple coneflower had yet to give way to a riot of sedum, chrysanthemums, and asters, but the summer flowers were looking tired. Their brightest, boldest hues were spent, the bees and butterflies had vanished, and all signs pointed to the end of their season. Soon, pumpkins and hay bales would appear on the shop stoops and the old flowers would be pruned or pulled.

Jane glanced down to her left and noticed a stepping stone partially obscured by a clump of ornamental grass. It said *Remembrance*.

The door to the bookshop opened and Eloise appeared on the stoop wearing a wide grin.

"When I looked out my window, I thought you were a model from one of Rossetti's paintings!" Eloise exclaimed, settling onto the bench next to Jane. "I love it when you wear your hair in a long braid over your shoulder. You're the picture of a fair maiden from a Victorian poem. All you're missing are flowers. Here, here, here, and here." She touched Jane's strawberry-blond braid. "Then, you'd be ready to be someone's muse."

It was impossible to be glum in Eloise's company, and Jane smiled. "I braid my hair to keep it out of my face while I'm riding. Could you imagine how often I'd end up at Doc Lydgate's if I rounded Broken Arm Bend at my usual speed with my vision obstructed? I'd need a punch card for casts or a BOGO deal on crutches."

Eloise laughed. "The truth is, neither of us can afford to break a leg. We have too much to do. If we could be waited on, hand and foot, like a member of royalty from one of Mrs. Pratt's romance novels, we'd have a ball with such an injury." She cleared her throat and raised her chin. In an exaggerated highbrow British accent, she intoned, "Oh, Montgomery, how thoughtful. Yes, if it's not *too* much trouble, I *would* like to have my breakfast in bed. A foot massage afterward? Well, if you insist. Though I *do* say—"

Seeing a pair of elderly ladies approaching, Eloise stopped her narrative. "Hello, Mrs. Cortez. Hello, Mrs. Hesse." She waved at her customers. "Make yourselves at home! I'll join you shortly."

"Eloise, I dropped by to ask you a quick question," Jane said before Eloise could resume her injured royalty fantasy. "And I know I'll see you tomorrow for our book club meeting, but this couldn't wait."

All the merriment drained from Eloise's pretty face and she covered Jane's hand with hers. "Of course. I'm always here for you. What is it?"

"Have you heard anything from Edwin? Anything at all?"

Eloise exhaled in relief. "Yes, I got a postcard in today's mail. Didn't you?"

"I . . ." Since Jane didn't want to divulge details about hers, she asked more questions instead. "Where was it posted? Where is he?"

"Edwin's in Turkey. Ankara. Which is a little surprising because he's been there before," said Eloise. "How many times can a travel writer cover the same place? Though I guess our world is ever changing. I look at a current map and think of how completely different it is from the map we studied in elementary school." She shrugged. "Anyway, do you want to see the card?"

Jane hesitated. Correspondence was personal. Even a postcard, which could be read by anyone handling it, seemed like a precious thing in a digital age. The mailbox had become a receptacle for bills, catalogs, advertisements, and requests for monetary donations. It so rarely held anything personal like a handwritten letter. Holidays and birthdays might be the exception, but Jane realized that the older she got, the more she cherished a piece of mail that wasn't generated by a computer.

Which was why she was conflicted by Eloise's offer. Part of her wanted to scrutinize every inch of Edwin's postcard. The other part wanted to let it remain a connection between sender and recipient. Brother and sister. But once again, a niggling voice whispered, *What if he's in danger?*

Reaching a decision, Jane said, "If you don't mind, I'd love to take a quick look at it tomorrow, before our book discussion. Can you come to my house a little early?"

"Sure." Eloise bounced to her feet. "I'd better get going. Mrs. Hesse doesn't have the greatest memory and she tends to forget which books she's read. When Mrs. Cortez tries to remind her, arguments can break out. I've learned to gently intervene by showing Mrs. Hesse her purchase record and making a few recommendations to suit both ladies. Though they always leave with smiles on their faces and books in hand, there have been times where I thought they might go at each other with their purses. Did you happen to notice the *size* of their purses?"

Jane hadn't, but Eloise assured her that Pig Newton could easily fit inside either one. With a final laugh, she darted back inside the shop.

Leaving her bike where it was, Jane made the short trip next door to the Daily Bread Café. She'd been avoiding Edwin's eclectic restaurant since his departure, and now felt abashed over entering with the sole purpose of questioning Magnus, the manager.

Magnus was delighted to see her.

"How lovely!" he cried, taking both of her hands in his. "It has been far too long. Are you on your own? Where is your enchanting aunt?"

"I just popped in for a quick social call." Gazing around the café, Jane wished she could stay for a cup of Vietnamese Egg Coffee or South Indian filter coffee.

In truth, she loved the café and regretted not stopping by sooner. She remembered when she'd first laid eyes on the renovated space. The transformation had been incredible. The café had gone from a lackluster lunch spot with aged booths and linoleum flooring to an exotic wonderland. The hardwood floors were now covered with kilim rugs, the walls were lined with antique maps and potted palms, and mosquito nets served as dividers between the dining room and a lounge area in the rear of the café. In this intimate alcove, patrons could relax on British colonial chairs with animal print cushions and set down their drinks on large copper kettles, African drums, or steamer trunks.

"You are always welcome, Jane. For any reason," Magnus said warmly.

Jane turned to him with a wistful smile. "I was reminiscing about the day of the soft opening, and of the honey lavender crème brûlée."

"Ah." It was an appreciative sound. "No one makes it quite like Mr. Alcott."

"He has a special touch," Jane agreed. And then, in what she hoped was a casual tone, she asked, "Have you heard from him?"

Magnus nodded enthusiastically. "Yes. Come see!"

Jane followed Magnus through the restaurant, where several patrons were enjoying a late lunch or an afternoon treat accompanied by an exotic drink. In the kitchen, Edwin's cook, who filled his shoes whenever he abruptly vanished, was chopping lettuce. His movements were so swift that he'd completed the task before the door leading from the dining room to the kitchen finished swinging. Only then did he raise his eyes to see who'd entered his domain.

"Hector, you remember Ms. Steward."

Hector was short, bald, and possessed the hooded and inscrutable gaze of a bird of prey. He dipped his head in greeting and started chopping a carrot.

Jane murmured a hello, too hypnotized by his flashing blade and the rapid decimation of the vegetable to manage anything else.

"Here," said Magnus, touching Jane's elbow. "On my board. See?"

Tearing her eyes away from Hector's hands, Jane looked at the bulletin board and saw a postcard featuring what she assumed was the interior of a mosque. She stared at the image for several seconds before asking Magnus if her guess was correct.

"Yes, it is the Sultan Ahmed Mosque from Constantinople. This is a vintage postcard. Edwin knows that I enjoy the old postcards and goes out of his way to find them for me." Magnus beamed.

"Was yours posted from Ankara?" Jane asked.

If Magnus found the question odd, he didn't show it. "It was. Did you also receive a postcard like this one?"

Jane was torn. She longed to confide in Magnus, just as she'd longed to confide in Eloise, but she couldn't. Edwin's secret belonged to Edwin. Even if she were worried over his safety, Jane could not expose his secret life as a Templar. She could never let anyone know that he came from a long line of men who stole books in the name of shared knowledge.

What are you stealing now? she wondered as she stood in the kitchen of Edwin's restaurant. Daily Bread was his cover job, just like being the manager of Storyton Hall was hers. His true vocation was to steal books. Hers was to preserve and protect them. The irony wasn't lost on either of them. They'd fallen in love despite their differences.

Dropping her gaze to the tile floor, Jane said, "No, I haven't."

It wasn't a lie. Her postcard hadn't been like Magnus's. It hadn't been vintage nor had it been postmarked from Ankara.

Interpreting her downcast eyes as disappointment, Magnus gave Jane's arm a brotherly pat. "I'm sure he sent you one. Have you collected today's mail?"

Jane hadn't, in fact. Though the postmistress had hand-delivered Edwin's postcard at Storyton Hall, Jane had yet to check her mailbox at home. She shook her head and Magnus grinned triumphantly.

"I bet there's one waiting as we speak!"

His optimism was contagious and, because Jane wanted to believe him, she pictured a second postcard buried among the bills and catalogs. "I'll tell you about it the next time I come for lunch. Which will be soon. I know Aunt Octavia's been missing everything about Daily Bread, including its charming manager."

Magnus performed a theatrical bow and showed Jane to the door. As for Hector, he never looked up from his work. His knife was a silver blur as it sliced through the pale flesh of an onion.

As much as Jane wished to ride straight home, she had her most pressing errand to attend to first, which was checking in with Sheriff Evans.

The sheriff's department looked more like an English country cottage than the local law enforcement hub. Even though Jane had visited the building on numerous occasions, she still found the idea of interrogation rooms and holding cells incongruent with the quaint brick building, flagstone path, and well-tended front garden filled with boxwood and rosebushes.

However, when Jane asked the desk clerk for a few moments of the sheriff's time, she was quickly reminded that they were not in a quaint English village. They were in Storyton, where two men were dead, and both cases were open and active.

"You can go on back, Ms. Steward." The clerk waved at Jane before reaching out to answer the ringing phone.

The door to the sheriff's office was ajar and Sheriff Evans was seated at his desk, so Jane tapped on the door with her knuckles.

"Ms. Steward. Excellent. This saves me the trouble of calling you." The sheriff came forward and shook her hand. The formal gesture unsettled Jane. The sheriff cleared a stack of file folders from one of his guest chairs and gestured at it. "Please, have a seat. There's been a development."

Jane sat down and waited for Sheriff Evans to speak. Her mouth had gone dry, but she wasn't sure why she felt such dread. She had no inkling of what he was about to say.

"I am prepared to make an arrest for the murder of Mr. Bartholomew Baylor," he said in a solemn voice. "Since you're here, I can tell you in person that the suspect is a guest at Storyton Hall."

Jane released a sad sigh. "I wish it were otherwise, but I'm not surprised. Whoever committed the crime was familiar with Bart's latex allergy and his habits." She steeled herself before asking, "Who is it?"

The sheriff touched the brown case-file folder on his desk. "Felix Rolf. And I intend to take him into custody without delay."

"Felix?" The sheriff's announcement stunned Jane. Not only had the book dealer convinced Jane of his innocence, but he'd persuaded Butterworth as well.

"I won't explain all my reasons behind the arrest at this time," Evans said. "However, I can share two things with you. The first is that Mr. Rolf's business is failing. I have this on direct authority from his accountant. It would take a miracle to save the shop."

A five-figure miracle? Jane remembered the note Levi Ross had left on the desk in his guest room. She also remembered the current market value he'd assigned to the cookbook.

"Do you think Mr. Rolf killed Bart over *Mrs. Tanner's Everyday Receipts*?" Jane asked. Without giving the sheriff a chance to respond to the question, she went on. "Even if that were true, he couldn't sell the book openly. He'd have to sell it through *other* channels or risk his reputation, which has already suffered a blow. Also, in selling stolen property, he'd earn a much smaller profit. It's hard to believe he'd commit murder for such a high-risk endeavor."

"Under regular circumstances, I'd agree with you." The sheriff laid his hands over the folder as if affirming the decision with his body. "But there are more than just Mr. Rolf's financial woes to consider. The second thing I'll share with you is that we have a witness who saw Mr. Rolf purchase a box of gloves from Storyton Pharmacy the day before Mr. Baylor's death. The gloves were identical to those Mr. Baylor favored. Purple. Size large. Latex free."

Jane wanted to feel confident that the sheriff was after the right man, so she asked, "Is that enough to arrest a man on suspicion of murder? Financial troubles and the purchase of a box of gloves?"

There was a glint of impatience in the sheriff's eyes. And something else. Exasperation? Jane realized she wasn't owed a detailed explanation of how the authorities had arrived at Felix Rolf as their suspect. She was fortunate that Sheriff Evans shared as much as he had. Not only that, but he was always tactful and courteous. What else could she ask from the man?

"Forgive me," she said. "I know these things will be revealed in due time. It's just hard for me to process the news because I spoke with Mr. Rolf at length the night of Bart's death and he confessed to having wronged Mr. Baylor. His regret was so sincere. He had me totally convinced."

Sheriff Evans nodded in understanding. "Remember when I told Deputy Emory that a killer is capable of great depths of emotion? I'm sure those expressed by Mr. Rolf when the two of you talked *were* genuine. You have no reason to be embarrassed because you believed him, Ms. Steward. He undoubtedly felt shame and regret and probably still feels it. Unfortunately, darker, more dangerous feelings dwell inside him too, and those are the feelings he'll now have to answer for."

"Well, I guess we won't need to use the cookbook as bait during tomorrow's Pre-Raphaelite dinner dance," Jane said. She felt no sense of relief or resolution. Only a feeling of sadness.

"No. We can skip the theatrics." Evans came over to Jane's side of the desk and placed a copy of the day's conference schedule in front of her. "After examining this, I have no idea of Mr. Rolf's current whereabouts. I called the front desk and was told that he wasn't in his room. Nor had he signed up for any excursions or activities. Do you know where he might be?"

Jane mulled this over. "In a reading room, maybe? Let me text Butterworth. He can alert the staff to report back with any sightings."

As Jane was typing the text, she noticed the time on her phone screen. Suddenly, she had a strong feeling that she knew Felix Rolf's exact location.

"Ms. Steward?" The sheriff watched her in concern. "Are you all right?"

"I—I don't know," she stammered. "There's a chance . . ." She trailed off and glanced at her phone. "I need to make a quick call." She started dialing. "He might be with my family. Having tea."

Sheriff Evans tensed and remained standing.

As for Jane, she couldn't move from her chair. The phone rang and rang. No one picked up.

"It's a nice day. They could be on the back terrace," she said, speaking more to herself than to the sheriff. Without hesitation, she broke one of Storyton Hall's technology rules by calling Butterworth's cell phone.

As expected, it took him several seconds to answer. When he did, his voice echoed slightly and Jane assumed he'd hurriedly ducked into the staff corridor. "Miss Jane? Do you need assistance?"

"Sheriff Evans will be taking Mr. Rolf into custody shortly," Jane said, trying to sound like a woman in control of her emotions. "I'm worried that he's having tea with my family. Perhaps on the terrace? Could you please check?"

"Certainly." Jane heard the sound of footfalls and knew that the butler was moving swiftly through the staff corridor. "Is there reason to consider Mr. Rolf an imminent threat?"

"I don't know," Jane said. "But if he's with my family, don't take your eyes off that man."

Butterworth whispered that he'd keep his phone on, concealed in his uniform pocket, and would report to Jane the second he had news.

The minutes seemed to stretch on and on before Butterworth's voice finally came through her phone speaker again. "They've just sat down. Only three adults, Ms. Jane. The twins are in the kitchen with Mrs. Hubbard. Your great-aunt told me this before asking me to find you. Apparently,

Mr. Rolf has selected books for you to peruse. And though I've stepped back into the staff corridor to speak with you, there are other eyes on that table."

Knowing Butterworth was referring to another Fin allowed Jane to relax just a little. "Please tell my great-aunt and -uncle to go ahead with their tea. I'll join them as soon as I can."

"And Sheriff Evans? Is he willing to wait until teatime is over to arrest Mr. Rolf?"

Because the phone was on speaker mode, Sheriff Evans had overheard the conversation. He now indicated his assent with a brief nod.

"He is," said Jane, and hung up.

Jane stood up and faced the sheriff. "Can we avoid taking Mr. Rolf out through the main lobby? I'd rather ask him to walk with me through the herb garden to the garages. With your permission, that is."

The sheriff was not amenable to this plan. "You'd be too vulnerable."

"Not if Sterling tags along. And there'd be nothing unusual about a chauffeur heading to the garages."

The sheriff refused to relent. "Mr. Rolf poisoned one man and hit a second man with a truck. His behavior is impossible to predict, Ms. Steward. Which is exactly why I need to take him into custody. I'll allow you one opportunity to isolate Mr. Rolf from the rest of the guests on the terrace, but that's all. For the safety of you, your staff, and your guests, we need to proceed with caution."

Eager to get back to Storyton Hall, Jane meekly agreed. She then followed Sheriff Evans out of his office and into a large room with multiple desks where Deputies Phelps and Emory stood at attention.

"Phelps, take a car and park by the garages. Emory, you're with me." The sheriff turned to Jane. "How did you get to town?"

"I rode my bike. Could I catch a ride with you?"

The sheriff gestured at Phelps. "Take the truck instead and load Ms. Steward's bike into the back. We have a little time to spare. After all, I've seen the teatime spread at Storyton Hall. Not even a killer could walk away from that."

Sheriff Evans agreed to wait in the herb garden for no more than five minutes. After that, he and Deputy Phelps would ascend the terrace stairs and ask Mr. Rolf to excuse himself from his present company in order to answer additional questions.

"If he resists, we won't hesitate to subdue him in front of your guests." The sheriff issued his final warning as Jane hurried away.

Now, breathless from exertion and fear, she approached Aunt Octavia's favorite table. Set apart from the others in its own little alcove, the table provided privacy while still allowing a splendid view of the gardens, the great lawn, and the majestic blue hills.

Jane smiled mechanically at her guests, the majority of whom had finished their tea and were reading or quietly conversing as they enjoyed the temperate weather and the serene vista.

Looking around, Jane saw that Butterworth had taken up a sentinel position on the terrace. He stood in a discreet space between two columns and appeared to be gazing outward, though Jane knew he was fixedly watching one particular table. His stoic posture reassured her. Nothing untoward had occurred since their phone conversation and nothing would occur as long as Jane could separate Felix Rolf from her family.

When she came upon the table, she could see that it had been cleared of foodstuff. In place of plates and platters, Felix Rolf had fanned an array of books across the starched tablecloth. Aunt Octavia was gazing at them with rapture while Uncle Aloysius toyed with one of the feathery flies poking out of his fishing hat.

Glancing up at Jane's approach, Aunt Octavia cried, "Look at the treasures I just bought for the boys! They have *no* idea what delights await them!" She elbowed Felix in the forearm while keeping her gaze on Jane. "Mr. Rolf read *me* just like a book. He sensed that I was more a Hardy Boys gal than a Nancy Drew gal and he was right! I read them both, of course, but if I had to choose, I'd pick the boys every time."

"That's because you were once a tomboy, my sweet," Uncle Aloysius said indulgently. "You could climb trees like a squirrel and skip rocks like a major league pitcher."

"Flattery will get you everywhere." Aunt Octavia blew her husband a kiss.

Felix smiled during this exchange, and Jane, who would normally jump at the chance to examine the books on the table, stared at the book dealer. She stared at his cloud of untamed hair and his wild brows and tried to envision him acting out a pair of unspeakable crimes. Could a man with the ability to make Aunt Octavia so merry, a man who bought and sold such magical books, be the same person who lined Bart Baylor's gloves with cyanide or mowed down Kyle Stuyvesant with a truck? And for what? To keep a bookstore afloat?

Jane watched Felix Rolf smile with what seemed like genuine warmth and wished—not for the first time—that people weren't capable of such incredible depths of duplicity.

Suddenly, Felix looked up and caught her assessing gaze. His smile faltered. She saw his expression turn anxious. But his concern wasn't for himself. "Ms. Steward? Are you all right?" He got to his feet and hastened to pull out a chair for her.

"I'm fine, thank you," she said, recovering her composure. "I just have too much on my mind. However, I could use your assistance with a book-related matter. If you have a spare moment, that is. Aunt Octavia, could you *guard* the gems Mr. Rolf wanted to show me for a few minutes?"

Aunt Octavia, who'd clearly been on the verge of protesting, immediately changed tack. "Of course, my dear."

"Forgive me. I will make things right. I promise you," Felix said by way of farewell to Jane's great-aunt.

It was such an odd remark that Jane asked him about it as they descended the terrace steps with Butterworth following at a short distance behind them.

"I intended to sell your lovely aunt the full set of the Grosset and Dunlap Hardy Boys novels, but one of the books has gone missing. I didn't notice until I laid out the set in order. The books were packed in New Orleans, and I checked the inventory as I always do upon arriving at Storyton Hall. Everything was accounted for. I can't explain how it's suddenly disappeared."

By this point, they'd reached the bottom of the wide staircase and Jane had turned toward the herb garden. She held open a low gate, and when Felix passed through it to find Sheriff Evans and Deputy Phelps standing on the other side, he glanced back at Jane in surprise.

"Is this about my book?" he asked her. "Has my copy of *The Sign of the Crooked Arrow* been stolen?"

Chapter Fifteen

The sheriff and his deputies had just pulled away when the twins burst through the loading dock doorway and ran over to their mother.

"Was that Mr. Rolf?" Hem panted.

Hem hadn't even finished with his question when Fitz asked one of his own. "What did he do?"

Jane looked down at her boys. The sun threaded gold into their sandy brown hair and highlighted the freckles on their noses. Their eyes, which reflected a mixture of curiosity, mischief, and innocence, made it difficult for Jane to formulate an immediate reply.

The world isn't an innocent place, she thought, and held her arms out to her sides.

"Take a hand," she said to her sons. "I want to talk to you."

Fitz and Hem exchanged concerned glances. Their mother rarely demanded physical affection and was willing to receive hugs and kisses when they felt inclined to offer them. They'd also told her earlier that summer that they were too old to hold hands with her or any other adult.

"We know we're supposed to look both ways before crossing the street," they'd explained one day when the three of them stood on the opposite side of the street from Geppetto's Toy Shop.

"And we'll never get lost. We know every road in Storyton! We could draw a map better than an explorer!"

At the time, Jane had recognized that her sons were asking for a small measure of independence. She'd granted it to them. Now, however, she held their hands for her own sake. She let go only when they arrived at the low brick wall surrounding the herb garden.

"Let's sit for a minute," she said.

The boys unslung their book bags, dropped them on the gravel path, and got comfortable on the wall. Hem hugged his knees to his chest while Fitz stretched out his legs and leaned back on his hands.

"Sheriff Evans took Mr. Rolf to the station to keep everyone safe," Jane said. "Our guests, family, and staff. The sheriff had to do this because he believes that Mr. Rolf hurt two people. You've both read *The 39 Clues, The A to Z Mysteries,* and the *Encyclopedia Brown* books, so you know that a detective gathers clues and evidence before making an arrest, right?"

"So the sheriff found clues that Mr. Rolf was hurting people?" Fitz squinted in the afternoon sun as he looked up at Jane. "Was there a clue in his wig? Because *I* thought it was a wig all along."

Hem rolled his eyes. "It's *not* a wig. I asked Aunt Octavia, and she said it's real. *I* bet he hid things in his books. You could put stuff in those pop-up books. In the spaces behind the pictures. Like a piece of paper."

Jane didn't want the boys to become distracted, so she clapped her hands together once and said, "The point I'd like to make is that Mr. Rolf wasn't the man we thought he was. All of us, including Aunt Octavia and Uncle Aloysius, thought he was a nice man. Right?"

Fitz opened his mouth to speak. Guessing that he meant
to boast about knowing that something was off about the
children's book dealer from the start, Jane gave her son a
warning glare. He said "right" in a small voice.

Hem took more time to respond. "I liked him because
I liked his books, but I think he was extra nice to Aunt
Octavia because he wanted her to buy his books."

This was an astute observation and Jane told Hem as
much.

"I liked his books too. What will happen to them,
Mom?" Fitz asked.

"I don't know," Jane said, feeling saddened by the
thought of a shop filled with rare and wonderful books left
abandoned for a prolonged period of time. She imagined vibrant covers dulled by dust and bookshelves festooned in
cobwebs. She saw a CLOSED sign with sun-bleached letters.
As the days passed, the air inside the shop would grow
staler. The gloom would grow deeper. The atmosphere of
neglect would spread like shadows until the worst would
happen: people would forget that such a marvelous shop
had ever existed.

Hem touched Jane's hand, bringing her out of her
morose reverie. "Mom? Are detectives ever wrong?"

"Yes," she said. "They're people, and people make mistakes. Even when they try their best not to."

"What if the sheriff made a mistake?" Hem asked.

"If he did, then he'll let Mr. Rolf go free."

Fitz abruptly swung his legs to the ground. He was no
longer relaxed. "But that would mean the bad guy is still
free."

This was the moment Jane had feared. Though the boys
had been receiving martial arts training from Sinclair,
archery lessons from Sterling, and outdoor survival skills
from Lachlan, they saw these as mostly recreational. They

were aware of their future Guardian roles, but were too young to take them seriously. However, they were old enough to be told that they'd have to be more careful around strangers. Especially since strangers constantly surrounded them.

"Yes," Jane finally answered Fitz. "And until Sheriff Evans can prove that Mr. Rolf is responsible for hurting people, we should keep our eyes open for unusual behavior. We've talked about what you should do if a stranger tries to grab you—"

"Yell for help!" Hem cried.

"*And* give them a quick jab in the throat if they're close enough," Fitz added, repeating Sinclair's instructions. "After that, we run like the wind."

Hem nodded enthusiastically. "To a place with lots of people. Or to a place where we can't be seen."

Jane made a time-out gesture. "What I want you to be on the lookout for is much sneakier behavior. I'm talking about not trusting people just because they seem nice. Do you understand what I'm saying? Unless you've known the person for a long time, you have to be careful. Got it?"

Sensing the seriousness of the moment, the twins replied "yes, ma'am" in unison.

"Good." Jane ruffled their hair to lighten the mood.

"Mom!" Fitz protested, and she tickled him just under the armpit until he squealed.

She went after Hem next, prodding his most ticklish spot, which was the top of his thigh.

"Race you home!" she shouted when they were both helpless with laughter.

Though she had a good ten-second head start, she didn't stand a chance. The boys were as fleet-footed as juvenile cheetahs. They zipped by her, issuing zealous whoops of victory as they ran.

Jane slowed her pace to savor the moment. Watching the small, lithe figures of her sons race over the great lawn and hearing their laughter rise into the September air like a bouquet of balloons, she was nearly overwhelmed with love.

I am so lucky, she thought as the boys turned to wave at her before disappearing into the house.

Jane walked to her mailbox. She'd just pulled out the mail when a shadow detached itself from beneath a large holly bush. Muffet Cat ambled over to where Jane stood and gazed up at her. His eyes sparkled like peridots, marred by a smudge of black pupil.

"Hello, Muffet Cat. Have you come to see if I received any tuna coupons?"

The portly tuxedo rubbed the length of his body along the mailbox post and yowled. Jane started when she heard the plaintive note of the feline's meow. This was a noise Muffet Cat reserved for times of acute distress.

Pinning the mail against her chest, Jane bent down and stroked Muffet Cat with her free hand.

He stopped rubbing the post and rubbed against her legs instead. He didn't respond to Jane's caresses by purring and he wasn't begging for food. And yet he clearly wanted something. Unfortunately, Jane had no idea what it was.

"What are you trying to tell me?" she asked him.

Again, he repeated his anguished yowl. He then nudged Jane on the arm holding the mail and several pieces fell to the ground.

One of these included a postcard.

Muffet Cat stepped on it with his front paws and began to growl.

"More cryptic messages, Edwin?" Jane murmured. "See? Even the cat thinks you could put more effort into your communication."

Giving the agitated feline a gentle push, Jane picked up the postcard and examined the image. Like Magnus's card, this one looked vintage and depicted a scene from Ankara. It wasn't the interior of a mosque, however, but a scene from a bazaar. There was a stall featuring baskets of colorful spices. The powdered spices were piled into high mounds and Jane wondered what it would be like to lean over, close one's eyes, and inhale a breath of pure saffron, cinnamon, or cardamom.

She flipped the card over, eager to read Edwin's message, when Muffet Cat let out another growl and trotted away, affronted.

"What did I do?" Jane called after him. She felt bad, for the animal was obviously upset. But Muffet Cat did what he did best, which was to ignore her and vanish as suddenly as he'd appeared.

After gathering the rest of the mail, Jane returned her attention to the postcard.

J—

My original objectives have changed. There is more work than I'd originally expected, so I won't be returning to Storyton for a long time. I can't ask you to wait for me, so please consider yourself free. I'll always be grateful for the time we had.

Yours, E

Jane touched the mailbox to prove to herself that she hadn't suddenly entered some terrible alternate reality. The feel of the warm metal against her fingertips told her that she wasn't dreaming and that Edwin's second message was every bit as bizarre as his first. Except that it was far more hurtful. Was he truly saying good-bye to her in a postcard?

This doesn't even sound like him, her inner voice protested.

She turned back toward Storyton Hall, hoping to draw comfort in its solidness. It had been the fairytale castle of her childhood. It was now her legacy. She loved every brick, stone, and piece of timber that fashioned its main section and two wings. She cherished its clock tower, its turrets, and even its endless problems and costly repairs. It was home. Home to her, her family, and to thousands of books. It was a sanctuary to those who traveled from all over the globe, searching for peace. She need only wake in the morning and it was there, waiting for her.

Jane slipped the postcard inside a gardening catalog and went into her house to join her sons. She needed to help them get ready to spend the night with Aunt Octavia and Uncle Aloysius. After that, she had to prepare for the arrival of the Cover Girls.

As promised, Eloise showed up a few minutes early. She knocked on the door and let herself in while calling out a cheerful "It's me!" After hanging her dress for the Pre-Raphaelite dinner dance on the coat rack, she dropped the book their group had chosen for tonight's discussion on the kitchen table.

"Here's my darling brother's postcard," she said, pulling it from between the pages of the book and handing it to Jane. "Ah, I see you're preparing our libations." She headed over to the row of glasses lined up on the counter, which is why she failed to notice Jane's wan expression.

"I've invented a cocktail in honor of our heroine, Lizzie Siddal. I hope it's good," Jane said before glancing at the card in her hand.

Eloise's postcard featured a rather cartoonish drawing of the country and its most famous landmarks. Across the top, a bubbly typeface proclaimed, "Greetings from

Turkey." A cruise ship traversed the waters along the bottom of the card.

Turning it over, Jane saw the Ankara postmark as well as Edwin's familiar handwriting.

E—
   *Just had coffee near the bazaar. A man was
telling his grandson the story of the time he
followed a jinn into the desert and saw his crystal
palace shimmering against a backdrop of sand. He
returned to his village and shared the story, but no
one believed him. Except his sister. The next day, he
showed her the palace. They stood in the desert
and held hands until the sun set. That's when the
palace disappeared, never to be seen again.
   The story reminded me of you and your faith
in what's not visible.*
                                        Love, E

Jane fought back tears. Though Edwin's missive to Eloise was short, it conveyed both tenderness and affection. It was as if Edwin was saying that his sister would also have believed the story about the jinn because she was incredibly loyal and put her heart and soul into what mattered most.

"I hope he sends me a magic carpet. You and I could travel to a remote beach on the other side of the world and be home before anyone missed us," Eloise said as she examined a bowl of strawberries on the counter. "Are these for our drinks or can I eat one?"

"Help yourself. I have a different garnish for our cocktails." Jane put the postcard back inside Eloise's copy of *Ophelia's Muse* and washed her hands at the kitchen sink.

When she was done, she found that Eloise was holding the dish towel ransom. "Tell me if you found anything in your mailbox today and I'll hand this over."

"A postcard," Jane said.

"I knew it!" Eloise tossed the towel at Jane. "Though honestly, my louse of a brother could do better than that. He could send an actual letter. Or a care package filled with thoughtful trinkets. How about a phone call? Is that really asking too much?" She sighed. "Why did we both fall for men who can't communicate? Yours jets off to exotic places and goes radio silent. Mine is right here, but getting him to talk is like pulling teeth."

Jane was going to ask Eloise when she and Lachlan had last spent time alone together when there was a brief knock on the door and the rest of the Cover Girls flowed into the house.

"We've arrived!" Mrs. Pratt trilled.

"In all our glory!" Mabel added boisterously.

The women hung their dresses on the coat rack, dropped their handbags on the table, and then gathered around the center island. Betty, who'd been the last to greet Jane, asked for an update on the investigation.

"Let me serve the drinks and I'll tell you," Jane said. "I named this cocktail the Lizzie Siddal to honor the young woman who served as muse to several Pre-Raphaelite painters and was also wife to Dante Gabriel Rossetti. Lizzie was probably best known for her lavishly long and thick copper-colored hair, but she *should* have been celebrated as a talented artist in her own right." As Jane spoke, she poured ingredients into a cocktail shaker.

"Excuse me." Phoebe pointed at the old-fashioned glasses on the counter. "Are those rose petals on the bottom of our glasses?"

"Yes," Jane said. "What would a Pre-Raphaelite cocktail be without a rose?"

After jiggling the shaker for several seconds, she poured a red-orange concoction into two of the eight glasses. The Cover Girls responded with appreciative noises.

"What a gorgeous color!" Anna cried.

"It's just like Lizzie's hair," Violet said.

Eloise held her glass to the light. "What's in it, Jane?"

"Half an ounce of Campari, an ounce of gin, rum, and fresh-squeezed orange juice. And to top it all off, a teaspoon of grenadine. It should be a cocktail of complex flavors. On the outset, it will taste sweet. However, there'll also be a hint of bitterness. It'll be vibrant and light enough to feel romantic, but will pack enough of a punch to serve as a reminder that people *can* die from a broken heart."

Jane immediately turned her face away to focus on preparing the next batch. She didn't want her friends to see her inner turmoil or how she was suppressing the urge to smash one of the glasses against the nearest wall.

"Wow," said Phoebe. "This is a serious drink."

Mrs. Pratt accepted her glass with a shrug. "It was a serious book. Poor Lizzie. She didn't deserve such callous treatment. I don't give a fig about Rossetti's temperamental artist nature. He was a jerk. Pure and simple. He ruined her life."

"In the beginning of the book, there was a scene where Lizzie tossed a flower in the river and asked for the waters to show her a sign that one day, she'd find love and be loved in return," Violet said to her friends. "After finishing the book, I thought back on that scene and found it so sad. The waters offered her nothing."

"She's famous for *being* Ophelia. A drowned woman. A woman who probably committed suicide because of unrequited love." Anna sighed and took a sip of her drink. "Lizzie drowned in her own way. It took years, but that's what the laudanum did. It slowly pulled her under."

Mabel set her glass down and held up her book, which featured part of the celebrated John Everett Millais painting. "So we don't get too gloomy, I want to say that I loved the art references in this book. You know that I adore color.

I adore creativity. I adore the messy, mysterious spaces where artists work their magic."

"You just described La Grande Dame to the letter," Betty said with a smile.

The Cover Girls laughed and the heavy mood that had descended during the start of the discussion lifted.

"Did you know that this painting shows flowers that bloom at different times because Millais worked on it over the course of five months?" Mabel went on to say. "Or that the ivy on the frame was seen as a feminine plant during the Victorian era or that it symbolizes resurrection?"

The rest of the women confessed that they hadn't done much research into analysis of the painting, but they'd all been so influenced by the combination of *Ophelia's Muse* and the upcoming dinner dance, that every one of them had taken the time to familiarize themselves with the most popular artwork from the Pre-Raphaelite period.

"Speaking of feminine, we need to get ready soon. But can you give us a brief recap first, Jane?" Eloise asked. "Do you need our help tonight? With the investigation?"

Since her friends already knew about Kyle Stuyvesant from Betty, Jane told them of the recent and unexpected arrest of Felix Rolf.

"You don't sound convinced that he's a murderer," Mrs. Pratt said when Jane was done. "Do you think the sheriff has the wrong man?"

"It's not that," Jane said. "I just don't want Felix to be guilty. I wouldn't want anyone so dedicated to books to be a killer. And it's hard for me to picture a man utterly enamored by the works of Beatrix Potter and Hans Christian Andersen lacing someone's gloves with cyanide or running over a drunk pedestrian with his truck. And for what? For the chance to steal a book he'd have to sell on the black market?"

Mabel grunted. "That is very volatile behavior for a

bookseller. The man isn't a character from an Ian Fleming novel, so I can see why you have doubts."

Jane looked at Anna. "One of the reasons Sheriff Evans suspects Felix Rolf is that a witness came forward claiming to have seen him buying a pair of purple latex-free gloves in Storyton Pharmacy the day before Bart died. Do you remember selling gloves to a man with a cloud of white hair?"

Anna frowned. "We have lots of customers with white hair. Do you have a photo?"

"There might be one on his store website," Eloise said. "Hang on a tic. I'll grab my phone from my purse."

By the time she returned to the kitchen from the living room, she'd pulled up the website and located a small black-and-white photograph. She showed Anna the image. "Here he is."

Anna stared at it for several seconds before saying, "I didn't ring him up. I'd remember his face if I had. He looks like a badger." She quickly glanced at her friends. "That's not a criticism. I like badgers."

"It's okay, Anna, I thought the same thing when I first saw him," Jane said.

"What if Felix shopped during your lunch hour? Is there a way to tell who entered the pharmacy on a given day?" Phoebe asked. "Do you have security cameras?"

Anna shrugged. "Only in the pharmacy department where Randall works. Not in the front half where I am. It's fine for me to be held at gunpoint as long as no one touches the drugs."

Mabel gave Anna a sympathetic, one-arm hug. "Oh, honey. We'd go after anyone who messed with you. That's probably why they don't. They know the Cover Girls have your back!"

"Thanks." Anna flashed Mabel a grateful smile.

"What about receipts?" Mrs. Pratt asked, ignoring the

exchange between Mabel and Anna. "You keep copies of credit card receipts, right? Are they itemized?"

"No good," Jane answered before Anna could. "The witness said that Felix paid in cash."

Violet put a hand to her chest. "Cash? Anna would remember someone paying in cash. I don't even get tipped in cash anymore. Everyone pays with credit cards, debit cards, or bar codes on cell phones. I don't even remember what my favorite presidents look like anymore."

"Keep your presidents. I'll stick with my favorite founding father. Benjamin Franklin," Betty said, nudging Mabel. "I find him very sexy. On paper, that is."

She and Mabel giggled like kids who've eaten too much sugar.

When the two older women settled down, Eloise turned to Jane. "I wish there was something we could do to lift your spirits. None of us like the idea of a book lover being a murderer, but it's over for now. Can you let it go? Maybe just for tonight? You should find a handsome bibliophile to dance with. Or an archivist. I won't tell Edwin."

"No crime in dancing, anyway. What *is* a crime is missing the first course of Mrs. Hubbard's decadent meal," Phoebe said. "And we still have to dress and do our hair. Jane, I'm with Eloise. You need a break from carrying the weight of the world on your shoulders."

"It's true," Violet agreed. "What's that line from *The God of Small Things*? The one about the woman wearing flowers in her hair and carrying magic secrets in her eyes? Let me put the flowers in your hair. Hopefully, there'll be enough magic in the air to help you forget about what's happened for a little while."

Jane smiled at her friend. "That's a lovely thought. However, you should all know that I've decided to use the cookbook as bait just in case Felix Rolf isn't the killer. I have complete faith in Sheriff Evans. He is party to elements of the investigation that I'm not, and I trust him. And yet . . ."

"The universe is telling you that something is still rotten in the state of Storyton," Mrs. Pratt said. Grimacing, she added, "I never could pull off a Shakespeare reference."

Eloise put a hand on Mrs. Pratt's elbow, poised to usher her out of the kitchen. "Never mind that. We need to get a move on. Jane needs us, ladies. Not only do we have to look our best, but we also have to be charming, gracious, and extremely observant." She glanced over her shoulder at Jane. "You're not in this alone. You're not in anything alone. You have us. We won't be much use in a fight, seeing as we'll all be wearing long gowns, but we're book people."

"Which means you might notice the secret in someone's eye," Jane said. Looking at her friends, she felt a rush of pride. "What would I do without you, ladies?"

"You wouldn't have this hairstyle, for starters," Violet said, producing a color printout from her pocket and offering it to Jane. "Don't show it to anyone. I want it to be a surprise. You're going to be more resplendent than Anthony Frederick Sandys's *Perdita*."

Thirty minutes later, Jane did feel resplendent. Violet had pulled Jane's strawberry-blond hair into loose, convoluted coils at the base of her neck. She'd then woven tiny faux pearls around the coils and crowned the top of her head with a diadem of fresh flowers.

Mabel had completed Jane's look by draping a stunning floral shawl over the shoulders of her gown, which was sapphire blue with loose sleeves.

"There," Mabel declared with satisfaction. "You truly look like you just stepped out of a Pre-Raphaelite painting. You're a vision."

Jane's favorite Rossetti painting was his portrait of Joan

of Arc. He'd painted his model kissing the blade of her sword and gazing into the distance with a look of rapture on her lovely face. It wasn't her expression that Jane connected with. It was the fact that Rossetti's Joan knew her life would never be a quiet one. Her life required her to wield a sword. Jane loved the fierceness of Joan's bearing. She loved that she wore gauntlets instead of jewelry and that her hair was free of flowers or any other ornament.

Gazing at her own reflection in the mirror, Jane realized what she admired most about the painting. It was the strength emanating from Joan's eyes—a willingness to fight for what she believed in, for what she held most dear. It was a light that shone from deep inside. Jane saw the same light shining from her eyes.

Jane's friends descended the stairs to gather by the front door, but she lingered behind. She wanted a minute of the privacy of her bedroom to remove her locket and plant a kiss on its book-shaped engraving before tucking it back into the bodice of her dress. A moment to prepare for all that might lie ahead.

Chapter Sixteen

The Madame Bovary Dining Room had been transformed into a Victorian banquet hall.

Diners entered the room and stopped, enchanted by the scene. They took in the pristine white cloths, polished flatware, glittering silver candelabra, crystal stemware, and massive floral centerpieces overflowing with greenery and roses in autumnal hues and felt a thrill of anticipation.

"It's breathtaking," Eloise said to Jane. "Whenever I attend a themed event at Storyton Hall, I'm always convinced by that theme. Just look at this space! It could have been plucked from the pages of any Victorian novel describing an upper-class feast."

Violet, who looked lovely in a cream-colored gown with a garland of purple asters in her hair, glanced around in wonder. "I feel the same. It's as if the rooms are capable of whisking us through time."

"I wish they could whisk me back to my thirty-year-old waistline," Mabel said, picking up one of the printed menus included with every place setting. "Seeing this has me ready for a fainting couch."

The rest of the Cover Girls laughed and craned their necks to examine Mabel's menu. Except for Mrs. Pratt. She seemed more interested in the other diners. "Did you assign the seats, Jane? In other words, will I be engaged in stimulating dialog with lust-worthy literary types or resigned to an evening of small talk with my neighbors? Not that there's anything wrong with our Storyton men, but it's refreshing to converse with strangers once in a while. Unlike the rest of you, I don't run a business, so I don't have many opportunities to meet new people."

Phoebe smiled at Mrs. Pratt. "You make it sound exciting, but it's not like I sit down with my customers for heart-to-hearts. For the most part, they order coffee or frozen yogurt, exchange a few pleasantries, and leave. Occasionally, we'll discuss the art on my walls. That's my only chance to engage them in a lengthier dialogue."

"What about the Book Junkies? Surely, those must have earned you a flirtatious comment or two." Anna was referring to the sculptures Phoebe had crafted using found materials like bottle caps, tin cans, vinyl records, road signs, wire, buttons, and cooking utensils. These seven pieces of art, which were displayed in the Canvas Creamery's back garden, were nude studies of the female form. The women were voluptuous giantesses caught in the act of reading. Their postures were of utmost relaxation while their expressions managed to convey guilty pleasure.

Phoebe shot Anna a coy grin. "Why do you think I have those ladies on display?"

The Cover Girls fanned out to locate their seats. Jane had left these arrangements to Butterworth, but as she wandered around the dining room, she could see that he'd taken great pains to intersperse the villagers among the rare book attendees.

Jane and Eloise found their nameplates, penned in Butterworth's meticulous calligraphy on ivory card stock, among three of the Robert Harley Society members.

"Austin and Aaron, I'd like to introduce my friend. This

is Eloise Alcott." Jane gave the brothers a moment to drink in Eloise's appearance. Eloise was the picture of a fair-haired English rose in a jade-green gown and a red shawl. Her golden tresses were captured in a loose hairnet and she'd eschewed any jewelry or accessories, allowing one to focus on her luminescent skin. "And this is Levi Ross."

Eloise shook hands all around and explained that she had the honor of running Storyton's only bookstore. Within seconds, she and Levi were comparing notes about the joys and heartaches of operating a book business. This left the Sullivan brothers to Jane.

"I hope you're hungry," she said, indicating the menu.

"We're always hungry. And it looks like we won't have long to wait." Aaron made a subtle gesture. "Here comes the bell."

Butterworth approached the dinner gong, which sat on a mahogany sideboard. He picked up the mallet, struck the gong twice, and waited for the sound to resonate through the room. It took several seconds for the hum of conversation to die down, but when Butterworth was certain he had everyone's attention, he introduced the members of the chamber orchestra who'd be playing Victorian-era pieces for the diner's pleasure. After the expectant guests finished applauding the musicians, the head butler concluded his short speech by listing the beverages accompanying the dinner and explaining when the dancing would start in the Great Gatsby Ballroom. He then wished them an excellent meal, issued a stiff bow, and withdrew to a corner of the room.

The waitstaff began moving around the tables, serving red or white wine. When it was Austin's turn to choose, he seemed unable to decide.

"He'd like red, thank you," his brother told the waiter.

"I'm sorry," Austin's apology was directed at Jane. "I'm missing Bart tonight. This dinner was his idea. He loved art and he was one of the few people who believed book collecting was an art form. As for art in the Victorian era, Bart was especially fond of the Arts and Crafts movement. Any patterns showing symmetry made him feel calm."

Aaron nodded and picked up his wineglass, though he didn't take a sip. "We should toast his memory."

Jane experienced a moment of déjà vu. She and her friends had just shared cocktails in honor of Lizzie Siddal. Lizzie had been dead for over a hundred years. Bart had been gone for only a matter of days.

"That's a lovely idea," she told Aaron. "Did Bart have a favorite quote?"

The Sullivan brothers exchanged knowing grins. "Funnily enough, he was very fond of one by John Ruskin," said Austin. "Ruskin was a great patron of the Pre-Raphaelites."

"I'll have Butterworth ring the gong again. Would one of you lead us in the toast?"

Hand to heart, Aaron obliged.

Jane caught Butterworth's eye and signaled for him to ring the gong. In the silence that followed, Aaron got to his feet and surveyed the room. "I don't mean to keep you from the delicious meal we're about to enjoy, but seeing as this night celebrates a famous brotherhood, my brother and I wanted to ask you to stand in memory of our other brother—the one we all lost this week." He paused for a moment to collect himself. "Bartholomew Baylor loved books. He loved this conference. He looked forward to spending time with his book brothers *and* book sisters every year. I'd like to think he's with us tonight."

He touched his brother on the elbow and Austin now stood up and raised his glass. "Bart's favorite quote, which was from John Ruskin, was this: 'One cannot be angry when one looks at a penguin.'"

The dining room echoed with soft laughter.

Austin waited a heartbeat before continuing. "Your laughter is an example of Bart's gift. He found ways to bring people together. And he always brought out the best in all of us, even though people didn't always see the best in him. To Bart."

"To Bart!" the diners repeated loudly and with feeling.

From that point onward, the meal progressed like a well-rehearsed symphony. The candles gently flickered, the music filled in any gaps in conversation, and poached salmon with mousseline sauce followed the vermicelli soup. After the fish course came the meats. There was veal stewed with mushrooms, garlic, and saffron, French pigeon pie, and roasted chicken. In addition to the entrees, the fresh vegetable dishes included green beans, new potatoes, and asparagus.

It felt like hours had passed when the waitstaff cleared the table to prepare for dessert. Most of the diners complained that they had no room left for sweets, but Jane knew better. There was a lull as the wineglasses were removed and coffee cups were delivered. The din of conversation grew a trifle louder. During this time, Jane raised the subject of *Mrs. Tanner's Everyday Receipts* to her tablemates.

"With all that's happened, I haven't had the chance to tell you that Bart's theory about our cookbook was spot on. It is, in fact, the cookbook also known as *The Devil's Receipts*. He was also correct when he told you that it was given this negative moniker because the recipes contained certain ingredients that could endanger certain members of the public."

Levi put his coffee cup down and stared fixedly at Jane. "How were you able to confirm this?"

"A happy accident," was all Jane would say. "But I'm grateful to be sharing a meal with two collectors and a dealer. You see, I'm not sure how to appraise this book or what measures I should take to ensure its safety until I'm given leave to sell it."

"You've already made that decision, then? To sell?" Levi

asked. There wasn't the slightest hint of eagerness in his tone. Merely curiosity.

Jane made an encompassing gesture with her arm. "The upkeep on this place costs a fortune, and I'd like to proceed with our spa project. I'm hoping that the sale of such a rare book would defray some of the building costs." She looked at Levi. "Do you have an idea what price the book would fetch at auction? You've seen it. You know its condition."

Levi hesitated. "Yes. The condition was worse than rough. However, I haven't seen the book's printed pages, which is precisely what would restore its value in the eyes of a collector. I couldn't give you a proper appraisal without seeing it again."

"Fair enough," Jane said. "The cookbook is still in the Henry James Library. Tomorrow, if you have time, perhaps I might show the . . . revised version to you."

"I would like that very much," Levi said, and dipped his chin in appreciation.

Jane turned to the Sullivan brothers. "The invitation extends to you two as well. Though the cookbook isn't American and isn't something you'd be interested in collecting, it—"

"Fascinated Bart, which means we could probably learn something from it," Aaron said with a smile. "Thank you, Ms. Steward. We'd love to see the infamous recipes."

"As long as there are no members of the press around to document the moment," Austin hastily added. "We've had our own public relations troubles over ingredients this year, so we don't need our critics connecting us, or our company, to that cookbook."

Aaron nodded vehemently. "Absolutely. We want to see it because of Bart. Because, well, it was the last book he saw." His expression became aggrieved. "I wish it had been a botanical or a book featuring engravings of the animals of Papua New Guinea. I just hope Bart's final thoughts weren't about food adulteration." He shot a glance at his brother. "We'd hate that."

Jane was stunned by the openness of the Sullivan brothers. Not only had they admitted that their company was under fire for food adulteration, but they'd also made it clear that they were concerned about their reputation. And yet they still cherished their friendship with Bart enough to honor his memory by looking at the cookbook. Jane was surprised that they'd been so transparent in front of her and Eloise.

"I hope the issues your company faces are resolved to everyone's benefit. And by everyone, I mean your family, the farmers, and the customers," Jane said. This was her way of expressing sympathy for the Sullivans while making it plain that she believed it wrong for consumers to be exposed to harmful chemicals in products claiming to be organic. "And while I can't offer you comfort in that quarter, I honestly don't think Bart was focused on the contents of the cookbook. In the end, I believe his final impression was of being surrounded by books. For him, it was more like a colorful image. Like a painting of books."

"How apropos, considering this evening's theme," said Levi.

The conversation switched to another subject, but was soon interrupted by the arrival of the waitstaff with the final course.

The desserts were a triumph. Mrs. Hubbard had contained herself to a quartet of Victorian delights. The diners could sample chocolate pudding, a cherry tart, Apple Charlotte, and floating islands. This delectable treat, which consisted of pieces of soft meringue drifting in a vanilla custard sauce, had always been one of Jane's favorites.

"Ms. Steward, would you please dance with me as soon as possible?" Aaron asked after dabbing his mouth with his napkin. "If I don't move, I might pass into a food coma right here at the table."

."Your chef is amazing," Austin said. "My compliments to him."

Eloise shook her head. "The head cook is *Mrs.* Hubbard."

Austin had the good sense to look abashed. "Forgive me. That was a sexist assumption on my part. Could I make it up to you, Ms. Alcott, and to Mrs. Hubbard, by discussing the head cook's favorite genre on the dance floor? I'd like to stop by Run for Cover tomorrow and purchase a gift for the person who was able to carry out Bart's vision with such panache."

The satiated diners left the Madame Bovary, heading for the Great Gatsby Ballroom at a leisurely pace.

Butterworth, a true Renaissance man, had taken up his conductor's baton and was leading the Storyton Chamber Orchestra in an opening waltz. He would conduct for several songs before passing the baton to his understudy and resuming his duties as head butler.

Aaron took Jane's hand and led her to the center of the dance floor. He pressed his palm against the small of her back, smiled at her, and then began to waltz in synch with the other dancers.

Jane knew that Aaron cut one of the most dashing figures in the room. While some of the men had opted for Rossetti's bow tie and a shirt with a shorter collar, Aaron had chosen a high collar and an elaborately tied cravat. Many men would have looked ridiculous in such a getup, but Aaron Sullivan did not. He looked like he'd stepped right out of a Jane Austen novel. With his fair hair, he couldn't pull off the perfect Mr. Darcy, but he'd make an excellent Captain Wentworth.

To Jane, he might as well be the Invisible Man. His good looks didn't matter to her one bit. And while she found his company pleasant, Aaron Sullivan couldn't keep her mind in the present.

It was Edwin she thought of now. And of a private dance she'd shared with him in this room. The music had been from Tchaikovsky's *The Sleeping Beauty*. The floor had been illuminated by thin beams of candlelight coming from tall candelabra stationed around the dance floor. Edwin had held Jane very close, as if willing any space between them to disappear. He'd moved her body as if she had no ownership over it, and she'd willingly surrendered to his touch.

At the end of the song, when she'd longed for nothing more than a long, deep kiss from the man clutching her so tightly, he'd lowered her into a dip and seen the owl tattoo on her left breast. It was at that moment that Edwin Alcott had discovered her secret identity. Later on, he'd confessed the complex details of his own.

No other man could compete with such a memory, Jane thought as the waltz ended and Aaron complimented her on her graceful dancing.

"I had an excellent partner," she said, before excusing herself under the pretense of having to check on the punch bowl.

Aaron had no trouble replacing her. By the time the second dance began, Rosemary was in his arms.

"They make a charming couple," Mrs. Pratt said, causing Jane to jump. "Sorry, I didn't mean to sneak up on you, but I assumed you'd want to know how the baiting of the hook went over at our table."

"I most certainly do. Let's find a quiet place to talk."

Jane and Mrs. Pratt left the ballroom and made for the Ian Fleming Lounge. After taking seats close to the door, the two women bent their heads together.

"I'll do my best to be brief," Mrs. Pratt began. "Though brevity is *not* one of my strong suits."

Jane smiled and made a waving motion for her friend to continue.

"Rosemary seemed as blue as her gown at the start of the

meal, but she perked up by the time the soup course was over. I sat with Violet and Anna—who are much closer to Rosemary's age than I am—and they were able to dispel her black cloud by asking her about the recent events held at the Library of Congress. That led to discussions about fashion, celebrities, best-selling novels, and so on."

When Mrs. Pratt paused for breath, Jane made a noise of encouragement.

"Despite our most valiant attempts to engage Rosemary at the end of the meal, she was glum again while we waited on dessert." Mrs. Pratt's mouth curved into a secretive smile. "There was no opening for us to slip in the subject of the cookbook. None. But help came from the most unexpected quarter."

Jane raised her brows. "Oh?"

"The gentleman seated to my left explained that he suffers from debilitating allergies. I use the word 'debilitating' considering his line of work. He's the special collections librarian at a large university in the Midwest, and the poor man is allergic to dust. He's constantly breaking out in hives." She shook her head in sympathy. "For once, and I doubt I will ever utter these words again, we were grateful to have Randall at our table."

Jane rolled her eyes. "Oh, no."

"Oh, yes." Mrs. Pratt squirmed in her chair—such was her delight over being able to share this anecdote. "As you can imagine, our local pharmacist pounced on this man like a cat on a lame mouse. The lecturing commenced and, as usual, we thought Randall would drone on forever. Again, we got lucky."

"I can't imagine how," Jane muttered, feeling sorry for everyone forced to listen to Randall Teague. "Why has he attended these rare book events, anyway? Is he trying to drum up business for Storyton Pharmacy?"

"I think that's part of it," Mrs. Pratt said. "But he also has a small collection of rare medical books. When he stopped lecturing and raised this subject, Rosemary really came to life. Her father also collects books on medicine and disease. His interest centers on the American Civil War."

Jane nodded. She was beginning to understand how this could lead to one of the Cover Girls raising the subject of the cookbook. "Did the ingestion of poison somehow enter their conversation?"

"It was far more distasteful, actually. Especially since I was *trying* to savor my tart!" Mrs. Pratt was clearly torn between wallowing in her indignation and continuing her narrative. Fortunately, her desire to reach the best part won out. "Somehow, Randall and Rosemary began talking about the food served to Civil War prisoners. Rat stew was one of the better examples. This led to a discussion on the troops killing and eating tens of thousands of passenger pigeons. Somehow, the subject returned full-circle to our meal and Victorian-era recipes."

"Who finally brought up the topic of *Mrs. Tanner's Everyday Receipts*?" Jane couldn't keep the impatience from her tone.

Mrs. Pratt glanced at the ceiling. "I believe it was Anna. She idly wondered if your cookbook contained a pigeon recipe, and if that recipe included dangerous ingredients. Rosemary replied that we'd never know because the cookbook pages were blank. You should have seen her face when Anna told her that they were no longer blank."

Jane exhaled. "Excellent. Now all remaining members of the Robert Harley Society know the cookbook's location, and that it's every bit as rare and wonderful as Bart predicted. Horrible, but rare and wonderful."

Mrs. Pratt surveyed the room. Other than a man and woman sitting at the bar, it was unoccupied. "What now?"

Jane checked her watch and said, "The trap is set. All we can do is wait for it to be sprung."

"And if morning comes and the book remains untouched?" Mrs. Pratt asked.

"Then my feelings of reservation were unfounded and Felix Rolf is the murderer."

Mrs. Pratt stood and adjusted the bodice of her gown. "I'm going to return to the ballroom and make it clear that I'd like to be swept off my feet. What will you do?"

"I think I'll say hello to Celia Wallace," Jane said. She couldn't tell Mrs. Pratt about Otto Frank's diary. It was bad enough that she and Sinclair had had to concoct a lie to feed to Celia concerning where they'd found the diary. Jane hoped that Sinclair had been able to pull off the fabrication. After all, it would be hard to believe that the diary had suddenly surfaced. And in perfect condition.

"We'll say it was tucked in with my great-uncle's books on Victorian transportation," Jane had suggested to Sinclair. "Celia's never been to his private library. She doesn't know the scope of his personal collection and she has no idea if it's orderly or in a state of complete disarray."

Mrs. Pratt rubbed her hands together. "If I had that diary, I'd skip to the last page. If you thought you were being stalked like wild game, wouldn't *you* write the names of your hunters in your diary? *I* would. Otto Frank was a man of science. He believed in facts. I'd bet my Victoria Holt collection that he documented everything that happened to him. He would have believed that in the future, people would read his diary and realize that an injustice had occurred. Not just to him, but to all those who purchased and ate adulterated food from crooked manufacturers."

Though Jane liked the picture Mrs. Pratt painted, she doubted the diary named Otto Frank's murderers. If it had, Sinclair would have contacted her by now.

However, as she was escorting Mrs. Pratt back to the ballroom, her cell phone vibrated in the pocket of her gown. Mabel never failed to sew a pocket into the skirt of all of Jane's theme dresses, and Jane made a mental note to thank her talented friend for her thoughtfulness when she had the chance.

"Enjoy the dancing," Jane told Mrs. Pratt before ducking into a staff corridor to read Sinclair's text.

Her phone screen shone as brightly as a full moon in the gloomy corridor. The narrow space was always cooler than the public thoroughfares, but it felt as cold as a tomb at this moment. The skin on Jane's arms and shoulders broke out in gooseflesh before she'd even begun to read Sinclair's words.

When she did read them, she was so overcome by terror that she had to lean against the rough wall to keep herself from crumpling to the ground.

Sinclair had written only two lines. The first was innocuous enough. All it said was **Meet me in the Henry James.**

The second line, however, was a dagger. It plunged between Jane's ribs and stuck fast in the center of her heart. It was a dagger made of five words. Five words that wrenched a high-pitched keen from Jane's throat.

She flung open the door and started running for the library. The five words echoed inside her head. Over and over again, they shouted:

The twins have been taken.

Chapter Seventeen

Sinclair was waiting for her just inside the library doors. Jane looked past him to where her great-aunt and great-uncle stood in the center of the book-lined room. Clad in dressing gowns, they were clinging to each other and exchanging frightened murmurs.

"What happened and where are my sons?" Jane's words tumbled out in such a rush that they were barely comprehensible.

"They snuck out of the apartment," Aunt Octavia replied through quivering lips. "They asked permission to call down to the kitchens for ice cream, and of course, we said yes. We always have a dessert tray delivered when they stay over. *Always!*" She began to wail, but tried to stifle the noise by burying her face in her husband's faithful shoulder.

Jane walked toward them with her arms outstretched in desperation. "Someone tell me what's going on!"

"We must have dozed off," Uncle Aloysius said. His eyes were hollow and his voice was haunted with guilt. "We didn't hear the bell signaling the arrival of the delivery. Nor did we hear the twins open the door. Something on the television stirred us, and by the time we were fully alert, the twins were already gone and the door to our apartment was ajar. When we called down to the kitchens . . ." He stopped and began again. "We were told that Wade had left with the ice cream twenty minutes earlier."

Sinclair stepped forward and took Jane's arm. He grasped it firmly, preparing to support her weight if necessary. "Wade never made it to the apartment. He was attacked as he exited the staff elevator. He was struck on the back of the head, stripped of his uniform, and left unconscious in the staff stairwell. Mr. Sterling was able to revive him with smelling salts. Unfortunately, Wade never saw his attacker. He was blindsided."

Jane's mind struggled to piece together the scenario. "So Wade's attacker dressed in his uniform, rang the apartment bell, and then what?" She glanced from Sinclair to her great-uncle and back. "He just grabbed the boys?"

"After spinning them a yarn about having dropped their ice cream, he probably implored them to come down to the kitchens where he could serve them a new treat," Sinclair said. "He must have preyed on their kindness and begged them not to say anything, else he'd be in hot water. Your sons, who understand what it's like to be in trouble, would want to spare him that unpleasantness. They'd have followed him without reservation. After all, he was wearing the Storyton uniform. Even if they didn't recognize him, he wasn't a stranger. He was a staff member. He was supposed to be safe."

A strange sound rose in Jane's throat—something between a growl and a sob. "No one leaves Storyton Hall tonight until my sons are found! Do you hear me! *No one!* Have Sterling shut and lock the main gates!"

Sinclair shook his head. His gaze was filled with regret. "It's too late for that. Locals have already left for home and guests have retired to their rooms."

"Then we'll rouse them!" Jane cried. "Pull the fire alarm! Get everyone out on the great lawn. They can stand there until dawn while we search this place from cellar to attic. I don't care about their comfort! I don't care about anything but finding my boys!"

"I know, my dear, I know," Sinclair said soothingly. "Nothing is more important, which is why Mr. Lachlan, Mr. Sterling, and Mr. Butterworth are already trying to track them through our video surveillance."

Jane shook herself free from Sterling's grip and shouted, "That never works! I don't know why we bother with these cameras. They fail us every time. *Every time!*" She heard her voice rising—heard the hysteria in every syllable, but she couldn't stop it. Especially not when she imagined the twins in a dark place, hunched together, with their wrists tied and their mouths gagged. The image made her sick and furious at the same time. These emotions were overwhelming her ability to think clearly. She didn't want to stand here and think, anyway. She wanted to act. She wanted to throw open doors, scan closets, rip apart large packing crates, and peer inside the trunks of cars. Her boys, stowed like luggage, were awaiting rescue. By their mother. And what was she doing? She was standing in a library, talking.

Jane was about to issue a command when Aunt Octavia suddenly pulled away from her husband's comforting embrace. Her mouth was stretched into a long oval of horror and, as Jane watched in confusion, Aunt Octavia's arm slowly rose into the air. Her index finger pointed in a straight line to the book cradle on Sinclair's desk.

The tableau on the desk was all wrong. First, the bin that had held *Mrs. Tanner's Everyday Receipts* was missing its lid. Second, the book displayed on the cradle had been placed carelessly. No blocks had been tucked under its delicate spine and its deteriorated cover had support only from the cradle. It wasn't enough, and fresh rents had appeared along the length of its gutter.

What was most out of place, however, was the bright

white piece of paper resting on top of the splayed book pages.

"It's a note." Jane's whisper was almost inaudible.

She flew across the room.

Sinclair warned her not to touch anything, but Jane didn't need to pick up the note to read it. It had been typed in all caps using Helvetica, a typeface Professor Piech had mentioned several times in his workshop.

GUARDIAN.
    DROP YOUR KEY AND THE EXACT LOCATION OF STORYTON'S SECRET LIBRARY IN THE POSTAL BOX OUTSIDE THE PICKLED PIG BY MIDNIGHT. COMPLY, OR YOU WILL NEVER SEE YOUR SONS AGAIN. COME ALONE, OR YOU WILL NEVER SEE YOUR SONS AGAIN. TRY TO DECEIVE ME, AND YOU WILL NEVER SEE YOUR SONS AGAIN.

Jane checked her watch and then swung around to face Sinclair. "We don't have much time! Call Sterling. Tell him to pull a car to the main doors and leave the motor running. Aunt Octavia, send Ned to your apartments for the key to that miniature carriage clock. He's our fastest runner."

Sinclair and Aunt Octavia jumped into action, and as Jane yanked open desk drawers in search of paper and an envelope, Uncle Aloysius sank into a nearby reading chair.

"You intend to switch the keys in your locket, I see. That should convince him, this devil posing as a human being," her great-uncle said heatedly. "But I don't see how you can fool anyone who knows as much as he obviously knows. If he detects so much as a whiff of trickery, then—"

"He must not be given the chance." Jane cut off her great-uncle before he could finish his grim prediction. Storyton Hall had other secrets besides its library. There was an underground passageway—long-since collapsed—

from the main house to the hunting lodge. There were secret panels in nearly every library and reading room. And of course, there was the space between the conference room walls. A space that could be accessed only through a broom cupboard.

The killer can't know where that narrow corridor leads, Jane thought. *For all he knows, there's a set of stairs at the end of that corridor descending into a basement chamber. Uncle Aloysius is right. The man who has my boys knows far too much about Storyton Hall, but he doesn't have all the answers. If he had, he wouldn't be forced to trade my sons for the final pieces of information.*

The tip of Jane's pen hovered over the paper. Was she taking too great a risk? Was she voluntarily putting her sons' lives into the hands of a madman?

She shot a lightning-quick glance at Sinclair. He'd finished sending his text and was now reading what was undoubtedly another urgent message. Sensing her gaze on him, he met her eyes. She found everything she hoped to find in his unblinking stare: strength, courage, loyalty, determination, and an unwavering love. He would sacrifice himself for Jane or her sons if necessary. Not because he'd pledged his life to them. Because he'd pledged his heart. The twins' lives were not in the hands of a madman. Their fate rested in the capable hands of the four men who adored them. And a mother who wouldn't hesitate to kill for them.

Jane began to write.

"He'll be watching that post office box," she said to the Fins as they gathered on the front steps minutes later. "Even if you left ahead of me and looped around, you might be spotted. We can't take the chance."

"I pulled up the water, sewer, and storm drain map of Storyton Village." Sterling pointed to the Pickled Pig's block. "That's how he'll collect the drop-off. This is no spur-of-the-moment plan. He's been preparing for this. He probably went down this manhole, which is only a few feet from the postal box, and drilled an access hole up through the sidewalk. Because it's under the box, people wouldn't notice right away. As for the box itself, I'm sure he's also cut an access panel into the bottom. It'll only take him a few seconds to collect your envelope, Jane, and there'll be no way to identify him."

"I didn't expect him to come out into the open," Jane said. "I also don't think he'll bring the boys to the pickup. He has them elsewhere. And while he's distracted by my delivery, you have to find them. That means figuring out who's missing from the dinner dance. Enlist the Cover Girls to help you with the locals and the Robert Harley Society members to help with the conference attendees." Suddenly remembering that there'd been a recent arrival to Storyton Hall, Jane looked at Sinclair. "Where's Celia?"

"In her room with Otto's diary," he said. "She isn't involved, Jane. She was with me tonight. That is, until your great-uncle called me."

Jane had little time to consider the part Celia may or may not have played in the twin's abduction. "But she hasn't been in Storyton this whole time. She could have driven the car that struck Kyle. She could have procured the cyanide. She was conveniently available when a forensic anthropologist was needed. There she was, serving as a visiting professor in our neck of the woods. And if she believed our lie about the diary, maybe it's because she wanted to believe it." She turned to Butterworth. "We can't afford courtesy. Speak with her. Find out the truth. I don't care if you have to drag her to that room beneath the garage and chain her to a chair."

Butterworth nodded to show that he understood and dashed back inside Storyton Hall. "The rest of you know what to do. I'll draw out my drop as long as I can, but I don't want to. Every minute that I stall means that my boys are somewhere, alone and scared. So find out who's missing and call me the second you have a name."

Jane didn't wait for her Fins to reply. She knew they'd carry out her orders without delay and that her friends would leap to help the second they heard Fitz and Hem were missing.

Alone in the car, Jane allowed the emotions she'd been holding inside to burst free. "Fitz! Hem! My sweet boys!" Her rage and terror materialized as violent sobs and, for a bit, she was nearly blinded by tears.

Gradually, her anger overcame her fear and she began to fantasize about the things she wanted to do to the man who dared to touch her precious sons.

"The archery range is lovely after midnight," she said to the dark night, her voice filled with quiet fury. "And I can always use extra target practice."

As she approached Broken Arm Bend, she could almost hear her boys singing the latest version of the song. Her venom dissipated. She pictured Fitz and Hem running across the great lawn toward their house and remembered how their laughter had floated back to her like a bouquet of multicolored balloons. She saw her sons pause at the mailbox and wave at her before entering their home. She saw their shining eyes. Their gleeful smiles.

"Mama's coming," she whispered.

Storyton was cloaked in sleep. Jane looked at the darkened windows and thought of how the twins should have been abed long ago.

Where are you? she thought, her heart knotting in pain inside her chest.

When she passed Daily Bread Café, she felt a fresh surge of anger in addition to the pain.

"Where are *you*?" she hissed at the storefront. "You're *always* leaving me! I hope you *never* come back!"

She hated Edwin Alcott at that moment. She hated his endless absences, his cryptic messages, and his knowledge of the parts of her life meant to be secret. For a second, and it was a second only, she wondered if Edwin was responsible for her current situation. Why would she suddenly receive a message about a false Fin from him hours before her sons were used as pawns in a game involving the world's greatest treasure: knowledge?

"No," Jane said to the empty road. "Edwin cares about my boys. I can see that whenever they're together."

Pulling into a parking space near the Pickled Pig, Jane got out of the car with the envelope clutched to her chest. Just across Main Street, the church she attended shone like a beacon in the moonlight. Its tall, steadfast spire calmed her and she walked toward the post office box with her head held high.

Though it was tempting to pause at the mailbox and examine its base for evidence supporting Sterling's theory, Jane knew she had to let the vile creature who'd taken her sons believe he'd outwitted them. So without hesitation, she dropped the envelope in the box and returned to her car.

Now came the hardest part. The waiting.

Jane had to wait for word from the Fins. They clearly hadn't had time to figure out which missing guest was behind this scheme, but she didn't think it would take long to find the man. After all, he would have left the Great Gatsby soon after the first dance, if not before, in order to execute his plan to grab the twins.

Jane drove back to Storyton Hall as quickly as she dared. On the way, she tried to decipher the kidnapper's motive.

"It's never been about the cookbook," she said to herself. "It must come down to Otto Frank. He was murdered at

Storyton Hall. Shot in the back by an archer. Then, he was hastily buried. But why?"

Suddenly, she remembered the arrowhead. Celia had first noticed it after she'd taken X-rays of Otto's bones. But she'd extracted the arrowhead from the shoulder bone later on, hadn't she? Jane had meant to ask if there were markings on the arrowhead—anything that might identify its owner. However, she'd been distracted by other events and hadn't gotten to it. Now, the question seemed crucial because Jane was sure that Otto's death, the premeditated murders of Bart and Kyle, and the kidnapping of her sons had occurred for the same reason.

Someone was on quest to find Storyton's secret library.

Jane parked the car by the loading dock and rushed into Storyton Hall using the terrace entrance. Her phone was already pressed to her ear.

"Sinclair? Where are you?"

"I'm with Celia Wallace and Mr. Butterworth in the Henry James Library. We're using tonight's seating chart to track down the guests. Mr. Lachlan and Mr. Sterling teamed up with Ms. Alcott and Ms. Doyle. They've begun a room-by-room search. The rest of the staff has been dispersed to cover the public rooms and the grounds."

Even though Sinclair couldn't see the gesture, Jane shook her head. "He won't have them this close. To find the boys, we must learn the kidnapper's identity." Jane passed staff members as she trotted down the hall. They shot her glances of sympathy before continuing on their way. "Ask Celia if there were any markings on the arrowhead removed from Otto Frank's shoulder bone."

By the time she reached the door to the Henry James Library, Sinclair was waiting for her in the hallway. Pulling her close, he whispered, "Otto Frank's killer was a Templar. After seeing the engraving on the arrowhead—it's barely noticeable, but I have no doubt of its meaning—I can tell you that the doctor's murderer was no Fin."

"Didn't Celia notice the marks?" Jane asked.

"Yes, but not many would recognize this symbol—especially since it's not a traditional Templar cross. It resembles a fine crosshair or reticle and is very faint and imprecisely done."

Jane struggled to make sense of this new information. "Why would a Templar kill Otto? To gain possession of the cookbook?"

"I assume so. The killer must have tracked the doctor to Storyton and killed him here. Edwin would understand this Templar's motives better than the rest of us." Sinclair squeezed Jane's shoulder. "Since he's not here, it's up to us to solve this riddle. What do you think? Is the man holding your sons also a Templar? Is this why he infiltrated Storyton Hall?"

Beware of false Fin. Edwin's message surfaced in Jane's mind.

"Look what he's done in the hopes of discovering our secret library," she whispered. "So yes, I think he's a Templar. But he's not like Edwin. Edwin wouldn't commit murder or kidnap children to obtain rare materials. Besides, he swore that the mission of his faction is to make broken books whole and to return stolen material to its rightful owners—no matter how long ago the theft occurred. Edwin has proved himself to me, Sinclair. He's already returned several pages that have been missing from our Gutenberg Bible for decades. And we have no idea what retrieving those pages cost him."

"I believe in Mr. Alcott." Sinclair released his hold on Jane's shoulder. "However, that's how *his* faction operates. We know the Templars splintered into multiple sects and we can never track them all. There are dozens of secret societies who claim the Templar Brotherhood as their foundation."

Jane thrust out her hands in frustration. "Right now, we need only find out which male guest is a Templar. Who has the intelligence to pull off multiple crimes under our noses? Who can move about without raising any . . ." She trailed off.

"Suspicion," Sinclair finished for her.

They stared at each other.

"What if he's not a guest at all?" Jane asked the obvious question. "What if he works for me? Or lives in the village and attended the rare book events over the past few days?"

"Then our search will be far more challenging. We'll have to . . ."

Sinclair continued talking, but Jane wasn't listening.

Several Cover Girls were heading her way, including Eloise and Betty, but Jane had eyes only for Anna. As her friend approached, Jane mentally reviewed the sequence of events since the conference started.

"Jane!" Eloise cried. There were black mascara tracks on both of her cheeks and her lips quivered. "Everything's going to be all right."

"We'll find Fitz and Hem," Betty said, her eyes damp with tears. "And if not us, someone will. I just know it!"

Anna was about to utter her words of encouragement when Jane cut her off with a look. "Anna, this is very important. Do you remember when I mentioned that the twins might have seen Kyle pocket something from the dig site?" When Anna nodded, Jane went on. "Did you repeat this story to anyone?"

Unlike Mrs. Pratt, a self-professed gossip, the other Cover Girls were more discreet when it came to sharing details about their private lives with customers. At any other time, Jane's question might have rankled Anna. However, heat flooded her cheeks and she said, "I did. I told my mom. I didn't think it would matter, seeing as she's in a nursing home in another state."

"What phone were you using?" Jane demanded. "Where did you make the call?"

"I—I was at work," Anna stammered in alarm. "In that closet that passes for a break room. Why? What does this have to do with what's happening?"

Jane held up her right hand, which was balled into a tight fist. "Randall Teague. He's been a figure in the background since the beginning. He attended every conference event open to the public. He was close enough to Bart several times during the garden party and could easily have overheard him telling the Robert Harley members what he'd discovered about the book found with the skeletal remains." As she spoke, she emphasized her points by raising her fingers. "He was at the Cheshire Cat the night Kyle was killed. Betty, do you remember when he left?"

Though Betty looked distressed, she took a moment to think about the question. "I'm not sure. I assume he took part in Trivia Night, but I don't remember him being there to answer the questions he'd usually answer."

"Call Bob and ask if he remembers more," Jane said. "If he doesn't, we'll call Sam or one of the Hogg brothers."

Betty was so accustomed to Storyton Hall's technology policy that she didn't even open her handbag to remove her phone until she'd stepped out of the public hallway and entered the Henry James Library. Sinclair followed her at a polite distance.

Normally, Betty's respect for the house rules would have made Jane smile, but she was incapable of mustering one. Turning back to Anna, she asked, "Did you see where Randall went after tonight's meal? Did anyone notice him in the ballroom?" She glanced at Eloise, including her in the question.

Neither of her friends had.

Beware of false Fin, Edwin had written in a hidden message. Whom was he talking about? Had he been referring to a man who acted like a Fin, but was really a Templar? That didn't describe Randall. No one had acted like a Fin. And how would Edwin be aware of what was going on at Storyton Hall in the first place? Wasn't he supposed to be abroad?

She shook her head in annoyance. She needed to organize her thoughts. The twins needed her to be sharp.

"Anna. Where does Randall live?"

Anna rattled off an address.

Jane knew the neighborhood. It was located up a curvy road overlooking the village. Each house was surrounded by at least an acre of woods. It was a lovely and secluded spot.

The perfect location for a person with something to hide.

But what would Randall have to hide, exactly? Was Randall a small-town pharmacist during the day and a Templar assassin in his spare time?

As Jane was processing these thoughts, Betty finished her phone call to Bob. "Bob helped me remember. The night Kyle was killed, Randall walked outside with another customer because he hadn't finished whatever lecture he'd started inside. He never came back inside to finish the trivia game, but I guess no one noticed."

"Or they were relieved," Eloise said. "That's Randall's effect on people. Other than a few hypochondriacs who'd gladly discuss their symptoms with him all day, most folks try to avoid him. He's insufferable."

Anna was staring at her friends as if they'd lost their collective minds. "This is Randall we're talking about. Do you really think he's capable of killing someone? Of abducting two children? The don't-forget-your-flu-shot-monotone-of-a-man I've worked with for five years?"

Jane believed it to be quite likely. "Can you think back to the day leading up to Kyle's hit-and-run, Anna? Did Randall take a longer break than usual? Did he leave early or mention needing to have his car serviced? Was there anything out of the ordinary? Anything at all?"

Anna gave Jane a strange look, but answered readily enough. "No, he was his normal, maddening self. He—" She stopped and her eyes widened. "But the *next* morning, well, he *was* different. He whistled while he filled scripts. I have *never* heard him do that before. And he whistled like a songbird. It was beautiful. He didn't give a single lecture to a single customer and he even told me that I was doing a good job and that he was lucky to have me as his right-hand person. That was the first and only compliment the man has ever given me."

"So it was almost as if he acted out of character," Eloise said.

Anna nodded. "That's exactly what I'd say. He acted *completely* out of character. Unfortunately, it didn't last. By lunchtime, he was himself again."

"Thank you, ladies." Jane turned toward the library.

"Where are you going?" Eloise reached out in a plaintive motion. "Can we help?"

Jane hesitated long enough to say, "Please continue your search for my babies. That's the best help you can give me."

She entered the library and, seeing that Celia was seated at a reading table on the opposite side of the room, gestured for Sinclair to join her near his desk.

"Alert the Fins," Jane commanded. "We're driving to Randall's house right now. And we're going armed."

Chapter Eighteen

Jane ordered Sinclair and Lachlan to remain at Storyton Hall.

"This could be an attempt to lure us off the premises," she said while pushing a folding knife into the back pocket of her jeans. After Ned had raced upstairs to collect the tiny carriage clock key, Jane had sent him to her house to fetch a pair of pants and a T-shirt from her closet. Clever Ned had returned carrying these and her tennis shoes as well.

In the privacy of Sterling's office, Sterling and Butterworth strapped on holsters and armed themselves with several other weapons from a locked cabinet. Sinclair accompanied Jane and his fellow Fins to the Silver Shadow and opened the back door. "Good luck, Miss Jane."

Jane didn't want luck. She wanted revenge against the man who'd kidnapped her sons. If that man proved to be Randall, she wanted him to know the same level of fear her boys had known before she turned him over to Sheriff Evans.

"Our biggest advantage is surprise," Sterling said as he drove through town. "And we'll achieve that only if he isn't monitoring our every move."

Jane gazed at the black hills. "If Randall is a Templar,

he's been cultivating his small-town pharmacy persona for years in order to collect information about Storyton Hall and my family. Is that really possible? Would a person invest all that time just for the chance of discovering our secret library? How fanatical *is* this sect?"

Her questions went unanswered, so she continued to stare out the window. She avoided looking at the shadowy trees, for they reminded her of the night they found Kyle's body. Instead, she looked up and searched for stars.

Just one, she thought. *One to wish upon.*

The hills seemed taller than usual. Jane felt like they were occluding the stars until Sterling crested a rise and parked the car. Here, above the somnolent village, the sky was rich with stars.

At Randall's mailbox, Sterling unslung his backpack and distributed pairs of night vision goggles. Though Jane had practiced wearing them before, it took her a moment to adjust, and she had to touch the mailbox to get her bearings.

It struck her that Randall's mailbox, like everything else about the pharmacist, was incredibly ordinary. He had done such a successful job in blending in that no one would have considered him a villain.

Sterling waited for Jane to signal that she'd adjusted to the goggles, then passed her another device. It looked like a small walkie-talkie.

"RF detector," he whispered. "It'll vibrate if it senses security cameras, listening devices, or cellular or Bluetooth signals. If Randall's tracking our approach, we'll know."

Jane gripped the black gadget and made a hurry-up gesture. She understood the need for caution. She knew that her sons' lives might depend on caution, but it was killing her to sneak around the back of Randall's house, threading around trees in what seemed like an agonizingly slow pace.

When they were facing the rear of the house, Butterworth motioned for Sterling and Jane to wait while he approached the door. As always, Jane was amazed by how swiftly and gracefully he moved.

She watched him point to the door's upper right-hand corner.

"Alarm system," Sterling whispered. "Your device will vibrate. Don't worry. I can jam the signal between the alarm and the door. Randall will undoubtedly have his system set up to detect jammed signals, but I have a solution for that too. Home security systems aren't very secure. Dogs are better."

Sterling fished around in his bag and produced more gadgets. Because Jane was wearing her goggles, she couldn't tell what he was doing. However, when Butterworth picked the lock on the door and pushed it open, no alarm bell sounded, which was all that mattered.

Fitz! Hem! I'm coming! Jane was dying to shout.

Butterworth held out his hand for them to halt and cocked his head. Jane heard nothing beyond the night noises coming from outside, but Butterworth had clearly detected a sound.

As he turned to track the source of the noise, he removed his pistol from its holster and carried it by his side. Sterling replicated the movement while Jane frantically glanced around, expecting someone to jump into her field of vision at any second.

Butterworth crept forward until he reached an interior door that looked like it might lead down to a basement.

The door was locked.

Butterworth did not produce his lock pick tools. Instead, he put his ear flat against the door and listened intently for several seconds. Drawing back, he turned to Jane and Sterling. Holding up his right hand, Butterworth used his left hand to quickly cover the tips of the fingers of the right hand. The gesture reminded Jane of an animal being bitten by a snake and she remembered that this was the sign for "trap."

You're no pharmacist, Jane thought, glaring at the doorknob. *Pharmacists don't booby-trap their houses.*

Suddenly, she heard something overhead. The noise could have been the settling of boards or the scratch of a thin branch against a pane of glass. But Jane had the distinct feeling that they weren't alone.

Jane pointed in the opposite direction and Sterling nodded. He'd heard it too.

They quickly ascended the stairs to the second floor. The stairs were carpeted, which allowed them to move silently. Still, Jane had a strong sense that Randall would not be taken by surprise. She believed they were dancing to his tune, and it was a tune without melody or rhyme. It was the steady tick of a metronome—a metaphor for all the time he'd invested in this scheme. And he wanted a return on his investment.

After hurriedly checking the bedrooms, they came to the end of a hallway and found another locked door. Not only was the knob locked, there was also a deadbolt. This time, after Butterworth listened, he didn't indicate the presence of a trap on the other side of the door. However, he pointed at Sterling and made a climbing motion with his fingers.

Sterling disappeared into one of the spare bedrooms.

As Jane waited for Butterworth to pick the locks, it occurred to her that most of the rooms in Randall's home were unfurnished and that he'd likely chosen the house for its location. It felt like they were in the middle of nowhere—that the rest of the Fins weren't minutes, but hours away.

Butterworth touched Jane's shoulder and she snapped to attention. He nodded and, after she nodded in return, indicating that she was ready to face whatever was on the other side of the door, he raised his booted foot and kicked the door an inch below the knob.

There was a loud *crunch* as his boot made a ragged hole.

Butterworth reached through the hole, popped both locks, and opened the door.

Jane didn't pause to wonder why he'd thrown discretion to the wind. Now that the door was opened to a narrow staircase rising into darkness, she heard a whimper. Her boys!

Butterworth bounded up the stairs with Jane a heartbeat behind. At the top, Butterworth turned in a swift circle and whipped off his goggles. Jane did the same, and waited as the butler snapped a green glow stick and tossed it on the floor. He pivoted and repeated the motion, raising his gun after each toss. After the third toss, his stick illuminated two shapes tucked into a corner where the rafters met the wall.

"Fitz! Hem!" Jane cried.

She rushed toward them, knife in hand. She was already on her knees beside the shapes when she realized that she'd mistaken burlap sacks for her sons. On the floor, in front of the sacks, a pair of men's glasses and a false beard had been tossed on top of a Storyton uniform. Wade's uniform.

Nearby, in the gloom, a man began to laugh.

Butterworth tossed another glow stick and Randall Teague's face was illuminated by an eerie green light. He sat on a chair in the far corner of the attic like a ruler of the underworld awaiting the arrival of new souls.

"Lost something, Guardian?" he asked. His eyes were black pools with glints of green.

"Give me my sons, you bastard." Jane lunged for Randall, but Butterworth grabbed her arm and held her in check.

Randall laughed again. "Is the butler in charge now? I thought *you* were the mistress of Storyton Hall." He swung Jane's locket back and forth like a hypnotist performing a stage act. "A pretty trinket. What's worth more: this or the lives of your ill-behaved, precocious sons?"

"I gave you what you asked for," Jane said. Her voice was a harsh rasp. "Tell me what you've done with my boys.

And so help me, if you've hurt them, you will pay. I swear by all that's good. *You will pay*."

The mirth vanished from Randall's features and he glowered at Jane. "This is just the beginning of our bargaining, Guardian. Even if you told me the truth, which I sincerely doubt, I can hardly stroll through the front door of Storyton Hall and start investigating this broom cupboard, can I? No. I need to keep your boys as leverage so that I can move freely around your ancestral home. Also, you left a pair of liveried bodyguards behind. You'll have to order them to come join you here. Right now, if you would."

Jane was too furious to formulate a reply. All she wanted to do was wrap her hands around this man's throat and squeeze. He referred to Fitz and Hem as if they were plastic chess pieces—disposable, valueless objects to be used as he saw fit. Jane wanted to hurt him for his disregard of those she held most dear, but she couldn't touch him. Not until her sons were safe.

"Assuming you're about to utter a clichéd line about our not being able to kill you because we'd be unable to discover the location of Masters Fitzgerald and Hemingway, do not waste your malodorous breath," Butterworth said. His tone was cool and haughty. "I once believed that Mr. Alcott was a loose cannon of the Templar order. You, sir, make him look like a Prince of the Realm."

Randall snorted in derision. "Alcott's a Robin Hood. His order is a lost cause. Altruism has no place in the modern world." He flicked his wrist. "But you need not concern yourselves over Alcott anymore. He was captured weeks ago. If he isn't dead, he'll never see sunlight again. Sorry to tell you this, Guardian, but it's best for those with secret lives not to indulge in romantic entanglements. In my order, such foolish relationships are strictly prohibited."

"That explains why you're so uptight," Jane snapped. "Maybe you should have stayed at the Cheshire Cat and finished the trivia game instead of running over Kyle Stuyvesant just to get your hands on Otto Frank's ring. *That* was foolish."

Randall resumed his glare. "I won't explain my order or my motives to you. You wouldn't understand. You Guardians are as outdated as rotary phones. You won't stand the test of time. Now, call your dogs. Tell them to come here without delay."

"No," Jane said.

Randall was stupefied by her answer. His mouth opened and closed twice before he finally managed to produce a sound. "*No*? Do you want your sons to die? Is a library more important than your own children? What kind of mother would sacrifice her own flesh and blood for old books?"

"I'm not going to sacrifice anything tonight," Jane said with a confidence she didn't feel. "I now know where my sons are hidden." She smiled at Randall. "You might not be aware, but we have an interrogation room at Storyton Hall. It's below the garages and is uniquely equipped for men of your ilk. We could keep you there for weeks. No one would ever find you. No one would hear you scream."

Randall didn't respond. He silently studied her and Jane returned his gaze without flinching.

"I should just kill him now, Miss Jane," Butterworth said, taking a step toward Randall. "The people of Storyton will certainly suffer when they learn that the man who pretended to care about their well-being also abducted two local children."

At this, Randall released a single, humorless guffaw. "I hope they suffer! I've had to deal with those sheep for *years*. I've had to listen to their endless ailments and petty gossip. To all the details of their *insignificant* lives. I've been patient. *So* very patient! When I heard my bleating coworker telling her mother about the exhumed cookbook and the possibility that the driver of the earthmover might have scooped up an item belonging to the dead man, I knew Otto Frank had been found. A member of my family killed him. Did you know that, Guardian?" His voice was taunting. "My relative posed as one of Walter Steward's Fins. Teague isn't my true surname. I'm a Rackley. Recognize the name? My family was one of the food manufacturing firms behind the publication of *Mrs. Tanner's Everyday Receipts.*"

"So your relative put an arrow in Otto Frank's back. How noble. How brave. How proud you must be," Jane said with a sneer.

Randall shook his fist. "I *am* proud. Otto, that inquisitive bastard, should have stayed in Germany." Lowering his hand, Randall grinned. "Funny that he ended up doing me a good turn all these years later. Just by being discovered, Frank confirmed my sect's theories that Walter Steward was a Guardian and that my ancestor, Reuben Rackley, wasn't crazy."

This line resonated with Jane, for many of Walter Steward's contemporaries had believed that he'd lost his mind when he'd dismantled his estate and moved it to a remote valley in western Virginia. But knowing that Randall also had an eccentric relative didn't mean that Jane felt an iota of compassion for a man who'd stoop to kidnapping two little boys.

"If Reuben was a Fin, then why did you spend years serving as a small-town pharmacist?" Butterworth asked. "Why don't you already have all the answers?"

"He posed as a Fin for a single night when Otto stayed at Storyton Hall," Randall murmured. "Reuben incapacitated one of Walter's servants, dressed in his livery, and approached Otto in the garden. The two men fought, but Otto was a scientist. He was no match for a Templar. Defeated, he turned to flee. That's when Reuben shot him."

"Your esteemed relative clearly lived long enough to

send a report of this event. It was his last report, I'd wager, before he was discovered by the real Fins." Butterworth stared down at Randall. The pharmacist was the first to look away.

Jane didn't want to hear another word about bygone killings. She wanted to see her sons. To Butterworth, she said, "I'd like to get my boys and go home. Can you shoot him in the kneecap before we leave? Just in case there's something he should be telling us now?"

Butterworth knew that Jane was issuing a threat, not an order. Randall took her at her word, however, and his eyes widened in surprise.

"Touch me and your sons die!" he hissed. He raised his hand, clearly intending to reach into his jacket pocket, but he never got the chance. Butterworth fired his pistol and the impact of the bullet caused Randall's hand to flail outward away from his body.

Randall howled in pain, and before Jane could even process what had happened, Butterworth had Randall's face pressed against the floorboards.

"Bind his wrists. Tightly." With his knee dug between Randall's shoulder blades, Butterworth held out a plastic wrist tie to Jane.

Though a little repulsed by the rivulets of blood leaking from the center of Randall's palm, Jane complied. Next, she searched his pockets and discovered two crucial items: Otto's ring and a cell phone. After scooping her locket off the ground, she handed the locket and the ring to Butterworth. The butler, who'd just finished binding a handkerchief around Randall's injured hand, nodded at Jane in approval.

Randall's phone was password protected, but the phone could also be accessed by touch identification, so Jane used her shirt to wipe the blood off Randall's right thumb. She then pressed his thumb to the phone's home button. Randall tried to foil her attempts by wiggling, but Butterworth threw his arms around the smaller man's chest and held him in a fierce bear hug.

Having gained access, Jane scrolled through the phone applications. There were no messages or recent calls and Jane didn't know how to track Randall's movements using his SIM card. Sterling or Sinclair could, however. She needed to turn the phone over to one of them.

"We should go," Jane said to Butterworth.

The butler hauled Randall to his feet. "Walk on, sir. If you resist, I will shoot your left hand. I do not make idle threats, but if you'd care to test me, I should warn you that I am fresh out of handkerchiefs."

As soon as Randall began moving, Jane hurried toward the stairs.

"Your sons are dead, Guardian." Randall's voice struck Jane like a hammer. "Your efforts are pointless."

Jane refused to reply or to allow her steps to falter. She descended the stairs and flipped on the lights in the hallway, making it easier to continue to the next staircase. She didn't notice a single detail about her surroundings. Her mind was fixed on Randall's horrible claim.

What kind of monster could say such a thing? He's lived among us for years, pretending to care about Storyton's residents, when all he really wanted was to steal from our secret library. He's a thief, a murderer, and a child abductor. A monster among us.

When they reached the ground floor, Jane stopped and turned to face Butterworth. Anger radiated off her body, but her voice was icy. "Since Randall went through the trouble to prepare a special welcome for us, I don't think we should leave until we see it."

Butterworth immediately understood her meaning. He pushed Randall toward the door leading to the basement.

Next, he pulled a key ring from Randall's pocket and unlocked the door.

For the first time since their arrival, Randall looked scared.

"If you do this, you'll never discover where your beloved Edwin is being held captive," he said, watching as Butterworth took out his lock-picking kit.

Jane sent a quick text message to Sterling. After telling him their location and what they planned to do, she pocketed the phone and stared at Randall. "As if I'd believe a word from your lying mouth. You're a mixture of flesh, blood, and deceit."

"If you don't rescue Alcott, no one will," Randall said. "He's not overseas, no matter what his postcards led you to believe. There are others who can write like him and secure those postmarks. Suffice it to say, he never made his flight. He's surprisingly close."

This information, which sounded legitimate, was too much for Jane to take in. Her mind was already a maelstrom of thoughts centered on finding her boys. There was no room for the possibility of another loss. It was too much. She felt as if she were coming apart—unraveling like a ball of string.

"Mr. Alcott knows how to extricate himself from difficult positions," Butterworth said. "We have complete confidence in his ability to do so in this instance as well."

Randall laughed. "The last time, he was imprisoned by an angry sheik. That's a walk in the park compared to his current situation."

Butterworth finished with the lock. Ignoring Randall, he arched a brow at Jane. "Do you wish to continue?"

Jane hesitated. It was Randall's modus operandi of deceit that led her to what was undoubtedly a rash—bordering on crazy—decision. But it was obvious that Randall wanted to avoid the basement. Why else would he attempt to bargain with her again? And why would he use Edwin instead of her sons to sway her? Because the trap was a deterrent—a way of dissuading her from searching the basement for her boys. She felt this in her bones.

"Yes," she replied. "My boys are down there."

Butterworth put one hand on the knob while trying to position Randall so that he'd face whatever was on the other side of the door, but Randall twisted with sudden violence and bolted straight for Jane.

Jane's reaction was a result of her martial arts training. She released a guttural shout and hit Randall with a flying front kick that landed in the center of his chest. He reeled backward into Butterworth's arms.

Butterworth wrenched the basement door open and pushed Randall forward into the void.

"Wait!" Randall shrieked, teetering wildly on the top step. The fear in his voice filled the stairwell. "If I fall, I'll trigger the explosives! If I die, your sons die!"

Butterworth yanked Randall out of the doorway while sweeping his leg under Randall's feet. Randall landed hard on his back, his head bouncing off the floor with a resounding thud.

"Coward," Butterworth said with disgust. After tying Randall's ankles together, he felt for Randall's pulse. "He's alive, but unconscious."

Though Jane was tempted to deliver a swift kick to Randall's ribs, she had more important things to do.

"Boys! It's Mom!" she shouted down into the black abyss at the bottom of the stairs. "Butterworth and Sterling are here too! We're coming to get you!" She listened for any sound to indicate her boys were alert and responsive, but what she heard renewed her terror. With all the talking and commotion, she hadn't heard the ticking before.

"Come away from the door," Butterworth said. "Mr. Sterling is working on the cellar window. It's barred, but Mr.

Lachlan brought blowtorches from our garage. It was clever of you to text your intentions to the other Fins."

"I'm going outside." Jane pointed at Randall's inert body. "Keep an eye on him. If he tries anything, shoot him. He was willing to sacrifice my sons."

Butterworth shook his head. "Randall Rackley is not the head of the snake. There will be more of his kind sniffing at our door. We should question him."

"Even incarcerated, he'll tell his sect everything he knows about us. What better reason to silence him?" Jane didn't subscribe to violence as a means to an end, but this man had threatened her children. Her emotions were displacing rational thought.

Outside, she saw the starburst sparks of blowtorch flames illuminating the night. Sterling and Lachlan crouched in front of a horizontal basement window. The glass had been knocked inward and two of the bars were already removed. One more, and Jane could slip through the opening.

"Did you hear anything from inside?" Jane asked Sterling.

"Not yet," he said.

Jane willed his torch flame to work faster.

Please, Lord. Let my sons be here, she prayed. *Please let them be okay.*

Lachlan had barely pulled the last bar away from its frame when Jane was on her belly, wriggling through the window.

"Wait." Sterling grabbed her. "You need to check for trip wires."

Jane felt like a fool. She was in such a hurry to save her sons that she could have killed them just as surely as if she'd shoved Randall down the basement stairs.

"Yes. You're right," she said, accepting the proffered flashlight.

The beam revealed an empty space.

"I see nothing. There's nothing here," she whispered, trying to fight the rising despair.

Sterling touched her shoulder. "Put that in your pocket and we'll lower you down. Stay close to the wall. When you get to the bottom, move slowly."

Jane gave a hand to each of her Fins. They lowered her as far as they could, but she had to let go and fall several feet before landing on the cold, concrete floor.

Pulling out her flashlight, she asked Sterling for his supply of glow sticks. He cracked them and dropped them down. Jane hurled a stick in every direction. Through a nimbus of spectral green light, she saw the bottom of the staircase and another door on the far side of the room.

Hugging the wall opposite the staircase, Jane moved toward the door. She continued to sweep her flashlight beam back and forth, but she still saw nothing. The space was completely empty. It was filled with only a damp darkness.

Jane reached the door, looked at it, and then returned to stand below the window.

"Will the blowtorch work on a padlock?" she called up to Sterling.

"Yes," he said, and passed it down to her. A pair of goggles hung from the top. "Be patient. It could take several minutes. Was that all? Just the padlock?"

Jane frowned. "No. There's a second lock requiring a key."

"Burn that too," Sterling said. "Keep the flame directed on the keyhole. Once it's melted, it'll be too hot to touch, so pry the lock mechanism off with your knife."

Jane ran back to the door and fired up the torch. She was relieved when the brass on the padlock started to bubble, but it was agony waiting for it to melt. To distract herself, she began to talk to the boys as if they were standing right beside her.

"They don't teach you lock melting in science class," she

said, and went on to share a story about the time her lab partner fainted when she was told to dissect a frog.

"I think it was the smell of the formaldehyde," Jane said just as the bottom half of the padlock separated from the top and fell to the ground with a satisfying *clink*. Turning her attention to the second lock, Jane continued her story. "Sally—that's the girl—wasn't the only student to faint. One of the biggest and toughest football players keeled right over before ever touching his scalpel."

Jane kept talking. The sound of her voice resonating throughout the empty basement was oddly reassuring.

"How's it coming?" Sterling called down to her.

"Almost done!" she shouted back as the metal surrounding the keyhole bubbled and sank inward. She unfolded her knife and pried it out. Next, she twisted the locking mechanism using the point of her knife.

At last, she had the door open. The beam of her flashlight landed on a world map marked with Templar crosses. To the right was a map of the United States marked with more crosses. Jane noticed that one of the crosses was in a neighboring state before she moved her beam to the darker shadows underneath the maps. The light fell upon two motionless figures on a sofa.

"*No!*" Jane screamed, rushing forward. "Boys! *Boys!*"

When she touched her sons—her hands moving from their cheeks to their hands, and finally, to their carotid pulses—some of her fear dissipated.

Fitz and Hem were warm.

They were alive.

Jane had found them. Her sons were safe.

They'd soon be back at Storyton Hall, tucked in their beds with the nightlight shining like a small crescent moon. Their mother would guard their sleep.

Scanning her sons for signs of injury, Jane knew that she could punish one monster. Randall Rackley would suffer for what he'd done. For killing Bart and Kyle. For toying with her sons' lives. Jane had to make an example of him. She had to be sure that history would never repeat itself—that no one would ever threaten her family again.

"My sweet, sweet boys," she whispered, drinking in the sight of her sons—the scattering of freckles on their noses, the sweep of their eyelashes, their tousled hair, their seashell ears. She kissed her boys on the forehead and prepared to lift them, one at a time.

"Mommy's got you," she said, her heart singing in relief. "We're going home."

Afterword

Jane carried Hem to the window where he was gently lifted up and out of the basement by Sterling. Lachlan took Fitz. Finally, the men pulled Jane back through the narrow opening.

"They've been sedated," Lachlan said, examining Fitz's eyes with a penlight. He looked at Jane. "They're going to be okay."

Sterling scooped Hem off the ground. "Should we drive them straight to Doc Lydgate's house?"

"No," Jane said. "I want them to wake up at home. I'll ask the doc to come to us. He won't mind."

"No, he won't," Sterling agreed. "He cares for these two. We all do."

Jane managed a grateful smile. Her throat had suddenly tightened, which was just as well, for she couldn't think of anything to say. She was suddenly flooded by emotions. She felt immensely relieved, but there was plenty of residual anger coursing through her too.

Glancing through the basement window, she wondered what to do about Randall. The eerie green glow provided no answer. Before she could give the question further thought, Butterworth appeared.

"I think you'll need these." He proffered a set of keys, his gaze sliding to the window. "Or perhaps not. Masters Fitzgerald and Hemingway? Are they . . . ?"

"Alive," Jane said. "The bastard sedated them and—wait. Is Randall still unconscious?"

Butterworth frowned. "As I was conducting a thorough search of his person, which is how I found these keys hidden in his belt buckle, he was showing signs of coming around."

Jane didn't want to deal with Randall. She wanted to be with her sons. Never did she resent her designation as Guardian more than now. Why should her duty to the secret library trump her role as a mother?

She took a deep breath to calm herself. "We should take him back with us. He spoke of Edwin being held captive. Not abroad, but here, in the States. And we need to learn more about Randall's warped faction."

"Agreed," Butterworth said. "Go to your sons, Miss Jane. I'll deal with Rackley."

The butler's use of Randall's surname illustrated his utter lack of respect for the man. It was his equivalent of spitting on another person's shoe.

Jane and Butterworth hadn't taken more than two steps before the explosion came. There was a cannon fire boom, the glass from multiple windows shattered and shot outward, and the ground shook.

Both Jane and Butterworth stumbled. Butterworth threw Jane to the ground and covered her body with his. A wave of heat rolled through the open basement window as a tongue of blinding flame burst into the night air.

"The bomb!" Jane cried, wriggling out from beneath Butterworth. "Who triggered it?"

Sterling, who'd materialized within seconds of the blast, helped to her feet. "It was Randall," he said, staring at the flames.

Butterworth stood up. After dusting himself off, he looked at his fellow Fin. "Are you certain? He didn't strike me as the suicidal type."

"He probably couldn't risk being questioned," said Sterling. "This was his version of a cyanide capsule."

For a few seconds, they silently watched as smoke poured through the basement and first-floor windows. The fire was gaining momentum. Jane could hear the telltale chewing sounds of burning wood and there was an acrid stench in the air. A chemical odor that Jane couldn't place.

"I think you're right." She touched Sterling on the arm to get his attention. "I saw two wall maps hanging in the room where I found the twins. One was a world map and the other, a US map. Each was marked with Templar crosses."

Sterling and Butterworth exchanged unhappy glances.

"They could be meeting places or treasure depositories. Locations where others from Rackley's faction operate." He gestured at the burning house. "We'll never know."

"Mr. Butterworth, why don't you return to Storyton Hall with Miss Jane and the boys?" Sterling said. "I'll call in the fire and wait for the sheriff."

Jane raised a warning finger. "Unless he's a Fin, the only man permitted inside my home tonight is Doc Lydgate. My sons have been through enough. As have I. Tell the sheriff that I'll speak with him in the morning."

"Understood." Sterling took out his phone and began to dial.

Jane ran to the car where her sons were waiting. Lachlan stood guard by the driver's door.

"I shouldn't have left Rackley alone," Butterworth said as Jane reached for the door handle. "We've missed our opportunity to question him. I apologize, Miss Jane."

Opening the door, Jane saw her boys stretched out on the car seat. Lachlan had used his jacket to cushion their heads. They looked like they'd fallen asleep during a long car trip.

Jane turned and put her arms around Butterworth. "All that matters is that Randall is gone and my boys are safe. Thank you, my friend."

For once, Butterworth's rigid posture relaxed. He gave her a powerful hug before releasing her.

"Let's go home," Jane whispered.

Butterworth nodded, his eyes shining with what might have been tears—Jane wasn't sure because he looked away too swiftly—and waited for Jane to settle in the backseat with Fitz and Hem before he joined Lachlan up front.

As Lachlan drove down the curved road toward the village, Jane watched Randall's house recede in the distance. As the burning house, which lit up the hillside like a primitive beacon, fell out of sight, Jane felt like her worst nightmare might finally be over.

Her fear, lodged firmly in her gut, lingered until Doc Lydgate confirmed that the twins were sedated and otherwise unharmed. In the privacy of the boys' bedroom, he conducted a full examination and decided that Fitz and Hem should wake in the comfort of their home.

"The effects of the sedative are unlikely to wear off for hours," he told Jane. "And when they come to, your sons might not remember what happened. What they do recall may just be confusing fragments. You're their mother, Jane, and a damned good one. You'll know what to say when they ask questions. My only piece of advice is to not let them see how scared you'd been. Be calm for their sakes. Make them breakfast. Follow your regular routine. Children feel safest in a predictable environment. I'd recommend they skip school tomorrow, however. They might experience headaches or sore throats and should take it easy for a day."

Jane took all the doc's advice to heart. She changed the boys into their pajamas, washed their faces, and put them to bed.

She also washed and changed. Afterward, she poured

herself a glass of wine and sat in the chair in the corner of the twins' bedroom. She sat, sipped wine, and watched her sons sleep. She listened to their breath and to the little noises they made as they slumbered. She closed her eyes only once. To whisper a fervent prayer of thanks.

Jane thought she'd stayed awake the entire night. However, it was clear she'd dozed off when a hand shaking her shoulder jerked her out of a fragmented dream.

"Why are you sleeping in our chair?" Hem asked.

Jane squinted, turning away from the beams of morning sun sneaking in through a crack in the curtains. Her sons stood in front of her. Their hair was disheveled and their cheeks were flushed pink with sleep.

All she could do was smile.

"Did you have a weird dream too?" Fitz asked. "Because Hem and I did. Do you want to hear it?"

"Yes," Jane said. "Come into my room. We'll snuggle and you can tell me all about it."

Huddled together under her covers, Jane listened as her sons talked. When they were done, it was her turn to speak. When she was finished, Fitz and Hem were unusually quiet.

After a time, Fitz said, "I have more questions, but I'm really hungry."

"Me too," said Hem. "Can we have pancakes?"

"Of course." Jane wanted to squeeze them even tighter, but she resisted the temptation and threw back the covers. "You can ask me questions while I make you a special shape. What kind of pancake art would you like this morning?"

The boys pondered this for several seconds until Fitz cried, "Can you make them look like ice cream cones? We never got our ice cream last night!"

Suppressing a laugh over her son's indignation because he'd been denied his dessert, Jane led her boys down the stairs and into a new day.

* * *

"I still can't believe it," said Eloise. She'd closed her shop, as had the other Cover Girls with businesses, and come to Jane's house bearing comfort in the form of food and company.

"*You* can't?" Anna spluttered. "I worked with that creep for years. I thought Randall Teague was a bore and know-it-all, but a thief? A murderer? A child abductor?" She shook her head. "I'm going to need therapy after this."

Mrs. Pratt looked at Jane. "Why *did* he take the boys? What did he want? Money?"

Jane and the Fins had prepared for these questions. They'd had to, seeing as Sheriff Evans had expected a detailed statement as soon as Jane was finished with breakfast.

"Justice," Jane said. "At least, that's what he believed it was."

Mabel's mouth fell open. "How could kidnapping two little boys ever be considered justice?"

Jane put her fingers to her lips, silently asking Mabel to lower her voice. Though the twins were in their room, listening to an audiobook Eloise had brought them as a surprise, Jane didn't want them to overhear unnecessary details about their ordeal. "Randall's last name wasn't really Teague. It was Rackley. In Edwardian England, the Rackley family was one of the major food manufacturers behind the publication of *Mrs. Tanner's Everyday Receipts*. After the warehouse fire where all the cookbooks burned, Otto's articles in the *Times* were given more weight and the food companies were forced to change their ways. Without adulteration, their bottom line suffered. The Rackleys went bankrupt and their reputation was forever tarnished. Because of this, Randall felt the cookbook belonged to him, as did anything buried with Otto Frank. After all, Otto ruined the Rackley family."

"But that was ages ago!" Violet cried. "People can't go around seeking revenge for something that happened so far in the past."

"Sure they can," Betty said. "I hear about things like this every night at the Cheshire Cat. Old wrongs done to someone's granny or to someone's great-great-uncle. These wrongs are passed down like genes. They're the bedtime stories told to some children on a nightly basis. The sense of injustice gets in their blood, like an infection. They can't help but become obsessed with it."

Phoebe shook her head. "That's sad. Every generation should have a clean slate—a chance to make their own mark on the world without the influence of their family."

"I agree," Jane said, thinking of her own destiny and of how it would one day be inherited by her sons. "But history is powerful. Consider the words the word 'history' is made of. His story. Stories of the past can shape people's lives. It's not easy to let them go. People want the next generation to remember what mattered to their generation."

Eloise, who'd been distributing plates, napkins, and forks while the others were talking, began to serve the Cover Girls slices of pumpkin bread.

"Don't you feel like we missed that, Jane?" Her voice held a note of sadness. "Because we both lost our parents when we were young, we missed out on those stories."

Jane nodded. "You had your grandparents and I had Uncle Aloysius and Aunt Octavia, but it's not quite the same. I guess that explains why I've made so many scrapbooks for the twins. They've gotten to the point where they run whenever they see a camera."

The women laughed and helped themselves to tea.

"What will become of the cookbook?" Eloise asked after they'd all had a sip or two of tea.

Jane shrugged. "That's up to Sheriff Evans. Celia Wallace would like to display it in a special food adulteration exhibit, along with Otto Frank's remains, but both the book and Otto's ring are pieces of evidence in a murder investigation. I suspect they'll be sealed and filed away in the sheriff's department basement."

"Maybe that's just as well. *The Devil's Receipts* is an appropriate name for that book. It sure seems to have some sort of evil attached to it," Anna said.

Jane was about to respond to this remark, but Mrs. Pratt beat her to the punch. "Nonsense. People are wicked. Books aren't." She studied Anna over the rim of her teacup. "Forget the book for now. What about your future? What will become of Storyton Pharmacy?"

Anna's mouth curved into a huge grin. "As you know, I'm a certified pharmacy tech. I didn't get as much experience working in the pharmacy as I would have liked because Randall liked to keep me out front, manning the register and stocking shelves, but I could do everything he did. I want to take care of the people of Storyton, so I've decided to go for my doctor of pharmacy degree."

Violet put her teacup down with a loud clatter. "Does that mean you're leaving us?"

Anna laughed. "I don't plan on going anywhere. Creighton University has an excellent online program. However, I might not be able to attend every book group meeting. I'll be juggling work and school, which won't leave me much time to read."

Eloise raised her teacup in a toast. "Congratulations, Anna. Your plan sounds perfect. Except that bit about the reading. You still need your moments of escapism. That's what'll keep you sane. To quote Philip Pullman, 'We don't need a list of rights and wrongs, tables of do's and don'ts: we need books, time, and silence.'"

"And friends," Jane added.

"And family," Mabel whispered, pointing to the ceiling.

Mrs. Pratt cut another slice of pumpkin bread. Before transferring it to her plate, she paused to ask, "Should we save some of this for the boys, Jane?"

"Heavens, no. Mrs. Hubbard already prepared a lavish tea spread for them. Despite my request to the staff to act normal, no one is acting normal." She sighed, but it was more a sigh of amusement than annoyance.

Betty leaned closer to Jane. "Fitz and Hem are really okay, though? No signs of trauma? Not even after being questioned by the sheriff?"

"Doc Lydgate told me that they might not remember much," Jane replied in a low murmur. "Thankfully, he was right. The last thing the boys recall was following a man wearing a Storyton uniform into the staff stairwell to get ice cream. They also have a vague memory of a bad smell. That's all. They woke up in their beds, wearing their pajamas, with headaches and a funny taste in their mouths. They were also hungry. Of course, that's not unusual. They're always hungry."

"Sounds like chloroform," Anna said. "No wonder they had a nasty taste in their mouths. Poor babies."

Phoebe made a noise of agreement. "But the lack of memory is a blessing. Will it come back, do you think? Later on?"

"Lord, I hope not," Jane said. "It was bad enough that I had to tell them they'd been taken by someone they'd seen in the village for years and that we'll all have to be much more careful from now on. No mother should need to have that conversation with her children, but this is the world we live in."

"We also live in a place where an entire community will band together to search for two of its lost lambs," Mrs. Pratt pointed out. "I have never been prouder to be from Storyton."

Tears sprang to Jane's eyes. "Thank you for reminding me of why this place is so special."

Suddenly, all of the Cover Girls were dabbing at their eyes and squeezing each other's hands.

Minutes later, Eloise poured fresh cups of tea and asked Jane if the Walt Whitman Spa project would resume.

"On Monday," Jane said. "Which leads me to a bit of good news. And an announcement. The good news is that the set of books Sinclair sent off to be auctioned has already surpassed its presale estimate via online bids. Considering there are another ten days until the live auction, we expect to make more than anticipated. This means I can pay for the second half of the spa project and contribute to Kyle Stuyvesant's memorial fund."

Betty cocked her head. "Who's the beneficiary? I thought Kyle was divorced."

"He is. However, he and his ex-wife had a daughter, and the memorial fund will ensure that Miss Stuyvesant is taken care of," Jane explained.

"That's good," said Mabel.

Trying to hide her smile of excitement, Jane said, "There's more news of a similar nature. I've decided to start a Golden Bookmark raffle. This program will provide a needy individual, couple, or family with a free Storyton Hall vacation. I hope to give away one Golden Bookmark per month."

Violet clapped her hands. "Move over, Willy Wonka. There's a new fairy godmother in town!"

"'So shines a good deed in a weary world,'" Phoebe declared, trying to sound like Gene Wilder's Willy Wonka. "Did you know that quote was originally from Shakespeare's *Merchant of Venice*? Roald Dahl was brilliant. As are you, Jane. This is a wonderful idea! So wonderful that I want to be involved. Your Golden Ticket winners can have treats from the Canvas Creamery. On the house, of course."

"Yes," Betty cried. "We can create an entire fan deck of Golden Bookmarks from the merchants of Storyton. It'll be a trip the winners will never forget."

Anna looked at Jane. "Speaking of trips people won't forget, has Felix been released?"

"Aunt Octavia and Uncle Aloysius collected him from the sheriff's office late this morning," Jane said. "They've been seeing to his every need since his return. The poor man. He was already fighting rumors about his reputation, and his bookstore suffered because of those rumors. What he really needs is a positive PR campaign."

Eloise spread her hands. "We can make that happen. The media is sure to descend on Storyton to cover the Randall scandal. The Cover Girls will spread the word that everyone giving interviews needs to sing praises about Felix's character. We should plug his shop too."

"Maybe Sheriff Evans should issue a public apology," Mabel said. "An arrest on suspicion of murder can ruin a person's life. I'm not talking about reputations." She touched her chest and her temple before continuing. "It can ruin a person here and here."

A silence descended following Mabel's comment and Jane sensed that there was truth in it. Still, Sheriff Evans was a good man who didn't make rash decisions or rush to make arrests as a response to public pressure. He did things by the book and she felt compelled to defend him.

"The sheriff had just cause to take Felix into custody," she told her friends. "I know that sounds crazy considering what's since come to light, but Randall set up the whole scheme. He came forward as the witness who'd seen Felix buying the latex-free gloves. He had your break room bugged, Anna, and has been listening to you for years."

Anna's mouth formed a wide *O* of surprise, but Jane went on before her friend could get a word in.

"And then, there was the missing Hardy Boys book."

Jane explained how Felix's copy of *The Sign of the Crooked Arrow* had been found under the passenger seat of an abandoned truck. The truck's front bumper and hood were damaged and, after further testing, revealed traces of Kyle Stuyvesant's blood."

As one, the Cover Girls gasped in horror.

"I didn't know about that detail until today," Jane said. "But Sheriff Evans has always been as transparent as he can be with me. As I told the boys, people make mistakes, even when they try their best not to. We can all help the sheriff to fix his."

There was murmur of agreement from her friends.

"We got off track after you told us about the Golden Bookmark. So what's your announcement?" Violet asked.

Jane thought back on her post-breakfast meeting with the Fins. As soon as she'd finished feeding pancakes to the boys and sent them upstairs to bathe—an order that elicited a round of robust protests—she'd asked Uncle Aloysius, Aunt Octavia, and the Fins to come over.

They'd met in her kitchen. Everyone stood except for her great-uncle and -aunt, who sat in ladder-back chairs and looked like a pair of aged monarchs, which, to the long-time employees of Storyton Hall, is pretty much how they were viewed.

It had taken several minutes to calm Aunt Octavia and to reassure her that Fitz and Hem were truly unharmed.

"I'll never forgive myself!" Aunt Octavia had wailed. "Neither of us will."

"There, there." Uncle Aloysius had taken his wife's hand. "We made a grievous mistake, it's true, but Jane has forgiven us. You must accept her forgiveness and listen to what she has to say."

After a few more sniffles, Aunt Octavia had fallen silent, allowing Jane to share her thoughts.

"This is about Edwin, the map I saw in Randall's basement,

and what Randall told me," Jane had said. "After looking at a map of the Southeast, I believe the Templar cross I saw close to us was marking the Biltmore in North Carolina. Furthermore, there's an upcoming conference for hoteliers at the Inn on Biltmore Estate. I plan on attending that conference."

Sinclair had responded to this news with a pensive look. "Do you think Mr. Alcott is being held at the Biltmore?"

"I don't know," Jane had replied. "Maybe. But if there are other Templars on that estate, they'll have information on him. Randall lied about many things, but I don't believe he was lying when he spoke of Edwin. Edwin is in trouble and needs our help. If our roles were reversed, he'd come for me."

"But your role—" Uncle Aloysius began.

"Needs to be redefined." Jane had cut him off. She'd softened her tone and added, "My role almost cost me my sons. I cannot lose the man I love because I am Guardian to Storyton Hall. I'm going, and I need at least one Fin to come with me."

Jane had refused to discuss the matter further. There'd be logistics to work out and the twins' care and safety to see to, which was where her announcement to the Cover Girls came in.

Looking at them now, Jane said, "As you know, I very rarely leave Storyton. But in a few weeks, as long as the boys are totally and completely okay, I plan to take a short trip. In my absence, I'll need one of you to look after Fitz and Hem."

Nearly all the Cover Girls jumped at the offer. Only Eloise remained quiet, staring at Jane with a mixture of surprise and confusion.

And why wouldn't she? Jane thought. *My sons were just abducted. Here I am, hours later, talking about leaving them.*

"Why do you need to go away now? So soon, after everything that's happened?" Eloise asked after the rest of the women had fallen silent.

Jane reached across the table and took her friend's hand. She loved Eloise's candor. She loved how protective her best friend was of Jane's entire family. She loved Eloise's loyalty and her passion for books, her neighbors, and her friends. It wasn't just for her sake that she had to rescue Edwin; it was for Eloise's as well.

"'Not all those who wander are lost,'" Jane said to her friend, repeating the line from Tolkien's *The Fellowship of the Ring*. "But some are. And they need the people who love them to find them and bring them home."

She saw that Eloise understood. Her oldest and truest friend smiled and quoted another line from Tolkien, "'Deep roots are not reached by the frost.' Let me keep the boys, Jane. It would make me so happy."

Jane nodded and, after glancing at the clock, told the Cover Girls that she wanted to spend the rest of the day alone with her sons. She thanked them for the treats, the company, and the comfort. As they passed through her gate, her hand automatically moved to touch her locket.

And then, she remembered.

She hadn't put the locket back on following last night's ordeal. It was in her jewelry box, sitting next to the owl brooch Edwin had given her.

Jane realized that Randall had been right about a few things and that it was time to update her role as Guardian. That included where she hid the key to Storyton's secret library. There would be many changes ahead, but like the new season, Jane had faith that they'd be for the best.

After taking a moment to breathe in the air, which was perfumed by fresh-cut grass warmed by the September sun, Jane went back inside to read to her sons.

Read on for a sneak peek of the next
The Secret, Book & Scone Society mystery,

THE WHISPERED WORD,

coming soon from Kensington Publishing Corporation.

Hide until everybody goes home. Hide until everybody forgets about you. Hide until everybody dies.

Yoko Ono

"That girl's got one foot in the grave."

Nora Pennington, proprietress of the only bookshop in Miracle Springs, North Carolina, glanced from her friend to the empty chair where she expected to find the fragile, slip of a girl who'd hidden in the stacks until past closing time. However, the girl wasn't there.

Recalling the hospital ID bracelet encircling the girl's bony wrist, Nora returned her attention to her friend. "June, did she say anything to you? Or to Hester or Estella?"

June grunted. "Oh, sure. She told the three of us her whole story. Yes, ma'am. She donated a kidney to the love of her life and the surgery took place without a hitch, but when the sweethearts woke up, Miss-Skinny-As-A-Broom-Handle found out that Mister Right was Mister Seriously Wrong. According to a news report, he was an escaped serial killer. No, that wasn't it. He ran a cult. So she bolted from the hospital when the nurses weren't watching, snatched a housedress from a clothesline, and hopped a train to Miracle Springs."

The woman behind June issued a throaty chuckle.

"June Dixon, I believe you could write fiction if you had the notion," declared Estella Sadler in an exaggerated Southern accent. Estella uncrossed her shapely legs and stood up. Jerking a thumb toward the back of the bookstore, she said, "Unless you need help evicting your bubble wrap refugee, I'm calling it a night. You know I live for excitement, but even *I* need a break. Besides, if I'm planning to add Good Samaritan to my resume—a title I *never* thought I'd add—then I could use a decent night's sleep. Sweet dreams, ladies."

Nora turned to Hester Winthrop, the fourth member of The Secret, Book & Scone Society, and arched her brows. "Bubble wrap refugee?"

"You'll see," Hester said as she picked up her handbag. "I need to get going too. The bread won't knead itself at five in the morning and I'll be baking extra loaves starting tomorrow to put in our secret gift bags."

June shook her head. "I don't know many people who wake up when it's dark out and work all day long without taking a break. With your freckles and endless energy, you remind me of Pippi Longstocking."

Hester grinned. "Except Estella's the redhead, not me."

June grunted again. "Estella's no Pippi. She's catlike. She moves with slow grace until it's time to pounce. Who does she remind me of?" She tapped her finger against her chin. "Shere Khan. That's it! The tiger from *The Jungle Book*."

"And what book character are you?" Nora asked, unable to avoid being drawn in by the subject.

June put her hand over her heart. "When I worked at the

nursing home, one of my favorite patients called me a Black Mary Poppins."

Seeing the shock on Hester's face, June burst into laughter. "Honey, I wasn't offended. This lady meant it as a compliment. She wanted me to know that she could see how I tried to put a little magic into the residents' lives."

Hester gestured in the direction of Nora's small stockroom. "I don't think there's been much magic in that one's life lately. What are you going to do about her, Nora?"

Nora shrugged. She'd moved to Miracle Springs in search of peace and privacy. She hadn't wanted a single responsibility beyond owning her tiny house and her one-of-a-kind bookstore. She hadn't wanted any pets. Or close relationships. She refused to join a place of worship or participate in charity events. She didn't sponsor children's athletic teams, enter bake offs or gardening competitions, or take sides in local politics. She didn't seek out anyone's company. Despite her reclusive nature, people sought her out.

Strangers came looking for her. People from other states and sometimes, other countries. People with skin of every color. People with an array of stories to tell. People carrying a burden they were incapable of putting down.

These weary souls came to her, the "woman who might have been beautiful, had she not been burned," or "the bibliotherapist with the burn scars." These were examples of how the Miracle Springs Lodge staff members referred to Nora. They made these remarks without malice, for the majority of the hotel and spa employees liked her. Or, more accurately, they liked her bookstore. It was difficult not to. In fact, it was virtually impossible not to fall in love with the place.

Meandering through the bookshop was like falling in love for the very first time.

In the beginning, Nora's customers would hesitate near

the front door in case they wanted to beat a hasty retreat. Many entered fearing the store would be stocked with only New Age titles and crystals—a reasonable concern in a town built upon the premise of healing.

People had been traveling to the region's hot springs and thermal pools for nearly two centuries in search of pain relief—whether of body or spirit—and the waters continued to draw the broken, the injured, and the spent to the remote hamlet. Because Nora had never bathed in the hot springs, she couldn't say if the waters had restorative powers.

But she believed books had the power to heal. She believed that the experiences of an author, rendered into carefully chosen words, gifted readers with the ability to let go of their painful past and continue their story anew.

Because of this, Nora's store was stuffed with books of every imaginable format and genre. There were the latest bestsellers with glossy hardcovers. There were dog-eared, yellowed, used paperbacks. There were first editions, signed books, and beautiful, leather-bound books with gilt lettering. Some books had no words at all, but were filled with exquisite illustrations or paper sculptures. To Nora Pennington, every book had value. Every story had meaning.

Faced with this overwhelming cornucopia of books, Nora's first-time customers needed a minute to get their bearings. After all, there was so much to see. A warren of shelves immediately invited them to wander—to become lost in a labyrinth of colorful spines. And yet, something close at hand also tempted them to pause. This temptation was often a beautiful book cover. At other times, it was a shelf enhancer.

Nora created the term "shelf enhancer" before ever opening Miracle Books. One day, when she was still assembling her initial inventory, she'd been rummaging through a box of books at the local flea market when she'd come across a pair of bronze owl bookends. They weren't in perfect shape. There was minor flaking to the bronze in several places, undoubtedly due to age. Regardless of their flaws, Nora liked the owls. Their gaze was stern, almost severe. And their talons were hooked over a stack of thick tomes, lending the impression that they were guarding the knowledge held within the books.

"If you buy the set of Nancy Drews, I'll give you a discount on the owls," the vendor had said to Nora while overtly studying her burn scars.

Though Nora was used to being stared at, she wasn't used to bargaining. Still, she knew that she'd have to buy every book at rock bottom prices if she wanted her business to succeed, so she turned the bookends over in her hands and thought of how much more interesting her future store would be if her shelves were enhanced by unique, eye-catching, vintage items. And then, she'd begun to haggle.

The shelf enhancers became impulse buys for locals and visitors alike. Now, as Nora moved deeper into the stacks, she walked by a wooden mortar filled with crushed lavender, a marble and brass letter holder, a picture frame in pink Lucite, a Victorian child's porcelain tea set, and an Art Nouveau trumpet vase. And those were just some of the treasures displayed in the Contemporary Romance section.

As Nora rounded the corner of a bookcase crammed with pulp fiction novels toward the back of the shop, she heard the loud clang of brass bells smacking against wood. The bells, which had once been attached to a horse harness, now hung from a strip of leather behind Nora's front door.

The sound meant that her friends had left.

Nora was alone with her books and the pale, thin girl.

And there she was, curled into a fetal position on top of a layer of bubble wrap and white packing paper in Nora's stock room. She looked like an undernourished Goldilocks who'd passed out after a night of too much partying.

Nora studied the stranger in the dim light. Though her lithe figure and pallid skin made her appear childlike, Nora guessed that she was well out of her teens.

"What am I supposed to do with you?" she murmured under her breath.

Nora had intended to live an uncomplicated life in Miracle Springs, but despite her attempts to keep people at arm's length, she'd recently become friends with three remarkable women and had formed The Secret, Book & Scone Society. In the middle of their investigation into the murder of a visiting businessman, Estella, June, and Hester had each shared their deepest secret with Nora. And eventually, she'd entrusted them with hers—the terrible truth behind the jellyfish burn scar swimming up her right arm and the pod of tiny bubbly octopi scars floating up her shoulder and neck to caress her cheek with their puckered tentacles.

I've already risked enough, Nora thought, staring down at the sleeping girl.

Miracle Springs was still reeling following the abrupt closing of the community bank. Dozens of people had lost their jobs. Others had been jailed. The town needed to recover. So did Nora.

But she was torn. Part of her wanted to shake the girl awake and tell her to move on.

"This is a bookstore, not a hotel," she could hear herself saying.

The other part of her remembered how the girl had caressed the book spines when she thought no one had been watching. There had been such tenderness in that touch. And longing. There'd been loss too.

Nora had seen herself in that moment. Because of that,

she strode to one of the shop's many reading nooks, grabbed the throw blanket from the back of the fainting couch, and draped it over the slumbering girl.

I wish I could sleep that soundly, Nora thought. But the girl's hospital bracelet and ill-fitting clothing hinted at a sleep that was anything but sound. This young woman's sleep was of the bone weary kind. It was the sleep of someone who'd been running and running and had finally run out of steam.

Nora lingered for a moment to consider why a person would run away from a hospital before she decided that she didn't want to know the answer to that question. She didn't want to get involved. She would give the girl food and shelter. For now. That was all.

After writing a brief note, Nora locked the girl in the bookstore for the night.

The next morning, Nora woke early. She hadn't slept well and her thoughts were focused entirely on coffee.

She was well into her second cup when she remembered her stock room Goldilocks.

"Damn it," she muttered. She showered, dressed, and made a plate of food for the girl.

Nora walked the short distance from her tiny house, affectionately dubbed Caboose Cottage by the townsfolk, and unlocked the back door to Miracle Books.

"It's Nora! The shop owner!" she called out upon entering. She didn't want to scare the girl and it was possible that she was still sleeping.

However, the stock room was empty.

Nora stood in the doorway and tried to comprehend what she was seeing. The room had been completely altered. The boxes had been flattened and lined up neatly along one wall.

There wasn't a shred of bubble wrap or packing paper in sight.

Moving through the store to the ticket agent's booth, Nora glanced around for signs of life. Had the girl used one of the hundred coffee mugs hanging from the pegboard to make herself a cup of coffee or tea? If she had, she'd already washed it and hung it back up.

"I have fresh bread. It's lightly toasted and buttered," Nora said, her voice resonating through the stacks. "Hester baked it. You met her last night. She's the one with the freckles and the frizzy, blonde hair." Nora continued on to the checkout counter. "I also have blackberries that I picked yesterday morning. And farmer's cheese. I could make you a cappuccino or a latte if you'd like."

By this time, Nora had reached the register. She set down the plate of food on the counter and stopped to listen. The girl was still here. She could feel her presence. But why was she hiding?

Nora threaded her way to the front of the store. She was immediately struck by the foreignness of the display window. It had not looked like that last night.

"What the—?"

Digging the brass skeleton key that unlocked the front door of what had once been the train depot for Miracle Springs, Nora rushed outside to view the window from the sidewalk.

What she saw was so magical that she could hardly believe it was real.

The scene had been created entirely out of packing materials. The central figure was a woman sculptured using clear packing tape. The transparent tape woman held a string fastened to an enormous balloon made of bubble wrap. Both woman and balloon were surrounded by hundreds of origami birds of various sizes fashioned from white paper. The birds swayed and spun, coaxed into subtle movement by the air exiting a nearby duct.

For a moment, Nora felt as if she were in motion. She almost glanced down, half-expecting the concrete slabs under her feet to have transformed into a moving sidewalk.

When she looked at the window again, she saw the books. Books with blue covers dangled from the ceiling. White string dug into each gutter, forcing the books to flap open, creating an illusion of wings. Nora found herself shifting left and right in an effort to read every title.

The girl—for she must be the artist behind this masterpiece—had selected books from a variety of genres. There was *Cat in the Hat, Go Set a Watchman, Wonder, All the Light We Cannot See, The Great Gatsby, Eragon, The Mystery at Moss-Covered Mansion, A Brief History of Time,* and a dozen more. On the bottom of the window, a whimsical set of cardboard letters spelled out the phrase, "MY BLUE HEAVEN."

Nora reentered the store and found the girl standing next to the plate of food. She hadn't touched it, but was hovering so close to it that her hunger was almost palpable.

"It's beautiful." Nora gestured at the window behind her. "Did you spend all night making that?"

The girl took a long time to reply. When she finally spoke, her voice was a faint whisper, like a breeze winding through reeds. "It took a few hours."

"I think you've earned your breakfast," Nora said, indicating the plate. "Come on. I'll make you a coffee while you eat."

Though the girl said nothing, she picked up the plate and followed Nora to the circle of chairs near the ticket agent's booth.

Nora tapped the chalkboard menu affixed to the wall next to the ticket window and asked, "What would you like?"

The girl stepped up to the menu. Her lips moved as she murmured every word aloud.

The Ernest Hemingway — Dark Roast
Louisa May Alcott — Light Roast
Dante Alighieri — Decaf
The Wilkie Collins — Cappuccino
Jack London — Latte
Agatha ChrisTEA — Earl Grey

Nora turned away. She didn't want to embarrass the girl by gawking at her while she tried to process the menu. Instead, she searched for the perfect coffee cup for her guest.

The majority of Nora's mugs, which were purchased at yard sales or flea markets, bore book-related sayings or humorous one-liners. Glancing at her collection, she decided that none of them were a good fit for this girl. She wished she had one of her handmade pottery mugs covered with a thick cobalt glaze from home, especially since the girl seemed to have an affinity for blue. Nora could give her one of the mugs she kept for when children asked for hot chocolate, but Cookie Monster, Batman, Snoopy, or Harry Potter cups didn't feel right either.

Nora selected a white mug with a donut covered in pink icing and rainbow sprinkles. The donut was flanked by the words, I to the left and CARE to the right. Giving the girl a questioning look, Nora wished, for the first time, that she owned an innocuous kitten or puppy mug.

"Anything tempt you?"

"A latte would be great, thanks."

Nora nodded and moved behind the espresso machine to make the drink. She hadn't asked the girl if she wanted sugar or special milk because she didn't make a habit of giving her customers too many choices. If they wanted sugar, they could stir it in themselves. If they wanted soy, almond, or coconut milk, they were out of luck. Nora didn't stock a range of items. She was neither a Starbucks nor a grocery store. Her espresso machine was a refurnished model that ran on a wing and a prayer, and Nora was always relieved when her customers stuck to a standard cup of coffee or herbal tea.

"What's your name?" Nora casually inquired over the hiss and sputter of the machine. She'd already made the espresso and was now frothing the milk for the girl's latte.

There was no answer, so Nora finished preparing the latte. When she was done, she set down the donut mug next to the dish of food.

The girl kept her eyes fixed on the offerings. "It's . . . Abilene. My name's Abilene."

Given the slight pause, Nora wondered if the girl had just made up a name. But if she had, it didn't matter to Nora. She would call the girl whatever name she wanted to be called.

"That's a pretty name." She gave the girl a friendly smile. "I don't like it when people watch me eat, so why don't you grab a seat and enjoy your food? I'm going to head to the front and take care of things I need to do before opening for the day. I don't need to mess with the window display, thanks to you. I won't want to change that for months. It's really amazing."

Abilene returned Nora's smile with a small, shy smile of her own. "Thanks."

Later, Nora was behind the checkout counter, circling promising yard sale ads in the paper when Abilene silently appeared. "Thanks for the food. The bread and berries were really good. And thanks for letting me stay last night. I'll show myself out."

She turned toward the front door.

Nora knew the girl couldn't show herself out because the door was locked and the heavy brass skeleton key was inside the cash register. As she watched Abilene and tried to decide what to do about the young woman so clearly in need of help, something occurred that would keep her from leaving Miracle Books anytime soon.

Without warning, the rubber strap on Abilene's left flip-flop snapped, causing her to lose her balance. She pitched forward, colliding with a floor spinner stuffed with paperbacks. The display was made of acrylic, and Nora gasped in dismay as an entire side gave way in a series of violent cracks. Abilene cried out in pain.

Nora dropped to her knees beside the girl who was cradling her right hand with her left. She tried to hide the blood seeping from between her fingers and the tear tracks wetting her cheeks, but failed.

"Don't move," Nora ordered and ran to get a dishtowel from the back.

When she returned to Abilene, the girl refused to let her look at her hand.

"I'm fine," she insisted stubbornly.

Nora scowled at her. "Bullshit. You're bleeding all over my floor. Come on. I need to see it."

Averting her gaze, Abilene offered Nora her injured hand.

Gently, Nora pried away the girl's fingers. Blood immediately welled from a deep gash across her palm. It was deep enough to require sutures. This was not a wound that would heal on its own.

"You need stitches," Nora said, balling up the towel and pressing it against Abilene's palm.

The girl drew back so abruptly that she nearly knocked Nora over. "No. I'm fine."

Nora realized that there was no way she'd get Abilene to an urgent care center or doctor's office. "Listen. I have a friend who can patch you up. He won't tell anyone about you. I'm going to call him. You're going to stay with me today. No arguments. You're going to rest and eat. No one will ask you questions. And if they do, you don't have to answer them."

Abilene shook her head and Nora feared that the girl would bolt the second she turned her back. She'd have to find another way to coerce her into staying put, which wouldn't be easy. It was obvious that Abilene was incredibly on edge.

Why? Nora silently wondered as she held the girl's hand. *What happened to you?*

"Look, Abilene." Nora adopted the firm, no-nonsense tone she'd employed during her previous life as a librarian. Pretending that Abilene was an unruly high school student, she said, "You broke my spinner and you've made a mess that needs to be cleaned up before I open at ten. The way I see it, you have two choices. You can run out through the back exit, leaving a trail of blood, and pass out in some field a few miles away. Your left foot will be wrecked because you have only one shoe that clearly doesn't fit. But what happens to your foot doesn't matter because your hand will likely get infected and you'll run a fever. Whoever finds you *will* call for an ambulance. Or they'll call the police. Is *that* what you want?"

Abilene refused to answer.

"Your other option is to let my friend patch you up. You can regain your strength, change into clothes that actually fit, and do a few light chores for me to earn your keep." Nora cocked her head. "Do you like books?"

Judging by the window display, the girl most certainly did, but Nora wanted to see if her question would elicit a response. It did.

Abilene whipped her head around. Her eyes were lit with twin sparks. Not the sparks of enthusiasm, but of anger.

"I love them," she declared in a voice that was almost loud.

Nora was relieved by this evidence of Abilene's passion. Whatever else the girl was, she wasn't weak. There was a layer of steel under that translucent skin. And Nora guessed it was strength that had carried Abilene this far. From wherever it was that she had come.

"I love books too," Nora whispered reverently to the girl. "In fact, they saved my life." She held Abilene's gaze. "So believe me when I tell you that this is a safe place for you. Here, among the books. With me, a woman who was rescued by them."

Abilene glanced around the shop and Nora recognized the girl's expression of longing. How long had she been running? Who was she afraid of, and was Nora being a fool for inviting more danger into her quiet world? After all, she'd just risked life and limb for a complete stranger and had vowed never to repeat such ridiculous behavior. She'd barely been released from the hospital and yet, here she was, offering shelter to a young woman who was undoubtedly being hunted. But by whom?

The thoughts churning around in Nora's head were interrupted by a buzzing noise outside the bookstore. Putting the towel in Abilene's left hand and forcing her to press it against the wound on her right palm, Nora stood and walked over to peer out the glass panel over the front door. What she saw made her breath catch in surprise.

A crowd had gathered on the sidewalk. The faces of men, women, and children were all turned toward the display window of Miracle Books. This collection of locals and out-of-towners were pointing, smiling, and snapping pictures of Abilene's creation with their cell phones.

Nora looked at her watch. It was nine-thirty, which meant the trolley from Miracle Lodge had arrived early and delivered Nora's favorite kind of customers: the wealthy kind.

"There's a group of people out there admiring your work," Nora told Abilene. "You see? I'm not the only one who thinks it's beautiful."

The compliment brought a rush of color to Abilene's cheeks and she seemed to glow with delight. The reaction was so powerful that Nora could see that the girl was unaccustomed to being praised.

"So? Should we see to that hand?"

After a brief hesitation, Abilene reached out with her index finger and held it over Nora's pinkie knuckle—over the empty space where the rest of her finger should have been, but wasn't.

"Did the books save you? After you were burned?" she asked in a timid whisper.

Nora snatched her hand away. "We all have a story. We all have secrets. But we don't have to share them. Not with everyone."

Someone knocked on the front door and Abilene gave a start.

Since Nora didn't recognize the man, she ignored him. He'd have to wait until she opened at ten.

"How did it get so late so soon?" she muttered to herself. Abilene's indecision was making her irritable. Not only did she have things to do, but she was also annoyed with herself for welcoming this strange girl in the first place.

"I like his poems too," Abilene said. "You were quoting Dr. Seuss, weren't you?"

When Nora gaped at her in surprise, the girl responded with a smile.

Finally, Abilene got to her feet and said, "Yes. I'd like to stay. For a little while, if I can. Here with you. And the books. These wonderful, wonderful books."